THE LAST SAFARI

Books by Richard Rhodes

Fiction

THE LAST SAFARI
HOLY SECRETS
THE UNGODLY

Nonfiction

LOOKING FOR AMERICA
THE OZARKS
THE INLAND GROUND

The Last Safari

RICHARD RHODES

Doubleday & Company, Inc., Garden City, New York 1980

The Last Safari is a work of fiction.
The author is aware of the liberties he has taken
with time and place.

A glossary of African words appears on page 347.

ISBN: 0-385-14243-9
Library of Congress Catalog Card Number 79-7207
Copyright © 1980 by Richard Rhodes

For Tim and Katherine

For if the last shall be first, this will only
come to pass after a murderous and decisive
struggle between the two protagonists.

FRANTZ FANON   *The Wretched of the Earth*

THE LAST SAFARI

PART I

Camp

One

Two MASAI HERDBOYS found the head. It was rolled away
from the body as if someone had kicked it and it had been
severed cleanly with a panga or a sword. The two herdboys
were brothers. They had driven their father's cattle from the
manyatta, the village, in the early morning and watered
them at the spring that the rhino and the greater kudu from
the forest had already visited and then they had driven the
cattle out onto the plain. The African sun soon heated the
morning. After the cattle had grazed they had retreated to
an acacia grove to chew their cuds. They were small bony
animals, white and red and black, each one named and
cherished. The boys had guarded them alertly, resting like
storks one-legged with the other leg cocked up and braced
at the knee and leaning on stout hardwood herdsticks.
When the boys noticed the vultures coming in one of them,
the older one, went over to investigate and there in the grass
was the head. The older one called to the younger and together they harried the vultures from the body. The vultures

didn't fly away but in the manner of vultures waited stinking nearby fluffing their dusty wings and picking their feet up and down in disgust at being driven off a delicacy.

The boys discussed the matter quickly. They were familiar with death and it was not shocking to them except that the dead man was white. They had never seen a dead white man before but they understood that the death meant trouble even though the country of Tanzania no longer belonged to white men but was the country now of the Masai as well as of the ugly and stupid peoples who farmed. They could not leave the cattle lest lions or wild dogs attack them. If they left the body the vultures would strip it to bone. Already it was open and black with flies although it had not been dead long. They decided to bring the body together with the cattle where one boy could guard both and the other boy could go to tell their father.

The older brother clamped his herdstick under his arm and harnessed himself between the dead man's legs. The younger brother picked up the head, giggling at the staring blue eyes. Then he noticed the paper folded in the cleft stick stuck into the ground beside the body and pointed to it and the older brother dropped the legs and pulled the paper from the stick. He turned it several ways in his hands. He would have cast it aside but unfolding it he saw that it was marked with the marks of words. Thinking to show it to his father and lacking pockets in his goatskin apron he folded it again and withdrew his shortsword from its scabbard at his hip and fitted the paper around it and sheathed sword and paper together and again picked up the legs. He dragged the body over among the cattle, calling their names softly to calm them, and his brother placed the head beside the body on the grass. Then he sent his brother to inform their father while he stayed to guard. The vultures moved back in to where the body had lain and picked at the grass spotted with blood but it was not the feast they had expected and one by one they flapped clumsily away.

Seth Crown's Land Rover bounced over the plain, jarring the girl beside him and making his friend ole Senkali in the back seat grin. The girl probably should have stayed in camp. Murder wasn't tourist business. But she was an entirely different class of girl from the trash and silliness he'd taken in over the years to warm his bed and she'd wanted to come along and he'd liked her beside him these last two days. She wanted to see Africa. She might as well see all of it.

Crown was driving too fast. He knew most of the people in the district, African as well as European, and it enraged him that one of them might be dead. There were always private *shauris* and sometimes people got hurt but no one cut off heads. That wasn't even a city trick. City tricks were knives and razors. That was an old Mau Mau trick and a nicety of the worst bigots among the old anti-Mau Mau settlers' brigades and Mau Mau and bigots alike were long gone.

Ole Senkali was the father of the two herdboys. When his son came running into the *manyatta* he had been playing the board game of stones and holes with his father-in-law, counting out his cattle stones in the six field holes on his side of the board and jumping over to steal his father-in-law's cattle stones if the count went his way. It had annoyed him to be disturbed until his son explained the reason. The murder of a white man so near his *manyatta* was sufficient reason and he had apologized to his father-in-law and graciously conceded the game although clearly he had been winning. He had set out then on foot to walk the five miles to the tent camp of Seth Crown on the lake of wildebeest at the edge of the plain. For any lesser personage he would have sent his son or one of his wives, but while Crown was

white he was also a senior elder of the Masai who advised
his fellow elders wisely on government matters including
matters of crime, and to send a son or a wife to him would
not have been respectful.

It was after the middle of the day when ole Senkali arrived at the tent camp. He found Crown working on his
lorry in the open thatched garage beside the main lodge of
the camp. Small parts of the lorry's engine were laid out on
a cloth on the fender and Crown was cleaning them with
petrol. The white woman who attended Crown in the garage, the same who rode with them now in the car, was tall
and had hair like a lion's mane. Ole Senkali had observed
her with interest and decided she was comely except for the
white skin and the hair. The hair was handsome in its way
and would have graced a man but ole Senkali found hair on
a woman's head barbaric if not obscene. Ole Senkali's three
wives quite properly shaved their heads.

Ole Senkali had greeted Crown and asked after his cattle.
The asking after cattle was a courtesy. Crown had kept no
cattle, so it was said, since his wife, the unfortunate Masai
daughter Sidanu, had been murdered at his ranch in Kenya
in Emergency days. Ole Senkali understood that Crown's
great wealth, wealth enough to buy many cattle, came now
from coins that he took from foreigners he allowed to sleep
in his tents and feed in his lodge, coins he then placed in an
iron box at the bank to multiply, but he asked anyway because Crown was an adopted Masai. Crown had asked in
turn after ole Senkali's cattle and following a brief but interesting conversation about the dryness of the season and
the prospects for the early arrival of the long rains ole Senkali had told him about the dead white man. Crown had
cursed and washed himself hurriedly and collected blankets
for wrapping the body and they had entered into the Land
Rover and the wind blew in the windows freshly and the
ride in the noisy machine was like the ride of the bulls that

ole Senkali had mounted as a herdboy when his father was not around.

"Okay, Cassie?" Crown asked the girl.

"Fine," the girl said. She smiled. The window at her left was slid forward and her arm was braced in the frame.

"Not much farther."

"I'm fine," the girl said.

Buff, white-bellied tommies with dark diagonal stripes on their sides, small Thompson's gazelle, ran before the car. Some of them played with it, cutting across in front and kicking up their heels. At another time Crown might have joined them, speeding and slowing to challenge their timing. He had grimmer business now and drove straight through. The tommies closed ranks again behind the car, flicking the flags of their tails, and lowered their heads to graze.

The girl's name was Cassie Wendover. She had come out to East Africa from California and found Crown at his tent camp south of Serengeti National Park and taken up with him and she still wondered at her luck. Three months ago her father had died. He died suddenly, without warning, at midlife. She was twenty-eight years old and she knew nothing about death. She'd had no chance to prepare. It was as if her father had disappeared. Recoiling from mourning she had thrown herself out to a place far from home, a place where death was visible and had weight. Traveling the game circuit among chattering tourists she saw that she would need a guide and then she found Crown. The first night in camp, two days ago, they had talked late on the screened porch of the lodge and he had helped her to her tent in the darkness and she had taken him to bed with something like ferocity. He was American, he had been born in Africa of missionary parents and had lived there all his life, he was fifty-three, he had been a professional hunter, he had lost a wife and somewhere a son, he was honest and he was passionate. His isolation drove to such depths that she still wasn't sure she could reach it, but they had made a strong beginning and she saw that he was going to be very good for her.

"To the left hand, my brother," ole Senkali said to Crown in Masai.

"Where?" Crown asked. "I see. The grove." He swerved left toward the feathery shading acacias where the cattle milled impatient now to graze but confined by the work of the boys. Closing on the grove he caught a flash of white in the grass and braked well short of it. He cut the engine, threw open the door and stepped to the ground and leaving the door open, Cassie coming out the other door and ole Senkali extricating his walking stick from the back, he strode across the short dry grass to the body. The belly was torn open and the guts swelling and he took in the severed neck before he saw the head turned away from him beside the body. He knelt and turned it up. "The sons of bitches," he said. With his left hand gently he closed the eyes.

At the sight of the head Cassie winced and stepped back but she steeled herself and stepped forward again by Crown. "Is it someone you know?"

"He was studying the rhino. He was doing the bloody definitive study on rhino." Crown turned the head aside and stood. "His name was Dominick van Meeren. He was Dutch. He was a zoologist at the Serengeti Research Institute at Seronera." He examined the ground as he talked and something was wrong. "We had dinner together last week. He needed some radio tracking collars. He wanted me to help him buy them." There wasn't enough blood: the body must have been moved. "Get the blankets, would you, Cassie?" The Masai came up carrying his stick and bent to examine the body and the girl walked back to the Land Rover. "I would speak to your sons, ole Senkali," Crown said in Masai.

The boys watched from beyond the cattle. Ole Senkali

called them. Cassie returned with the blankets and spread
them overlapping on the grass and Crown rolled the body
onto them, stirring a buzzing cloud of flies, and laid the
head in its place at the neck. They wrapped head and body
together so that they could lift them into the car. The boys
waited now beside their father, politely bowing their heads.
Behind them the small zebu cattle saw their chance and
moved out onto the grass. The older boy told Crown how
they had found the body and explained that yes, they had
moved it to guard it from the vultures. He led Crown to the
place where the body had lain but blood was scant there
too. Whoever had murdered the poor bastard had murdered
him somewhere else and dumped his body here. The grass
was matted where a vehicle had driven in, a lorry from the
spead of the tracks, but the ground was too dry for tire im-
pressions.

Crown and ole Senkali had lifted the dead man into the
back of the Land Rover and closed the door before the older
boy remembered the paper. He pulled his shortsword from
its scabbard and unfolded the paper and handed it to
Crown saying that he had found it on a stick beside the
body. It was a small sheet of lined paper torn from a pocket
notebook, printed crudely in block capital letters. Crown
held it so that Cassie could read it with him:

ONE NOW
BUT LATER
MANY MORE.
RUKUMA

Crown translated it into Masai for ole Senkali. Ole Senkali
pursed his lips and spat.

"I don't understand," Cassie said. "It sounds like a
threat."

"*Rukuma*'s not a name," Crown said. "It's a black club
the Masai chiefs carry as a sign of office." He spoke to ole

Senkali in Masai: "Do you know of this Rukuma, my brother?"

"Nay," ole Senkali said. "He can be no Masai. No Masai would behead an unarmed man. The panga is not a weapon of the Masai."

"Have you seen a lorry in the area?"

"*O*. The white people in the buses striped like *il'oitigoshi*, like zebra, came here once to stare at the herd of black buffalo but the buffalo left the area many seasons ago. The machines that come here now are only those of the government men who go among us with medicines and bad advice."

"What did you ask him?" Cassie said.

"If he'd seen a lorry. He doesn't know anything about it."

"It doesn't make sense. Why would someone dump a body in the middle of nowhere and leave a note?"

"There was a herd of buffalo here years ago. We used to bring people out for game viewing. But it's close to ole Senkali's village."

"If we are finished, my brother," ole Senkali said, "I will return with my cattle to the *manyatta*."

"Thank you for helping us," Crown said. "We will take the body to the police in Arusha. The matter is theirs to study and resolve."

"Let them do so. It is the work of cowards." Ole Senkali nodded respectfully to Crown. "May your cattle prosper."

"*O*," Crown said. "And yours also." The Masai walked off to join his sons. "Let's get going, lady," Crown said. "Where's that note?" Cassie handed him the note and they got into the Land Rover. It stank of the body. Flies buzzed above the blankets and bounced off the windows. Crown reached up behind him and unlocked the trap in the roof and flipped it open. He started the engine and looked over the scene once more, shaking his head. Then he shifted into gear and pulled away.

Back at camp Crown sent Cassie to collect box lunches from the cook for the six-hour drive to Arusha and went looking for Abdi, his camp manager. The tourists had returned from a day of game viewing in the park and assembled on the porch for sundowners and he found Abdi inside the lodge tending bar. Abdi was nearly Crown's age, a tall, capable Somali. He'd been green as Crown when Crown hired him as his gun bearer in 1946. They'd learned the safari trade together and when Crown gave up professional hunting after Uhuru and bought the camp he'd kept Abdi on to run it.

Crown collected a beer from the refrigerator and led Abdi into the dining room where the tourists couldn't hear and told him about the dead man.

"It is very bad, Effendi," Abdi said when Crown finished. "If it is as you describe there is much arrogance in the note. The camp may be in danger."

"Maybe, except that Dominick wasn't working around here. He was working on the forest rhino up in the highlands." Crown drank deeply of the beer.

"But the body was brought here."

"Near here. If it's a warning to anybody, it's probably a warning to the Masai."

"But the man was not Masai. He was a *mzungu*, a white man."

"True," Crown said. "It was probably Dominick's bad luck. The forest's a pretty good hideout. He may have stumbled onto something." He studied his beer. "I honestly think it's a fluke, *mzee*—old man—but why don't you load up the guns when you get the time? No sense taking chances."

"I will do so."

"Did you get the engine back together?"

"*Ndiyo*. Yes. It runs smoothly."

"I've got to take the body into Arusha. Everything under control?"

"Everything is in order, Effendi, except that we are short

of toilet paper. A shipment waits in Arusha that might be picked up."

"I thought you went in for supplies last week."

Abdi pulled on his earlobe. "The shipment was late out of Dar-es-Salaam."

"Christ," Crown said. "Explain to me sometime why we have to get our toilet paper from the People's Republic of China, will you? And then explain to me why it's always pink." He drained the beer.

"The plastic sandals that many are wearing from the Chinese are also pink," Abdi said, taking the question seriously. "They like the color very much. Also the shirts. But the other material is not much used in Tanzania, Effendi. The people are poor. I do not think that they are very civilized."

"Right. The Somali are civilized."

"The Somali are very civilized."

"That's a civilized great scar on the side of your head."

"My enemy acquired many more scars."

"I remember. You ventilated him." Crown got up and pushed back his chair. "Okay, *mzee.* If I can roust out our supplier in the middle of the night I'll pick up the paper, but don't count on it. That Indian's too rich to sleep in the back of his *duka.* I can't hang around Arusha all night. The girl's going with me."

Abdi grinned. "She is a very fine woman. She has redeemed you from old age."

"You ought to know with your four wives."

"They are also very fine women although sometimes they are wearing."

"I'll bet they are." Crown turned to go and turned back. "You might call Seronera on the radio and have them tell the institute about their man. Tell them I've taken the body to the police in Arusha. They'll have arrangements to make. Oh, and ask them if they've got any toilet paper to spare."

Abdi stood then. At six feet he was three inches shorter

than Crown. "As you wish, Effendi. But if you do not pick up the paper and Seronera has none to spare us?"

"Then our guests will just have to use their thumbs, *mzee*. Your average civilized Somalis do."

Crown drove eastward across the Serengeti following the parallel dusty tracks where the tires of tourist cars had killed the grass and the sun set red behind them. The Crater Highlands that they would ascend and cross on their way to Arusha barricaded the eastern plain and robbed it of water. The highlands rose westward of a rift that was slowly splitting the continent apart and the spew of ash from their chain of volcanoes that were now forested and extinct had formed the plain. Up to the foothills twenty kilometers away it rolled out flat, one vast expanse of lion-colored grasses devoid of trees and featureless except for the moving game, tommies and zebra and herds of wildebeest and an occasional lone eland. The lions, the hyenas, the wild dogs that preyed on the game they could not see, but the predators moved there as well, gorged from hunting or preparing to hunt.

They turned southeast at Olduvai Gorge, the branching canyon eroded below the level of the plain that exposed in its layered beds the latest three million years of human history. Olduvai marked the upgrading of the track to a broad gray-dirt road and they followed the road southeast and began winding up into the highlands in the dusk and the dirt of the road altered color to rust-red. The view from altitude to higher altitude opened out into immensity as if they were circling upward in a plane, distances and farther distances of the Serengeti now graying and the sky deepening to dark and darker blue, mountains dimming far away to the north and the land to the south mottled with thorn scrub and empty of obvious habitation all the way to the horizon. They drove into montane forest then and the view was lost.

The air chilled and dampened with mist and the car slipped greasily on the red mud. Crown shifted to a lower gear for traction. Through the trees in the failing light Cassie saw a farmer plowing a narrow hillside field. He wore his iron-red blanket tied around his waist and he guided a crude wooden plow shaped from the forked branch of a tree. Cassie looked for oxen as the trees momentarily cleared but instead of oxen found the farmer's wife pulling the plow, the woman's head shaved and her upper body bare, her flat stretched breasts flapping, the leather traces hauled taut over her shoulders, her body bent far forward in strain, her long gaunt legs muscled to sinew and her bare feet breaking the maize stubble as she pulled and then they were past and the smell of woodsmoke blew in through the window pungent in the cool air.

Cassie hadn't expected the smells. They decoded Africa for her as sight alone could not. When she was twelve her father had taken her to Yellowstone National Park. She had delighted in the pictures of the geysers he had shown her in the encyclopedia before they left—Old Faithful, the Grotto, the Giant, the Castle, the Oblong with its rainbow basin—but nothing had prepared her for the stink of sulfur pouring from the basins and the mud pools and it sickened her until she adjusted to it and it was what she remembered first of all about Yellowstone now. African smells didn't sicken but they surprised her, the smell everywhere among Africans of sweat, the smells in Nairobi of hot peanut oil and rotting vegetables and the high-compression exhausts of small, right-hand-driven cars, the Masai potent with the cattle manure the women used to plaster their houses, the soil metallic with iron and the fragrant tropical trees and from every village and the yard of every house the smell of woodsmoke.

In Africa woodsmoke meant habitation as in America electric wires did. Her father had been an experimental physicist. As a graduate student at Caltech, during the war, he had been recruited to work with Hans Bethe at Los Alamos. He told her once—sadly or nostalgically, she wasn't certain which—that in the last weeks of the Manhattan Project he had held in his hands the spherical gold-plated plutonium core of the Nagasaki bomb. A woman sweating on an African hillside pulling a cruel wooden plow and her father holding the core of the Nagasaki bomb cupped in his hands. It was warm, he had said. It was no bigger than a softball and it made its own warmth.

The road leveled at altitude and curved around to the south through dense forest. In the dark now, the headlights sweeping the road, Crown shifted to higher gear. "Can you sense it?" he asked.

"What?"

"The crater."

She listened. Following out the noise of the engine she heard an expectancy in the air of space dropping away. "Yes. I think so."

"When we get back I want you to see it. It's the finest scenery in the world. We're a little below the rim. There's the turnoff to the lodge."

"Which crater? Ngorongoro?"

"Not so much emphasis on the 'n.' It's more like a hum—nngorongoro. The floor's two thousand feet down. You can't get in without four-wheel drive. There's a cabin down there the game boys use. We can stay overnight. No one ever gets to see the place at night except the Masai, and they don't give a damn for the game."

"They live there?"

"One village. Otherwise it's all game. Everything you find on the Serengeti." The car skidded in the mud and the body shifted behind them, thumping against the back seat. "Goddamned murderers," Crown said, angered again. "Ten to one it's some bloody dreamer working up some bloody cause. I'd take the Mau Mau any day. At least the Kikuyu had legitimate grievances. No one's got anything to complain about in Tanzania. It's a damned fine country except that it's poor."

"Did the Mau Mau murder your wife?"

He stared ahead. The car fishtailed and he slowed and swore.

"Seth? I'm sorry. I want to know you. I need to know you. I can't if I don't know how you got here."

"Where?"

"Here. In this time and place. Where you are."

"You want to know? Fine. I'll tell you just the way Abdi told me."

"Abdi was there?"

"He was there. It didn't matter. He couldn't help. He tried. What mattered was that I wasn't there."

"I'm sorry. Tell me. It will help me."

"Right," he said. "Why not. It's ancient history now."

After the war, Crown said, after he got back to Kenya from service in North Africa, he took up safari hunting and bought a ranch on the edge of the Masai reserve in Kenya, south of Ngong. His parents' mission had been on that reserve. He'd grown up there. Hell, a Masai woman had wet-nursed him. He spoke Masai before he spoke English. He still felt more Masai than American sometimes. He didn't know which he was. He was proud to be both.

Sidanu was mission-educated. They'd grown up together. She was the first Masai girl, the first one in the Purko division at least, who'd been educated beyond the reserve. He went off to North Africa and she went off to Nairobi and trained as a nurse. They reconnected after the war. She'd come back to the reserve to work with her people. They walked out to *ngoma* together. Those were the dances, a lot of activity in the bushes afterward among the young men and the young girls. They talked. They talked through a

whole year. When they decided to marry he went to her father. The old man was down in the mouth about her. He
didn't think he'd see any return on her because she'd been
educated and because she'd refused to be circumcised. That
didn't stop him from negotiating a stiff bride price, though.
Fifty white cows and ten fine young bulls and thirty goats.
They were married within the tribe. The British didn't sanction intermarriage.

They had a son the next year, Crown said. He named
him Joseph after his father. He took Sidanu and Joseph with
him on safaris. He lost a few clients, bloody British and
southern gentlemen from the States, but most of his clients
let it alone. They were interested in the hunting, not his private life.

The Mau Mau Emergency dried up the safari trade.
Scared most of the clients away. He arranged papers for
Abdi and his wives, two wives then, and settled them with
him on the ranch. He ranched through the Emergency and
tried to stay clear of it. Put in some time pacifying the
Masai. They didn't give a damn for the Kikuyu anyway. The
Masai were on their way to routing the Kikuyu when the
white man came in the first place and their own land was
secure. The settlers went hysterical over Mau Mau, pistols
under their pillows at night, everyone wearing side arms.
Nairobi looked like Dodge City. Some of the more fanatical
settlers suspected him of sympathy with Mau Mau because
he'd married across the color bar. They tried to pick fights
with him in the streets. He'd never taken Sidanu with him to
Nairobi because of the color bar and he couldn't take her
during the Emergency because it was dangerous and because Africans had to have special passes to move around.
He went only when he couldn't avoid it.

The bastards were right, too, he did sympathize with Mau
Mau. Not the terrorism but the Kikuyu demands for land
reform and an end to the color bar and for voting rights. Not

the counterterrorism the British and the settlers laid down either. They bombed the Aberdare forests where the guerrillas were based. They tortured prisoners. They packed the Africans into barbed-wire compounds where they couldn't grow enough food and they set up mass detention camps.

Do you know the numbers? Crown asked Cassie angrily. Everyone heard about the Mau Mau atrocities. That fascist Robert Ruark saw to that. Did you ever hear the numbers? The Mau Mau killed thirty-two white civilians in four years of fighting and one hundred sixty-seven soldiers and police. And the British Army and the Kenya Special Branch—the police—killed eleven thousand, five hundred and three guerrillas and god knows how many more noncombatants. So much for atrocities.

And one day in the last year of the Emergency, Crown said, in 1955, when the worst of it was over, when the Special Branch was hounding the last bands of Mau Mau out of the Aberdares, rounding up Mau Mau Prime Minister Dedan Kimathi so they could hang him, he went up to Nairobi for supplies. There was an outbreak of rinderpest in the district and he had to get vaccine for his new crop of calves. He left Sidanu and Joseph behind with Abdi. When he got back he found Abdi waiting for him at the gate. Abdi'd been beaten so brutally he could hardly talk, but he was holding the loaded Winchester he carried on safaris and he was guarding the gate.

"She was working in her *shamba,* the place you call the garden," Abdi told him afterward, sitting exhausted in the grass of the yard before the house now stained and obscene, gesturing across the yard. "It was early afternoon and the sun was warm. She wore the skirt of beaded goatskins and the four beaded collars of orange and blue and colored stripings that are the dress of the Masai woman honored in marriage. Her maize was ripe and she was picking it. Effendi, Effendi, her arms were full of the ears of yellow maize and she was happy. The boy Joseph was playing in the rows. The herdboys had driven the cattle to the grazing lands. My wives visited their *shamba* beside the watercourse, an hour's walk away. I only was with her, holding the basket to receive the ears of maize as she instructed me to do.

"We heard a lorry. At first the sound came from far away, from the Magadi road, and we hardly marked it, but the noise of the engine increased steadily and we heard it turning off onto the track that passes the ranch and coming fast this way. She imagined that it was you and she laughed and joked of your early return, that you could not stay long away from her, but I said, 'No, daughter, it is not the Effendi's car. It is a lorry.'" Abdi paused and shook his head. "I have no wisdom, Effendi. I have no wisdom or I should have understood. Men do not drive freely through the country in these evil times."

Go on, Crown had said.

"They stopped to open the gate. We could not see the gate from the *shamba* but we could hear them stop. Then they accelerated at great speed to the track in front of the house and suddenly braked, making a show, making the brakes squeal and raising a plume of dust. I saw through the dust that it was a lorry of the army, with the patches of paint on its body like a wild hunting dog.

"They had hardly stopped but they jumped out. Two white men. They were not dressed as soldiers. They wore the rough clothes of settler farmers and the belts of bullets across their chests—"

Bandoliers, Crown had said.

"—the bandoliers. They were armed with Sten guns, the ugly black guns that frequently jam on automatic fire and must be loaded with a tool. They called out your name, 'Crown! Crown!' and also they swore at you. They called you a Kaffir lover and worse things. They ordered you to come out of the house. They must have been drunken. No man would take such a risk of you unless he was drunken.

"All this happened very quickly, Effendi. The boy Joseph, knowing only friends at your house, would have run to them. I caught him and caught your wife and pulled them back into the maize, thinking that we could hide, but I saw the head of one of the men snap around in our direction and I knew that he had seen us. We heard one clatter across the porch and kick open the door and the other running toward us and then he appeared at the end of the rows of maize and ordered us to come out. He was big and puffy, with the paunch of a *fisi*, a hyena, and we obeyed because he menaced us with the Sten gun.

"His mouth was smirking as the *fisi* smirks when it corners its prey. 'Then this is the little family,' he said. He spoke in a way that I cannot imitate. He spoke English, but I believe that he was Boer. The other man called from the house, 'The bastard's not home, Jacob! It's just as I told you! I saw him making for Nairobi!' He looked from the window and saw us standing at the edge of the *shamba* and ran from the house and came over to where we stood.

" 'Well, well,' he said, 'the Kaffir whore and the half-breed *toto* and the faithful nigger. Just what we need.' His face was red and ugly and he was short but with powerful arms. 'Where's your master?' he asked us with much anger.

"Your wife was not afraid, Effendi. 'My husband is near,' she told him. She held the boy Joseph close against her side.

" 'Your *husband's* in Nairobi,' he said, and he called her the word for her sexual parts.

" 'What do you want?' she asked him. Her words were very cold.

" 'What do you want, *Bwana*,' he corrected her fiercely.

"She did not respond to his taunts. 'Whatever you want,' she said with dignity to the short man, 'you must leave here and not harm us. My husband is a great hunter. If you harm us he will hunt you down.'

"It was then that I acted. I did not want them to gain more control over us than they already had. I thought that I could occupy them and your wife and the boy Joseph could run away. I had no weapon but I jumped the paunchy one and carried him to the ground. I hit him in the face and tried to wrest the Sten gun from his hands but the other one hit me with his gun hard and knocked me out. It was nothing to do but it was all that was possible."

Crown had gripped Abdi's arm then. You didn't see the rest? he'd said.

The Somali had looked up and there were tears in his eyes. "Yes, Effendi, I saw much of the rest. But it is difficult to tell. She was your wife, but she was one of my daughters in the love I bore for her."

Crown had loosened his grip, looked away to the red sunset across the valley, looked back. Yes, he had said. I'll know all of it.

Abdi nodded. "It is what I would wish also." Crown had let him go then and he rubbed his right hand absently on the grass and stared ahead. "When I came back to wakefulness, I found that they had dragged me into the house. I was tied to one of the posts in the living room of those that support the roof. I opened my eyes first to the twisting horns of the greater kudu above the fireplace and then I saw the great stone fireplace with the fresh logs laid on for the evening and then my sight cleared and I saw the Boers in the middle of the room. The short one was holding the boy Joseph with his arms pinned behind him and the paunchy one was lying on your wife with his pants dropped around his ankles and he was raping her. She had fought them and her head and face were bloody where they had beaten her unconscious. They had ripped open her goatskin skirt and torn off her beaded collars and there were beads of bright colors scattered across the floor. The paunchy one was panting like a pig.

"The boy screamed at them in the tongue of the Masai. I do not know much of that tongue but he screamed things I had not thought a boy of seven years could know. I shouted also and cursed them but they paid me no heed. When the paunchy one had finished he stood and pulled up his pants and retrieved the boy, slapping him to silence, and the other, the short one, took his place over your wife on the floor.

"I struggled to break the bonds that held me to the post but I could not. I could hear each sound separately in the room and the light was bright from the western windows. It seemed to me that the sounds were equally loud, the breathing, the sound of the bodies, the sound I saw in the boy's staring eyes. The light was moving and breaking over the room and I thought that what I saw could not be happening. I would gladly have died to protect her from this. They did this vileness more than once, Effendi. To protect her from this and to protect your son from seeing it.

"With each act of filthiness they grew more violent. When they tired of holding the boy they cuffed him senseless and left him lying on the floor. I understood that they were working themselves up in the way cowards have, and I cursed them more vigorously in the hope that they would turn their anger to me. Finally they came to me and kicked me and berated you. They said they meant to teach you a lesson. They said you were worse than Mau Mau. They said your marriage to your wife violated God's law. They had the vileness to call on God's law when they were committing this filth. They said they would make Kenya a proper place for white men to live. I did not hear all that they said, Effendi. Sometimes I was unconscious from the kicking. But they left me again for your wife.

"The paunchy one attempted a last filthiness but it seems he was unable to perform. He rocked back on his knees, felt behind him and found his sheath knife and released it from

its sheath and brought it in front of him and looked to the
short man as if confirming an agreement. I shouted 'La! La!
—No! No!' but hastily the paunchy one raised the knife and
stabbed Sidanu your wife and raised it and stabbed her
again and rocking back he cut her belly cruelly. He scrab-
bled backward then like a crab and staggered to his feet and
dropped the knife and there was much blood and her limbs
were moving although I believe she was unconscious
throughout the attack and did not know the filthiness they
had done to her nor feel the pain of the stabbing and then
the short one shot her with the Sten gun and the noise of the
Sten gun firing and firing was terrible in the house.

"I thought that they would kill the boy next and then kill
me but they only tied the boy's hands and left him on the
floor. The short one came over to me. I was prepared to die
but he wanted me to give you a message. He was breathing
hard and there was madness in his eyes. 'Listen, you Kaffir
bastard,' he said, 'tell Crown we'll be up in the Aberdares
making a private safari. Tell him to come and get us if he's
got the balls for it.' He kicked me in the head then, Effendi,
and I knew nothing more until my wives returned in the late
afternoon and revived me and then you returned shortly
after."

And Crown had sat silently, staring at the dark line of the
distant rift wall where the sun had set. Abdi waited. Then
Crown in a choked voice had said: Yes. I did.

Beside him in the car, silently crying, the car speeding now
northeast to Arusha on the macadam road beyond the highlands, Cassie said: "Why?"

"Why? Because that's the way it worked. Do you wonder
the Africans wanted them out? It's no different in Rhodesia
and South Africa. It wasn't that much different in Vietnam."

"No," she said. "It wasn't. My god."

In Arusha they delivered the body to the police. Crown

gave them the note and made a report. He drove around to the Indian's and raised a watchman but the watchman was suspicious and refused to open the shuttered door. They left Arusha after midnight and drove back through the long darkness that in equatorial Africa contends from season to season equally with day, back over the highlands, Cassie awake beside Crown and watching, and dawn lightened the Serengeti before they pulled into camp.

"Let's get some sleep," Crown said. "And then let's go up to Ngorongoro. You can see what this country looked like before the apes arrived."

"What apes?"

"The black apes and the white apes and the brown apes. All the bloody apes that foul their own nests."

Two

THE CRATER WAS the best of it, Crown thought, Ngorongoro, the best place in all of Africa, and descending from the rim with Cassie in the Land Rover, cautiously maneuvering the unbarricaded hairpin curves of the steep dirt road wide enough for only one car in four-wheel drive and the lowest low gear, he hoped she'd think so too. No one remotely like her had come into his life since Sidanu. She rode beside him cool in a white shirt and tan safari shorts with her tawny hair tied up in a square of blue silk. He enjoyed that of her too, her beauty, her poise, but that wasn't the difference. She was upper-middle-class American. She ought to have been as spoiled and selfish or unfinished as the other American girls he'd known who came out to Africa on their own to party or earnestly to view the game. She was none of those and she had come out for other reasons. He didn't know all the reasons yet but he meant to find them out and in the meantime he meant for her to see the best that he could show her, because in bed or beside him at table or merely riding at ease with him in the car she made him feel at home. It was a simple feeling and many ordinary people took it for granted every day but he hadn't felt it securely anywhere or with anyone since Sidanu died. The times he got closest to it were the times he visited the crater. Bringing Cassie to the crater ought to do it nicely for him then and he wished the same for her.

They had driven up from camp before dawn, the death and the trip to Arusha a day and a night behind them, and eaten breakfast at the fine new lodge on the rim at seventy-six hundred feet. After breakfast they stood outside on the tiled terrace watching the clouds, the clouds that sometimes covered over the crater at night like curtains drawn before a stage, roll and break into streamers gilded and rainbow-edged by the morning sun and drift away. From the terrace the forest along the watercourses on the crater floor, umbrella thorns and fever trees and figs, reduced in the distance to lines of dark green running through the lighter green of the savanna to the shining golden-pink lake. The crater floor spread out that far below them. The opposite rim was sixteen kilometers away. She had marveled at the view and he had felt as if he were not only showing it to her but giving it to her, as if between them, in the sharing that had already begun between them, a view that the other hadn't seen or something that had happened to you that the other didn't know were the most important gifts that you could give.

Ngorongoro was not properly a crater at all but the caldera of an ancient volcano, the bowl that formed when the cone collapsed. Time had worn its lava to soil and wind had blown in the seeds of grasses and shrubs and trees. When the bowl was pastured and forested, game had found its way up from the Serengeti and discovered a gap in the rim and proceeded down onto the crater floor to take up permanent residence, blue wildebeest and zebra, elephant and ar-

mored rhino, hippo fat in the pools, black-maned lions, dark
buffalo, hyena, ostrich, giraffe, tommies and Grant's gazelle
and topi and hartebeest and all the lesser game and descending into the crater from the air all manner of birds,
crowned cranes and bustards, herons and sacred ibis and
avocets, weavers and spoonbills and vultures and dour
marabou storks.

The crater guarded a model Serengeti within the fastness
of its walls. For Crown it also guarded the Africa that once
had been. Even the Masai who lived in the crater and
grazed their cattle there belonged, because the Masai in the
wisdom of their arrogance credited the twentieth century
not at all except in veterinary matters. His parents had labored among them for two decades and hardly made a dent.
His parents were the only missionaries the Masai had ever
allowed on the reserve and the Masai allowed them only because his father had been a cattle farmer and showed far
more interest in improving their cattle than in improving
their souls.

Other cars had left the lodge before them. When they
reached the crater floor and entered the open acacia forest
that hugged the lower margins of the wall they found three
tourist Range Rovers stopped ahead of them blocking the
track. They looked beyond the cars to locate the obstacle
and there were elephants, six cows milling in the track, two
of them with calves, and the largest of the cows faced the
lead car as if daring it to move. She was baggy in her bulk,
black, her withers and her rump dust-reddened, with fan-
shaped, ragged ears like battened sails and one tusk broken
off halfway down its length and she towered up into the
trees. From her size and the weight of her ivory Crown put
her age at above fifty years, a matriarch. He pulled aside
and slowly passed the other cars and the drivers frantically
gestured to him but he pulled onto the track again and took
the lead.

The elephant loomed ahead. Cassie gripped the seat. "What are you going to do?"

"Move them out. They'll face you off for hours unless you give them a push." He inched forward, disengaged the clutch, raced the engine in a growl. The matriarch flapped her ears irritably and he engaged the clutch and inched forward again and stopped and growled the engine. The matriarch swayed her massive head and hoisted her trunk and advanced toward the Land Rover. Crown hurriedly shifted into reverse and backed up to his starting point and placated she stopped.

"I can think of other places I'd rather be right now," Cassie said.

"Peace," Crown said quietly, keeping his eyes on the elephant. "We're having a little discussion here."

When the matriarch lowered her trunk he shifted into forward gear again and moved ahead and stopped and growled the engine and this time the elephant watched him without displaying. He growled the engine once more, louder, and suddenly she trumpeted and Cassie gripped the seat harder but he inched forward again half-clutching so the engine would race and abruptly the matriarch gave way, her body going around in parts, the head first led by the trunk and then the forelegs working the reddened withers and then the belly and the boxcar rump and the other cows moved with her into the forest, the calves quick among their legs, and the road was clear and behind them they heard the tourists cheering.

"Crown, buddy," Cassie said, "I'm glad you know what the hell you're doing because I thought we were goners."

He grinned and patted her hand. "Don't tell anyone, but I did too."

"Wonderful. Do we also get eaten by lions?"

"Now you know why the Africans don't care much for the game."

"There's a lesson here."

Driving on: "There's always a lesson."

"Yes," she said soberly, settling back in the seat. "There is."

They left the forest and came out onto the savanna. It was not flat as it had appeared from the rim but rolling. Wildebeest striped vertically at the shoulders and black-bearded grazed on low, grass-smoothed hills intermingled with ostrich and tommies and families of fat zebra. Small white egrets harvested the insects the grazers disturbed. The animals fed as peacefully as cattle pastured on a farm but more noisily, the wildebeest chorusing in grunts, and they hardly marked the car as Crown drove among them.

"That's a very funny animal," Cassie said.

"Which?" Crown stopped the car.

"The wildebeest."

"Odd sense of humor. Most people think they look mournful."

"They look as if the grass never made it to the rear end."

"They do have runty behinds, don't they."

"I saw some hyenas before we got to your camp. They were built that way too."

"Makes more sense with them. They need the muscle up front to carry off your leftover head or leg."

"Are they a kind of cattle?"

"The hyena?"

"No, you madman. The wildebeest."

"Antelope. But they're cattlelike. They fill the cattle niche out here." He pointed. "Look over there. See that bull standing and pawing?"

"Where? Oh, I see."

"Then see the bull beyond him? And the one over there? And there?"

"They're all doing it."

"Those old boys have taken up territories. They pretty

much hold territories year-round in the crater. They try to entice the cows into their patch of ground and keep them there. The young bachelors come in and try to pick them off. Actually, it's just past calving time. It's a hell of a show. The cows all calve together in the space of about a month."

"Amazing. How do they manage it?"

"They synchronize it. I suppose it's the smell. They can hold off calving up to three weeks. The idea is to swamp the predators. Drop so many calves they're glutted. Even then the hyenas get about three quarters of them every year."

Cassie watched the nearest bull. A cow grazed toward an invisible line and the bull trotted over to it and shouldered it back. Beyond the wildebeest, beyond the near hills, blue in the distance, the crater wall rose up and white clouds held back by the heat rising from the crater floor poised at the rim like a surf. "I'd always heard them called gnu," she said to Crown. "Is wildebeest the African word?"

"Gnu's the African. It's Hottentot. It's supposed to sound like that bellowing snort of theirs. *T'gnu*. Wildebeest is Afrikaans. Boer."

She started at the word. He'd said enough that night and she hadn't asked. "What happened to the Boers? The two men?"

"We chased them into the Aberdares." Pain in his face, and that quickly his voice had gone hard. "The Special Branch loaned us one of its pseudo-terrorists, one of the Mau Mau they'd turned. He knew the trails, but it took a week. We found them up high, near the bamboo zone. The Mau Mau found them first. And the vultures. There wasn't much left of them." He looked at her sharply. "I appreciated the Mau Mau and the vultures but I'd rather have done the job myself."

"What about Joseph?" she asked quietly. "Was he all right?"

He shrugged, turned away, watched the bulls at post among the herd. "I raised him as best I could."

"At home?"

"At first at home. He wouldn't let me near him. I was his father, but I was white. He never cried. He just fought me. He had nightmares. He'd wake up screaming. Abdi's wives helped. He spent a lot of time with Abdi. He got used to me again. I thought everything was squared away. I kept it jolly. I didn't try to raise him as a Masai. I taught him how to shoot. I taught him how to handle a spear. I took him with me on safaris when they started up again after the Emergency. He had to go to school so I sent him to school in Nairobi. We'd get together between terms. He was a very solemn boy but he was one hell of a student. He went up to university in Nairobi. That's when I bought the camp. I figured he could take it over after he finished his degree. But he got mixed up in politics at the university, veered off in his own direction. The *Mzee* was tightening up the ship at that time and Joseph must have said the wrong things in the wrong places. The authorities sent him down."

"Who's the *Mzee?*"

"Jomo Kenyatta. The Prime Minister of Kenya." Despite the open windows the Land Rover was heating in the morning sun. Crown levered out the breeze vents under the windshield, on Cassie's side first and then on his. "That was halfway through his third year. He stayed with me for a month and then we had a row and he took off."

"Where?"

"Nairobi. He cleaned out the cash box and stole one of the Land Rovers. We found it in Nairobi. He'd sold it. I looked for him all over hell and gone. He had a network of friends by then. He just disappeared. I've never heard a word from him since."

"How long has it been?"

"That was 1968. Ten years. He'd be thirty now."

She looked down at her hands. "Then he never got over it. How terrible for both of you."

"He got over it. After he changed to fit it in. But right," Crown said, shifting into gear, moving on, "he never gave up hating me. Can't say I blame him."

They drove to the soda lake and stopped back from the shore. Around the wide shore and far into the lake, pink-and-black flamingos waded the shallows seining for the algae that bloomed there, hundreds of thousands of flamingos on pink stilt legs doubled in reflection in the still silver water heavy with alkali.

"So that's why the lake looked pink," Cassie said.

Crown nodded absently. The flamingos unminding fed, curving their sinuous necks, their heads under water swaying, and a salt breeze blew through the car. Joseph retreating from Nairobi all the way to the camp in a battered taxi, his cabbie friend dropping him off. Fueling the taxi and sending it back, a city machine ridiculous in the bush. His angry son denouncing, pacing the porch, tall as a Masai but thicker, Crown's blood, bigger-boned, lighter than the red-brown Masai and no less fierce. He called the authorities fools for sending him down and cursed them, cursed Crown as well through the long month of argument. He didn't want the camp, the camp was vulgarity and greed, the camp was another outpost of black *totos* and white bwanas, he wanted a share of his inheritance, he wanted to go abroad. Leave this ugly place of fools and corruption, Kenyatta's men already fair imitations of the British before, black colonials exploiting the people on the model of the whites. New exploiters: *wabenzi:* the people of the Mercedes-Benz. There will be a day of reckoning, Joseph shouted, shouting his rage, there will be a day of reckoning!

And the last night, when they both had taken as much from each other as they could take, the argument exploding

into violence, fighting each other in the bar, father and son
wrestling on the floor, Crown trying to restrain Joseph and
not to batter but enraged by his ingratitude and by his
taunts at the failure before, and Joseph in the thick of it
flashing a knife, and Abdi, Abdi who had understood the
need for purgation and stood unhappily by, Abdi pulling
Joseph off, forcing the knife from his hand and pinning back
his arms and then remembering the earlier time and as if the
pinning of the arms had burned him Abdi let Joseph go.
And Joseph silent in his room until the camp slept and stealing the cash then and the Land Rover and running away.
Even now, after ten years, Crown would welcome him
home.

A hyena strolled past them to the shore. It stood at the
edge of the water studying the flamingos and then stretching its neck, its dark tail raised straight up and its ears
turned forward, it dashed into the shallows and scattered
the nearest birds. They flew up noisily and settled, making a
clearing around the hyena. It waded to shore and studied
and dashed again without apparent aim.

"That's odd," Crown said. "They don't usually hunt
flamingos."

"I'm surprised they even go into the water," Cassie said.

"They don't mind it. I've seen them feeding on drowned
wildebeest in water over their heads. Dive like ducks and
come up with a mouthful and stand there on their hind
legs gulping it down."

"They're horrible animals."

"Give them a chance. You haven't seen them hunting at
night. They're not the bloody scavengers everybody thinks.
They scavenge less than the lions. The lions steal their kills.
They'll go out of their way to take on a lion if it's alone.
Hell, get enough of them together and they'll take on almost
anything. They're very tough and very efficient. They don't
kill and then eat. They kill by eating."

"That's even worse."

"Depends on your point of view. It has a certain purity about it." He raised his hand. "Watch. Here he goes."

Stretching its neck again, its tail up, the hyena raced through the water avoiding birds nearer at the side. It was chasing one bird that was slow to take flight and it closed on the slow bird as it lifted from the water, the hyena jumping and catching a leg, the bird's black wings flapping helplessly, and pulled it down and took it under. The wings beat on the water and the hyena flashed up and bit into the body and the wings went limp and it gulped feathers and all, blood and feathers sticking to its muzzle and the wings severed from the body floating separately away. The body devoured, momentarily the hyena considered the wings and then forgot them and swung around and waded calmly to shore. It shook itself like a dog and sniffed curiously in their direction and softly grunt-laughed, its tail going down between its legs, and slunk off the way it had come, looking back again and once again at the car.

Cassie turned from watching. "From now on I'll shut up until I know what I'm talking about."

"You have a right to think what you want to."

"I don't when it's ignorant."

"It wasn't ignorant." He winked. "Maybe uninformed." She took his arm. "Do you realize I wanted you ten minutes after I saw you?"

"We wasted a lot of time then."

"I don't mean sexually. Well. That too. I mean to know you. To be with you. Why is that when you were a complete stranger?"

"Listen, lady, I'm doing well just to figure out these beasts around here."

"Did you feel that way?"

"I'm older," Crown said, smiling. "My reflexes are slower."

"Don't joke. It isn't reflexes. It's more like imprinting. I know why with you. You remind me of my father."

"Oh, very good. That's going to help us a lot in bed."

"Seriously, Seth. I must remind you of someone too."

He hadn't realized. "Sidanu," he said.

"But she was so different."

"Maybe not."

"I'm like her?"

"She was straight. She was completely honest."

"You think I'm like that?"

"So far. Yes, I think you are."

She looked away, looked out toward the lake. "Thank you."

"My pleasure," he said.

She turned to him. "I'm happy with you. Seth? You know?"

He took her in his arms, her head against his chest, and looked beyond as she had looked. "I know. I'm just beginning to feel it. I had a longer wait than you."

He held her in silence, a space of silence. They listened to the crater, the breeze rustling the grasses behind them, the flamingos lifting their heads dripping from the water and plunging them back, rippling. They separated then and Crown drove toward the shore to turn around and as the lone hyena had been unable to do, the machine put the flamingos to full flight, pink birds with black wings flapping away from the shore, a field of pink beating black in a curving plane flaring radiant against the overcast.

They drove around the lake to Loitokitok Springs to picnic but found the area pre-empted by tourists eating box lunches and dodging the black African kites that swooped like bats to snatch at their food. Instead they turned and followed the curve of the lake to the Munge River on the southeast shore. The river channel cut deep into the floor of the crater, overgrown with dense bush and riverine trees hung with vines, and the river ran narrow and clear from the headland of the wall to empty into the sink of the lake. They followed it south to the cabin hidden in a grove above its banks. The cabin was built of logs and shingled like the old lodge on the rim and small four-paned windows had been set high in its walls. Inside, the rooms were dark and cool. Crown came out from inspecting them and opened the back door of the Land Rover. He passed Cassie the picnic basket and collected two cold bottles of Tusker beer from the ice chest. They spread out their picnic on the cabin's front stoop. The cook had packed them fried chicken and papayas and English chocolate biscuits sealed in thin foil. Cassie halved and cleaned the papayas, scooping the black seeds into a piece of waxed paper. Crown sorted out linen and silver and levered the caps off the beers. The sky had darkened. The air was fresh and smelled of distant rain.

After a while Cassie said: "I keep remembering what happened."

"Van Meeren?"

"Yes. Will the police do anything?"

"I suppose they'll send out a team. Look around, ask around. There's not much to go on. They'll steer clear of the highlands. They're city boys." Crown picked up his beer, drank, set the bottle down. "The Masai pretty much run their own show out here. I should talk to ole Kipoin. He's the paramount chief of this section. Ole Senkali's probably already passed the word. Ole Kipoin ought to alert the *moran*. They'd keep an eye out."

"The *moran?*"

"The young warriors. The word really means cattlemen, guards. They guard the cattle and the villages."

"Are you really a Masai?"

"No. I'm officially a Masai."

She had finished her papaya and she wrapped the skin in the waxed paper with the seeds. "It's weird. It's like meeting someone and discovering later he's a rock star."

"It's not so strange. You had men in the Old West who were taken into Indian tribes."

"Are they as primitive as they look?"

He laughed. "We've got two Oxford men on the Council. They'd find that question hilarious."

"They went off to college and came back to herd cattle?"

"And help run things. The Masai are wealthy as Africans go. Cattle and land. They're developing it and trying to keep the old ways alive at the same time. It's working. You'll meet your detribalized Masai, but the people have kept together. There'll be some grim business about the murder. They've never had much crime and they don't like it on their land."

"This is their land too?"

"The crater? It's a game reserve area, but it's Masai."

"Some land," Cassie said.

Thunder had rumbled above the crater as they ate. As they repacked the basket and carried it to the Land Rover the rain blew in, light rain misting through the trees and across the cleared space in front of the cabin. They pulled their travel bags from the car and slid the windows closed and ran inside. "In here," Crown said. He led her through the kitchen into the larger room of the cabin. A stone fireplace was built into the wall at the end of the room and beside it was a table with canvas camp chairs. Nearer the kitchen wall two camp beds had been made up with sheets and olive-drab blankets. A kerosene lantern with a smoke-darkened chimney stood in the center of the table and another stood on the low table between the beds. There were candles in tin holders stored in the rough board bookshelves built onto the wall at one side of the fireplace. "It looks like

we're in for the afternoon," Crown said. "We could try it in
the rain but we wouldn't see much."

Cassie went to the beds and began turning one down.
"Why don't we try it in the rain?" she said, looking back at
him and grinning. He laughed and tossed his bag onto the
other bed and came to her.

They caressed each other in the narrow bed, mounting up
to love. His body was lean and hard, younger than his
weathered face with its lines at his eyes and his mouth and
on his high forehead and when they made love she sought
the muscles that worked at his shoulders and in the small of
his back. She lost them in pleasure, lost her hands and her
arms and sight failed and he waited for her to return to him
and moved again and when he cried out the cries like cries
of pain no longer surprised her. She held him close then in
her arms, hearing his breathing, and the tenderness that
flooded her brought tears to her eyes. Silently between they
rested, discovering each other by touch, and made love
again and rested and the small rain sounded on the shingled
roof and altered by cloud-blow the light grew and dimmed
from the windows.

Naked at the head of the bed, Crown leaned back against
the rough wall. He had drawn up his legs. Cassie leaned
against him and traced the curving scar she found on his
knee.

"Shrapnel," he said. "I caught it in North Africa in the
war. Some bastard kraut made me a present of a grenade.
They sent me over to the States to fix it up. First time I'd
been there. When they let me out I took a train to Missouri
and visited the family farm."

"Where?"

"Near Independence. It's not in the family anymore. Fine
land though. Three hundred sixty acres. My father left it to
his sons by his first wife. My half brothers." He winked at
her. "Lovely breasts you've got there."

She smiled and pushed back her hair. "I always thought so. You're not half bad-looking yourself."

"A modest person," he said. "Don't overdo the praise."

"Well, for an older man."

"I feel about twenty-five right now." He growled, clowning. "Go fight *simba*. Go pick up *ndovu*, swing him by trunk, throw him over fever tree."

Laughing: "If you've got all that energy, maybe we should make love again."

"*Ndiyo*. Make love again. Put spear in ground." He left it to admire her. "You're a very beautiful woman."

"Thank you. I'm glad you think so."

"I think so." He moved down beside her, his hand on her shoulder, their faces near. "We have time now," he said gently. "Tell me about your father."

She closed and opened her eyes. "How he died?"

"More if you want to. I remind you of him."

"I'll have to sit up for that."

"Don't sit up. Stay here. If you sit up you'll go away into it."

"I haven't told anyone."

"I know. Tell me. Let it go. Let it go, and I'll try to let what I've got go too. It's past. Put it there and maybe I can put what I've been carrying there."

She moved down farther in the bed, her head against his chest so that he not only heard her words but felt them through his body.

"He wasn't old. He was only fifty-eight. I thought we had years. Years to help him and years for my own life after that."

"What were you helping him with?"

"His work. He was an experimental physicist. He was associate director of the Lawrence Livermore Laboratory."

"Where?"

"In Livermore. In California. That's where we lived. He

was very involved in government energy policy. He spent a
lot of time in Washington working with Congress. I was sort
of his aide. We flew back and forth."

"What did he look like?"

"He was tall. Almost your height, but thinner. Too thin. I
used to try to feed him up. He worked too hard. He looked
Scandinavian. Bony, loose. Long arms. Long legs. Light
brown hair that was going gray. Just long enough to comb,
the way men wore their hair in World War II. Glasses. I got
him into aviator frames. He wasn't handsome but he was
boyish. Shy when he wasn't working. Intense when he was
working and absolutely sure of himself. In California he
wore string ties. You know, turquoise and silver slides. That
was from the war, from New Mexico. He'd been a graduate
student at Caltech and they recruited him for Los Alamos to
work on the atomic bomb."

Crown whistled.

"After the war he went back to Caltech and finished up
his doctorate. Edward Teller recruited him for Livermore. It
was just starting up."

"Who's Teller?"

"He started Livermore. He built the hydrogen bomb."

"Your father worked on that too."

"He wasn't proud of it. He thought the United States
should have it first. He thought that was less risky than the
Russians having it first. He was proud of his career. His father was a garage mechanic in Oklahoma City and his
mother was a schoolteacher. He'd gotten a scholarship to
Caltech. But not of the bomb work. Do you remember the
Cuban missile crisis?"

"Very well. Even out here."

"I was only eleven. I didn't understand what was going
on. I came home from school that week and found him at
home watching TV. He just sat there all week watching TV.
At the end of the week, in the worst of it, when the ships

were about to confront each other in the Caribbean and everyone thought we were on the brink of nuclear war, I came
in to him and he didn't say anything but he took me on his
lap and held me as you're holding me, as if he wanted to
protect me from some terrible danger. I realized later that
he felt the most awful guilt, that the weapons that were
threatening the United States, Russia, everything, were the
weapons he'd helped build. He told me once that a friend of
his at Los Alamos had gone back to New York after the war
fully convinced that life on earth wouldn't survive more
than a few more years. I think my father felt that way too.
He lived that way, intensely, every day. He taught me to
live that way too.

"He talked to me. It's the earliest memory I have. He and
my mother weren't close. Her father had made a bundle in
real estate in Santa Barbara and she thought she was better
than my father. She did the garden-club number and the so-
cial number and she wasn't interested in his work. I was the
oldest child, so he talked to me. He was good with my
brothers too but he talked to me. When I got to school I
found out the other kids had heard about Winnie the Pooh
and the wind in the willows. I heard about subatomic structure and the evolution of stars. It was just as magical. It still
is."

She stopped, remembering.

"He coached me for exams. He took me with him sometimes on hunting trips. He talked me through a political
phase when I was out protesting the war in Vietnam and
even though his politics were conservative he saw the point
and came over to my side and made himself unpopular in
Washington for a while. And the little things. He taught me
to shoot pool. My mother was horrified. My senior year in
high school I broke my wrist skiing and couldn't type, the
cast was too heavy. He rigged a sling to a rope and ran the
rope through pulleys in the ceiling of my room and

weighted it to counterbalance the cast and I could type again. My sophomore year at Stanford he saw me through an abortion."

"That's not so little," Crown said.

"No. He never said a word." She shifted, moved back to look at Crown. "He was strong for me. Do you understand? He nurtured me and gave me strength. He was my closest friend."

"I understand."

"Yes." She hugged herself and shuddered and Crown gently separated her arms and she opened her eyes and he stroked her hair. "Livermore is working on laser fusion. We'd been at Fermilab, in Illinois, going over the problems with some of the men there. We flew from Chicago to San Francisco and he brought the car around and we drove around the bay to Livermore. He seemed distracted. He missed a turn. It surprised me because he always knew where he was, even in a strange city. We got home about six o'clock. He let me out and put the car away and I went on inside. He came into the front hall and looked at me and smiled and said my name and then his hands went up to his head, pressing on his temples, and he just folded up and collapsed on the floor. I ran to him and tried to lift his head and see what was wrong. He wasn't breathing and I couldn't find a pulse and I screamed for help but nobody was home. I ran into the living room and dragged the phone into the hall and started giving him cardiac massage and artificial respiration and in between I got the operator and she called the paramedics. I thought he'd had a heart attack. It wasn't a heart attack. It was a massive stroke. He was dead when he fell.

"No one murdered him. It's not exceptional. It happens all the time." She was whispering now and staring. "People die in the prime of their lives. But it emptied me. He taught me how close it's possible to be to another human being. I felt as if I'd died with him. One moment we were together and then I looked around and he was gone. Everything was unreal. Water came out of faucets. Food grew in supermarkets in little plastic bags. Clothes that strangers had made came out of closets and were put on and taken off and hung back in closets in the dark. Streetlights turned on by themselves and turned off again in the morning. There weren't any facts anymore. My father had died. My closest friend had died. That was a fact. That was the only fact I knew. I thought of it as a new kind of physics. I had to design a whole new world. I tried to think where it would lead, what followed from it. The first thing that followed from it was that I had to go as far away from Livermore as possible, to a place as different from Livermore as possible. Somewhere where all the facts were different so that the hole where my father had been wouldn't show."

She stopped then and reached for him, letting it go, her voice changing as the crying began: "But I never thought I'd find you out here. I never thought I'd find someone to be close to again."

Crown held her as her body shook, held her long, longer the grief, the grief she'd held back, and took the release of it in his arms for the gift it was.

"Neither did I," he whispered when she quieted. "Cassie?" Tears in his eyes: the room blurred. "Love? Neither did I."

Later they built a fire. Crown went out to the Land Rover for the chop box and the sky had cleared. They cooked dinner on the kerosene stove in the kitchen and ate at the table beside the fireplace. After dinner they took blankets and drove in darkness to a hill near the center of the crater. They parked on the crest of the hill and climbed through the trap in the Land Rover to the roof and closed the trap and spread the blankets and lay under the night sky. Hyenas whooped in the crater, the clans gathering to hunt. The moon had not yet risen. No city lights dimmed the stars. Looking up from the crater was like looking up from a well. The crater walls raised the horizon, marking a circle that seemed of the sky, but below the circle was blackness without stars, the black walls, the enclosing earth that was not like a star and did not burn.

"Can you see my hand?" Crown asked. "Follow where I'm pointing. Pick them out. Sirius. Rigel. That red star—Aldebaran. The Pleiades. Andromeda. And the Big Dipper upside down. But look the other way, over your head. The Southern Cross. You'll never see it better. Below that, Alpha Centauri. Over there, that dim glow—the Large Magellanic Cloud. Canopus. Achernar. The South Pole's between Achernar and the Southern Cross, and you can't see the North Star at all." He lowered his arm. "That's how far away you are. Even the stars aren't the same."

"They're beautiful," she said. She took his hand and they watched the sky and she felt as if she were floating, safely tethered by his hand. "Seth?" she said then. "I haven't asked you if you want me here. I haven't asked you how long I should stay. I invaded your life and I don't have to stay any longer than you want me."

"Don't think about it," he said. "Don't even wonder."

"I did invade you."

"There's no way we can know."

"I know now."

"So do I, but you came out here with grief and until the grief is over you can't really know."

"I do know. I just don't want you to feel invaded."

"I don't feel invaded. I'm just coming back to life."

"I don't want to hurry anything or push anything but do you think when you're completely back to life you'll want me to be part of that life?"

He was silent then and the silence was frightening to her.

He was thinking: the camp, the plain in its seasons, walking
out on the land. The simple, ordinary days and the nights.
All that he had loved that had emptied away and the years
of bitterness and the sterile years when he got on with it and
that now was refilling. The place below the high blued hills
cool where the clear stream ran down through fernfalls
where they'd camped with Joseph, where Joseph laughed
and the waterbuck came to drink. Maybe a child, children.
She would want them. It wasn't too late. He had given it all
up but it wasn't too late and what he had seen he could see
again freshly through her. The odd thing was the trust. That
it came so quickly. He supposed he was primed for it. She
was too. You got a chance to remake your life about every
ten years. Everything could go to hell and then you'd wake
up one morning and you had a new chance, if you saw it.
The wonder of it was that it was the same for her. And that
they knew. If you cheated on yourself and lied to yourself
then you missed it. Many people missed it. Maybe most people missed it, from dishonesty or because they didn't see.
But if you were honest with yourself and you saw it then
you knew. And even if it didn't last forever you had it and
they couldn't take it away from you. It never lasted forever.
No such bloody luck as it ever lasting forever. But while it
was there it was everything.

"Seth?"

He raised himself beside her and looked into her eyes.
"You are that life," he said simply.

"It is good that you are back," Abdi greeted them the next
morning. "A General Nguvu of the Army of Tanzania has
radioed from Arusha that he wishes to speak with you of the
death, Effendi. He will fly here from Arusha early in the afternoon. Also, Robert Fuhrey is here."

"Robert Fuhrey?" Cassie questioned Crown. "Is he American?"

"He's a Harvard paleontologist. He's working on a hominid site west of here at Oloito Gorge."

"That's amazing," she said. "I know him. I didn't realize he was out here."

"Also, Effendi," Abdi finished, "we have acquired a great reserve of toilet paper. Unfortunately it is once again pink."

"Busy times," Crown said.

Three

"I'D APOLOGIZE FOR dragging you two away," Robert Fuhrey said happily from the back seat of the Land Rover, "but it's no good just seeing the tooth. You've got to see the site. Cassie's a virgin in these site matters, Seth. Anyway, this is a new high in paleontology. I should say new low. I want your flabbergasted witnesses. I want to hear some *ooh-ahs*." They neared Oloito Gorge on the track that ran west through thorn scrub from Crown's camp, at midmorning. "The bitter reality," Fuhrey said, pitching his voice deeper and pretending shame, "is that my man Bwana John Kegedi found the tooth. I was still poking around doing the site survey."

Cassie turned smiling to look at him and he grinned. Her honorary older brother. He had been a senior at Stanford when she was a sophomore. He dated her roommate and ate and studied and sometimes slept at their apartment. He knew he was going into paleontology and he talked endlessly about East Africa. It was the world center for hominid studies and from books and maps he'd memorized it. Listen, he said to her once when she was moping around the apartment after the abortion. Listen to this. You need a little perspective on this venereal matter, my child. Kiambu and Moshi, he recited, proudly rolling the place names and beating out the time like a conductor, Lake Turkana and Homa Bay, Endashat, Kericho, Tsavo, Laikipia, Loolmalassin and Keekorok. How can you be depressed when you haven't even been to Keekorok? What's the worst line Hemingway ever wrote, daughter? he asked her. You don't know? You're a sophomore at a respected university and you haven't even taken up Hemingway-baiting? Whatever will the English Department think of you? Okay, Fuhrey said, this is the worst line Hemingstein ever wrote. Are you ready? *Highly humorous was the hyena obscenely loping, full belly dragging, at daylight on the plain, who, shot from the stern, skittered on into speed to tumble end over end.* How can you be depressed when Hemingway's highly humorous hyena is obscenely loping somewhere out there shot from the stern? God, he said, I love that 'skittered on into speed.' Speed! Took him hours to find that word. You'd better read *Green Hills of Africa*, daughter. No way to be depressed when you read *Green Hills of Africa*. Even with the bad line it's a golden oldie. That Papa could really sing.

Fuhrey's talk was one of the reasons she chose to come to East Africa. He made it real to her even as he showed her its distance from her life. He was skinny then and pale, and all his charm left him when he turned his talk to science. It was his deity in those days and he was humorless about it. She was glad to see the change. He'd graduated and gone on to Harvard and they'd lost touch. Now he was almost stocky, tanned, his beak of a nose sunburned and peeling, his curly auburn hair lighter than before, sun-bleached, his face matured with a dark red beard. His association with Crown and his new self-confidence delighted her. He was one of those rare friends whose loyalty survived years of separation,

who met her again at Crown's as if he'd talked to her only
the day before.

He leaned forward and patted her on the arm. "Ah, Cassie, me darlin', yir a sight for sore eyes."

"Is he always like this?" Cassie asked Crown. "He was
much more dignified when I knew him."

"Stuffy," Fuhrey corrected her. "The operant word is
stuffy. I thought paleontology was a branch of undertaking."
He snapped his fingers, jiving. "Roll dem bones, Doc
Fuhrey, roll dem bones."

"He's just giddy," Crown said. "Hard to blame the wee
lad. He'll be famous if he pulls this one off. He's got a handle on the bloody missing link."

"Jesus, 'missing link,'" Fuhrey said. "So much for enlightened patronage. Did I mention that it's your site?" he asked
Crown. "The lowest bed at SCK?"

"Is it? Restores my faith in honest bribery, Robert."

"Have you been encouraging this crazy?" Cassie asked.

"I throw him some scraps now and then. It's earned me
the dubious honor of having a ravine named after me."

"That's the custom," Fuhrey said to Cassie. "The Leakeys
started it at Olduvai. Oloito's shot with side canyons. We'd
call one a ravine. *Korongo* in Swahili. You designate each
one with a name. So SCK, Seth Crown's *Korongo*. That's
where John found the tooth. It eroded out of a bed near the
bottom of SCK. We've got to follow it back into the bed and
see if we can find the rest of it."

"Show me the tooth again," Cassie said.

Fuhrey coaxed the bundle from his shirt pocket,
unwrapped tissue and then cotton on the palm of his hand.
"It's a molar. It's distinctly hominid."

"You've told us that four times," she said. "I'm keeping
count." She touched the tooth. It was hardened to rock,
brownish white, with its cusps worn away so that a ring of

enamel surrounded porous hardened pulp and with broken roots.

"They'd shoot me if they knew I was carrying it around in my pocket. Totally unprofessional. It ought to be in a safe somewhere." He checked ahead. Cut below the plain, the gorge was hidden from view, but his field tent and the open thatched shelter beside it in the distance shimmered in the heat. "Veer to the south, Seth. It's about three quarters of the way along the side." He folded the wrappings around the tooth and returned it carefully to his pocket. To Cassie: "There's a notorious gap in hominid evolution between nine and four million years ago. Nobody's turned anything up yet. Before nine million years we've got *Ramapithecus*, who was small and apelike. After four million years we've got two kinds of *Australopithecus*, early *Homo* and a late *Ramapithecene* too. So *Homo* probably split off between nine and four, and that's SCK site."

"But you said you can't date the tooth."

"Not from placement, because it eroded out. But I think I know which bed it came from. Where to start digging. That's why I wanted Seth to see the site. I wanted his advice."

"On paleontology?" Cassie questioned Crown.

"He used to hang around Olduvai."

"I watched the Leakeys," Crown said. "Sometimes I helped them out. They didn't have any water over there and I've got a well."

"He's being modest," Fuhrey said. "He put some money into their work. They've got National Geographic funding now—Mary Leakey does, Louis's dead—so he puts the money into mine instead. Just beyond that umbrella thorn, Seth. You can park there and we'll walk down. Does Cassie know where the money comes from?"

"I tax the tourists," Crown said.

"You tax the tourists? Did you tax me?"

"No. The tourists who use my airstrip. They get charged a pound a head for landing rights. Then I turn the money over to Robert. I figure he needs it more than they do."

She laughed. "So you really are a patron. Are you going to tax the general?"

"You don't tax generals in Tanzania, lady," Crown said, shutting off the engine. "Generals tax you. But you're not taking this business seriously. I'll be enrolled in history as the name of a gully. Seth Crown's Gully, the gully where man was born. Slip Robert a fiver and he'll make you famous."

Fuhrey opened the side door and got out and opened the front door for Cassie. "Be careful going down. We've had rhino around here. When it rains they take over the water hole. We drink rhino piss for tea. Puts curl in your hair."

"How is your water supply, Robert?" Crown asked, coming around the car.

"That's one of the reasons I paid you a visit. I'll load up some cans when we get back. I didn't have time before you came in." Fuhrey guided them along the narrow path that led to the edge of the *korongo* and steeply down.

The gorge had looked ugly to Fuhrey when he first saw it the year before, Crown riding out with him from camp to show him the way, both of them hung over from a night of celebrating the new dig. Good sites were hard to find and the best of them were badlands where desiccation had succeeded conditions of moisture and preserved the hardest parts of whatever creatures had lived there, teeth and bones and sometimes, if the creature was man, the post holes of his housing and stone tools. But Oloito Gorge was scruffier than most. It looked like a scoured, unrestored strip mine dredged from a sere plain of whistling thorn and wait-a-bit thorn and scattered dark termite mounds. Its steeply eroded *korongos* were spotted with clusters of sisal, thick yellow-green serrated blades that slashed like bayonets. The

korongos connected to a central canyon that meandered
west in the direction of Lake Victoria and gave out onto an
old sink long ago dried to bitter dust. The water that cut the
korongos and the canyon during the seasonal rains dried up
into pools where rhino sometimes wallowed and wandering
bachelor lions sometimes drank and then the pools dried up
and the rhino and the lions moved on and the gorge hosted
desert fauna, lizards and scorpions and poisonous snakes.
Gritty, crumbling, colored a monotonous dirty gray, its walls
treacherously decayed, the gorge could easily be mistaken
for a flow channel on the back side of the moon.

But it no longer looked ugly to him. Living beside it, sur-
veying it, digging at it on hands and knees with fine small
brushes and dental picks, he began to populate it with life.
At its higher levels he had already found the fossil vertebrae
of extinct crocodiles, turtle scutes, the skulls and horns of
giant buffalo, a pig tusk fully a meter long and fossil fish and
shellfish, and his crew had begun uncovering what would
probably be a complete skeleton of *Deinotherium*, a swamp-
feeding mammal with a massive body and backward-curv-
ing tusks that would have looked to modern eyes like a fab-
ulous hybridization of walrus and elephant. High on the
sloping side of one *korongo*, digging back through erosion-
rotted rock, following a trail of fragmentary bones scattered
from the carcass of a giant Pleistocene pig, he had found
solidified in the stone that once was mud a bowl-shaped
depression, a basin, with gouges in its sides that fitted the
fingers of a human hand, and at the edge of the basin what
might be the footprint of a five-year-old child. A gouged
channel led into the basin from what had once been the
shallows of a lake. The basin was almost two million years
old. The lake would have been salty even then, though fed
by fresh watercourses. It would have been blue, and the sky
blue and the plain green with grass. Small dark hominids
lived on the lush shores in thatched shelters not different

from the shelter his crew had built on the plain above the gorge, and not yet knowing fire, a woman dug in the mud a basin that filled with salt water and a man brought pig meat and cut it with chipped stone and dipped the meat into the water to flavor it and a small child played. Oloito was alive to him now and beautiful, and now before he expected it he had won the tooth and the possibility of a skull.

An African met them at the bottom of the *korongo,* a blue-black African with close-cropped hair and prominent veins at his temples, shirtless, powerfully built, sweating in the heat in ragged safari shorts. He greeted Crown warmly in Swahili and Fuhrey introduced him to Cassie as John Kegedi. Kegedi led them along the *korongo* to the point where it debouched into the main canyon and pointed proudly to a metal tent peg driven into the ground.

"This is where I found the molar," he said in English. "It was fixed in the crust of the talus slope."

"You can see where that's coming from," Fuhrey said. "It runs back up to this bed here." He pointed low on the side of the *korongo.* "We'll have to cut back into the wall to excavate it." His hair blew in the hot wind and he brushed it from his eyes. "The question is, Seth, should we cut a vertical test trench or go ahead and cut the whole thing down?"

Crown studied the site. "You'd keep the sequence clearer with the trench. If you found anything you could extend it laterally easily enough."

"But if we didn't find anything we'd be out the time."

"If you're in that much of a hurry you could always bulldoze it."

"No, seriously," Fuhrey said, grinning, "this is too important to wait on. What do you think?"

Crown inspected the talus slope and followed it up to the wall. He examined the wall and turned back to them. "I'd go for the test trench. That skull's got to be scattered all over hell and gone. The odds are good you'll turn up some

fragments on one distinct level and then you'll know where
to extend."

"Agreed," Fuhrey said. He looked to Kegedi. "John?
What do you think?"

"I also agree."

"Then go ahead and stake it out from Bed Three down to
the floor. Be very careful of that talus slope. There just
might be more fragments in it. In fact, why don't you sift it
first and see what you find? Then it'll be out of the way. I'm
going to give Mama Cassie here a tour of the joint and then
I've got to go back to Seth's and load us some water and
pick up the Land Rover. I'll drive over before dark and we
can begin excavating in the morning."

"*Vizuri*," Kegedi said. "*Kazi nzuri na maji mazuri.* Good.
Good about the work and good about the water."

"*Si kitu.* Don't mention it."

Parked at the edge of the airstrip, Crown and Cassie
watched the light single-engine scout plane come in high
and fast and expertly stall and touch down and bounce once
and taxi to a stop opposite the car. They got out and walked
over to meet it. It was painted in patched camouflage above
and silver below and as they approached the starboard wing
the pilot cut the engine and the door opened on their side
and a small, light-brown, gray-haired man in olive-drab fatigues emerged and briskly stepped down to the grass followed by a younger man also in fatigues carrying a black
leather briefcase. The older man turned and appraised them
and his expression was pleasant but he did not smile.

"I am General Nguvu," he said. "This is my aide, Colonel
Mongali. You are Mr. Crown. Who is the young woman?"

Crown introduced Cassie. The general's handshake was
quick and hard. He was short, no more than five-seven, but
wiry, alert, aggressive, his body tensed as if ready to spring.
He wore a patch of gray mustache on his lip in the style of

Julius Nyerere, the President of Tanzania, and two silver stars on each shoulder and an automatic pistol in a black leather holster at his hip. His fatigues were tucked into polished black paratrooper boots. "We can drive back to the lodge," Crown said. "Would you like your pilot to join us?"

"The pilot will stay with the aircraft," General Nguvu said. He took Cassie's arm as they walked to the Land Rover. "What brings you to Tanzania, Miss Wendover?"

"I've been touring, General."

"Good. We encourage touring. It gives our people employment. You are from the United States. Which is your native state? I should guess somewhere west of the Mississippi."

"California," Cassie said, surprised. "Have you been to America, General?"

"I graduated from Cornell and later from the U. S. Army Command and General Staff College at Leavenworth, Kansas. In both places I learned something about snow. You will find no snow in Tanzania, Miss Wendover, except on Kilimanjaro. As with California, that is one of my country's virtues."

Cassie smiled. "I agree with you."

"Excellent. There are few things in life so pleasant as an attractive woman's agreement."

The aide sat with Crown, Cassie with the general in the back, the general's arrangement. Crown turned the Land Rover on the airstrip and headed north to camp wondering why a murder in the bush produced a general from Dar. Either the Dutch were raising hell with Nyerere or Rukuma was big fish. Or the Tanzanian Army didn't have enough to do. Or all of the above, Crown thought.

"I am interested in this man who was murdered, Mr. Crown," the general said. "Who found the body?"

"Two Masai boys," Crown said over his shoulder. "Sons

of an elder of this district, ole Senkali. His village isn't far from where the body was dumped."

"How do you know the body was dumped?"

"It's in the report I gave to the Arusha police, General. There wasn't enough blood on the ground and there were lorry tracks."

"I have read the report, Mr. Crown. There are always nuances that do not appear in reports. You were a professional hunter at one time?"

"Yes."

"Then you would be knowledgeable of blood and tracks. And if the body was dumped from elsewhere, then there is no point in Colonel Mongali and I personally examining the site. So we may proceed directly to your camp, Mr. Crown."

"We're there," Crown said evenly. He turned off the track into the entrance under the adze-hewn wooden sign with the lettering CROWN'S TENTED CAMP chiseled out and painted gold and drove past the water tower and parked behind the lodge.

"There are four lions under your water tower, Mr. Crown," the general said. "Are they guests of yours?"

Crown looked back at the general. The little general with the big mouth. "They're cubs. They wandered in starving last month. My camp manager and I have been teaching them to hunt."

"I had not heard of that custom before," the general said, reaching for the door handle. "I hope it does not become prevalent."

"We're taking them out later this afternoon. Perhaps you'd like to join us."

"I see. An entertainment." Finally Nguvu smiled. "Yes, if there is time after our conversation, why not?"

They settled on the screened porch at the front of the lodge, looking out on the lake. The cook's boy came to the porch and Crown offered drinks and when the boy returned with their orders, tea for the general and his aide and Cassie, a gin and tonic for Crown, he brought hot roasted cashews in wooden bowls and a bowl of fruit.

"This man who was murdered, Mr. Crown," the general said, stirring his tea. "Did you know him?"

"Yes."

"He was a friend?"

"An acquaintance. He was a scientist studying rhino at the Serengeti Research Institute."

"It's a pity. Do you know where he was working? Where he might have been when he was killed?"

"I think so. In the Crater Highlands, up high, near the bamboo zone."

The aide had followed the questioning since it began in the car and he had written each answer down. The general cocked his finger and his aide set aside his notebook and produced a map from the briefcase and unfolded it and smoothed it on his lap and passed it over.

"Can you locate the co-ordinates?" Nguvu asked Crown.

Crown bent at the general's side and the general oriented the map to him. His finger found the Serengeti where it abutted the highlands. He traced the Arusha road, the oval of Ngorongoro's rim, and traced north to a mountain that rose to higher altitude. "About there."

"On the western slope of Olmoti Crater, is it?" the general said, glancing at his aide. "Northwest of Ngorongoro?" The aide wrote in his notebook.

Crown straightened and returned to his chair. "He may have been working elsewhere as well. Almost certainly he was working in Ngorongoro. But when he went out overnight he camped on Olmoti."

"We do not know that in this instance he went out overnight, Mr. Crown."

"That's true. We don't."

"Are you aware that the body was stripped of identification? Assuming the man carried a wallet and wore a wrist-watch, the wallet and the watch were gone. This may have been no more than a particularly vicious robbery." The general sipped his tea. Cassie watched him wondering if he were hostile to whites or if brusqueness were simply part of his manner, his style of generalship. She had met generals before with her father. They were almost always either flamboyant dandies or efficient, no-nonsense administrators. This one seemed to be a combination.

"Robbers don't leave notes," Crown said.

"The note itself is not conclusive. All it informs us is that Rukuma, whoever Rukuma is, is literate."

That would do it, Crown thought. That would bloody well do it. "If you know it all already, General Nguvu, why the hell did you fly clear out here to talk to me?"

The general flashed strong white teeth and turned up his hands. "Good, Mr. Crown. I see you are a man impatient of the obvious. I did not fly 'clear out here' merely to interrogate you. I flew here to give you information and perhaps to enlist your help." He leaned back in his chair, his hands on the arms, and drummed his index fingers against the ends of the arms in unison and then in counterpoint. "Let me tell you about this Rukuma." He saw Crown's look of surprise. "Yes, he is not unknown to us. He is, as you seem to have suspected, a so-called guerrilla. He was based at one time in Dar with the brave volunteers of Zimbabwe who have worked from Tanzania to free their country of colonial domination." Nguvu stopped and looked to Cassie. "The racist state of Southern Rhodesia, Miss Wendover, which until very recently your country supported handsomely in return for a supposedly strategic trade in chrome. The chrome, of course, went onto the bumpers of your country's excellent automobiles." He turned back to Crown. "Since Rukuma was acceptable to that group and his papers appeared to be in order, we did not inquire closely into his background. His passport was Algerian. He entered Tanzania from Algeria and he had important Algerian backing. Money, access to weapons and so on."

The general stopped to finish his tea and his aide stood quickly to pour him another cup. He's got them jumping, Crown thought. That's a good sign. "No more *chai*, Colonel," the general said. The aide picked up his notebook again. "Three years ago Rukuma left us. Poof. Overnight he was gone. We traced him to a flight to New Delhi, where he seems to have boarded for Bangkok. Where he proceeded from there we were unable to discover. We heard no more about him until three weeks ago. Three weeks ago a gang of men driving an unmarked lorry attacked an army post at Kajiado in Kenya on the Nairobi-Arusha road. They were armed with U.S. M-16 automatic rifles, an unusual weapon in this part of the world, and they killed four men and wounded seven others. Since they attacked in the dead of night, and the post was not properly picketed, they escaped without casualties. They looted the post of its arms stores. Among other weapons, they acquired a supply of grenades, four Bren light machine guns and an undetermined amount of ammunition—at least ten thousand rounds." The general sat forward. "They left behind a note implying that they were operating out of my country with the permission of my government. The note, Mr. Crown, was signed 'Rukuma.'"

"So he's back," Crown said. "What's his game? He can't be so stupid as to leave all these notes around from sheer egomania."

"No. I agree. I think not. The incident at Kajiado was obviously intended to foment trouble between Kenya and Tanzania. I give away no state secret, Mr. Crown, when I tell you that relations between Kenya and Tanzania are not of the best. Rukuma has put us to much trouble to convince the *Mzee*'s government that Tanzania was in no way responsible for the incident. And of course the Kikuyu are much too suspicious to believe us. But I must confess that, like you, I am puzzled by this recent murder. I do not see the point of it. If, as we suspect, Rukuma and his band are based in the highlands, then he has given himself away. If he has ambitions of taking on the Tanzanian Army, then he has, as they say in the States, bitten off more than he can chew."

The general stood and walked to the end of the porch and looked out through the screen. "Your camp is excellently sited, Mr. Crown. I am told you have an outstanding reputation as a hunter."

Here it comes, Crown thought. "What can I help you with, General?"

Nguvu turned around and leaned against the porch frame compactly at ease, his hands clasped behind his back. "Within a week, Mr. Crown, I shall have established a base camp in the highlands near Ngorongoro. I understand you know the area well."

"I've hunted there."

"I should like you to consider joining us from time to time to aid us in hunting Rukuma. You have cause in the death of your friend, but you would also be paid at the rate of a colonel." The general came back to the group then and stood at the opening of the semicircle of chairs. "And there is another reason," he said. "It is distinctly to your advantage, commercial and otherwise, that the area be secure."

Abdi had discovered the lions one morning under the water tower when he went out to start up the generator. He had crossed through the private compound that was built on behind the lodge and rousted Crown from a thick early-morning sleep and Crown had pulled on shorts and chukka boots and gone out to look at them. They were adolescent cubs rather than full-grown lions, four males about two

years old. Only one of them showed even the scraggly beginnings of a mane. All of them showed ribs and jutting hip-
bones and faces so gaunt with hunger that they looked more
like dogs than cats. Abdi speculated that they had been separated from their pride before they learned to hunt and had
survived by scavenging. They were obviously on their last
legs or they wouldn't have risked coming into camp. The
choice was chasing them off and letting them die or giving
them hunting lessons.

Crown opted for the hunting lessons. The more wild lions,
the better. He went out that morning and shot a tommy and
skinned it and cut the meat into cub-sized chunks. He slit
the chunks for stuffing and stuffed them with fat pink cap-
sules of tetracycline from his medicine stores and then he
pulled the Land Rover over to the cubs and fed them out
the back door.

After a week of feeding them at the water tower they
looked strong enough for a lesson. Crown began dumping
the meat in a line out the back door of the Land Rover
while Abdi drove it slowly along the track past the camp. As
the cubs learned to follow the Land Rover, Crown found
that he had developed a certain affection for them and he
considered naming them. He worked out the names at night,
drunk as he often was in those days before Cassie came into
his life, driving the Land Rover up and down the track like
Mother Goose with the cubs docilely following behind as
the feeding from the back had conditioned them to do.

The one with the mane could be Curly, he decided. The
eager feeder could be *Uhuru ni Kazi,* which was the Tanzanian national motto and meant in Swahili *Freedom Is
Work.* The humorless one that occupied itself during rest
periods licking the others' genitals could be Deacon and the
smallest and thinnest of the cubs could be Eats.

But on further considering the matter Crown repudiated
the names. He decided late one night that he'd leave the

naming of lions to the Elsa-lovers of the world. The Elsa-
lovers of the world, he decided, knew far more about game
management than he could ever hope to learn. They were
game-lovers and they loved to name the animals but they
didn't believe in shooting them or cropping them or clearing
them off the land.

He got them at the camp. They abhorred the shooting of
game even for the pot. If they ate meat, which most of them
did with gusto, they never offended their fine sensibilities by
shooting it. They let someone else shoot or slaughter it for
them and collected it cooled out at the market. One night in
camp the conversation had turned to cannibalism, and a
game-loving woman of good family had wondered aloud
what part of the human anatomy cannibals ate. The meat,
someone had said. But human beings didn't have any meat,
the woman had said. Animals had meat, as well as such unmentionables as muscles and organs and bones, but human
beings had only the unmentionables. It emerged on further
questioning that the woman believed meat outcropped on
animals in special pockets at the rump, the rib, the sirloin
and so on. That was a game-lover for you.

The game-lovers liked to have the animals around. It
made them feel good. They felt much better about animals
than they did about people. If it was a choice between animals and people they'd take the animals every time. One of
the things they liked to do was helicopter rhino around
Africa. You could helicopter a rhino almost anywhere in
East Africa for twenty thousand dollars, which was only two
hundred times the annual income of the average Tanzanian.
When the Elsa-lovers put one of Elsa's cousins back in the
bush after suitable retraining it got tangled up with a wild
lion that already occupied that particular corner of the bush
and such was the logic of the Elsa-lovers that they shot the
wild lion. On the other hand, when another tame lion that

they'd retrofitted for the bush ate one of their Africans, the shooting of it made them queasily unhappy.

The Elsa-lovers, the game-lovers of the world, princes among them and pioneering Aryan pilots, were lovely spiritual people, Crown decided that night, and he'd leave the naming of wild animals to them. He'd concentrate on giving some scraggly cubs a leg up on what he hoped would be excellent careers, and maybe in the fullness of their wild lives a game-lover or two would come their way. And not long after that Cassie had arrived and he'd turned the cubs over to Abdi. Now that he and Cassie were settled in he could pick up the training again.

In deference to the general's rank Crown stationed him in the left front seat of the Land Rover for a better view. Cassie and the general's aide sat in the back seat with Abdi between them fondling the Winchester and they drove out in the late afternoon. Abdi had previously assembled the tourists. They followed at a distance in their zebra-striped Volkswagen microbuses and between the Land Rover and the microbuses came the cubs. The cubs were sleek now and strong after a month of feeding. They loped along keenly, their faces relaxed and their mouths open, indifferent to the dust from the car. A kilometer north of camp Crown swung off the track and the Land Rover bounced through the open forest toward the plain.

"I am glad you have agreed to work with us, Mr. Crown," the general said. "You might also alert the Masai in this district. They should certainly be informed."

"Was that in my file too, General?" Crown said. "That I'm a Masai elder?"

"Of course, Mr. Crown. You are a most interesting man. You might after all have been merely another droll colonial. Instead you are something of a hero, certainly a hero among the Masai. You played a very valuable role in supporting African nationalism in colonial days. It hasn't been forgotten,

even here in Tanzania. Nor has the sacrifice of your wife."
Crown said nothing. "I see," the general said. "Then that
subject shall be closed between us. But about alerting the
Masai?"

"I've planned to. I'll talk to the paramount chief of the
section before I see you again."

"Good. They are a very talented people, if also stubborn
and backward."

"They aren't much impressed with progress, General.
Even Tanzanian progress, which they respect more than
most."

"Yes." The general sighed and turned around to look at
the cubs. "Explain this entertainment for me, please," he
said to Crown, facing forward again.

"These boys missed out on their hunting lessons, General
Nguvu. Poachers likely got their pride when it was away on
a kill. We're giving them make-up work. Once they get the
hang of it they'll be on their own." Crown stopped the Land
Rover at the edge of the forest. Beyond it on the grass a line
of tommies grazed. The cubs moved up to the general's side
of the car, using its body as a screen.

"My opinion has not been sought in the matter," the general said, "but I would gladly arrange to shoot all the game
outside the parks and free the land for agriculture. All the
colonial powers did so long ago, yet they press us to remain
a savage country where schoolchildren fear for their lives.
There are no bison in Kansas, Mr. Crown."

"I couldn't agree with you more, General," Crown said,
liking him better, "but in the meantime, I'm not allowed to
shoot lions in a reserve area and if I left the cubs alone
they'd be a nuisance and a danger. So I'm giving them the
same challenge all Tanzanians have—*Uhuru ni Kazi*."

The general laughed, a restrained laugh, a chuckle deep
in his throat.

"May I shoot now, Effendi?" Abdi asked from the back.

Crown looked out through the rear window. "Have the buses come up? Yes. Whenever you're ready, *mzee.*"

The general went intent, leaned forward in the seat. Behind him Abdi cautiously lifted the trap in the roof and folded it aside and the cubs pushed up from the crouch they had taken and almost seemed to point. A few of the nearer tommies raised their heads and studied the Land Rover but these were park gazelle grazing south from the boundary and they were used to cars. Crown could see only Abdi's scarred brown legs in the mirror; the rest of him stuck out through the roof.

They watched the sun-flooded plain while Abdi found his target, the silence broken by the panting of the cubs, and then the Winchester cracked and the tommies spronked and scattered in zigzags away from the sound and the cubs took off. One tommy, the one Abdi had gut-shot, staggered behind. Bounding like kittens and tripping over their paws but expressionless with intensity the cubs neared the wounded tommy and the largest male, the one with the beginnings of a mane, assembled itself into an approximation of a run, caught up with the tommy and efficiently batted it down. The tommy lay obedient in shock, not even struggling, while the male moved over it and bent and bit its neck, holding on to strangle, but the bite broke its spine and it kicked wildly in reflex and quivered and stilled and the other males rushed up to it and snarling and swiping at each other, selfish as lions always were at a kill, tore it apart. And that quickly the vultures came in and stood aside impatiently like the beginnings of a mob, a hooded vulture first settling and preening and shortly afterward an Egyptian and then an ungainly marabou stork. The cubs withdrew with their trophies and but for the chewed skull and a patch of hide that showed its side stripe the tommy was gone, and blood stained the brown-golden grass.

"Bravo, Mr. Crown," the general finally said, breaking the

silence. "I can see that they are not yet skilled, but they are learning. Perhaps when you have finished with the lions you would consider training some of our troops. Too many of them feed under the water tower and do not know how to hunt."

"You'll shape them up, General," Crown said as Abdi slipped back into the car. "But I'll be glad to help you track Rukuma."

"Good," General Nguvu said. "Then if you will drive us directly to your airstrip, we will return to Arusha and thence to Dar. I shall call you when we are on station."

"Damn it, Robert," Crown said to Fuhrey in the bar of the lodge, "you need some protection. You're completely exposed over there. I don't want to find your head at the bottom of the gorge."

"I've never fired anything bigger than a twenty-two rifle in my life," Fuhrey said.

"Then it's time you learned." Crown unlocked one of the polished ebony gun cases built onto the inner wall of the bar. He lifted a belt and holster from its hook inside the case next to a rack of rifles and unsnapped the holster and drew a heavy blue-black Colt .45 automatic. With a flannel he wiped it clean of oil. "You can handle this bastard. Just point the son-of-a-bitch. It'll knock down anything you can hit smaller than a rhino. You ought to have some armament out there anyway." He unlocked the other case and scanned a rack of shotguns. "Here's a twelve-gauge. It's good for forty yards. Let's go out and practice."

Fuhrey shrugged. "If you think it's necessary."

"I think it's necessary." They left the bar by way of the porch and Cassie was there. "Can you handle a rifle?" Crown asked her.

"I've hunted deer."

"Thirty-ought six?"

"Yes."

"How about pistols?"

"No."

He went back into the bar and took a .38 revolver and a box of rounds from the case and returned to the porch. "Let's go learn to shoot," he said to Cassie.

Walking out, Cassie said: "Do you think you'll be able to locate Rukuma?"

"It's not going to be easy," Crown said. "The long rains are due any day."

Four

EACH YEAR, at the beginning of the long rains, the wildebeest migrated through the camp. Crown had learned to expect the migration and even to prepare for it but he had never learned to like it. Elsewhere on the Serengeti it was a spectacle of awesome proportion with great appeal to tourists. At his camp it was three days of unremitting carnage.

The rains did not begin all at once. After the short rains of November and December the Serengeti dried out through the first two months of the new year. Then, in late February, as the prevailing winds shifted from east to northeast, scatterings of white, fleecy, flat-bottomed cumuli drifted down the plain toward the highlands, playing with the light. From day to day they thickened and increased, assembled into crowded advancing fronts and darkened, built to mountainous heights and blackened and threatened and echoed through their roiling breaks the rumble of distant thunder and blew in the smells of wet grass and wet earth and moist, lightning-freshened air. The wildebeest that had grazed er-

ratically back and forth between plain and woodland began
then to follow the scent north toward the land already
under rain where the new grass had started. Solitaries joined
with small herds and smaller herds assembled into larger,
moving and feeding and moving on, the cows with calves
now hungry for grass more urgent, the bulls pulled in off
their territories, the herds falling into lines and the lines
streaming together into one great line drawing out across
the land no more than a dozen animals abreast and often
enough single file down washes and through forests and
even on the open plain itself, the migration irresistible on a
fixed, ancient trail that the older wildebeest remembered
and the younger wildebeest learned. The trail ran through
the camp, ran through the lake itself, Lake Engat, the lake
of wildebeest, because the lake was newer than the trail and
lay across it, and in the confusion of swimming the lake
calves drowned by the hundreds and lions and hyenas and
vultures crowded the line to scavenge and to kill.

Wildebeest were easily the oddest of the antelopes,
Crown thought. They were antelope advanced almost to the
status of cattle. They weighed as much as young cattle,
three hundred fifty to six hundred pounds. They stood four
feet at the shoulders and they were colored slate gray except
for the darker vertical stripes on their forequarters. They
were ox-like in their forequarters with powerful shoulders
brushed by horse-like black manes and noticeably humped.
Their heads were more like the heads of bison but narrowed
in at the sides and flattened and elongated downward at the
muzzle with black beards and black inward- and forward-
curving horns. The resemblance to oxen and bison stopped
behind the shoulders and their hindquarters were spindle-
legged and slightly built but they had tails like the tails of
horses that the Africans had long prized for fly whisks. They
herded like cattle and grazed like cattle but they didn't defend themselves like cattle. If a hyena dashed among them

they responded by bunching up into dense, snorting masses but they failed to protect their calves inside the bunch and face outward to threaten the attacker with lowered horns as even eland did and that was one reason they lost so many calves. They lived by numbers. They defended themselves by sacrificing individuals and followed each other blindly like sheep. Not many found them more than mournful or ridiculous but submersion in the mass was a survival strategy as good as any other, the strategy of choice of termites and bees and even some of the poorer and more populous nations of the world. The wildebeest thrived on the Serengeti despite their losses. In the years Crown had owned the camp their numbers had doubled to something more than six hundred thousand head. And of that six hundred thousand at least a third passed through the camp on their regular migration northward at the beginning of the long March rains.

"Seth?" Cassie questioned sleepily from beside him. "What time is it?"

He turned to her. He could barely see her in the gray light of early dawn. "About six-thirty. Go back to sleep if you want to."

"Why are you sitting up?"

"I was thinking about the wildebeest."

"What about the wildebeest?"

"I'll tell you later."

"Are you all right?"

"Absolutely. I've rather neglected the tourists, you know?"

"Abdi's taken care of them, hasn't he?" She stretched and smiled. "What about the wildebeest?"

"We're going to have hundreds of thousands marching through the camp in the next few days."

"That sounds like fun."

"Don't count on it."

"Will you wake me when you're ready to dress?"

"I'll do better than that."

"Lovely. Something to look forward to."

She turned over and Crown listened to her breathing slow as she drifted back to sleep. He could hear the cook in the kitchen across the compound rattling pans. In the dining room, setting out plates and clicking bowls, the cook's boy warmed up a lover's song, lyrically demanding and explicitly anatomical. Soon Abdi would start the generator. By day it powered the refrigerator and the pump that delivered water from the lake to the two shower buildings behind the row of tents to the west of the lodge, the eight tents raised off the ground on wooden platforms and sheltered under thatch. At seven Abdi would go from tent to tent waking the tourists. The sun would not yet have risen above the highlands, but the sky would be blue, the last bright stars dimming, and if there were clouds they would stream pink in the early light and the light would silhouette the flat-topped umbrella thorns black against the lake. Serengeti dawn, the game moving out onto the plain to feed without memory as if every morning were the first morning of the world.

He'd been remiss about the tourists. In the past they'd interested him almost as much as the Serengeti game and between Cassie and the murder and Robert and the general he'd neglected them. Abdi managed them well enough in normal times. During the migration they needed handling. They'd signed on for what most of them believed to be a pleasant tour of a large and benevolent outdoor zoo. They didn't realize that a natural disaster might be part of the package as two free cocktails at their Nairobi hotel and a guaranteed window seat on their tour buses and three meals a day inclusive were. He could easily hire a crew of Africans to help him with the wildebeest but he'd found in the past that the tourists, some of them, were willing to do the work and grateful for a chance to mix with the animals instead of

watching them from the confinement of their buses. If the
Serengeti was a zoo then the people rather than the animals
occupied the cages. The best of them welcomed a chance to
get out and walk the ground.

He read the fates of nations from the tourists who showed
up at his camp. When he first bought the camp, in the mid-
1960s, most of them had been Americans. The Americans
who could afford to travel to Africa were usually middle-
aged, Republicans, businessmen and merchants and their
wives whose children had grown and who had come out to
see the world. They wore safari suits they'd bought from Indian tailor shops in Nairobi and they drank moderately and
worried about the healthfulness of the water and they liked
bathroom jokes. Some of the Americans he got now were
younger, with longer hair and political sympathies that bor-
dered on the anarchist. Among the younger Americans the
conversion from tailored safari suits to proletarian jeans and
tee-shirts stenciled with depictions of the hemp plant ro-
mantically in full leaf was almost complete. But through the
late sixties and the early seventies he'd begun getting sturdy
West Germans and then Japanese loaded with cameras and
ingenious personal electronics and lately he'd even had a
few Arabs. The Arabs behaved badly. They flew down from
Nairobi with a bird on each arm and did everything they
weren't allowed to do at home. They sinned very imagina-
tively and they weren't as bad as they behaved. They
praised the Serengeti. It looked lush to them after their native dunes and they respected it. Unlike some of the Americans, they never said the game was cute.

His paying guests fluctuated according to the conditions
of their national economies much as their currencies did and
he wondered which nationalities he would see next. The
Chinese were a possibility except that the Chinese had neither time nor inclination for game viewing, believing as they
did that the best of everything could already be found in

China. The British couldn't afford the indulgence any more even on the national dole. The likeliest prospects for future travelers were the elite of the oil countries, who were rapidly buying up the world. He expected to see more Arabs and probably Venezuelans and eventually Mexicans but despite their oil reserves he would see few if any Nigerians. They preferred the pleasures of civilization. The preeminent pleasure of civilization for the Nigerians, as for most prosperous Africans, was lording it over the old colonial powers. For game viewing they safaried to Paris and London and New York.

Right, Crown thought. That's enough jolly innkeeping for one morning. Now let's see about this lady. What a fine wonder she is to wake to.

"Looks like we've got a full house," Crown said to Abdi in the dining room that afternoon, going over the register. "Do you know much about them?"

"There are altogether ten and five, Effendi." Abdi pointed out the names. "These are Germans. A man and wife and a young daughter and two sons in early manhood."

"Dieter Friedrich. What's he do?"

"He is an engineer. This is an American businessman. He is employed by an oil company in Europe and he has come here on furlough."

"J. Malcolm Tobin."

"His wife travels with him. Her name is Marsha and her voice is very shrill."

"What about the one from New York? David Kahn?"

"He is a painter of pictures. It seems he sold one for a large sum of money and has used the money to come out on safari. The young woman who is with him has only one name. If she were African I would say that she is underfed. She takes the sun in a bathing suit so small that it hardly covers her breasts and her sex."

"That's never bothered you before, *mzee*."

"It would not be distasteful except for the thinness."

"She must be his model. What's her name? 'Aura'?"

"That is what she has written. These two are Japanese."

"Husband and wife? I can't read it."

"I also cannot read it and they have spoken very little to me. They are two bwanas. These last are older Americans who arrived only yesterday morning. They are owners of many cattle."

"They're registered from Wyoming. They must be ranchers. Mr. and Mrs. Ferd Wells and Mr. and Mrs. Gib Gossett. If they can handle cattle we can use them."

"The Bwana Gossett is very thin and his wife is very large and the Bwana Wells is very large and his wife is very thin. It seemed to me that they might wish to exchange wives."

"Good idea. You should talk to them. See what you could arrange. Maybe they'd give us a trial run on the bar after dinner."

"I understand that Americans do not exchange wives, Effendi, although I have seen them do so on many occasions here in camp at night, trading from tent to tent. Many over the years have also visited you and you have not sent them away."

"Yes. Well, we won't mention that to Cassie, will we."

"No, Effendi. Will you draw upon the guests to do the work with the *nyumbu*, the wildebeest?"

"Right. That's why I want to check them out."

"Their drivers will return them from Ngorongoro in the early evening."

"I'll put in an appearance."

"They will be glad to see you. They have asked me much about you."

At first, at sundowners and dinner, Crown found the guests slow going. They had the innocent good will of travelers new to a country who have come there frankly expecting marvels, who see it freshly but do not yet understand the way it lies or how it works, so that, hearing them talk about it, a native of the country feels renewed pride in its virtues but also wonders if he got off at the right station that day. Marsha Tobin, the oil executive's wife, told Crown at sun-downers about the black-maned lions they had stopped to watch in Ngorongoro—the driver had called them "very fierce" and Crown saw them crouched black-maned and hair-triggered in their fierceness in the tall grass—but she then asked Crown where all the tigers were. At dinner he overheard Ferd Wells, the rancher, comparing the Serengeti favorably in its fecundity and the variety of its game to the great plains of western North America, but Wells also seemed to believe that a meteorite had gouged out Ngorongoro.

The guests puzzled at the absence of jungle in East Africa but admired the coolness of the night air; the grace of a lone leopard scattering tommies at the forest edge; the taste of the game Crown's cook served up, roast eland and curried guinea fowl and lesser bustard and Hottentot teal; the majesty of Kilimanjaro bulking immense and snow-hooded on the land. Crown would rather have guests who were appreciative but confused than guests who were cynical. He remembered a Serengeti tourist, a New Yorker, who instructed his wife to film him petting one of the park lions while it guarded a kill. She froze at the camera and the footage she took home to New York along with her husband's remains was a vivid indictment of cynicism. Confusion he could at least repair.

It was better after dinner, in the bar. Abdi mixed the drinks strong. Crown guided a tour of his gun cases and trophy heads. Looking splendid in a floor-length madras print gown, Cassie attended the wives. The lodge's genet cat, Kanu, came awake draped over a joist, up under the thatch, and dropped down onto Crown's shoulder as he sat in one of the big wicker armchairs by the door to the porch. The genet was spotted like a small leopard, its long, full tail ringed like a raccoon's, and hands reached out to pet it that it batted playfully away. When the petting subsided it went looking for Cassie, reconnoitering the backs of couches and brushing startled heads, and settled purring on her shoulder and wrapped its tail around her neck.

David Kahn, the painter, Crown liked immediately. He was brash and tough and very alert. He could have banked the painting commission, he told them, but he'd broken into five figures for the first time and he wanted to celebrate.

"I don't believe these collectors," he said. "They're nuts. Good taste in art, but nuts. This guy that bought the painting? He's from Indiana originally. Fort Wayne. He's about thirty-five and he's loaded. Second-generation money. He's also a poor slob. He's a hundred pounds overweight. Took him five years to get through Princeton. He marries this tall, cool blonde and she never gives him any. Everything he tries he flops at. He studies math because he figures he's a hell of an investor. They give him a desk down at the brokerage house because just investing his own money they clean up on the fees."

"Tell them his name," Aura, the model, said. She wore coils and coils of blue Masai beads and with her tan and her dark hair she was lovely to look at.

"Yeah. Donny. Donny Nichols. Donny likes cars. He's pretty good with them. He takes you out driving, he'll stop on the parkway and adjust the tappets. Doesn't wrap his thumbs around the wheel, keeps his hands set at ten o'clock and two o'clock just like the big boys. So after the brokerage business he buys a Porsche dealership. Blondie doesn't like that. She went to Smith on a scholarship but now she's rich and car dealers are *très gauche*. Donny gets walked over. All those macho Porsche salesmen eat him for breakfast. But there's this tight-assed little secretary that comes with the dealership, right? She knows Donny's a live one and she makes a big play for him. Blondie gets wind of it and she comes down hard. He pulls out and sells the operation for a loss."

"He sure sounds pitiful," Gib Gossett, the other rancher, said. "He sounds like my brother-in-law."

"Wait," Kahn said, grinning.

"Let him tell his story, Gib," Mrs. Gossett said.

"He's tellin' it. I ain't stoppin' him."

"But the secretary's still in town," Kahn said. "She's still after him. Blondie decides she wants to live by the ocean. They sell the mansion and move to La Jolla. Donny's going crazy. He's horny all the time and he hasn't got anything to do. Blondie's surrounded with gay guys. They feed her ego and they don't make demands. But one of the gays tells Donny his problem is physical. He's all tensed up. He steers him to this little Japanese lady who gives him Shiatsu massage, the works."

"Shiatsu? Shiatsu?" one of the Japanese gentlemen said. Neither one spoke much English and they hadn't been listening before.

"Shiatsu," Kahn said, massaging the air.

The Japanese gentlemen bobbed and smiled. "Shiat*su*, shiat*su*," the other one said happily. They leaned in to follow the story.

"Donny goes bananas. No one's ever touched him like that before. It's an instant conversion. He's found his calling. He starts taking Shiatsu lessons from the Japanese lady. Blondie gets worried. He's running off to seminars in Functional Integration and he's wiring up ion generators all over the house and he's talking back." Kahn stopped and sipped his drink.

"So finally he kicks Blondie out. He's found his manhood. He's Francis Macomber. Divorces her. Marries the Japanese lady. Big Shinto ceremony. He gets to be a black-belt Shiatsu specialist. He drives all over the country giving massages. He's got a nice life and his wife loves him. She thinks he's a *sumo* wrestler and she helps him spend his money. He's still a slob, but he's a happy slob. He's a millionaire masseur."

They were all laughing.

"Now that's a damn fine story," Ferd Wells said. "I could use some a that shatsue myself, damn back's always givin' me trouble." He looked at Crown. "You ever hear about huntin' coyotes with dogs, Seth?"

"No," Crown said, "I haven't. What kind of dogs?"

"Oh, greyhounds and them Russian wolfhounds."

"Is it coursing?"

"Yeah, you could call it that. Hunt 'em from a pickup."

"Gives us somethin' to do all winter," Gib Gossett said.

"Yeah," said Wells, "see, we put up these here dog boxes in the back of the pickup. They got doors on 'em you can drop from the cab. Go out onto the range, check all the draws. Shoot over 'em with a pistol. Coyote comes out, you get up near him and drop the dogs. Sometimes they run 'em down, sometimes they don't. Gib here got him a hundred-fifty coyotes last year. Dog coyote's the hardest kind to catch."

"You killed that many coyotes last year?" Aura asked Gossett. "Why?"

"Na. I don't kill 'em. Dogs kill 'em. Just like them lions yesterday."

"What'd they ever do to you?" Aura challenged.

"Don't get your back up, honey," Mrs. Gossett said soothingly. "They kill calves. Calves and sheep. They can have the sheep, but they're a pest."

"Oh. I didn't know that. Excuse me."

"See," Wells said, "you got your rats in New York an' we

got our coyotes. Don't make much of a dent in 'em anyway. Seems like there's more every year."

"How did hunting with dogs get started, Ferd?" Crown asked.

"Now that's interestin'. I don't rightly know who done it first of all. Seems like it kind of spread out west from Kansas. They got these dog races down there, so that's where the greyhounds probably come from. I expect it goes back to the old buffalo days. My grampa hunted buffalo. Ain't no buffalo left, and there's seasons on antelope, so we hunt coyotes."

"Something like that happened here," Crown said. "Lion used to be considered vermin. Pests. The noble beasts were elephant and rhino. Giraffe, believe it or not. Black buffalo. The colonials would knock off lions whenever they got the chance and to hell with bloody sportsmanship. But then the game thinned out, and gradually they added lion to the list. Now he's the king of beasts. But the prejudice carried over. No one eats lion."

"Yuck," Marsha Tobin said. "Have you? It's a cat, isn't it?"

"It's delicious. It tastes like veal."

"Don't that beat all," Wells said. "I never did hear of that. Don't hold for coyote, though. Coyote tastes terrible."

"When did you ever eat coyote?" Mrs. Wells said.

"I ain't, but I heard about some o' them old pioneers who had to."

"Man'll eat anything if he gets hungry enough," Gossett said.

"I'll drink to that," Kahn said, winking at Aura and raising his glass.

Later in the evening Tobin cornered Crown. He worked for Esso in Belgium and the low-energy African economy had excited his imagination. Running on pure gin and tonic, he constructed for Crown a continental power grid cut through trackless jungle and strung across desert wastes north and south and east and west. Megavolt power lines quartered the Serengeti bringing clean, efficient electricity to every impoverished village to run treadle sewing machines and stone maize grinders and Tobin foresaw two cars, preferably American-made, in every *banda*. The Tobins wore matching white tennis outfits with matching green LaCoste alligators sewn on and green running shoes. Marsha Tobin's thighs were tanned but matronly and amply insulated with cellulite. She disapproved of Cassie, and when Cassie came to rescue Crown she unloosed a salvo of condescension.

"It must be wonderful working as a hostess in this lovely place," Marsha said.

"I'm not a hostess," Cassie said. "I'm a guest just like you."

"Oh, I'm sorry. I just assumed you worked for Mr. Crown. You seem to know your way around."

"I'm in love with Mr. Crown."

"Oh, I beg your pardon. It must have been the gown."

"No," Cassie said. "It wasn't the gown. It was the fantastic sex."

The fantastic sex collapsed the Tobins and they left shortly afterward to retire, collecting their pressure lantern from Abdi and retreating to their tent. Long after they left the bar and even over the snorting of the wildebeest that were gathering at the lake, Marsha's shrill nasal voice drilled through the night.

Crown noticed the Japanese gentlemen holding hands.

The German, Friedrich, was an engineer for Krupp, a quiet, thoughtful man. His daughter was shy, dimpled, a little overweight, but his wife and his two sons glowed with the ruddy health of mountain climbers. They were all mountain climbers, the daughter reluctantly. They had already climbed Kilimanjaro. Crown discovered that Friedrich had fought in North Africa. They compared notes and joked about the snafued strategies of the campaign, and inspired by the cognac Crown produced to toast their postwar prosperity they agreed that good wars made good neighbors.

The Germans were fine, Crown concluded. The ranchers, the painter, possibly the Japanese gentlemen if he could contrive to make them understand what was needed. They were obviously drunk, as who was not. Tobin might work out if he could get away from his wife and keep his mouth shut. Tobin's solution to the problem of the wildebeest drowning in the lake would probably be to pave it.

Crown briefed them on the migration. He promised them it would be something to write home about. They were eager to help him.

Cassie brushed her teeth for bed in the small bathroom of Crown's apartment in the private compound behind the lodge, by lantern light. She had drunk less than the others but enough to carry her within herself and at the same time outside. She looked in and looked out. The water she brushed with she had poured from the thermos into the glass. It was cool and tasted of iron. Her bare feet were cool on the planked wooden floor. She wore a pale yellow nightgown and her breasts moved beneath the nightgown loose against the cloth. Her breasts held the gown away from her belly but it fitted at her hips. Seth waited in bed for her. Her shadow in the yellow kerosene light moved on the wall. He waited in bed for her and she was opening to his waiting.

He used two wooden-backed hairbrushes. Small brass screws attached the backs. His hair was dark and thick, graying. He made white lather for shaving in a porcelain mug with an ivory-handled brush. He shaved with a straight razor of scrolled German steel. Its folding case was fitted with ivory plates. A worn leather strop hung on a hook beside the mirror. The sound of him stropping the razor was a

new sound added to the morning. He used witch hazel and
a styptic pencil. He washed with plain hard soap and showered in a tin-lined shower in the soapy alkaline water
pumped from the lake.

She was learning his rooms. The armchair in the sitting
room was slipcovered with canvas. Beneath the canvas was
worn burgundy damask. The table beside the armchair held
a rack of pipes he no longer smoked. There would always be
more than she could know. He was twenty-four when she
was born and his wife had already given him a son. He had
covered the floor of the sitting room with the skins of animals he had shot. A lion at the entrance. A zebra centrally.
A leopard at the chair. His men had skinned them and their
hands remembered the hot flesh and Seth had seen them
running alive and remembered that and remembered watching the skinning.

A framed photograph of the mission station hung on a
wall of the bedroom. His parents stood on the station's long
thatched porch squinting in the sun. They faced east or west
and it was morning or afternoon. His mother was small and
tightly corseted. His father was big, a farmer, clean-shaven,
with a farmer's patient weathered face. Masai milk gourds
hung on the bedroom wall, arm-length gourds narrow and
smooth as pumpkin seeds. When Seth was fourteen he had
left his parents' house and gone out alone and killed his
manhood lion alone with a spear. When he was fifteen what
had he done? When he was sixteen what had he done? It
was not possible to know both velocity and position at the
same time. History at the same time. The floor of his bedroom was carpeted with soft yellow-brown hyrax skins sewn
together. The hyrax skins were gifts from Masai initiates he
had sponsored. Before they hunted lions they hunted hyrax.
Hyrax were small animals like large rabbits. They screamed
at night going up trees and coming down. The initiates
hunted hyrax with bows and arrows in the forests of the

highlands. Each hyrax was a tree's voice brought back from the highlands and spread on the floor and stilled.

His bed was brass. His mother and father had slept in that bed. He was born there. His parents had brought it over in 1918 and he had inherited it and the brass still shone. How had his parents died and where were they buried? Sidanu had slept in that bed. Other women since. Other women since had visited the camp and found him. They came and went and left no trace. The rooms stopped. Would she come and go and leave no trace. And who did not? And who did not?

Her father had died at fifty-eight and Seth was fifty-three. He lived outward on the land, fitting it. The muscles of his chest began to define themselves through the flesh, but his belly was flat and his arms veined with strength. Strong veins in his hands, his shoulders strong, his mouth fresh for her. He was alive to her and urgent even before they touched. There had been boyishness and girlishness and there was lust, lust coming up from deeper and too thick for calculation. He had held his in check. She had known hers and carried it unused. It had never been met before or welcomed. They had five years or ten or none. They had bodies first. The rooms stopped, his and hers. Those were facts. He kept no clock at his bedside. He slept in darkness and woke to light and went out into the day. They.

He was waiting for her. She wanted him. She was wet with wanting him. She lowered the flame of the lantern. She slipped the nightgown to the floor, her body in the flame. She carried the lantern into the bedroom and he was there.

Five

By MORNING THE migration through the camp had begun and they watched it at breakfast from the lodge. The wildebeest came out of the forest south of the camp and passed to the east of the lodge where the grounds were open and grassy and sloping toward the lake. The morning breeze blowing across them blew in the smell of the tarry wax they exuded from glands within their hoofs to mark the trail and the cattle smell of manure and dust and the gamy smell of antelope. Nervous of the camp and crossing the grounds at a fast walk, skittish, the wildebeest snorted and grunted and bellowed, the cows hastening with their calves trotting at their sides to keep up, the young bulls cavorting in a stiff-legged rocking canter and the older territorial bulls working to corral their cows even on the move. The older bulls dropped to their knees and rubbed their muzzles on the ground drawing boundaries of scent with their preorbital glands. When challengers crossed their boundaries they pushed to their feet and lowered their heads and thrust for-

ward their horns and charged. At best they deflected the
younger bulls to the outside of the lines. The cows had no
time for corraling. They moved forward steadily, pressed
from behind. The bulls abandoned their territories and
moved with the cows and the lines of noisy, pressing animals, blue-gray and ranked, emerging from clouds of dust,
stretched back out of sight into the forest.

Most of the migration would have to pass before the lake
could be cleared, but after breakfast the men helped Crown
get ready. They lifted wooden pallets mounted on sleds
down from the rafters of the garage where they were stored
and set them on the ground behind the two camp Land
Rovers and chained them to the rear axles. They pulled the
big snub-nosed Mercedes lorry out of the garage and fitted
its flat bed with stake racks. Years before, when Crown first
encountered the migration, he had commissioned long-
handled gaffing hooks from the Kunoni blacksmiths who
made iron for the Masai. He retrieved them now from the
tool board at the back of the garage and loaded them onto
the lorry bed. Leaving the Land Rovers behind, Abdi bringing along the Winchester, Crown picked up the other guests
and drove them in the lorry down to the shore.

At the shore the milling, bellowing wildebeest plunged
into the shallows and waded out to swim. They massed
through the lake and across the lake they emerged and into
the distance the lines moved on. The lake was black from
near shore to far shore with wildebeest snorting and buck-
ing in the brackish green water, their manes bedraggled,
their wide-set eyes bulging, their heads straining high. Some
of them swam in panicked circles but most swam ahead,
climbing the backs of the animals in front to stay above the
water, kicking with their sharp hoofs, churning up foam,
and calves went down under the weight of the adults that
climbed over them. Already there were drowned carcasses
shining slick and black spotting the shallows. Incongruously

in that volcanic landscape they looked like wet glacial rocks.

The commotion attracted every predator in miles. After lunch, when Crown returned with the guests to the shore, he counted twenty-seven lions, including the four camp cubs. Spotted hyenas patrolled the shore in crowds, whooping and chasing and madly giggling, and a silent, impatient audience of vultures darkened the trees.

The cubs had left their rest area under the water tower late in the morning, bounding along beside the moving lines of wildebeest like sheep dogs at herding. Coming down to the lake they charged clumsily into the lines for calves, but outrigger bulls swerved with hooking horns to chase them off and the cubs tucked their tails and ran, falling over each other, and when the bulls left them to rejoin the lines they sat back on their haunches bewildered and watched the stampeding mass go by. They imitated the older lions at the shore and by afternoon they had learned their trade. None of the lions entered the lake. They had enough to do on the shore. Yellow and lethal, their muscles rippling under their loose pelts, they charged the bunched wildebeest pawing at the water and leapt onto their backs, clearing a space to bring down the animals they rode. They clamped mouths over muzzles and slowly smothered while the mass broke around them. Glutted with prey they left the dead uneaten and leapt to bring down more.

Hyenas working alone waded into the shallows and tore the carcasses where they found them. Packs of hyenas on the shore singled out terrified wildebeest and chased them aside and ripped their bellies open, the guts dragging on the ground, but no more than the lions did the hyenas stay to feed. In a frenzy of opportunity they killed and kept on killing. Jackals and even small bat-eared foxes fed on the abandoned kills. The vultures flapped down from the trees as the kills mounted and pecked at the carcasses scattered in the grass outside the moving lines and endlessly through the

day, bellowing and snorting and bunched stumbling together, running the corridor the predators made, the wildebeest crowded on.

No one slept well in camp that night and the second day
was worse, the carcasses thick on the shore and piled tram-
pled in the shallows. Late in the afternoon Crown organized
his crews. By the third day the main body of the migration
had passed and only stragglers crossed through the camp.
Most of the predators had withdrawn and the crews were
working efficiently.

Cassie and Mrs. Wells drove the Land Rovers. Gossett
drove the lorry. Abdi in a cartridge jacket guarded the salvage crew, firing the Winchester into the air to scare off
hyenas and keep the vultures back. Crown and Kahn waded
up to their waists in the shallows. They gaffed the bloated,
stinking carcasses and dragged them in to Friedrich and his
two sons, who hauled them out of the water and swung
them onto the pallets or up onto the bed of the lorry. The
drivers carted the loads half a kilometer eastward of the lake
to a dump Crown had designated. Tobin, Ferd Wells and
Mrs. Gossett, riding with the loads, cleared the carcasses
from the pallets and the lorry bed and left them for the mob
of vultures at the dump that milled now too gorged even to
fly. Tobin was better help than Crown had thought he'd be.
He was a former Marine. He'd seen combat in Korea and
away from his wife he was likable. Marsha, Aura and Friedrich's wife and daughter observed from the safety of the
porch, and on the grass between the lodge and the lake the
Japanese gentlemen set up tripods and filmed.

They were laboring in the stench of death and in foul,
scummy water. Crown had stowed a supply of whiskey in
the cab of the lorry. Each time Gossett drove the lorry back
from the dump they stopped work and passed the whiskey
around, Cassie and the ranchers' wives drinking from the
bottle like the men. The whiskey cut the stench and kept

them going. At noon the cook spread a picnic on tables outside the lodge and they stopped for lunch, but they worked steadily through the day.

Crown and Kahn separated as they cleared the carcasses from the lake. The Germans alternated behind them on the shore. They were working behind Crown when he noticed the cubs watching Kahn from the grass. They faced him in a line like sphinxes, tensely switching their tails, and Crown wondered what they were up to. Kahn hadn't noticed them yet.

Abdi fired off the Winchester. The crack of the rifle startled Kahn and he slipped on the muddy bottom and went under and came up thrashing and the cubs were on their feet and running.

"David!" Crown shouted. "Look out!"

Kahn found his footing and swung around. He took in the cubs and looked across at Crown and the cubs had reached the shore. They couldn't be hungry, Crown thought. What the hell were they doing? The rifle. They'd been conditioned to chase from rifle fire and watch for the odd animal. That's what he'd taught them. He was a bloody Elsa-lover after all. But maybe not. Maybe they were really on their way. Maybe they just needed the fear of god in them now, a little send-off now to teach them to leave the two-legged killers alone.

"Stand still!" Crown shouted to Kahn. He splashed his way through the muck toward the painter and the cubs were in the shallows. "Abdi! Watch them! Shoot if you have to but hold off as long as you can!"

"I am ready, Effendi!" Abdi called.

Seeing Crown approaching, the cubs faltered in their dash and stopped in the shallows and there was still danger and Crown kept on and then he reached Kahn's side. The man was grinning and brandishing his gaff.

"God *damn*," he said, "this is fantastic. You live like this all the time out here?"

"Don't talk," Crown said, "and don't stare at them. A stare's a challenge. Keep that gaff in front of you and walk in with me. When we get a little closer, start shouting. Let's hope they back off, because Abdi can't shoot all four of them at once."

"I spend the day dragging corpses and now I'm herding lions. Fantastic, man."

With Abdi covering them they waded toward the cubs but the cubs had been blooded by the frenzied killing of the wildebeest and held their ground. Crown started shouting then and Kahn shouted beside him but instead of retreating the cubs switched their tails and bared their teeth and snarled. Crown had decided to shout to Abdi to shoot when he saw Cassie in the Land Rover racing along the shore. Honking the horn she swerved into the shallows, dragging the empty sled and churning up water and flinging mud, and headed straight for the cubs. When they saw her bearing down they bounded from the water and skidding around, blowing the horn, she chased them up the slope and all the way past the lodge into the forest. The German boys cheered. Slapping each other on the back, Crown and Kahn waded out of the lake.

Cassie had turned and gunned the car down to the shore to meet them. She threw open the door and jumped out. "Was I good?" she called, running over. "Was I good?"

"You were fantastic," Kahn said. "Absolutely fantastic."

"You bloody well saved our lives," Crown said. "That's it. That's enough of the salvage brigade. We've cleaned up the worst of it. Tonight everything's on the house." He held Cassie away from him. "And you," he said. "And you. I want to talk to you. Where the hell did you learn to drive like that?"

"Did you see those goddamned lions?" Kahn asked Friedrich in the bar after dinner, not for the first time. "Did you see those bastards coming after me?" They were drinking Crown's champagne.

"It was very dangerous," Friedrich said. "Fraulein Wendover was most correct."

"Were they really after you, David?" Aura said.

"Bloody right they were after me."

"You don't say 'bloody.' Seth says 'bloody.'"

"Anything Seth says is fine with me. What a place this is." He strolled over to Crown in the wicker armchair by the couch. "We were supposed to move on tomorrow," he said, "but if you've got room I'd like to stay a few more days." He raised his voice to include the others. "Wouldn't everyone like to stay around a few more days? Isn't this place fantastic?"

"It sure as hell is," Gossett said. "Yeah, we're here another week."

"Long as we ain't got to drag no more carcasses," Ferd Wells said.

"No danger of that," Crown said, setting down his champagne. "We got the worst of it. The vultures can clean up the rest. Did anyone keep count?"

"I did," Tobin said. "I counted about six hundred."

"We had seven hundred last year, but we worked longer. You're all welcome to stay. No one's booked in before the beginning of next week. I've got to drive over to a Masai village tomorrow, but it's near here. I'd be pleased if you came along. I hope you know how much I appreciate your help."

"Hell," Gossett said, "our pleasure. Never seen nothin' like that before."

"It is like that every year," Abdi said from behind the bar.

"I'd go broke if I lost that many calves."

"The *nyumbu* continue to increase," Abdi said. "They are stupid but they are also prolific."

"I have read that the Serengeti holds more than five hundred thousand now," Friedrich said.

"I'd put it above six hundred thousand," said Crown.

"You'd think the lions and the damned hyenas would keep them down." This was Gossett.

"They weed out the weak, but the limiting factors are disease and parasites."

"Hey, guys, this is getting awfully country," Aura said. She took a gold cigarette case from her purse and opened it and held out a machine-rolled joint. "I'm going to smoke. Is that all right, Seth? Anyone want to join me?"

"It's all right with me," Crown said.

"I will." Cassie was sitting on the couch next to Crown's chair. "Seth will too if I twist his arm."

The Japanese gentlemen grinned and nodded.

"I smoke not *cigaretten*," Mrs. Friedrich said.

"It's not a cigarette. It's dope."

"It's great stuff," Kahn said. "We got it in Mombasa. What's it called, Seth?"

"*Bangi.*"

"Yeah. *Bangi*. It's better than Colombian."

Marsha Tobin bounced to her feet. "Is that *marijuana*?"

"Yeah," Aura said. "You want to try it?"

"What are you, a pusher? I think that's disgusting."

Tobin told his wife to shut up.

"What? What did you say?"

"I said sit down and shut the hell up."

She looked at him blankly and then abruptly sat down.

"So," Aura said. "Who wants to turn on?"

"Honey," said Mrs. Gossett in her deep voice, "you probably think us hayseeds never seen that stuff before."

"Have you?"

"Honey, we was smokin' that stuff before you was born.

Only we didn't call it dope. We called it locoweed. Sure, light up and pass it over. It'll give this old man here some ideas. He ain't had so many ideas these past few years."

"Hey, you don't need to be tellin' that," Gossett said.

"I love ya anyway, honey." Mrs. Gossett opened her powerful arms. "I think I just about love everybody here. People sure can work together when they got a mind to."

Aura lit up then and the joint went around. Crown smoked in turn and drifted at ease among friends.

Abdi's religion forbade him alcohol, but he took to the *bangi* with enthusiasm. After a while he began inventing drinks, working dreamily behind the big polished ebony bar. The drinks had a base of coconut milk. He mixed in rum and bitters or a fiery banana gin of local manufacture called *waragi* or any of several liqueurs and whipped everything to a froth. The drinks were refreshing after the dry champagne, foamy in the dewy glasses and decorated with slices of small sweet oranges from Zanzibar. Abdi talked to himself quietly as he worked.

The guests had formed a circle around Crown on the couch and on the floor. He reminisced about the days of hunting safaris. When he finished one story Cassie said: "I noticed an autographed copy of *Green Hills of Africa* with your books. Did you know Hemingway?"

"I hunted with him," Crown said.

"Hey, really?" Kahn said. "When?"

"He was over here in 1953. He'd hunted with Philip Percival in 1934. That's what the book was about. Philip was hunting him again. He asked me to come along and help out. Philip'd been through a nasty bout of tick typhus and he wasn't up to snuff yet."

"What was he like?" Aura asked.

"Hemingway?" Crown smiled down at her. "Big. Energetic. Moody. Told very funny stories. He was carrying a lot of weight. He was six feet tall and barrel-chested anyway and he had a belly on him. Let's see, in 1953 he would have been about my age now, about fifty-three or -four. I think he weighed close to two-thirty when we started out. He trimmed down with the hunting. He didn't do too well. He had trouble with his eyes. I really think he was a better fisherman than a hunter, but he tried hard enough. Wouldn't shoot elephant, though. Thought they were too noble to kill. Had a thing about hyenas. Knocked hell out of hyenas. You remember his Kilimanjaro story. Hyenas were death sniffing up to you."

"He was always talking about rummies," Aura said. "Was he a rummy?"

"Not the way he meant it. He meant someone who'd drink himself into a stupor all day. He didn't do that. Polished off a bottle of wine at breakfast and had his nips during the day, but he could carry it. Got drunk enough at night. Amazing what he'd do at night. Go out and stalk a leopard with a spear, that sort of thing. Damned dangerous. Court some local belle."

"Wasn't he married?" Mrs. Gossett asked. "I thought he had a whole pack of wives."

"Miss Mary put up with it. That's the way the other wives lost him. She wasn't about to lose him. It was harmless enough. He needed his wives. Got absolutely black depressed without them."

"*Über wen sprechen sie?*" Mrs. Friedrich asked her husband, aside.

"*Er war ein amerikanischer Schriftsteller,*" Friedrich explained. "He was an American author. *Er erhielt den Nobelpreis.*"

"*Wie hiess er?*"

"Ernest Hemingway."

"*Ach ja.* Der alte Mann und das Meer. *The Old Man and the Sea.*"

"*Nicht sein bestes Buch. Du hast seine besten Bücher*

nicht gelesen. You haven't read his best. Der Sieger Geht Leer Aus—*The Sun Also Rises.* Wem die Stunde Schlägt—*For Whom the Bell Tolls.* Tod an Nachmittag—*Death in the Afternoon.*"

"*Ich erinnere mich.* I remember. *Ein Sportfreund.*"

"*Ja,* a sportsman. A fisherman and a notable hunter. But also a great writer, one of the greatest."

"*Er beging Selbstmord.* He killed himself."

"*Ja.*"

"*Es ist traurig.* It's sad. Why did he do it? He had sons. Wasn't he wealthy? He had so much to live for."

"*Ich weiss es nicht.* I don't know."

"*Es ist sehr traurig.*"

"I liked him well enough," Crown said. "We were all rather innocent in those days. Mad, really. The most extraordinary thing I saw him do was bullfighting."

"Where?" Kahn asked. "Here? In Africa?"

"Right." Crown looked at Aura. "You wouldn't like to contribute another joint to the proceedings, would you? Might just loosen up the storytelling a bit."

"Bloody good," Aura said, finding her cigarette case.

"Now you're doing it," Kahn said.

"Hey, babe, place to do it." She lit the joint, expertly inhaling, and passed it to Crown.

"Right," Crown said, the joint moving on. "Well, we were camped at Figtree Camp, up in Kenya in the Rift Valley. The camp was on a stream bank in a grove of trees. Figs, obviously, among others. Fine place. The stream was clear. It came down out of the rift wall on the west. What was it called? The Oleibortoto, I think. Lovely clear stream. I'd taken to bathing in it of a morning and that morning I'd had a rhino chase me out. Rather hairy there. I was naked as the day I was born and the stream bed was loose rock. Hard on the feet. I managed to skin my way up the bank and get out of range. The rhino went on down. For some reason we didn't go out that day. By lunch Papa was hitting the bottle pretty hard."

"You called him Papa?" Cassie asked.

"I was asked to. I was twenty-eight and he was a distinguished older gentleman and I'd called him Mr. Hemingway, but he wasn't having that. I got used to it. So he's Papa for me. Papa Mr. Hemingway. He was really a rather boyish man, very quick with his enthusiasms and very quick to anger. He could pout, too, when he didn't have his way with things. Since we'd started out at Philip's he'd shot at lions, zebras, a wart hog and a baboon and missed them all. He wasn't in the best of moods. I suspect that's why he was hitting the bottle. Anyway, he started telling us about bullfighting. Very much about bullfighting. He'd been to literally thousands of bullfights in his time. He had the names of hundreds of bullfighters at his fingertips. And all the terminology. *Veronicas* and *gaoneras* and *mariposas* and *farols* and I don't know what all. *Serpentinas.* I remember him mentioning *serpentinas.* Something about citing the bull, which was making him charge. And the bull picking out his terrain, his *querencia.* And bullfighters who went *rabioso* when the crowd taunted them and bullfighters who were cold and scientific and bullfighters who had *cojones.* He did go on about it."

Everyone was listening now, and Abdi had come over from the bar.

"Then he had to demonstrate how it was done, how the matador handled the cape. Miss Mary had shot a tommy for the pot the day before and we had this flyblown head with the tommy's straight corkscrewed horns. 'That's about the size of the goddamned bulls they fight in Spain these days, Lunk,' Papa said. He called me Lunk. It was an—what's the word? The *bangi*'s taking me away, chaps. Cassie? What's the word for a word made up from the first letters of other words?" Cassie was sitting on the floor beside Crown and he reached for her hand.

"An acronym?"

"That's it. An acronym. An anachronistic acronym. Man had a way with the nicknames. Respected you, you understand, but wanted just a little edge. Papa and Lunk. Miss Mary. Flattery there. His little girl."

Cassie's cheek against his arm. "Seth?" she said. "What was Lunk?"

"Right. 'Uneasy lies the head that wears the crown.' *Henry the Fourth*, Part Three. U-L-H-W-C. Doesn't quite scan, but he got it there. Dropped the U. Said it was the Swahili plural and I was entirely singular."

Crown straightened and concentrated. "Anyway. He went off to his tent and came back with a big plaid blanket he'd brought along from Abercrombie & Fitch. 'Hell,' he said, 'it ought to be percale. A good cape is percale. Percale on one side, raw silk on the other. Stiff, too, and it's supposed to be colored yellow and cerise. A muleta's scarlet serge. Make a good suit except for the color. Fairy color.' He spread it out on the table and proceeded to cut it in half. Did something to it with the table knives left over from lunch to weight it. Miss Mary raised an eyebrow at the cutting but she knew better than to interfere. Then he took a swig of his drink and winked at me and walked me out to the clearing in front of the tents. Set me to running at him with the bloody tommy head.

"'Watch the cape,' he said. 'Don't watch me. Bulls watch the cape.' I'd run at the cape and he'd swing it slowly in front of me, standing straight with that big chest stuck out and holding the cape with both hands and bringing me close past him, the tommy horn just missing his chest, and I'd watch the cape and come up with it and then he'd turn me after I was past. That was to tire the bull. I got rather tired of tiring the bull. Papa was explaining it as he went

along, calling out the figures. He was re-creating a series of
passes he'd seen. He said the best he'd ever seen. I forget
who. Very decadent, he said. He said the killing was the
point. The killing was classical and the cape work was decadent but properly executed it was fine and true. And that
was all right. We had fun with that. But then he remembered the rhino I'd had to dodge that morning. He remembered the rhino and he wanted to look it up and fight it."

"Christ Almighty," Gib Gossett said.

"*Mafahali wawili hawakai zizi moja*," Abdi said, drifting
back from the *bangi*.

"Abdi's quoting. That's a Swahili saying. 'Two bulls can't
live in the same farmyard.'"

"I knew the Papa," Abdi said proudly. "He was *fahali
halisi*. He was himself a brave and genuine bull."

"Naturally we all did our best to dissuade him," Crown
went on. "Unfortunately, Philip Percival wasn't in camp at
the time, and Philip was the only one of us he really listened
to. I see. That's why we stayed in camp. Because Philip had
gone in to Magadi to see to some repairs. I'd forgotten. So
Miss Mary flared up at him. Papa. Little lady told him to
bugger all. Said she wasn't going to stand around watching
him knock himself off and stalked away to her tent. It just
egged him on. He'd had *nynigi* whiskey-sodas at that point.
Too many. We piled into the Land Rover and away we
went. Me, his gun bearer N'gui, a tiny little man, and Papa.
After the rhino chased me out it'd passed downstream. We
thought it had laid up in the tall grass a ways down the
stream on the other bank. Back from the stream the grass
was shorter. We forded below the rhino's cover. I wish I
could tell it the way he'd tell it. I'm surprised he never told
it. It was bloody amazing. He'd brought along his old
Springfield that he'd been shooting with, and the bottle, and
his plaid cut-off blanket cape weighted with the cutlery. We
parked the Land Rover and got out. It was hot in the sun.

The grass was the color of wheat and the wall of the rift rose up wheat-colored behind us but higher up blue. We were almost under it. It wasn't exactly sinister but it was a barricade off in the distance and the whole landscape changed there and elevated and the valley was wide enough that the eastern wall looked like low clouds. It was one hell of a *barrera.*

"Ahead of us maybe thirty yards was the tall-grass cover. We were pretty sure the rhino was in it. Papa looked over the terrain. 'I'm giving it one goddamn pass,' he said. 'Then we get the hell out of here. N'gui, I want your ass in the Land Rover ready to go.' 'This is crazy, Papa,' I said. 'That's your opinion, pal,' he said. 'Papa's inventing a new sport here. Fine thing for Kenya. Best thing that ever happened to Kenya. Make up for all the goddamn coffee plantations with the lesser nobility stalking the wild red coffee bean. You'll get all the sportsters out here again. Suck in the *maricóns,* too. They like to watch the boys blooded and they bring in the gentry. What you want is the Mau Mau working rhino. Get the Mau Mau working rhino and you've got a damned fine package, Lunk.' Then he faced the cover and unfolded the cape. 'Let's get down to it,' he said. 'Take the Springfield, Lunk, and cite the bastard. Scare him out of there.'

"I knew it wasn't very smart but I wasn't very old and I figured we could all run around behind the Land Rover if we had to and I couldn't very well take the man off at gunpoint with his own gun or knock him out. So I fired a round from the Springfield over the tall grass. We heard shuffling in the cover but the rhino didn't show so I fired twice more, lower. Then we heard him snorting and then he came out of there. Slowly. Curious. A big dark bull with that ugly swaybacked head of his low and swinging from side to side, beady eyes looking around, body like a tank car but armored, and twitching those pig ears and already testing those horns, jabbing the air and then twisting, tearing away at the air, bloody indignant to be disturbed, looking for a victim—arrogant, really, just damned bloody arrogant—and I backed away fast enough. But Papa stood his ground. I'll be damned if he wasn't staring back at the rhino and his head was going the same way. They might as well have been wired together. They were both jabbing and twisting and Papa was jutting up his chin. He had a white beard and it was a little long in the chin and he looked a little like one of those Spanish grandees he liked in El Greco with a long chin and he was doing a little spastic jut with the chin.

"It was still a great lark for him. He jutted at the rhino and the poor beast jutted the air. Then his face opened up in that big Clark Gable grin he had and he flicked the cape like someone shaking out a rug. He called 'Huh!-huh!-huh!', calling the rhino like a matador. The rhino heard him and shook its head and looked up and saw the cape flicking and the man behind it and it pawed the grass, pawed the grass and then it charged. I can't imagine what Papa was thinking. He'd stood down charging animals before, so he knew how it felt and how to hold himself together for it, but always before he'd had the business of getting ready to shoot, sighting in and looking for a shot and making sure his feet were in place and the butt of the gun well into his shoulder and his aim true. Now it was nothing more than a sawed-off piece of blanket and tons, Christ, bloody *tons* of rhino coming down on him. I thought he'd run. I swear I did. I'd have run. I'd never have done it in the first place, but if I got that far I'd sure as hell have run. He didn't run. He stood as still as a stone. It wasn't that he was drunk, either. He'd stopped being drunk the second the rhino came out.

"Because it wasn't the one we'd seen that morning," Crown said, looking around at the silent expectant faces. "It was another one about twice as big. I don't know where it came from or where the other one went. But when it

charged, it sobered him instantly. He sobered up instantly
and another thing that happened was that he stopped grinning. The big grin disappeared and his face took on a look of
great intelligence. He didn't actually furrow his brow but
you could almost hear him thinking, almost hear a high-
pitched hum like a dynamo winding over as he took it all
in and ran it through the equipment and realized suddenly
where he'd put himself and what the stakes were and what
he'd have to do about it to save face on the one hand and to
get out of there in one piece on the other. Your average
hunter on his first stalk with a lion coming at him couldn't
have looked any more suddenly intelligent or any worse.

"But he did a lot better than that. The rhino came on and
the rhino came on. It all slowed down the way those things
always do. I saw things I'd never ordinarily notice. The
head was marked off with a network of scratches like a
crude map of a hillside with peasant fields with oddly angled borders. The right ear was torn or possibly marked
with a little hooked notch that I could see the sky through
and I swear I could actually count the ticks crawling on the
folds of the bastard's neck as it went by me. Papa's shirt was
soaked with sweat. I hadn't noticed that much sweat before.
There were great brown patches spread out all the way to
the center of his chest that met in the middle and overlapped, I could see the salt lines overlapping and spreading
on and those piercing eyes of his looking straight at the
rhino and those big brown hands clutching the cape and
then the rhino was into the cape, into the cape and the horns
lifting it, that big black tank-car body coming in, the cape
caught on the horns and the body passing Papa and the
cape and the rhino and Papa making one solid figure, the
body of the rhino passing with inches to spare between the
wall of the rhino's side and that barrel chest, the wall clanking on, maybe the air rushing the way it would rush through
a narrow high canyon, the wall clanking on, and Papa just

let it take the cape, I think he figured we could get away
while it had the cape on its horns and that it would probably take out its rage on the cape, the poor cut-off plaid blanket of a poor cape, the cape going up into the air with the
lifting of the head. And that was it. There was Papa and the
cape and the rhino and then he was running toward the
Land Rover shouting at me to get the hell into the car, let's
get the hell out of here, and the rhino was tossing the cape,
hooking it, molesting it brutally, trying to gore it, losing it
on the ground and finding it and stamping on it and hooking
it up again. The rhino hadn't seen us yet. We jumped in and
N'gui gunned around with the doors swinging and Papa and
I trying to pull them shut against the turning of the car and
Papa was swearing and laughing, 'That goddamned son-of-
a-bitch rhino! That son-of-a-bitch goddamned rhino! Did
you see that son-of-a-bitch, Lunk? Did you see him? Did
you see him take the cape? Did you see him go by? Did you
see old Papa run the bastard, Lunk? Did you see it?'

"That was the nerves talking then, afterward. It really
wasn't quite sane and he knew it. Standing down a rhino
with a blanket wasn't quite sane. He was shaken. His hands
were shaking and he was holding himself, hugging himself
to still his hands and he was shivering. The rhino was chasing the car. N'gui was driving like a madman. Grinding up
through the gears. We left the rhino in the dust. Papa
calmed down. He chugalugged from the whiskey as we
drove back. He could hardly get out of the car. We put him
down for the afternoon. He looked damned old then. Old
and worn.

"But what he'd done, you see," Crown said, looking
around him, "was stand stock still. Stand stock still and execute a perfect pass on the animal. Figure out its charge as it
came on with no help from picadors or banderilleros, no
knock-up in the morning, no study, no harpoons in the neck
muscle, no help at all. Nakedly shift himself into position,

tons of animal coming down on him. So that when it went
by he didn't have to move an inch. Just guide it with the
cape. He had to let go the cape because the horns weren't
bull horns, weren't spread out to the sides but were rhino
horns parallel on the midline of the ugly little funnel of a
head. Not so little, either. But otherwise he did it perfectly.
Hell of a show, just a hell of a show."

Crown sat back then exhausted and spontaneously, Kahn
starting it, they applauded. The party continued late, the
light streaming out from the lodge, and a little after midnight it began to rain.

Six

THE *manyatta* OF ole Kipoin was located an hour's drive southeast of the camp. Because of the late party they didn't get away until shortly before noon. They drove south on the track through the forest, Crown and Cassie in the Land Rover and the guests following behind in the two tour microbuses, and beyond the forest where the track continued south through bush country they turned off east and drove across rolling open plain. The rain had stopped but the sky was heavily overcast. The low places were muddy from the rain. Crown avoided them for high ground. The watercourses ran east and west and only once was it necessary to make a ford. They forded at a riffle where the stream spread out over gravel shallows and the muddy banks had been cut down, gunning the car and then the buses one by one through the cut and across the riffle and spinning up the other side. There was less game on this Masai pastureland than on the reserve area nearer the park but looking back toward the ford after they had passed they saw two giraffe,

a bull and a cow that had been browsing at the watercourse
trees, moving away from the noise of the machines, their
long necks swaying as they walked, and here and there on
the plain families of zebra fed. Eastward rose the highlands,
black under the overcast, their heights shrouded in fog.

The *manyatta* as Crown's party approached it looked like
a great circle of brown, crusty loaves set down in the grass,
the loaves the rectangular, barrel-vaulted houses of the
Masai, the crust the mixture of mud and cattle dung with
which the house framings of *leleshwa* bush were plastered.
Smoke curled blue from holes in the roofs of the houses, and
nearer they could see the *boma* that surrounded the *manyatta,* a dense barricade of thorn bush that protected the
cattle from predators when they were herded into the circle
at night. Black and red and white cattle grazed into the distance around the *manyatta.*

Children came running to greet Crown when he left the
Land Rover outside the main entrance, small naked boys,
girls in beaded aprons. They bowed their heads for the
blessing of his hand. He spoke to them in Masai and laughing and pointing they ran confidently among the tourists pil-
ing from the buses parked behind.

Cassie joined Crown. "It smells like a barnyard," she said.

"It is a barnyard." He turned back to the buses. "Wait
here!" he called. "I'll arrange for you to see the village!"

Women greeted Crown as he crossed the common inside
the circle of houses and girls in red blankets ran up to kiss
him. Holding his hands, following behind him or walking
backward in front, they pointed to Cassie and questioned
and laughed, slim red-brown girls with shaven heads and
layers of beaded collars at their necks, the married ones
wearing heavy coils of copper wire burnished on their legs.

Cassie smiled at them. "What are they saying?"

"They're asking me if you're my wife. They say you have
a mane like a lion."

"Tell them we're in love."

Crown spoke in Masai.

"Aii!" the girls cried, laughing, and as they had done with Crown they crowded around Cassie and took her hands. Their hands surprised her; they were broad and thick and calloused.

Ole Kipoin greeted them in front of his house and the girls scattered. He embraced Crown and Crown introduced him to Cassie and he embraced her in turn. He was tall, tall as Crown, but slimmer, his body under his red blanket smoothly muscular. He wore a black woolen skullcap and brass earrings and he carried a black wooden club, the shaft the thickness of a shotgun barrel with a doorknob-sized ball carved at the end. "I am happy to see thee," he said to Crown in Masai.

"And thou also," Crown said. "I hope thy cattle are well."

"They are well now that the long rains have begun, my brother." Ole Kipoin turned to Cassie and spoke in English. "Welcome," he said. "I have little English only. You surely are welcome here."

He raised his hand and Cassie understood the gesture and bowed her head and he rested his hand on her hair and lifted it away.

"It's a great privilege to visit your village," she said when she straightened.

Ole Kipoin smiled. "This man good man. My brother. We know each other from childhood."

"He's a wonderful man," Cassie said. Ole Kipoin said something to Crown in Masai and Crown laughed and answered him. Cassie looked at Crown and he winked at her but he didn't explain the exchange.

"Let us go out and sit under the trees," ole Kipoin said to Crown. "Thou hast come about the dead man and we have much to discuss."

"I have brought people with me," Crown said. "They are

guests at my camp but they are more than tourists. They aided me in clearing the lake of *il'engat* after the march to new grass. They are friends. Wilt thou allow them to visit thy *manyatta?*"

"*O*," ole Kipoin said. "If they are friends of thine then they also are welcome. Will they take *il'oipi*, the photographs?"

"They would wish to."

"They may photograph me if they choose without payment, but they should pay all others here."

At the buses Crown introduced ole Kipoin and translated his greeting. He explained about the photographs and suggested rates and ole Kipoin directed the children to guide the guests through the village. Crown and ole Kipoin walked with Cassie to a grove of trees nearby where the elders of the *manyatta* lounged in the grass or sat with their knees drawn up and covered by their blankets playing the board game. The elders greeted Crown warmly and after the greetings, deferring to ole Kipoin, they moved away.

Seated under the trees, the Masai brought out a buckhorn from beneath his blanket and offered it to Crown. Crown declined and ole Kipoin unstoppered the buckhorn and tapped snuff onto the back of his wrist and snorted it and sneezed.

"I speak in Masai," ole Kipoin said first to Cassie.

"Seth will explain to me later," she said. "I'm glad just to be here."

"Good," ole Kipoin said, and to Crown in Masai: "Ole Senkali has informed me of the murder. I am ashamed that such could happen in the section of the Serengeti Masai."

"The man was murdered elsewhere, my brother," Crown said. "They only carried the body here."

"*O*. I know of that, but is there more that thou should tell me?"

"Yes. A high officer of the Tanzanian Army came to me some days ago. This Rukuma is a warrior of the bush."

"This Rukuma is an insult and a dangerous joke," ole Kipoin said sternly. "*This* is a *rukuma*." He brandished the black club.

"I know, my *olaitoriani*, my chief. A man of unknown origin who stirs up war has taken the word for the staff of thy office as his name. The high officer of the army told me of him. He is African but he came to Tanzania from another country. He trained in Dar-es-Salaam with other warriors of the bush to whom Tanzania is favorably disposed but he has broken off with them and makes war on his own against the Kenyans and now also in Tanzania. He has caused Tanzania much trouble. He is believed to be camped in the *il'doinyo orōk*, the black mountains. That is where we believe the man worked who was beheaded. The high officer now sets up camp near Ngorongoro and will hunt this Rukuma. I have agreed to help him. I come to thee now because this Rukuma left a paper with the body threatening to kill others. I thought that thou might wish to alert the *moran* to guard the Masai against such a danger. The man has many guns."

"How many are with him?"

"The high officer did not tell me or did not know."

"The *moran* have seen them," ole Kipoin said.

Crown sat forward. "Where?"

"A machine passed a *moran* encampment on the night before the sons of ole Senkali found the body. The encampment was west of the track that descends to the plain from the crater mountain Olmoti. The machine was an army lorry and there were four men in the back in soldier's clothing and two men in the driving house. The men in the back carried guns."

"Then they did come down from Olmoti," Crown said.

"That is what I told the high officer, because the dead man worked there."

"O. It would appear so."

"Six men," Crown said. "There are almost certainly more. Were the *moran* able to describe them?"

"Only that they were African, and the clothing. The machine passed them at great speed."

"I believe there is danger, my *olaitoriani*. This Rukuma has raided an army post in Kenya and escaped with many guns. He has at least one machine for rapid movement and at least five men. He has left a note in this area threatening further atrocities. I wished thee to know of this so that thou might prepare a defense."

"Thou need not insist," ole Kipoin said. "I welcome thy council. It is already done. The *moran* have been alerted and even now they guard the *manyattas* of the section."

"With spears," Crown said.

"With spears. The high officer has guns. Let him use them. The government is quick enough to collect taxes from the Masai."

"I will go to the high officer's camp tomorrow, my brother, and discover when he begins his search."

"Send word to me when thou knowest. Tell the high officer the Masai are prepared to help him in his hunt."

"O," Crown said. "I will do so."

"Why has this man taken a name from the Masai? We have no quarrel with the white men or with the Kenyans. Does he mean to paint us with his treachery?"

"I do not know."

"Thou art an elder of the Council. I would have thee find out who this Rukuma is. If he is Masai then we will insist on dealing with him ourselves. By our own laws. Our representatives in government will affirm the right of this demand. It is part of our agreement of confederation with the other peoples of Tanzania that we administer justice to our own. If this Rukuma is not Masai but an imposter, let the high officer take him. In any case, I authorize thee to stand for the Masai in this matter."

"I will do so, my *olaitoriani.*"

"Keep me closely informed."

"*O,*" Crown said.

Crown translated the conversation for Cassie on the drive back to camp. "What did he say to you," she asked him then, "when you laughed and winked at me?"

"I don't recall laughing and winking at you."

"Ah, he's going to play dumb. After you introduced us, Kimosabe."

"After I introduced you? He said you were a fine-looking woman."

"Oh no. He asked you a question and you answered him."

"Do you really want to know?"

"Of course I want to know."

"He asked me if you were good in bed."

"Yes. Just what I suspected. Great matters of state between the chief and his blood brother. What did you tell him?"

"I said you were fierce as a lioness in bed."

"Wonderful. I'm surprised he didn't ask to borrow me for the afternoon."

"He would have."

"Why didn't he?"

"Because he knew we weren't married yet."

"What if we had been?"

Crown grinned. "You'd still have a veto, but it wouldn't be easy to turn him down."

Cassie's grin matched Crown's. "Maybe I wouldn't want to," she said.

At Oloito, under the canvas awning he had set up to protect the site from rain, Robert Fuhrey worked on the test trench.

When he and John Kegedi had sifted the talus slope they had found it barren of other fossils. They had turned then to the wall of the *korongo* and begun cutting down the trench. They dug the trench half a meter wide and if they were forced to cut it all the way to the bottom of the *korongo* it would extend back three meters into the wall. Fuhrey had reached waist level, a meter and a half.

The layers he had already removed had alternated among soft sandstone and loose shale and tuff. The sandstones derived from the shores of the ancient lake, the shells from the muddy shallows, and their alternations revealed the lake's history. During pluvials, geologically wetter periods, it filled to cover its former shores with water and with mud; during drier interpluvials it receded and buried the mud under sand. The tuffs announced the successive eruptions of ash from the eastern volcanoes, and Fuhrey worked now at a level where tuff directly overlay sandstone. He suspected the talus slope had eroded from that level and with it the tooth. He was always careful, but he excavated now meticulously, isolating even the smallest cinders of ash with his dental pick before removing them, easing away the debris with a soft camel's-hair brush.

The gorge was cool. Last night's rain had washed torrentially through its central canyon and filled its water holes. Up on the rim the night had been black, the sky lowered like the ceiling of an immense cave. Fuhrey had sat in the thatched shelter after dinner talking with John and his two assistants, Mohammed and Kulaka, by lantern light, but when the lightning began he had put out the lantern and silently they had watched the storm blow in. The lightning had illuminated the plain like a strobe, each thorn bush silhouetted stark and black in the blue-white air, and as the flashes fired from quarter to quarter the bushes had seemed to dance. Thorn populated the plain and the gorge was a grave but for a time the rain would relieve the barrenness

THE LAST SAFARI   *111*

with wild flowers and new grass and on the slopes of the
korongos the sisal would bloom.

The lightning and the rain had reminded Fuhrey of home,
of line storms advancing on Kansas City from the prairies
that opened beyond it to the west. At the end of February
the season of storms was only beginning in western Missouri, the tornado weather of midwestern spring; at the end
of February there might still be snow. One of the reasons
Crown had welcomed him so heartily to the Serengeti was
the coincidence of their common origin in Missouri, he from
Kansas City, Crown's parents from an Independence farm.
The bond was tenuous, an accident of place, but in enormous Africa they were lucky to find any bond at all.

Fuhrey brushed at the tuff, exposing a patch of the buff
underlying sandstone. The tuff was dark gray, an easily
crumbled mixture of coarse and fine ash compressed into
rock almost as loose as soil. As a child he had dug through
sod and dark loam in his back yard for bottle caps and
shards of broken glass. His father was a trucking executive,
a burly self-made man who had sired eight children and installed his family in a worn mansion on the south side of
town. His father approved his excavations and encouraged
them and once, two feet down, a pup tent propped overhead as the awning was propped above the trench, Fuhrey
had found a rusting horseshoe and his father had arranged
to fix it in plastic for display on the bedroom shelves with
his other collections—wasps and butterflies, fossils chipped
from Kansas limestone, geodes cracked open like coconuts
to reveal their crystalline meat, a Visible Woman and a Visible Man with blue and red and yellow organs contained
within their smooth transparent skins. On his summer vaca-
tions from high school, assisting a University of Missouri
paleontologist, Fuhrey had shoveled the bones of mastodon
from the muck of an Ozark spring, and later, on a Stanford
expedition to Arizona, he had exhumed a mummified Indian

buried flexed in the dry dust of a cave among offerings of pottery and miniature ears of maize.

Here were no such riches. The layers of the trench he had cleared had been empty of everything but broken shells and he had already picked his way cautiously through two million years, back to seven million years ago. If hominids walked there they had left no trace despite the homely mud basin high above, in another *korongo*. Their discovery could be the work of years. Louis Leakey had first searched Olduvai in 1931 and Mary Leakey had found the two massive premolars and then the skull of *Australopithecus boisei* in 1959, after a twenty-eight-year effort. Fuhrey already had the clue of the tooth from deeper layers than any at Olduvai, but clues were scant; hominids, protohominids, were as rare in those incomprehensibly distant ages as abominable snowmen were rare today. They were not rare in retreat: they were rare in origination. From this almost barren trench or near it and from a few others like it the human race had arisen to dominate the earth.

The walkie-talkie squawked in the toolbox at his feet and Fuhrey withdrew from the trench and knelt to answer it. "Go ahead, John," he said.

"It is noon," Kegedi said, his voice emerging thin and metallic from the small speaker. "Will you stop to eat?"

"I don't think so. I'm on the interface between the tuff and the sandstone. It's about half clear. I think I'll work through."

"Food might be brought to you. Before long it will rain."

Fuhrey looked up at the gray sky, the flat underside of the cloud cover dimpled with pockets of turbulence. "I'll stick it as long as I can. How's the *Deino?*"

"The femur is almost exposed. Mohammed complains of a toothache."

"I'll look at it this afternoon. Talk to you later."

"*Vizuri*," Kegedi said. "Good."

Fuhrey set the walkie-talkie back in the toolbox and lifted the canvas water bag from the awning pole and unscrewed the cap and tilted the bag and drank, the cool water clearing the dust of tuff from his throat. He replaced the cap and hung the bag back on the pole, stretched his shoulders, bent again into the trench and continued working outward from the center, picking away the tuff.

The lakeshore was Eden, one of a few dozen Edens, but it was never a paradise. So early in the history of man there had been no burial: the dead lay where they fell. There had been no language but grimaces and signs, ape language, and there had been no hope of heaven. An alteration in the width of a pelvis, one minor variation in the expression of genes that even modern man shared above ninety-eight per cent with the chimpanzee, meant more to the future of humanity than fire, a slight enlargement of a brain less than half the size of modern man's meant more than the wheel, and not God or reason or love but the thinning and retreat of the forests that once had covered East Africa had determined the direction of human evolution. The enlarging savannas filled with herbivores and offered opportunity to a predator that could run down game in the heat of the day. An ape with limbs preadapted by tree-swinging to upright walking shuffled out from the forest margin, shrunk its fur to nakedness, evolved sweat glands, straightened its pelvis and its spine, taught itself the chase. In five million years it learned to eat meat, in two million more to pick up a stone. Its females gave up the recurring cycles of estrus and males and females bonded permanently in heat. Males hunted then in groups and females carrying offspring on their hips and in their bellies gathered food and lifespans lengthened and brains enlarged. And whatever man was now was a consequence of those beginnings, his culture and even his language an excrescence of the last one hundred thousand years of an evolution that required ten million.

Fuhrey remembered the class at Harvard early in his first year of graduate school, the tall, soft-spoken scientist reading his opening lecture sadly in the old, high-windowed room: *No species, ours included, possesses a purpose beyond the imperatives created by its genetic history. . . . The reflective person knows that his life is in some incomprehensible manner guided through a biological ontogeny, a more or less fixed order of life stages. He senses that with all the drive, wit, love, pride, anger, hope and anxiety that characterize the species he will in the end be sure only of helping to perpetuate the same cycle. Poets have defined this truth as tragedy. . . . In a word, we have no particular place to go. The species lacks any goal external to its own biological nature.* He meant, Fuhrey thought, that in some irreducible sense men and women did what they had to do, worked and begot children and died: that their genetic inheritance directed their destiny as certainly as, if less specifically than, the gods had directed Agamemnon and Oedipus and Medea. Digging down in the earth, digging back in time, made it plain enough. Here was no caesura of the sun, or broken tablet traced with holy fire, or any gear of ancient astronauts: somewhere in this trench was naked man, the animal's bare accommodation to chance, and Bethlehem was a village like any other.

Brushing away the tuff, Fuhrey saw the point of white before he recognized it for what it was, and turned away and jerked his head back to stare. Keeping his eyes on it, he lay down his brush and found the pick and slowly, delicately, picked the tuff away. The point of white became an edge and he brushed the debris aside and the edge showed a surface and he picked. It was no bigger than his little fingernail and it was embedded at an angle in the sandstone. He didn't dare to touch it for fear it would crumble. He picked at the sandstone below it, making a pedestal, and brushed away the sandstone and the fragment stood exposed and awed he

held his breath: a smooth, brownish-white surface weathered over with a network of fine cracks, a thin edge: bone.
He backed out of the trench and knelt at his toolbox and
fumbled with the walkie-talkie and dropped it and grabbed
it up again and pressed it to his cheek, with his other hand
pushing back his hair. "John! John!" he called. "John! I've
got it! Come down! I've got a skull fragment! It's exactly
where we thought it would be!"

It was raining in the highlands and foggy and the Land
Rover's wipers smeared the windshield. Crown didn't see
the guard step out to challenge them on the road north
from Ngorongoro until the guard's wet nylon poncho glared
in the headlights. Crown hit the brakes and Cassie gripped
the arm rest and braced herself against the dash and the
Land Rover skidded sideways to a stop, spattering the poncho with a spray of red mud. The guard jumped aside and
unshouldered his rifle. Carrying it at port arms, glaring, he
waded to the window. Crown slid forward the window
panel and quickly stated his business. At the mention of
General Nguvu the guard's expression changed and sullenly
he ordered them to wait. He conferred with another guard
outside a tent beside the track. The rain washed the windshield clear. Then he was hauling open the side door of the
Land Rover and climbing into the back seat, his rifle clacking against the metal doorframe. He slammed the door shut
and ordered Crown to drive on. In the heated car the wet
poncho steamed the windows. Crown started the defogger
fan. The rifle was a Kalashnikov AK47. The guard cradled it
in his wet lap with the long banana clip that projected from
the block in front of the trigger curving toward the back of
the front seat. It was going to need oiling.

Farther up the road the guard directed Crown to turn off
into the forest. The Land Rover plunged through the dark
cedars on a firm track bedded with cedar needles stained

brown by the rain and the fan drew the resinous smell of the
cedars into the car. Crown saw the second guard post and
prepared to stop but a guard came out and waved him on
and the Land Rover emerged at a clearing that Crown recognized as the site of an abandoned logging camp. On the
left a crusted, weathered sawdust pile rose up gray against
the trees. On the right, under a canvas shelter, mechanics
serviced a line of muddy vehicles, aging troop lorries and
jeeps. Two rows of field tents faced each other down the
length of the clearing across a stretch of mud. At the end of
the rows, in front of a peaked headquarters tent, the Tanzanian flag hung wet and limp from a raw cedar pole. The
guard told Crown to park beside the vehicle shelter. He led
Crown and Cassie toward the headquarters tent and as they
passed the vehicle shelter the mechanics stopped their work
to watch.

In the headquarters tent General Nguvu stood behind
a portable table spread with maps, frowning above the
white glare of a pressure lantern. "Mr. Crown, Mr. Crown,"
he said, "you are premature. I have not called you yet."

Crown stepped forward and extended his hand. "General
Nguvu. I've got some information for you. I didn't have your
call signals so I thought I'd drive on up."

"Ah. That is different. You are welcome. And you especially are welcome, Miss Wendover."

"Thank you, General," Cassie said.

General Nguvu's aide emerged from the shadows and
took their raincoats and directed them into chairs.

"The rain has slowed our preparations," Nguvu said, sitting at the table. He looks unhappy with the rain, Crown
thought. He looks as if he'd like to order an all-out assault
on the rain. "But what is your information?"

"I spoke with ole Kipoin. He's angry about the murder.
He's alerted the *moran*. He'll co-operate with you any way

you want. Some of his *moran* saw Rukuma's lorry the night of the murder."

"Yes? Where?"

"On the track running west from Olmoti. It passed an encampment. They counted six men. Armed. The body must have been in the back."

"Then it is Olmoti," the general said, tapping one of the maps. "Of course they could be anywhere in the highlands. They ran into Kenya from much farther north. But we confirmed with Seronera that the dead man was on Olmoti that night. The rhino were rutting." He leaned forward, his elbows on the table. "I am glad to hear of the Masai. It will make things easier. I have refined my plans since we last spoke, Mr. Crown. It is clear that my first purpose must be to prevent any further raids across the border. We must confine Rukuma before we hunt him."

"There's a lot of ground to cover," Crown said.

"The British succeeded in the Aberdares. We shall also succeed. I have a company of men here, and I am authorized to increase my force to battalion strength if necessary."

"Do you think Rukuma's got any popular support?"

"No, I do not. I think he is running his own show, to what purpose I have not yet discovered. We do not yet know the location of his base. Aerial reconnaissance has not been possible with the rain. We do not yet know his numbers. We know that he is highly mobile, and that his transport must be deployed somewhere below the highlands. You cannot run lorries through these forests."

"Then you'll guard the roads and the tracks out of the highlands?"

"Yes. We are already doing so."

"Are you guarding the main road?" Cassie asked. "We didn't see anyone on the way up."

"You were observed, Miss Wendover. Be sure of that. We have no wish to frighten off our tourist guests." He looked at

Crown. "The rest will be familiar to you. We will alert the villagers in the foothills and set up stop lines, concentrating on the many trails out of the highlands. We will then begin a systematic search and hope to capture at least one of Rukuma's men to aid us. They must come down for supplies. When they do, we will know."

"Just like Mau Mau," Crown said.

"Whatever else one may think of them, the British ran an excellent campaign."

"Then you won't be needing me for a while."

"No. I expect it will be several weeks before we begin the tracking phase."

"Right. I've been thinking about building a water hole at the camp. Seronera's loaning me a bulldozer. Maybe I can get the job done before you want me up here."

"Do not concern yourself any longer for the safety of your camp, Mr. Crown. No more unmarked lorries will travel west from Olmoti."

"Good, General. I'm glad to hear it. I think I'll keep my guns loaded just the same."

The general smiled. "As you wish." He pushed back his chair and stood and Crown and Cassie stood after him. "Since you are here, perhaps you would like to tour the camp. My aide will show you around. I apologize for the rain. Afterward we might have lunch. I should like to go over these maps with you, Mr. Crown. It would interest me to know where you think Rukuma might choose to locate his camp. You could also identify any trails you know that lead from the highlands."

"I'd be glad to, General Nguvu."

Nguvu called his aide. "Show them the camp, Colonel. Instruct the cook to serve us lunch when you return." And to Crown and Cassie: "Enjoy your tour. Despite the mud, you will find the camp in good order."

"I noticed you've got Kalashnikovs," Crown said.

"Yes. The Soviets supply us. It is not an unmixed blessing. With each shipment they would like us to take on a detachment of Cubans." The general winked at Cassie. "It is rather like a premium, Miss Wendover," he said, "rather like your Green Stamps."

Crown and Cassie returned to camp about four in the afternoon and by then the rain had ended. The overcast broke up into clouds outlined in golden light scudding south low over the plain and dappling the plain with sunlight and shadow. The sky through the broken clouds was blue, swept clean by the rain, and the sunlight was golden and the plain had greened. The rain had freshened the lake and filled it. The trees on its shores were darker green. Raindrops clung to the leaves like dew and sparkled in the changing light until the sky cleared and they dried. Crown walked out with Cassie to inspect the site east of the lodge where he intended to build the water hole. The grass was wet and there was new grass where the wildebeest had worn the ground bare on their march. Farther east, at the dump, the vultures still circled in to work the remains of the carcasses but the carcasses were downwind and the vultures only dashes of black against the blue sky.

The tourist buses returned. Some of the guests came out to join them. Crown explained the water hole and asked for their advice.

"You will need a drainage mechanism or the water will stagnate," Friedrich said. His wife and daughter had gone to their tents to change for the evening but he brought along his sons.

"It's got to hold the water," Crown said.

"It will hold the water. The limitation of the water I understand."

"Wouldn't a dam do it?" Kahn asked.

"I figured a dam."

"*Ja*," Friedrich said, "there must be a dam. But with a mechanism for flow." He took a small notebook with a pen clipped to its cover from the pocket of his shirt and opened the notebook and sketched. "In this way. A pipe sunk at the side, so. With the mouth below the water and the pipe going through the dam. Also with a valve." He showed the sketch to Crown. "The valve is open only a little and the water runs through the dam. This makes it fresh, because there is flow. Close in the driest time the valve and the water is conserved. You see?"

"Right," Crown said. "I'll have a hell of a time finding a drain like that and a valve."

"Ah. I have drawn them so large. This is ideal, but you need not so large a pipe. Ordinary water pipe will serve if you build a box to screen the opening. And a faucet tap for the valve."

"That I've got. Good, Dieter. Thank you."

"You are welcome. When will you build this dam?"

"I hope in the next few days."

"Perhaps I may help?"

"By all means."

They stood looking out across the lake toward the plain.

"I've never seen anything turn green so fast," Aura said. Kahn had his arm around her waist. "It's gorgeous. I wish we could stay here forever. Can't we stay here forever, David?"

"Got to get back and paint, babe," Kahn said.

"Now that you've seen the Serengeti," Cassie said, "will you paint it?"

"My work's abstract, but I can feel some changes coming on. I've never had such an incredible sense of space before."

"I can't get over how beautiful it is," Aura said. "I really hate to leave."

"So do I," Kahn said. "We're still here. Let's enjoy it while we can."

That evening at sundowners Crown heard the distant sound of a lorry. Coming across the plain it was steady, a faint beating in the air. From time to time through the hour he listened for it and it got louder. It changed pitch as the lorry left the plain and started up the gradual rise into the forest and he followed it past the camp and it changed pitch again turning back north. When he heard the driver gearing down and heard the air brakes hiss Crown excused himself and went out behind the lodge and up the track came the big flat-bed lorry from Seronera with the yellow bulldozer. The bulldozer was a relic of the war, long and high with a rusty exhaust pipe and high stanchions in front and a broad rusty blade and steel crawler treads. Crown had borrowed it before to scrape out the track to the camp. He helped the driver unchain it from the lorry bed and set the ramps and then he started it up and backed it off the bed. The crawlers shrieked when he worked the brakes to turn. He turned in beside the water tower and shut the bulldozer down and thanked the driver and walked back to collect his friends and lead them out to see it.

"Look," he heard Cassie say as he emerged from the breezeway. "Down at the lake. The cubs. They've come back."

"Hey," Kahn said. "My lions. Those lions. I'll never forget those bloody lions."

Crown swung open the screen door and stepped up to the porch and he was smiling. It's a damned fine camp, he thought. It really is a damned fine camp.

Seven

CROWN DREAMED BURSTS of machine-gun fire on a battlefield of liquid and twisted sand. A head lobbed in exploding flash and smoke and a shard of glowing cherry-red steel stuck from his knee. When the smoke blew past, Sidanu's riddled body impact-jumped flailing on the sand and Crown fell into the horizon and through it, and bold awake and scrambling from bed he heard what he had heard in the dream, the fast high pocking of automatic rifle fire outside in the night in the direction of the tents.

"Jesus Christ!"

"Seth?" Cassie sat up startled. "Seth?"

He was on his feet, pulling on his pants, kicking into his chukka boots, already running into the sitting room, shouting back. "They're attacking the camp! Stay here! Get down!" Screams from the tents came muffled through the walls and he flung open the door to the lodge and the screams went shrill and beyond the dining-room windows he saw the orange flaring light. The rifles pocking he ran

through the dining room bent at the waist dodging tables
and chairs, through the doorway to the bar, to the gun cases,
fumbling in his pants for the keys, rattling the padlock
around. He rammed in the key, flipped back the padlock, hit
it away, knocked the latch aside, jerked open the case. The
.45. He found the .45 and shucked a round into the cham-
ber. And the Weatherby. Five rounds in the Weatherby. He
clawed at the bottom of the case for extra clips. The rifles
stuttered outside and there were screams. A man shouting.
"*For GODSAKE!*" Another burst.

M-16s. They sounded like .22's. Who else? You didn't
think it was the general, did you? He hooked his arm into
the Weatherby, the steel cold against his bare back. Now
easy. They're out there. Over to the wall by the door. Open
the door. Easy. Push it back. The porch. The tents were
burning, the bastards, the tents were burning. They had the
light in their eyes. The screen door. Stay low. Ease it out.

AtAtAtAtAtt! Bullets tore the door, slammed it back
against the wall, wood splintering and splinters flying up in
the light and Crown ducked back, backed off the porch and
into the bar.

"Effendi." Crown spun around bringing up the .45.
"Effendi! *La* Effendi!"

"Abdi. Jesus Christ. The door's covered. They've fired the
tents. They're hitting them as they come out. Get a rifle.
Draw their fire. I'm going out the back."

"If it is covered, Effendi?" Abdi was already at the case
pulling out the Winchester and Crown ran through the dining room.

Cassie in the sitting room with the lantern, dressed, her
face white. "My god, Seth, what is it? What can I do?"

"Help Abdi. In the bar. Load for him. I'm going out the
back."

"Be careful. Please god be careful."

Abdi's wives were out inside the compound, the tour-bus

drivers, the cook farther down. The children. *"Nenda ndani!
Kaa ndani!* Go inside! Stay inside!" The women grabbed for
children and doors slammed behind him as Crown reached
the kitchen. He threaded tables and dodged smoke-
blackened pots and found the back door. It wouldn't be covered. You stupid son-of-a-bitch, it might be covered. They
wouldn't attack the camp, either. They wouldn't attack the
camp because a general of the Tanzanian Army said they
wouldn't attack the camp. And you believed him. The Tanzanian Army. All right. The door. Ease it open. Good. Open.
Good. Now out!

He sprinted across the lot looking everywhere at once, the
water tower ahead, the bulldozer, the entranceway, the
shower buildings, the light from the burning tents beyond
the garage yellow on the trees, sprinted the last yards to the
bulldozer and jumped up onto the crawler and crouched
low behind the seat pumping the choke, working the throttle lever and hitting the starter. The starter chirred and
cranked over. Oh you bastard *start.* He pumped the choke
and hit the starter again and the big gasoline engine fired
and he worked the throttle lever, nursing it, and the engine
roared and reaching up Crown engaged the hydraulic and
raised the blade. He climbed into the seat as the blade came
up and then the blade was ringing like a great bell and he
saw muzzle flashes beside the tree between the shower
buildings and the tents. The .45. He stood and braced the
.45 with both hands, dropped one hand to the hydraulic,
dropped the blade, the hand up—and fired! fired! fired!
Again! Again! He's down! Now go. Now *go.*

Raising the blade Crown pulled back the throttle and
threw in the clutches and the engine raced and throated
down taking the load and the bulldozer lurched forward
clanking up the lot past the garage. He threw out the right
crawler clutch and hit the brake and shrieking the bulldozer
spun right and he let go the brake and threw in the clutch

and the bulldozer ground ahead up the alley between the
garage and the tents. Abdi's rifle cracked and the automatic
rifles sprayed back, one and then another, glass breaking,
two of them, another one raking the tents, three of them, the
tents with their thatched overshelters popping in the heat,
orange-yellow flames swirling up and waves of heat shim-
mering and bodies scattered on the ground thrown at odd
angles and bent. Tobin and then Friedrich came running toward the bulldozer from the trees, the guerrilla beyond the
tents firing at them, the rounds walking up behind them
spitting dirt into the light, and Crown fired the Weatherby
from the waist and then booming from the shoulder and the
guerrilla ducked back behind a tree out of the light and the
men cut behind the bulldozer and climbed onto the tow bar.

"Get the bastard," Tobin hissed. "Get the son-of-a-bitch."

"Hang on," Crown said. He threw the bulldozer into reverse and with the two men clinging to the seat he ran the
machine backward and shrieked around the garage out of
the line of fire. "Let's go," he said. He left the engine running and jumped to the crawler and down to the ground.
With the men behind him he sprinted across the lot and
through the kitchen and across the compound, through his
apartment into the dining room calling to Abdi. Abdi and
Cassie had knocked out the window to the porch. They both
had rifles and they fired through the screen out into the
flickering light. Running low and banging into tables Crown
and the men crossed the dining room into the bar and back
to the gun cases. "Who's left out there?" he asked. He was
unlocking the case of shotguns and he threw it open and
pulled down two twelve-gauges and handed them over and
found boxes of shells.

"They're all dead." Tobin. "They're all dead. Marsha's
dead."

"Go back the way we came. Work around the garage. Get
that son-of-a-bitch at the tents. Pinch him. Go around be-

hind the tents and work in from the west. Watch yourselves.
We've got two in front of the lodge. Don't take chances.
Push him over this way. I think there's only three." He
looked at Friedrich. "*Verstehen sie?*"

Friedrich snapped up straight. "*Jawohl.*"

"Go! Be careful!" They turned and ran low through the
dining room. Two out of fifteen. You stupid hopeless bastard
two out of fifteen.

He crossed to Abdi and Cassie. "Keep at them. Keep
them pinned. I want one of them alive." His arm at Cassie's
waist. "You all right?"

"Yes. What about . . . ?"

"They got them. They're all over the ground."

"Oh no."

"Listen. Abdi? Listen. Keep up a steady fire. Blast the
hell out of them. I'm going around the lodge. We'll have
them pinched from the west. I'm bringing around the
dozer." The shotguns boomed. "Keep at them, okay?"

"*Ndiyo.*"

Firing loud, Abdi and Cassie. Crown heard one of the automatics as he came out the kitchen door, a burst beyond
the tents, and the shotguns answered and then he was up on
the bulldozer and he spun it around and headed it forward
past the garage, turned at the compound and turned again
at the corner by the kitchen, the engine throating and his
ears still ringing from the rifle fire in the enclosed space of
the bar. He switched on the headlights, the light flaring
back from the trees east of the lodge where he'd planned the
water hole, turned north shrieking and gunned ahead and
turned back west at the corner of the porch and threw out
the clutches and caught in the lights the two guerrillas
dropped prone behind the trees. Nailed and braced to one
of the trees he saw the elephant skull he'd mounted there
years before, its long yellowed tusks reaching out to the
burning tents like arms. He brought up the Weatherby. The

guerrillas had shifted behind the trees for better cover but the one under the elephant skull panicked and came up running and a rifle cracked from the lodge and the round hit him and threw him sideways and his arms flung open and the automatic dropped and he dropped with the automatic. The other guerrilla was scrambling to his feet and Crown followed him in the scope and fired and his leg jerked out and screaming he was down with his leg twisted at the shattered thigh. Crown jumped from the bulldozer and sprinted over to him under the tree as he clutched for the automatic and furiously Crown slammed the butt of the Weatherby down on his hands and the bones snapped and the guerrilla's scream cut off as he passed out and his head bounced.

Crown sucked in breath. He looked toward the tents. The other guerrilla was out in the clear and running. Crown brought up the Weatherby but a shotgun boomed and the running guerrilla's head exploded spraying red into the firelight and in the ringing silence Crown heard the moaning from the people on the ground.

He snatched up the automatic. Its clip was empty. He dropped the empty clip and searched the jacket of the guerrilla he had wounded and found a full clip and shoved it in. That's all of them. How'd they get here? Maybe that's all of them. Bastard's bleeding.

"Abdi!" he called. "Get over to the tents. Tobin! Friedrich! Cover him! Check those people! Someone's still alive!"

Abdi came out the door with Cassie running behind him. Crown knelt beside the unconscious guerrilla and pulled off the man's belt. The wound gaped, the femur jutting out bloody. He threw the belt around the thigh high up and tightened it for a tourniquet and the bleeding slowed to an ooze. Keeping you alive, you bastard. Where's Rukuma? Where's our friend Rukuma? Bloody coward didn't come, did he. We'll see about Rukuma.

White flakes of thatch, patches of blackened curled canvas blew in the night wind, the collapsed wooden platforms still glowing, embers like a bonfire burned down. Crown ran over. Friedrich and Tobin stood guard and Cassie and Abdi worked among the bodies. Crown passed Abdi the M-16. "It's on automatic. They could still be out there. Go around in back. If you see anything, fire a burst."

"*Ndiyo,* Effendi."

"Go." Crown went on to Cassie. Aura lay on her back, moaning. Her model's eyes stared wide. Her lower jaw was shattered and one cheek had been shot away. Cassie was shivering but she worked to staunch the blood. "I'll get the kit," Crown said.

He ran to the lodge for the first-aid kit and saw the elephant skull, the two guerrillas, the porch screens blown out, the splintered door, shell casings on the floor of the bar by the window. He found the kit in the storeroom and ran back out to Cassie. "Here's a compress. Who else?"

"The Gossetts." She pointed. "Over there."

Gossett lay drawn up near his wife, holding his belly. Crown looked for Tobin. They needed light. Tobin had given up guarding and knelt beside Marsha. Crown called him. He stood dazed, looked around, saw Crown and came over.

"She's dead." His voice was flat. "She's just gone. Just gone."

"Tobin!" Crown said harshly. "Listen to me!"

"What."

"Listen. Are you listening?"

"Yeah. What."

"Abdi's behind the lodge. Get back there. Let him know you're coming. Tell him if it's clear to start up the generator. We need some light. Tell him to send his wives to help. You got it?"

"Yeah. He's behind the lodge. Get the generator started. Send his wife."

"Let him know you're coming."

"Let him know I'm coming." He stumbled away.

Mrs. Gossett gagged and Crown moved to her. A froth of blood bubbled pink at her mouth. Carefully he turned her on her side and she gagged blood and cleared. He ripped back her nightgown. The wound sucked air beside her heavy, pendulous breast. "Cassie!" he called. "Throw me some tape!" The tape sailed white and he caught it. He peeled off strips and sealed the wound. The generator started and after a time the spotlights came on from the lodge.

"What the hell," Gossett kept saying, "what the hell. What the hell." Crown examined him. Belly. Maybe hemorrhaging. Crown got morphine from the kit, a glass vial and a syringe, scored the end of the vial and snapped it off, loaded the syringe and injected Gossett and laid him out on the ground. He opened his eyes. "Where's my missus?"

"She's here, Gib. She's hurt but she's alive."

"Beat all. What'd they want to do that for?"

"I don't know, Gib. Take it easy."

"What the hell. What the hell."

Crown stood and looked for wounded. Two of Abdi's wives came off the porch and ran into the light, his senior wife heavy in a cotton wrapper and his youngest wife big-bellied, far gone in pregnancy. "Three are still alive," Crown called in Swahili. "Go and bring camp beds from the storeroom. Bring blankets to warm them." The women nodded and turned and trotted back to the lodge.

Friedrich. His daughter, dead. His sons dropped where they had run from their tent. Dead. Dead. His wife on the ground in front of the other tent. Dead. "Dieter?" Friedrich moved among them arranging them. He didn't answer. Marsha Tobin, her chest bloody. Dead. Crown looked for the

Wells and saw them and looked away. Wells cut nearly in half, dead. His wife's head shattered, dead. Where was Kahn? The Japanese?

"Seth? Aura needs morphine. I don't know how to do it."

He injected Aura. Her eyes watched him from above her bandaged face. She couldn't talk. She slapped the back of her hand on the ground. Her eyes followed him. Slapping. He took her hand. Her eyes teared and she looked away.

Then Abdi was beside him. "There is nothing, Effendi. I looked but there is nothing. If they were here they have gone."

"Get on the radio. Call Arusha. Call in the air ambulance. Tell them we've got three wounded." Crown remembered the guerrilla. "Four wounded."

Abdi nodded and left. He still carried the M-16. Where was Kahn? Crown looked at the remains of the tents. The platform of the tent the Japanese occupied hadn't burned. The things there. They were lying on the platform, the ash sifted over them. They were holding each other. Dead. Dead.

He walked around behind the row of collapsed platforms, looking for Kahn, and found him. He'd come out the back of his tent bent over, running crouched, and the rounds had caught him in the top of the head and in the shoulder. He was nude. Dead.

Crown found the guerrilla he had shot from the bulldozer beside the tree where he'd seen the muzzle flashes. The .45 slugs had entered frontally and ripped out the guerrilla's back. Long, braided hair. He rolled the mess over and collected the automatic.

So of the camp two alive and three half-dead and ten dead. Of the guerrillas one half-dead and three dead. The girl mutilated and Gossett critical and maybe his wife would live. Crown went around to the front of the tents again. Cassie worked with Mrs. Gossett. He knelt beside them. "How is she?"

"She's in pain."

"We can't give her morphine. She's got a chest wound. Abdi's calling Arusha. They'll fly out here. Take about an hour. Stay with her. Are you holding up?"

"I'm holding up."

"Good girl."

"How did they get through?"

"I don't know. They must have stashed their transport somewhere and come down on a trail."

"Why? Why here? These people weren't involved."

"I don't know. We're white. That could be enough. Just that we're white. I should have closed the camp when they got Van Meeren."

"You can't blame yourself. How could you know?"

"I'm supposed to know. If anyone's supposed to know, I'm supposed to know."

"Even the general didn't know."

"The general," Crown said, standing. "Who knows what the general knew." They only had to get past the patrols, he thought. How could he have trusted the patrols? You never expected them to come after you. That's why they were the wrath of god everywhere in the world. Work down any number of trails the patrols hadn't found yet. Might never find. Roll out at night with the lights off. Figure everyone's asleep or leave the lorry or whatever a few kilometers back. Hike in and fire the tents and shoot when the fire drove them out. But if they knew that much about the camp they must have known about the guns. Why didn't they clear out? It looked like a suicide squad and why the camp? But then why not the camp? For a terrorist attack that would make the papers all over the world, why not the camp? Thing to do is to ask the man. Splint the leg and ask the man.

"One of these bastards is still alive," he said to Cassie. "I'm going to check him." He laid down the automatic. "We think we got them all, but keep this with you just in case."

"Okay."

The elephant skull loomed ahead of him in the trees. His souvenir. The stink had carried for miles. With his crew he'd homed on the stink like any other scavenger and found the carcass settled on the plain like a stew. The vultures got there first. They'd crawled in through the anus. They were working away inside and their backs tented the belly skin. He knew a trophy when he saw one. His crew disconnected the head and they dragged it back to camp behind the Land Rover. Had to keep the hyenas away from it. The hyenas even ate bone. Hyena dung was white as eggs and they dropped it in nests. So the vultures and the ants cleaned up the skull and he wired the jaw back on and braced the thing against the tree.

It was big but pinheaded, not rounded like a human skull. The tusks were scratched with scars. They were two-hundred-pounders and they curved like scythes but they were cylindrical, thick, the working one blunted and short-ened, and they socketed into matched casings of bone jammed up into the base of the forehead. There weren't any eye sockets in front because the eyes had looked out oppo-site from the sides. Where eye sockets would have been on a human skull, below the middle of the forehead, the bone curved inward to shape a dark oval slot as if one unlidded cyclopean eye had run there back and forth on tracks.

The forehead with its tracking eye and the joined casings jammed up from below formed a keyhole. Insert a key into the white keyhole of the skull and the front would swing back and open into a room. Something splashed there in the darkness. He knew the room. He had entered it before. For a long time he had lived there. In the room, relentlessly, nothing mattered, and fantastic shapes were thrown up onto the walls. The shapes dissolved and reassembled and dissolved and reassembled and slowly they were leveling. Through the room's oval port the camp was colorless and the plain beyond it and the trees intermingled with the bodies and the bodies intermingled with the ground.

No. He had left that room. There was no single tracking eye and no port. The hole had anchored the muscles of the trunk, the trunk that sniffed the ground and sprayed cool water over the living body and delicately picked berries from the tops of trees. The plain was golden and greened in season by the rain and each one of those who were lost that night would be mourned.

He went on to the guerrilla. The guerrilla was dead. With broken hands he had released the tourniquet from his thigh and released himself from interrogation.

The black club was a bold sender of messages, Crown thought. The first message Rukuma sent was for him and for the general and the Masai. They'd dawdled too long before answering. So Rukuma had sent another message. This time the message was fourteen words long. Ten of the words were white and four of the words were black. There were four German words and two words in Japanese and four American words and four of the words were African.

The ten white words were ornate. They announced Rukuma to the world press. They said he was a terrorist. They said he had a cause and he meant his cause to be known.

The four African words were plain. They said that Rukuma was a man men would die for.

Then he'd have to meet this Rukuma. Look him up. You didn't meet a man men would die for every day. Crown had words for Rukuma now too and wasn't it his turn to talk?

PART II

The Hunt
for Rukuma

Eight

STILL SLEEPY, drinking good Kilimanjaro coffee from a mess tin, Seth Crown stared down at the map of the Crater Highlands spread on General Nguvu's table in the headquarters tent at the army camp north of Ngorongoro. With a red pencil Nguvu's aide had crosshatched the sectors of Olmoti they had searched so far. In a week of slogging they'd hardly made a dent.

The map was a cheerful green and white, the work of some breezy desk-bound cartographer, with faint brown contour lines and blue watercourses and cultural features overprinted in black. Olmoti had no cultural features. It was trackless wilderness, without settlements or roads. It had no grassy caldera like Ngorongoro or like Empakaai to the northeast across the Embulbul Depression. It peaked above ten thousand feet and descended steeply, veined with fast, cold feeder streams, all the way to the eastern Serengeti. Eight torrential rivers ran down its western slope. The map didn't show the black forest that bound the mountain, forest

thickly canopied and laced with choking vines, the forest
floor matted deep with needles and leaf mold that obscured
any sign of passage. It didn't show the belts of bamboo
higher up, canebrakes of crowded bamboo pipes tangled
thirty feet overhead that shut out the light as effectively as
the forest canopy and gave cover to silent, vicious rhino.
The Mau Mau had called the rhino of the Aberdare bamboo
belts their Home Guard. The other game got used to men
moving in the forest and came in time to ignore them, but
the rhino never did, and the Mau Mau had relied on the
rhinos' hostility to alert them to patrols. The Olmoti bamboo
belts were equally deadly. A man could wander them for
hours, losing all reference, risking the rhino trails and cut by
slashing leaves, and end up back where he'd begun. The
map showed none of that. Nor did it show the rain.

"Damn this rain," Crown said. "Rukuma's had any
amount of time to slip away."

General Nguvu's teacup clicked in its saucer. "He will not
slip away," he said. Despite the rain, the general turned out
every morning in crisply pressed fatigues. "If we cannot
move, neither can he."

"Don't believe it. The Mau Mau moved in the worst kind
of weather."

"We are not dealing with Mau Mau, my friend. The Mau
Mau spent years up there. Rukuma may have forest skills. I
doubt if his men do."

"They manage to get about, though, don't they."

"Please sit down," Nguvu said, but Crown continued
standing, staring past him at the dark back wall of the tent.
"Seth, Seth," the general chided, shaking his head.

Crown sat then. "I know."

"No one is sorrier than I about the attack on your camp."

"I know. It's just bloody infuriating that we haven't had a
clue to the bastard's whereabouts."

"I have apologized to you in all sincerity."

"I don't blame you, General. It was my fault those people weren't protected."

"Terrorism is a form of warfare. It isn't possible to protect every noncombatant. The state would be an armed camp if every noncombatant were protected. We could not close down all tourism in Tanzania because of the murder of one man. If we had done so, in any case, Rukuma would simply have attacked our own people. I almost wish he had. President Nyerere has heard from Jimmy Carter. Carter asked him for guarantees. Nyerere is a sensible man, but he was not pleased."

"When did he hear?"

"At the end of last week, after the American ambassador had completed his investigation. Nyerere has ordered me to evacuate any Americans in the area."

"Does that include me?"

"I specifically asked that you be exempted. You have joint Kenyan-American citizenship, do you not?"

"Yes." Crown drank the last of his coffee.

"That would seem excuse enough. And that you are working for us in a military capacity. But there is the matter of Miss Wendover."

"She couldn't be safer than right here in your camp."

Nguvu tapped the table. "So long as we do not know Rukuma's location, we cannot consider any place in the highlands truly secure. Not even this camp. No, the farther away from here the better. I had thought to suggest that she be removed to Dar, but I understand that you wish her near you despite the risk."

"Bugger the risk," Crown said vehemently. "I want her near me so that I can protect her. She has a stake in this. They were her friends too. She saw them murdered too."

"I said I *thought* to suggest Dar. I understand your feelings, and Miss Wendover's, and do not do so. But what if she returned to your camp? Your Somali is there. I would happily provide guards."

Crown nodded. "Right. Then I'll be going along with her."

Nguvu pulled his mustache. "There is also the problem of the scientist. Dr. Fuhrey. You know we are temporarily closing Seronera and Ngorongoro. He should not be out there."

"Guard him. He's in the middle of the most important paleontological find ever made. He's going to prove that the human race originated in Tanzania."

The general flicked a wry smile. "I am not at all certain that is a distinction." He shrugged. "All right. I need you here. Miss Wendover may stay. Temporarily. I should like you to consider her removal at the earliest possible time."

"When we get a handle on Rukuma's whereabouts."

"Yes. I shall consult with Nyerere about Dr. Fuhrey. No doubt he will agree. Dr. Fuhrey's work is valuable in its own right. It might also deflect the journalists from Tanzania's troubles." General Nguvu looked at Crown. "I shall be below today directing patrols. We continue to locate trails. Firewood trails, poachers' trails. Perhaps Rukuma uses them. You are attempting the bamboo?"

"As close as we can get," Crown said. "Up high." He sat forward and pointed on the map. "Here."

By nine o'clock Crown and his three-man patrol had crossed northward into the forest and had begun to climb. Now above seven thousand feet the rain fell as mist that dripped from the moss-bearded, spidery cedars and the high, dark-leaved canopies of the hardwoods. The hardwoods forked low to the ground and they were green with soggy lichens. The men wore ponchos, but the continuous dripping fell heavier than rain and worked under their ponchos and soaked their clothes. Like the others, Crown carried his Kalashnikov slung upside down on his shoulder. Spare clips weighted the pockets of his bush jacket. The two privates, easygoing Chaggas from Kilimanjaro, packed pangas; the sergeant's battered binoculars bounced loose in a stained webbing case on his hip. It was dark in the forest and foggy, the air damp and cold, and for long stretches they couldn't see the sky. They stumbled over fallen logs, slipping the rotten bark and crushing the acrid brown crumble the termites made. The forest smelled of termites and must but the dominant smell was cedar. They followed an abandoned game trail, working toward the bamboo. When vine blocked the trail the Chaggas slashed a path with their pangas, disappearing ahead into the fog. Where the trail was open, Crown and the sergeant took turns leading the way.

The sergeant's name was Mugwa. He was a short, tough Kaguru from the Mpwapwa District in east central Tanzania, far southeast of the highlands. Before the Germans colonized Tanganyika and ended tribal warfare his people had eked out a living in pocket valleys high in the mountains. All but the poorest of them had long since moved down into the lower river valleys. Mugwa was a pocket-valley man who had abandoned the poverty of the mountains for the luxury of army life. His neck was as thick as his chocolate-brown, splayed-nosed face and his thighs and his muscular calves bulged his fatigues. Like most Kaguru he was witch-ridden. His years in the army had convinced him that automatic-weapons fire dispelled all but the nastiest witches but he still hated the night. He sneered at the hardships of mountaineering. Crown had worked with him now for a week and felt the pull of climbing in legs and back, light-headed at altitude. Mugwa rolled on.

They'd gone out at dawn. Crown had left Cassie sleeping. He could tell her about Nguvu's worries when they got back. Outside the camp a colony of black-and-white colobus monkeys had set up a racket growling in the canopy. The loud swallowed belching of the growls had followed them

into the forest. This deep in the forest there wasn't much
game and the canopy was still. They moved within an enclosed, moving space, their sounds returning to them muffled
by the fog. The fog streamed through the trees like smoke.
Closer to the bamboo he would stop the panga work. He
was certain the guerrillas were camped in the bamboo. He
didn't want to confront them yet, only to locate them, count
heads. He would take the men up silently and watch for
sign. In a pinch they had grenades: light, pressed-steel Chinese M32s. The grenades hung from their belts like small
black pots and handled like heavy baseballs and they were
shrapnel-loaded and charged with TNT.

The trail turned across the slope and leveled. It led them
to one of the rain-swollen rivers. They stopped in the forest
within sight of the river to rest. The channel was cut down
sharply below the forest floor. The river tumbled white and
roaring down the dark volcanic rock of its bed and the channel bloomed with spray. Trees grew to the edge of the bank
and then a space opened across the river. The space opened
to low cloud cover like the space above a forest road. The
cloud cover meant that they would climb into thickening
fog and might have wasted the day.

Anyway they would climb. Crown chose a rocky outcropping to sit on where he could look upriver through the trees.
Even one sign would be a start. He watched the river and
listened to it roar, the roar changing harmonics as the water
loaded cul-de-sacs in the riverbed that resisted the loading
as they filled and then overflowed, scoured, and accepted
the loading again. He remembered fishing the untouched,
spring-fed streams of the Aberdares with his father, pulling
out the fine small mountain fish as fast as he could cast his
line, smelling the forest and the smoking burley of his father's corncob pipe and the sweet flesh of the fish when he
cleaned them. Even on Olmoti the native fish had probably
been extirpated by the brown trout the British had stocked

everywhere in East Africa. The British had tried to make
over the uplands of East Africa into home. They stocked it
and planted it and tried to shoot it out. It was what any people did. The Africans did it too, and if they changed it more
slowly that was only because their technology was cruder.
There were no noble savages in Africa, not even the Masai.
You used up and threw your trash over your shoulder and
moved on, marauding someplace new. People like Robert
and the Leakeys dug up trash heaps all the way back to the
Pleistocene. The Bantu moved in with iron and agriculture
and drove the aboriginal Wandorobo into the forests, the
Masai came down with cattle and implacable ferocity and
confined the Bantu, the British snaked a railroad across from
Mombasa to Victoria with Indian labor and dominated them
all, and now the Rukumas with their feral terrorism crept out
from stagnant backwaters everywhere in the world. They
had flown the wounded to hospital, the gut-shot man, the
lung-shot woman, the model with half her face blown away.
Then they sent a larger aircraft and flew the bodies out,
what was left of them. The two charred Japanese shriveled
into one, all their camera lenses exploded. I wonder why I
care, Crown thought. I ought to take Cassie and pack up
and get out. And go where? *Kikulacho ki nguoni mwako,*
the old men said, drunk on scummy *pombe:* That which
bites you is in your clothes.

Mugwa sat on the wet ground with his knees drawn up,
watching the Chaggas. They had gone off to urinate and
when they came back, whispering and chuckling, they made
seats of their ragged ponchos and sat together leaning
against a tree, their pangas flapped out to the side and their
Kalashnikovs laid across their laps. One of them searched
under his poncho and retrieved a pack of cigarettes and
they both lit up. When the one with the cigarettes flipped
away the match Mugwa growled *"Usivute sigara!"* and the
Chaggas morosely pinched out the ends and worked the cig-

arettes back into the pack. Mugwa stopped watching them
and before long they were whispering again and nudging
each other. They got up together and strolled to the river-
bank. At the bank the one with the cigarettes hocked and
spat out over the river and the other one grinned and
hocked and tried to spit farther. "You privates!" Mugwa
barked in his guttural Swahili. "Get back off that bank!
Damn foolishness!" They retreated then to their tree and
stood beside it whispering, their hands in their pockets and
their heads down, scuffing their boots in the mulch.

Mugwa got up and blew his nose between his stubby
fingers. He studied the drainage and then flicked it away
and came over to Crown. "Damn privates," he said. "Stupid
I think. Damn bandits see them, tear out their butts." When
he wasn't using his arms they hung at his sides like sausages.
His eyes were set deep in his face and they were yellow
with rheum.

"You have felt that they are up there?" Crown asked. He
spoke in Swahili: Mugwa had no English.

"Damn bandits up there all right." Mugwa spat. "Make a
mess up there. We get wind of them today."

"Good. We have run out this trail. It will go faster now if
we follow the river. The way will be steeper. Can we cross
the feeder streams?"

"Wade them easy. Maybe some places work upstream.
Ugly crap mountain." Mugwa turned to the Chaggas and
jerked his thumb. "*Twende*," he ordered, barking it out.
"Let's go."

They climbed hard through the forest without benefit of a
trail, paralleling the river but keeping well back from the
bank, Crown leading silently, the pangas sheathed. The fog
thickened, hanging in layers that whitened upward into the
trees. It swirled around them as they moved. The air grew
colder. Their hands stiffened and they felt the wet cold on
their faces but they sweated under their ponchos from the

work. They waded the feeders as they came to them and
Crown saw the brown trout holding station undulating in
the pools, their gills pulsing, headed upstream. The forest
was opening. There was bush now in the understory and
they started small animals that squeaked in fright and rus-
tled off down escape runs laid out under the mulch. They
still fought the vines, going on hands and knees now that
they couldn't use the pangas, but gradually the hardwoods
were giving way to clear stands of cedar that let down more
light.

When they had climbed for an hour from the stop at the
river Crown stood aside and let the Chaggas pass and
tapped Mugwa and the sergeant pushed ahead and took the
lead. He quickened the pace. The river was heading out and
he turned away from its dividing channels to guide through
the natural openings in the forest. They began to encounter
fog-filled glades and stunted in the glades the first green
stalks of bamboo.

Rounding a copse filling in where an old cedar had fallen
Crown found the Chaggas stopped in place. He looked for
Mugwa but the sergeant had disappeared into the fog. The
Chagga with the cigarettes signed that the sergeant had
halted them and gone on alone. But the Chaggas looked
worried. Right, Crown thought, the man knew what he was
doing. He unshouldered his Kalashnikov and released the
safety and signaled the Chaggas to do the same. The automatic rifles restored their confidence and he positioned them
well apart under stout cedars where they could sector the
upslope with fire. He returned to where they had stood, putting the dark copse behind him, and draped the cold rifle on
his arm. Now they would wait. He hoped not for long. Visibility was down to thirty feet and it was bloody cold. They
had the fog to their knees now. It wasn't going to get any
better. They couldn't go much farther with the ground obscured. And what was the gentle sergeant up to?

Half an hour later Mugwa stepped soundlessly into view. He signed to the Chaggas to stay where they were and beckoned Crown to follow. Crown caught up and Mugwa led off confidently through the fog. They climbed through thinning cedars past a small spring, one of the sources of the river, and curved around to the left across the slope. For a while they seemed to be going slightly downhill. They were working into an old, decaying cedar stand. It was couched in the lee of the ridge that divided off the river's watershed and the trees were larger and some of them were fire-scarred.

Crown heard buzzing and realized that Mugwa must have heard it long before. He was guiding on it. Deep into the stand the sergeant stopped under a big cedar and pointed up the trunk. At twice Crown's height the black African bees swarmed at a ragged hole. The hive was open and the comb torn away and honey had bled down the bark. The green, velvety lichen had been stripped from the bark in a line where a man's boot had sought purchase sliding down.

Bull's-eye, Crown thought.

Mugwa signed patience and led him farther into the stand. In ten minutes he showed Crown two more honey trees. Neither hive had yet been raided. Mugwa signaled for Crown to bend down and whispered into his ear, whispered so softly that Crown strained to hear the words.

"They come for honey." Mugwa tapped Crown on the chest and gestured up the ridge. "Bamboo no good. Too much damn fog. We go back, come up again soon. Stake out trees. Catch us damn bandit. Bandit tell us where camp. *Haya?* Okay?"

It was a good plan, the best that they could do. If it worked it would make the whole thing simple. They could surprise the lot. Crown nodded, agreeing. Mugwa nodded gravely in return and led them back to the waiting

Chaggas. When they reached the lower trail, late in the afternoon, he gave up caution and crashed off to camp. Crown let him go. He'd done splendidly that day. If his witches meant to take him, tonight would be the night.

Cassie was waiting for Crown when he came into the tent a little after dark. She had set out a washbasin, soap, a washcloth and a towel on the camp box he had upended to make a table, and while he stripped off his wet clothes she carried hot water from the mess, groups of bantering soldiers passing her in the dark and the rain, and filled the basin. She sat on her cot watching him sponge-bathe. He soaped himself mechanically, unaware of her. He had hung the brutal stamped-metal machine gun on the tent upright and dropped the grenades on his cot. They had rolled together into a nest. Steam rose from the basin in the lantern light. She was wearing one of his bush jackets against the chill and she tucked her hands into the sleeves.

He told her about the honey tree, the raided hive, the lichen stripped from the trunk.

"Then you know where they are," she said.

He didn't hear her. He was thinking: Mugwa and the Chaggas. Maybe two more good men. The fewer the better. They ought to be the best Nguvu had. Too bad Abdi wasn't there.

"Does that tell you where they are?" she asked again.

"We're closer." He was dressing now, buttoning his shirt. "It's the first real clue we've had." Mugwa could handle it. Mugwa was the best tracker he'd ever seen. He looked up. "How are you?"

"I'm okay. Are you all right?"

"Sure. Just worn."

"Do you have what you need?"

"What's become of my hairbrushes?"

"I put them away." She opened the other camp box at the

head of his cot. His supplies: scotch and gin, tins of beef and sardines, chocolate biscuits, spare boots, rope, flashlights; his revolver in its holster wrapped in its belt. The first-aid kit.

"Get my sweater too, will you?"

She found the hairbrushes and the sweater, a thick cable-knit of oiled wool, and he pulled the sweater over his head and brushed his hair.

"So," he said, looking around. "Want to pack those grenades?" It was all mind and senses. You screwed them down tight, the tighter the better. Until you weren't even there. Until you were out ahead and coming up behind and everywhere on the sides where they could ambush you. That's why Mugwa chewed out the Chaggas. If you did it right you weren't even conscious and it was the hardest work there was. He'd done it long enough. He'd lived that way. And Cassie standing there beside the cot, her scrubbed face and her fine head, the hollow shadowed at her throat, and now there was room for her and he went to her and held her. "Sorry," he said into her hair. "I wasn't back yet."

"I know. How could you be?" She kissed him, her mouth opening, until his body relaxed against her, and smiled against his mouth and stood away. "Now I'll see about your grenades."

With his hands in his pockets he stretched his shoulders. "What did you do today?"

"I read. I would have done a washing, but I didn't think anything would dry." The cold grenades. They seemed as lethal as their weight. She carried them carefully to the camp box and closed the squeaking lid. His name was stenciled on the lid and his Arusha mailing address.

"Better lock it," he said. "What did you read?"

"*The Flame Trees of Thika.* Elspeth Huxley." She turned back to him. "I wish I'd known you then."

He smiled. "That was before the first war. I'm old, but I'm not that old. I didn't come along until 1925."

"Whenever it was, I wish I'd known you."

"It wasn't a bad time, allowing for the convenient fiction that it wasn't a bad time."

"You mean the blacks."

"The Africans. It's there in Huxley. Not so obviously in *Flame Trees*. That's a fairly recent book. The white man's burden isn't so fashionable anymore. But it shows up in some of her early books. You know, the land was empty and the natives were murdering each other. Blokes weren't civilized."

"Were they civilized?"

"What's civilized? Your father's little bombs?"

She looked at him. "No."

"Shall we go find the general? I ought to make a report."

It came and it went. Because they had a handle on it now. Because now they would do to Rukuma what Rukuma had done to David and the Friedrichs and the Wells. More or less. A little more drawn out. You could justify it because there was a government behind it, laws behind it, but that was all window dressing really. Really it was kill or be killed and you had to do it. You didn't have to like it, but you had to do it.

Going out, she said: "Are you angry?"

"Not at you. I'm sorry if I seemed so. I'd just managed to forget for a few years how bloodthirsty it all is."

Colonel Mongali, Nguvu's aide, had been in touch with the general by radio. He was delayed, but he would be up within the hour. They went on to the officers' mess for dinner. The officers had heard about the honey tree and they cheered Crown when he came into the mess and all through dinner they were jolly.

Waiting for Nguvu in the headquarters tent after dinner, the duty sergeant working in the glow of the lantern at the desk beside the entrance, Cassie said: "I feel so useless. You go out into that jungle and I'm afraid for you and there's nothing I can do. I can't even speak Swahili." Crown started to answer and she stopped him, shaking her head. "I'm not complaining. I just wish there was something I could do."

"Nguvu wants to move you out of here. He thinks you'd be safer in Dar." Crown sat up. "We could move you into Arusha."

"No," she said quickly.

"I didn't think much of the idea either. There is something you could do."

"What?"

"It depends on how things go. Until I know for certain that Rukuma's immobilized I want you here. For safety. I told Nguvu if he tried to move you out I'd go with you. He figures he needs me, so he's letting you stay."

"Why doesn't he want me here?"

"Nothing personal. His government's leaning on him. They're afraid this business will scare off the tourists. Tanzania pulls in about a third of its foreign exchange from tourism."

"But what is it I can do?"

"I won't give up on Rukuma, whatever the army does. He's got to be stopped. But I'm not going to close down the camp and I'm not going to live in a garrison. We're not. We've got a good life and an honest life and we've every right to be here." He shifted in his chair to face her. "Once we know what's what I want you to keep the camp going while I'm up here. Work with Abdi. Get it back together. When Rukuma's out of the way we'll open it up again."

"Wonderful," she said. "I'll do a damned good job, too. When can I start?"

"Nguvu's willing to loan us some guards. I'd say soon."

Cassie hesitated. "Will I see you?"

"I'll be back and forth. Once we've really pinpointed the

camp, Nguvu will handle the rest. That's all I signed on for anyway. I'd just as soon avoid the fire fight if I can."

The general burst in then, hailing Crown, throwing off his trench coat, charging over to greet them. "I heard the good news, my friend," he said to Crown, smiling and going around behind the map table. "You have searched for only one week and you have found them. Bravo." He began unbuckling his pistol belt.

"Pretty close, General. Your Sergeant Mugwa did the work. He's a hell of a tracker."

Nguvu dropped the pistol belt onto the table and remained standing, leaning across to them. "Good. I will see that he is commended. But let me not waste words. We have been equally successful below. North beyond Olduvai there is a badland of lava waste at the base of Olmoti that my men had searched before. We were returning at the end of the day from searching farther north. I think perhaps that the light was wrong before, because we made out faint traces of a track that we had not previously seen. We followed it up into the badlands. The area is cut by many dry *korongos* very dense with thorn. You see what we found, my friends. In one of the *korongos* farthest in. Laid over with mattings of cut thorn, completely camouflaged. We passed by twice before we saw." Nguvu straightened and clapped his hands. "We found Rukuma's transport."

Crown slapped the table. "Bloody marvelous!"

"Yes. Yes. Two lorries and a Land Rover. We discovered a petrol dump nearby. There was a bloodstained canvas in the back of one of the lorries, almost certainly the canvas that was used to wrap the scientist Van Meeren's body when it was brought down the mountain." Nguvu took a turn behind the table. "And so our work is doubly fruitful, above and below. Without transport Rukuma is confined to the mountain, and with the discovery of the honey tree you have narrowed the targeting of the camp." He stopped pac-

ing and sat down in his chair. "But tell me in detail how it
went."

Crown told him and guided him as he marked the map.

"And you are quite certain it was one of Rukuma's men
who raided the tree?"

"There have to be a few Dorobo wandering around in
there, General," Crown said, "but I doubt if they get up that
high. Anyway, a boot scraped that tree. Nothing a Dorobo
would be wearing."

"We have had much luck today," the general said, sober-
ing. "Rukuma is within our grasp."

"What do you think of Mugwa's plan?" Crown asked.

"The lorries argue against any great numbers of men
under Rukuma's command, perhaps no more than twenty.
His willingness to sacrifice four men in the raid on your
camp, however, argues otherwise, or else he is rashly fa-
natic. I believe our only remaining weakness is our lack of
information about his numbers. Yes," Nguvu said, nodding
and sitting forward, tapping the table, "it would be wise to
attempt to capture this honey collector." He turned to Cassie and smiled. "Our work today also clears up the matter of
Miss Wendover, does it not? You would not now be averse
to returning below where there is sun, Miss Wendover?"

"Seth and I have already discussed it, General Nguvu."

"Right," Crown said. "Without transport, Rukuma's not
going to pull off any more raids. I'd still like a detachment of
guards. He could always break out on foot."

Nguvu nodded. "Of course. How many?"

"Five should do it. My manager can stand in for a sixth if
you'll issue us an extra automatic. That would make three
shifts of guards around the clock."

"Consider it done. Is there any reason why Sergeant
Mugwa cannot execute the capture of the honey collector?"

"I'd trust that man with my life, General."

"Then perhaps you would relieve me of one additional

concern by escorting Miss Wendover down to your camp tonight."

"Tonight?" Crown said, surprised.

"Tonight. She would then be out of danger. Tomorrow
you could make arrangements for the safety of Dr. Fuhrey
and return to us at your convenience. Soon enough, I hope,
to talk to one of Rukuma's so-called guerrillas and to participate in the planning of a decisive campaign."

"Tonight it is then. Cassie? Okay with you?"

"It's fine with me," Cassie said, standing. "I'll need a few
minutes to pack."

"There is no hurry," Nguvu said warmly. "Sergeant?" he
called. "Find Colonel Mongali and tell him I wish to see
him immediately." He turned back to Crown. "While Miss
Wendover is packing we may discuss the composition of
Sergeant Mugwa's patrol. In the meantime my aide will arrange for the guards and the extra rifle. You must convey
them yourself in your car. As you know, even with the addi-
tion of Rukuma's vehicles we are painfully lacking in
transport."

Cassie lay awake. Seth slept exhausted beside her. She was
glad for the warmth of the Serengeti after a week in the
highlands, relieved that for a day or two at least he could
rest. Abdi had met them warily, stepping out of the darkness
at the entrance to the camp ready with a shotgun, his rifle
on his shoulder, and when he identified them he had
beamed. They made up camp beds in the dining room and
installed the guards. Two kept watch now on the ap-
proaches to the camp. Abdi had repaired the porch screens
and replaced the door but there was no glass in the window
between the bar and the porch and from the porch, looking
west, she had seen the black mounded silhouettes of the
burned platforms. There was work to do. This camp would
be her home.

She had not known she could do what she did that night.
Kneel at a window and shoot to kill to protect what was
hers. She had watched herself at the window without recog-
nition. An edge of hysteria had trickled sweat down her
back and she had followed that cold track as carefully as she
had sighted the rifle and remembered it with equal clarity
now. Inwardly she had jumped at each explosion; Abdi
firing beside her, the boom of the shotguns, the stuttered
pocking of the automatics; her decoupled muscles hadn't
moved. Worse were the wounded, but she knew the motions
of emergency. Worst were the dead. Open blind eyes were
terrible in their vulnerability and the body dead was de-
spoiled. Death was not in wounds. Death was in eyes and
in the thrown contortion of a body fallen to the ground. She
learned even from that. It was no betrayal to learn. She
learned that the difference between life and death was absolute. She learned with finality that her father was dead,
fallen in a hall, and her apprenticeship was ended.

There was an old way to live. Africa in its brutal simplicity had preserved it. Fires of wood, shelters of thatch, plain
clothing, work. Food grown and gathered, animals shot and
the meat butchered out. Knowledge of the sky, knowledge
of the seasons, sweat, the tangle of the bed. Sometimes the
landscape beyond was a storeroom, sometimes a mystery.
The mind within, the heart within, the unrecognized driving
imperatives, ran outward and connected. Nothing was su-
pernatural and the body took and gave and the mind
watched in wonder.

No home before had been her own. The camp was her
first home, the lodge, the compound, the platforms they
would rebuild, the open grassy park between the buildings
and the lake. The deaths anchored it and rooted them there
despite the danger. They lived the old way already,
modified to their station and their time. He had always lived
that way, or he had learned after Sidanu. They started that

way together and despite the violence and the death they went on. Every day filled up and emptied into memory and the next day enlarged. It was what she wanted. When she rebuilt the platforms she would know to the end of her life the contours of the wood. When they went out together onto the plain she would know to the end of her life the colors of the light.

If it had been possible she would have stayed with him in the highlands until he was done. If she had the craft she would have gone out with him, searched with him, guarded him as he risked himself to guard her. If even by leaving this place, if even by leaving him, she could protect him, then she would leave and live with the knowledge that he was safe. She was not given those choices. She would wait with Abdi and prepare the camp. There was nothing to waiting. It was another kind of work.

But oh Seth, she thought, my darling Seth, please be careful. Be very very careful. Do what you have to do and do it well but do it with great care. Take care where you go and carefully watch. Because I've only just found you. I've only just found you and I love you very much and I couldn't bear it if anything happened to you now.

Nine

SHE OPENED HER eyes to his smile in the bright morning room. He was braced up on his elbow with his head on his hand and the sheet around his waist so that his shoulders and chest were bare.

"Hello," he said. "I wondered when you'd wake. Your eyes were moving."

"I must have been dreaming. I don't remember." She shifted to face him on her side, making a rest of her hands under her cheek. "I didn't get to sleep right away."

"You're ravishing. I wish I could draw you."

"You were watching me sleep."

"I couldn't decide if your hair is gold or brown. I think we'll have to call it golden-brown. You're all one color, you know. Your skin's golden too. It's not white or pink or ruddy or olive. It's golden. And no freckles. As light as you are, you'd think you'd have freckles." His hair was tousled with sleep.

"I have freckles."

"News to me. Here, let's do this properly. Turn the way you were."

She turned onto her back. "I'll fall asleep again."

"I'm afraid there's no talking. Distracts from the work." He traced lightly with his finger. "Quite a high forehead. No widow's peak. We can be grateful for that. It's wide, too, but nicely rounded. Smooth. Fine eyebrows. Like down. A little darker than the hair. Sets off the face." He touched between them. "Do you pluck here?"

"They grow that way."

"Ah. They grow that way. Very good. Very sensible of them. You see how well it's all arranged. They grow that way. Now the nose. How do I describe the nose?"

"What about my eyes?"

"All in good time. I'm doing a profile at the moment. It's certainly not a pug nose. It's not a beak or a hawk nose. It's somewhere in between. It's of a good size, and it's not too narrow or too wide, and it's straight, and the nostrils flare. Don't they though. And there's this slight turning up at the end. Really a very excellent nose."

"That's the worst description of a nose I've ever heard."

"You've moved now. Back on station, please. This isn't Leonardo here. That's it. Good. Had a glimpse of the eyes. Gold flecks in the eyes. Clear whites and flecks of gold in the brown. Long lashes and then again the tips of them are golden."

He stopped.

"Your mouth is extraordinary," he said then. His voice had changed. "Do you know how full your lips are? What is it? Roses? Tulips? Fuller than that. Something tropical. Ripe." She turned to see and he was staring, his eyes dilated and dark and widened and the thickness in his voice. "Pomegranate," he said. "Cassie. Cassie." And his body came warm against her and his face close above her in the morning light and he was stroking her hair, looking at her

hair and looking again, looking into her eyes, looking at her
mouth and saying her name once more and then in the good
rested freshness of morning he kissed her.

Kissing her he still traced her, traced her with his hand,
traced her neck and smoothly her shoulder and her breasts,
describing them with the tips of his fingers, waking her,
tracing down her body and stopping to touch and stopping
again to touch and then to caress, lingering, finding, opening,
giving gently and with great delicacy and tracing her then
also with his mouth, uncovering her, grazing her, kissing her
each and each and each where he had touched as if she
were golden in the light, leaving her then cool and welcom-
ing and coming back to her, his weight that she received,
helping him, and now the light and the silence in the room,
the slow tender filling and the light, the giving in care and
the golden light and for her then the heating from gold to
blue and then to white, white, white near but not burning
and then cooling, the danger, cooling through blue to gold,
cooling to red, the shattering night, the stuttered pocking
laying waste, but here and now and certain, here and now
the morning and all the gold, and for him the eyes moving
asleep and the life, the gift, the golden-brown hair and the
eyes, the mouth that was fruit and the mind, the clarity, the
courage that flowed instinctively as the body flowed and the
body flowing, enclosing, holding and surrounding intimately
and always in welcome, always in welcome against cold,
against dark, against the shadow that he saw once and now
no longer could not see except now in this light and for both
of them then the light heating through gold, going white,
the light everywhere radiating and all edges going and featureless and bodied deeply but unbodied and the light, the
light, the light and the burning blinding light. The light.
The light. Cooling the light. Together the light. The morning light and each other then and the dew on their bodies
and again they could see.

Cassie lay aside in the tumbled bed, her heart slowing. She listened to the sounds of the camp. Abdi's children called in the courtyard. The cook was singing in the kitchen. The hammering meant that Abdi was starting on the platforms. The sun was shining. That was the light. That wasn't all the light. Not nearly all. And to have it and to have had it.

Mischievously he touched her. "So much for the drawing," he said. "Didn't get very far, did I." He was up on his elbow again and smiling.

"I like your drawing. You can draw all you like. Except noses."

"Bloody noses."

"Not puns. You're not going to do puns."

"Bloody puns. What puns?"

"Bloody noses." She sat up. "I'd better get us some coffee. We sound like idiots."

"Will you look at that. It's like two great spinnakers filling out."

She crossed her arms, lifting. "Do they sag? I'm sorry if they sag."

"Who said sag? It's the fine weight o' them, lass." He winked. "Sure it's coffee we'll be needin' now." He watched her swing her feet over the edge of the bed. "You're like a piece of unfinished sculpture, you know? These fine legs tapering down and then these huge coarse feet."

"What's wrong with my feet?" she said happily from beside the bed. "I like my feet. They're masculine."

He grinned. "Damned if they are. Never saw more womanly feet. All the ladies around here have feet like that." Shaking her head she faced away from him to put on her robe. "Ah," he said, "now I see the freckles. Can't think how I missed them before."

She faced him again, belting her robe to go. "I'll tell you

how you missed them. You've been reading that part of my anatomy by Braille."

"Bring that coffee around," he called after her through the door, laughing, "and we'll have a hand at it."

She crossed to the kitchen through the courtyard. When she returned with the tray he was sitting up in bed. He had shaved and brushed his hair. The bed was straightened and he had propped their pillows against the dark brass uprights of the headframe and opened a window. A warm breeze drifted the curtains. He was watching the curtains and as she came in he turned to her. She set the tray in the middle of the bed. The cook had made the coffee fresh and there was fresh bread and butter churned fresh that morning that still glistened with milk.

"Provender," he said, and looking up: "You will abandon that robe, won't you?"

She left the robe, the tray between them. "It's beautiful out. I didn't see a cloud in the sky."

"There'll be more, but we've had the worst of it. I wonder if Mugwa got off."

His voice had gone hard. She shouldn't have mentioned the sky, she thought, or brought coffee or even left the bed. She should have shuttered the windows and locked the doors. Outside was all the rest of it and even a word brought it back. It involved his honor and his sense of duty and perhaps also his pride and it could easily become obsessional. Planning was part of it. He had to plan and he'd been too exhausted last night. He did simulations, living and reliving it. He programmed as much of it as he could so that he wouldn't be surprised. It was one of the ways he tried to reduce the risk and if she went through it with him they might have time.

"What will they do?" she asked. "When they find out?"

He set down his cup. "Not much they can do. If Rukuma's smart he'll break out. It means someone's after

him. He's got to know about the patrols. He's got to know
about Nguvu's camp. He probably has a rough idea of the
numbers. He'll see they're regular army and discount ac-
cordingly, but unless he's stronger than we think he's not
going to want a head-on fight. But Christ, the man's completely unpredictable. Nguvu thinks he's got him down. The
hell he does. Why didn't he leave a message when he attacked the camp? What's his game? How many men has he
got? Who's he working for? Who's supplying him? We don't
know any of it. I hope to hell Mugwa comes up with a live
one. Right now we don't have a clue."

"I know you don't know about Rukuma," she said. "What
about the ones who raided the camp? I thought they took
their fingerprints." The guerrillas had been laid out at the
airstrip the morning after the raid and she had gone among
them to see. She saw that they were African and well-fed
and not Masai. She saw that bodies bloated quickly in the
sun.

"Nguvu ran a check. That doesn't mean a hell of a lot in
Tanzania. Army recruits get fingerprinted, police suspects,
but there's no central file. Didn't turn up a damned thing."

The ugly anonymity made it senseless and horrible and in
a reflex of self-protection she pulled up the sheet. "What
kind of people *are* they?"

The question was rhetorical but he answered it. "They
could be detribalized. Spivs from out in the district or from
Dar or Nairobi or who knows where. They could be religious types who've twisted it around. They could be politicos. My guess is they're all that. It doesn't take much out
here. This isn't the States. There's absolute poverty and the
whole world looks rich. Someone with two pairs of shoes
looks rich. A private in the army looks rich. Nyerere goes
around the country trying to get people moving. He
preaches a lot. You know what he tells them? He says the
Americans and the Russians are going to the moon while Af-

ricans are still eating wild roots. He means to spur them on,
but the contrast's there for anyone to see and not all of them
think that hard work's the answer. They've seen their parents work hard all their lives and it hasn't gotten them anywhere."

He had buttered bread but left it uneaten. He worked the
edge of the lacquered tray with his thumb. "But around
every corner there's been a revolution. Half the countries in
Africa came out of revolution. Algeria, the Congo, Mozambique, Kenya—you name it. Zimbabwe now. South Africa
any day. And the men who led the revolutions ended up in
power. They see that, they hear that. So whatever Rukuma's
personal game is, he can take his pick of followers. The spivs
want to get rich, the politicos want to try on their favorite
ideology, the religious types need a prophet."

He stopped and shook his head. "It's not murder, you
know. Swooping down on a sleeping camp and massacring
tourists out of burning tents isn't murder. It's theater. It's a
way to make the world pay attention. Ask a terrorist about it
and he'll tell you about Israeli raids into Lebanon or French
torture in Algeria or people hung upside down over fires in
Mozambique. The Mau Mau had their atrocity stories too.
Hell, even Idi Amin. Things have always been bloody in
Uganda between the tribes. Some of the early missionaries
talked about walking down the street and seeing people just
mutilated, missing hands, missing noses, people with their
cheeks cut off. If you're counting heads, Uganda's not as
bloody as Vietnam was. How do you average it out?" He
reddened with anger. "But Rukuma can't do it to me, Cassie. By god he can't."

"When do you go?" she asked then, quietly.

"I'll radio Nguvu this morning. I ought to get back up
there tonight. If Mugwa's come in with a prisoner the whole
thing can move that much faster. If he hasn't then I ought
to go out and help him. I'm worried about Robert. He's

probably safe enough during the day, but I'd like to see him check in here at night. It's not that long a drive back and forth."

"I can do that," she said. "Abdi and I could drive over."

"Good. Don't let Robert talk you out of it. Even with Rukuma's transport down he shouldn't be alone. He's not properly armed and now that he's digging out that damned skull I doubt very much if he's watching. One or two of those bastards coming in on foot with automatic rifles could do the job. I wouldn't leave you here except for the guards. Keep on them, will you? If they start to slacken get Abdi after them or call me on the radio and I'll be down here like a shot. Okay?"

"Okay." She left the bed with the tray and came back onto the bed to tell him. "I know you have to go," she said, kneeling before him. "I know it's right." Tears filled her eyes and she shook her head angrily to clear them. "But I *hate* it, Seth. You don't know how much I hate it." He raised his hand and she caught it and pulled it down. "*No*. Listen to me. You can't yet. I won't let you. I want you first. That's all I've got to give you and damn it, you have to take it. Take it. Make love to me again. So we'll have it." She didn't care now that her voice broke. "So you won't forget what we have. So you'll *know*. I want you to *know*."

Before there had been light but now there was pain: in clutching, lewd, in thrashing: the body took the burden and beat: to brand: and the mountains were shut out and the camp, the curtains drifting at the window, loose transparent nets, the room, the bed tangling: to have now without restraint, tawny, black-maned, driven, urgent: to deny, engulfing: turgid: flesh ordained and slipping, slipping, flesh confessing flesh and interceding: our flesh which art in flesh hallowed: pray for our flesh now and at the hour of flesh, now at the only hour, now, now: and short and sharp flesh came home: from wandering flesh came home: flesh crying came home, came home: flesh came home.

Mugwa had his bandit. He was just such a man as Mugwa had expected him to be, full of his own importance and careless. He had not even carried a damn rifle, only a knife. That damn Chagga had a big slash on his forearm to show for the knife. Behind on the trail he carried that arm in a sling he'd tied up from his shirt. The arm would have to be sewn. It was a stupid business.

They went out before the sun. At least the damn rain had stopped. They laid up in ambush at the two honey trees, the two assigned privates at the one deeper in the stand and he and the Chaggas at the one nearer the raided tree, the one the bandits were more likely to visit next. The ants had bitten them like hell. A small red duiker had come down through the trees and sniffed them and whistled and dived into the bush. They just waited. It was like any other day. Mugwa had waited many days hunting in the forests at home. At home in the forest he would have taken the duiker with his bow. You caught the ants and pinched them between fingernails like lice.

Then the one bandit had come without caution, noisily, pushing through the forest to the honey tree where Mugwa and the Chaggas hid as if he owned the damn mountain. He had lit a twist of grass to smoke the bees. He was afraid of their stings, a weakling. When he started to climb the tree Mugwa had pointed silently with his lips and the Chaggas had rushed him. Mugwa came up behind with his Kalashnikov. That one damn Chagga had grabbed the bandit and pulled him off the tree and the man had dropped the grass twist and found his knife and cut that Chagga and then Mugwa had clubbed him with the butt of his Kalashnikov. The Chagga should have clubbed the bandit instead of grabbing him. But that was all there was to it. They caught a damn bandit as the general had ordered and collected the other two privates and sent them ahead and now they were returning to the camp.

To make sure that he would not run away Mugwa had tied the bandit with a rope. The rope was tied around Mugwa's waist and ran back to the bandit's waist. Also the hands were handcuffed behind. The Chaggas followed some ways back of the bandit to bring up the rear. The bandit had good fatigues and boots. The fatigues were much bloodied from the slashing of the Chagga and from the wound of the rifle butt. The blood from the head wound had matted the bandit's greasy braided hair. He was gagged to stop him from shouting. Mugwa kept up a fast pace down the trail to bring the man in before his loss was discovered at nightfall and the man breathed raggedly because of the gag. Let him gasp for air and let his damn mouth dry until it cracked. Let him understand that Sergeant Mugwa was in charge of his damn life now.

Mugwa had wondered at these bandits. They lived on top of the mountain and they remained there even at night. It might be that they danced there at night. It might be that they whitened themselves with ash and walked the mountain trails upside down on their hands. It might be that they rode through the sky at night slung under the bellies of hyenas and possessed *uhai*, the powers and the potions of witches, and coupled with their mothers and fathers and ate the flesh of the dead. That was what witches did. Mugwa had suspected at first that all the bandits were witches. Now he saw that this bandit at least was no witch, or why had he not turned himself invisible to go honey collecting? If he were a witch his powers would inform him of the ambush, would they not? Unless he were only a weak witch or had only purchased his *uhai* and could not make *uhai* himself from the seminal fluid of cats or the skulls and teeth of the dead. The ones who had raided Bwana Crown's camp on the plain below were almost certainly witches who wanted the strong material of European skulls and teeth for their potions. Without doubt the leader, Rukuma, was a powerful witch. He had to be or why would he have such authority over men that a general of the army would come out personally to attempt his capture? There was a story of a head and witches were known to be able to invert the heads of their enemies on their shoulders.

Mugwa jerked the rope and the guerrilla stumbled. The damn bandit was not so full of his own importance now. He was only a little taller than Mugwa. He was thinner and not so strong and his skin was an ugly dark shade of brown. Mugwa wished he knew the man's tribe. No, he could hardly be a witch. The witch was Rukuma and perhaps there were others among the bandits as well. When it was night they would come out looking for this man. The thought cautioned Mugwa and irritably he jerked the rope again.

"Hurry it up!" he called to the guerrilla. "Damn bandit! Move along!" The gag pulled back the bandit's lips and exposed his teeth. His eyes were reddened and one ear was crusted with blood. Mugwa had searched him and found only pocket items, matches and a charm, and a pouch of snuff. Since it might not have been snuff but a *uhai* powder Mugwa let the Chaggas take it. If it poisoned them then he would know. It gave him no worry. He had potions of his own. He was not himself a witch, never having committed incest or devoured human flesh, but at home on leave he regularly made certain purchases from an uncle who was.

Closer to camp, on the lower trail, Mugwa saw that they would arrive well before dark. There was time then. He knew that the general and Bwana Crown would want to interrogate the bandit. It was not his place to do that work but he could make it go faster for them. He had seen that he could help Bwana Crown before by following the bees to the honey tree. Bwana Crown had praised him and he could help him again now. Bwana Crown was a man of great wealth and authority who knew the ways of the forest almost as well as a Kaguru. Almost as well as he, Mugwa, knew them.

"You privates!" Mugwa called. "Come here!"

The Chaggas trotted into view. When they reached the guerrilla they pushed him ahead of them until they came up to Mugwa. He gestured and they untied the gag and the guerrilla worked his mouth and licked his dry lips. Mugwa untied himself and tossed the end of the rope to the Chaggas. Then he stepped up to the guerrilla and hit him hard in the mouth.

The guerrilla grunted and fell backward and the surprised Chaggas caught him, the one with the slashed arm using only his good hand, and stood him on his feet and looked wide-eyed at Mugwa. He ignored them and watched the guerrilla, neither smiling or frowning. It was just work, softening the damn bandit for interrogation. The bandit's mouth was bleeding and he was spitting ropy blood and glaring.

Mugwa swung at the guerrilla again. The guerrilla saw the blow coming and jerked his head aside and the blow landed on his ear. He shook his head and started to struggle.

"Hold him," Mugwa said. The Chaggas gripped the guerrilla's arms and moved in behind him.

"Damn, man," the guerrilla said, "why do you hit me?"

Mugwa slapped him sharp across the face and his eyes watered. "Shut up," Mugwa said. While the guerrilla's vision was blurred Mugwa pulled back and punched hard from the shoulder into the man's belly just below the ribs and the guerrilla whooshed and bent forward gasping for breath and the Chaggas pulled him back upright gasping and Mugwa stepped in and ripped the heel of his boot down the man's shin and he shrieked and tried to twist away.

Then Mugwa stood back and waited for him to catch his breath.

"Damn mother-defiler," Mugwa said harshly, "you listen up." The guerrilla looked at him with fear. "We get you to camp, you talk. General Nguvu ask you to talk, you talk, see? Bwana Crown ask you to talk, you talk. Damn cook's boy, damn monkey ask you to talk, you talk. You hear that?"

The guerrilla flinched, watching Mugwa's fist. "I swore an oath," he said nervously.

Mugwa stepped forward again and held the guerrilla by the shoulders and thrust close his face. "Forget that damn oath," he said, gripping the shoulders hard. "You talk or they give you to me, bandit. You want them give you to me?" And still holding the guerrilla's shoulders Mugwa jammed his knee up into the man's groin feeling the testicles flatten and the man screamed, his head snapping back, and passed out.

"You privates," Mugwa said, letting go. "You bring this damn bandit on. One of you tie on that rope. No damn talk of this." They nodded and Mugwa turned and rolled off down the trail. That was no witch. That was a weakling and stupid as a bush pig. That one would talk for sure.

Nguvu saw that the guerrilla had been beaten. His head might have been bloodied during capture, but his lip was split and one of his ears was puffy. He walked painfully and bowed his legs. Nguvu was not displeased. Beating was crude but acceptable. The problem in interrogation was to shift a man's loyalties. When a man saw that his life no longer depended on loyalty to his group but on the good will of his interrogators he would usually co-operate. Fear could build a foundation, although it was inadequate alone. Alone it produced sullenness or useless passivity. Nguvu wanted active co-operation. That required subtler methods.

Nguvu had the guerrilla's handcuffs removed and arranged for a medic to treat his injuries. Flanked by guards, the guerrilla was served a hot meal at the duty sergeant's desk in the headquarters tent while Nguvu worked quietly at his table. Officers and NCOs came and went, conducting the normal business of the camp, consulting Nguvu, and the guerrilla watched them covertly from his meal. After the guerrilla had eaten, Nguvu sent him off with his guards, shepherded by Colonel Mongali, to see the camp. Mongali showed him the two captured lorries and the Land Rover, pointing out the bloody canvas they had found in the back. He guided him to the vehicle shelters, the enlisted mess and the officers' mess and allowed him to view the armory tent stocked with mortars and boxes of grenades and racks of automatic rifles. In the meantime Nguvu debriefed Sergeant Mugwa and by then Crown had come in.

Mongali returned to the headquarters tent with the guerrilla. Crown studied him. He was hardly more than a boy. Mongali settled him in a chair where he could see Crown at his left and the general across the table authoritative in the lantern light. Mongali sat at the end of the table and picked up his notebook. Then Nguvu dismissed the guards. The guerrilla turned surprised to watch them leave and turned back nervously.

"*Jina lako nani?*" Nguvu asked in a pleasant voice. "What is your name?"

The guerrilla hesitated, looking them over. Then he shrugged. It could not hurt to give his name. "*Jina langu Tomasi,*" he said.

"*Karibu,* Tomasi. Welcome. I am General Nguvu of the Army of Tanzania." Nguvu gestured. "This is Bwana Crown. You have met my aide, Colonel Mongali."

"*Jambo,*" Crown said. "Hello."

Tomasi cleared his throat. "*Jambo.*"

"You are feeling better, I hope?" said Nguvu.

"That man," Tomasi said, touching his crotch. "He beat me."

Nguvu looked sympathetic. "Yes. But you are not with Sergeant Mugwa now, Tomasi. You are with us and you see we do not beat you. What is your given name, my friend?"

"Kunambi."

"Tomasi Kunambi. Very good. Now, Tomasi Kunambi, what is your country?"

Tomasi looked away.

"Come, come," Nguvu said genially, "it can do no harm to tell us your country. You are Tanzanian, are you not?"

Tomasi nodded, feeling his swollen lip. The medic had painted it with iodine and it had stung.

"And what is your tribe, Tomasi?"

"I was Hehe."

"Are you not Hehe now?"

The guerrilla said nothing.

"Can a man give up the tribe he was born to?"

Tomasi shrugged and slid lower in the chair, spreading his legs.

"Tomasi," Nguvu said, "how old are you?"

"I am four and twenty."

"You are young. It is excellent to be young. You have much life before you." Nguvu smiled. "Have you wives?"

"I have no wives," Tomasi said.

"That is unfortunate. Wives enrich a man." Nguvu leaned forward, folding his hands on the table. "Who is Rukuma, Tomasi?"

Tomasi's eyes darted to Crown and back to Nguvu and then he looked down. "I know of no Rukuma."

"How came you to be on Olmoti?"

"I was collecting honey."

"Yes. But the Hehe live far from Olmoti."

"I was collecting honey."

"Ah, I forgot. You are no longer Hehe. If you are no longer Hehe, Tomasi, what are you now?"

Tomasi swallowed.

"You told Sergeant Mugwa that you had sworn an oath. What oath, Tomasi?"

"I know nothing of any oath," Tomasi said.

"You swore an oath to Rukuma, did you not?"

Tomasi continued staring at the floor. The lantern sputtered and Mongali adjusted the wick.

Nguvu played with a pencil. "Look at me, Tomasi. Good. You saw the transport we captured? The lorries and the Land Rover? You saw the camp? The great force of soldiers? Yes? Then you understand that we will soon also capture Rukuma and all his men. They have murdered many people. We will capture them and they will be tried for their crimes and hung. The hangman's rope will choke them to death, Tomasi. But before they are hung they will tell us about you. If you do not tell us then they will tell us and you also will be tried and found guilty of murder and hung."

Tomasi shook his head stubbornly. "I took no part in any murders. I know nothing of murders."

"But you will nevertheless be blamed, Tomasi. Your comrades will blame you. They will say you beheaded the European who followed the *kifaru*, the rhino."

Tomasi jerked himself straight. "It was not I."

"They will blame you just the same. They will say you attacked the tourist camp under cover of night and brutally murdered ten Europeans in their tents. That was a hateful crime, Tomasi. It has caused us much trouble. It has shamed the nation of Tanzania throughout the world. The President of Tanzania is personally interested in that atrocity, Tomasi. He has personally asked me to make sure that those who raided the camp are brought to justice. Were you one of those, Tomasi?"

"I was not one of those," Tomasi said vehemently.

"But you are one of Rukuma's band. It will not matter that you did not kill with your own hands the European who followed the *kifaru* or the Europeans at the camp. You will be just as guilty as those who did."

"I did none of it." Gingerly, Tomasi adjusted his crotch.

Nguvu sighed. "Tomasi Kunambi. Tomasi-who-is-no-longer-Hehe. Listen to me. Do you know what will happen if we return you to the mountain? That is what we will do if you refuse to talk to us. Return you to the place where we found you, a simple honey collector who cannot afford wives but who wears a fine military uniform and costly boots. How will Rukuma repay you for this strong loyalty of yours, To-masi? By now he has missed you. He is hunting for you. He believes you have been captured or perhaps have run away. If we return you to your honey tree he will find you. And what will he do then, Tomasi Kunambi? Will he welcome you with open arms? Will he inquire after your journey and give you *pombe* to drink and roast meat? What will a man so suspicious as Rukuma do to a careless youth who goes alone and unarmed to collect honey from honey trees and is captured and held by Rukuma's enemies and then returned to the forest? Think, Tomasi. If you help us then you will be spared. You will not be returned to the forest. You will not be hung. You may even be rewarded. It may be that Julius Nyerere, the President of Tanzania, will personally reward you. Think carefully, Tomasi. Who is now your friend?"

Tomasi pressed his hands against his knees and stared again at the floor. They waited, but when he looked up his face was a mask. "I have no knowledge of these matters," he said.

Crown caught Nguvu's eye and the general nodded. "We know you didn't attack the camp, Tomasi," Crown said. Tomasi watched him warily. "The four men who attacked the camp were killed."

"No!" Tomasi blurted.

"Yes. Rukuma gave them no means of retreat. He sent

them in to die. He sent them in alone and left them and they were killed."

"They were *not* killed," Tomasi said. He was agitated now.

"If they were not killed," said Nguvu, picking it up, "why did they not return to your camp?"

Tomasi looked back and forth uncertainly. "Because they were sent on a further duty."

"No," said Nguvu. "That is what Rukuma told you. He lied. They were killed." Nguvu turned to his aide. "Do you have the photographs, Colonel?" Mongali dug in the black leather briefcase beside his chair and found the photographs and laid them on the table. "See for yourself," the general said to Tomasi. He pushed the photographs toward him.

They were photographs of the bodies laid out at the airstrip. Tomasi snatched them up. Pain came to his face as he shuffled them and at the third photograph he stopped, staring. He rocked his head from side to side. "I have sworn an oath," he whispered.

"On what was the oath sworn?" Nguvu quickly asked.

Tomasi lowered the photograph, not comprehending.

"Was the oath sworn on a goat? Was it sworn on earth or by bleeding?"

"It was a new oath," Tomasi said, distracted. "Rukuma said the old ways must be abandoned. It was sworn on the lives of the people. On my life and the life of my family." He lowered his head. "It does not matter." Then his head came up and angrily he struck the table. "One of those at the camp?" he said to Nguvu. "One of those who was killed?" Nguvu nodded. "One of those was my brother."

"And Rukuma left him there to die," Crown said.

Tomasi looked at Crown and looked back to Nguvu. "I have been with Rukuma now a month. I joined him because my brother joined. Now my brother is dead. It is useless." He shrugged. "I will tell you what you wish to know."

Ten

A LITTLE LATER Nguvu asked: "Will you take *chai*, Tomasi?"

"I would prefer beer," Tomasi said. "For a month I have not tasted beer."

"*Chai* for me," Crown said.

"Colonel?" said Nguvu. Colonel Mongali called to the duty sergeant for beer and tea. The sergeant nodded and left the tent.

Tomasi shifted in his chair. "I am very sore in my manhood," he said, aggrieved. "That soldier should not have beaten me. He should be punished."

"He will be dealt with," Nguvu said, glancing at Crown. Crown rolled his eyes.

"When he beat me I swore to myself that I would kill him."

"There must be no more killing. Already your brother is dead, Tomasi. You will honor your brother and redeem the name of Kunambi by helping us prevent further killing."

"But you will kill Rukuma. You will kill men who have given me friendship."

"No. We will not deliberately kill anyone. They will be captured and tried by law. The law is fair. The law will decide."

"You said I might be rewarded. How much reward will there be?"

"A good reward," Nguvu said. "Also, you will not go to jail."

Grinning, Tomasi said, "And will I meet the President?"

"It may be that you will meet the President. I will see what I can arrange."

"Do you speak English?" Crown asked Tomasi. He asked: "*Unasema Kiingereza?*"

"*La.* No. *Unasema Kiswahili na Kihehe.*"

"He's feeling his oats," Crown said in English to Nguvu.

"Yes. He is an arrogant young man. It is necessary that we humor him, however."

"Rather than, say, kick his butt."

Nguvu smiled. "Rather than." He touched Mongali's arm. "You need not note that down, Colonel."

"As you wish, sir," Colonel Mongali said.

"What do you speak of?" Tomasi asked in Swahili.

"That we are proud of you," Nguvu said.

Tomasi beamed.

The sergeant came into the tent with a tray and left his flashlight at his desk and brought the tray to Nguvu's table and set it down. It held a pot of tea, a bowl of sugar, a small pitcher of milk, a stack of cups and saucers and three bottles of beer. He served them tea, disdainfully passed a bottle of beer to the guerrilla and returned to his desk.

"There is much that we wish to know, Tomasi," Nguvu began then. "It will go faster if I question you. Answer carefully only what you are certain of, what you have seen with your own eyes or heard with your own ears. If you report

what others have told you, say who did the telling. Do you
understand?"

"*Ndiyo*." Tomasi drank deeply of his beer.

"*Vizuri*. Good. Then we may begin." Nguvu folded his
hands in front of him on the table. "How many men has
Rukuma on Olmoti?"

"I have tried in my head to count them. It seems that
there were about fifty before the raid on the tourist camp."

"Then there would be about forty-five now?"

"And four women," Tomasi added.

Nguvu raised an eyebrow. "What is the status of the
women?"

"They cook and wait on Rukuma."

"Are they trained with weapons?"

"Yes. They are very fierce."

"Are these people all of Rukuma's followers?"

"He has spoken of others. He speaks to us like a preacher.
He says he has many followers and that the number is grow-
ing every day." Tomasi drained the first bottle of beer and
set it on the tray and picked up a second bottle. "The beer is
good," he said.

"Drink slowly, my friend," Nguvu said. "You require a
clear head. These other followers. Is there more than one
camp?"

"Not that I have seen or heard of."

"Rukuma's inflating his strength," Crown said to Nguvu
in English.

"Perhaps." Nguvu switched back to Swahili. "Of course
you know the location of the camp," he said to Tomasi.

"*Ndiyo*."

"Later I shall ask you to show us on the map. How is it
armed?"

Tomasi started to swig his beer, thought better of it and
sipped. "All have the American-made rifles that fire rapidly," he said, lowering the bottle. "I myself was trained

with them. There are grenades. There are the tubes that fire
the rockets—"

"Mortars," Crown said in English.

"—and the weapons captured in Kenya."

"Did you participate in that raid?" Nguvu asked.

"No. It occurred before I was recruited, but my brother
did."

"What other weapons?"

"I have seen machine guns."

"Other than the ones captured in Kenya?"

"I do not know."

"How much ammunition?"

"Very much."

"As much of weapons and ammunition as you saw with
Colonel Mongali tonight?"

Tomasi frowned and worked his free hand in the air as if
he were measuring. He shook his head. "I am not sure. I
would say not as much."

Rain began to patter on the roof of the tent and they
stopped to listen. Mongali laid his pencil on his notebook
and stretched his fingers.

"Tomasi," Nguvu resumed. "What is the situation of the
camp?"

"It is located within the belt of bamboo. In a place where
the bamboo thins. It is about a kilometer north of where I
went to look for honey."

"We were closer than I thought," Crown said to Nguvu.

Nguvu nodded. "What structures?" he asked Tomasi.

"They are built of bamboo to disguise them from the air.
Rukuma's *banda*, his cabin, is large. There are smaller *banda*
for the men. The women live separately. Behind Rukuma's
banda, deeper in the bamboo, there is a *banda* for the stores
and another for the ordnance. That one is guarded."

"Is the entire camp guarded?"

"Yes. By day and by night. Above the bamboo," Tomasi

finished his description, "where it is open, there is a place where we go to take the sun."

"Excellent, Tomasi. What about trails?"

"There are many trails. The one most used leads to the hiding place of the lorries, but it is very well hidden." Tomasi thought and then shrugged. "They go in all directions. I myself came up a trail from the east, over the mountain. My brother brought me."

"Are there other lorries besides the ones we found?"

"I am sure not, because there was talk of attempting to capture more. We had not enough for all to ride and there was the possibility that you would discover those on your patrols."

"Rukuma knew of our patrols?" Nguvu asked.

"But not about losing his transport, apparently," Crown said in English. "He'll know soon enough."

"He knew of the patrols," Tomasi said. He finished the second beer and played with the neck of the bottle. "He laughed at them."

"Why did he laugh?" asked Nguvu.

"He does not believe that you will attack him until after the long rains. He says you will not be here by then. He says you have a surprise."

Intermittently there was thunder. The rain was pounding now on the roof and draining down the sides of the tent. Nguvu raised his voice over the pounding. "Do you know what he meant by a surprise?"

"No."

Nguvu looked at Crown, who turned up his hands, and then looked back at Tomasi. "How is Rukuma supplied?"

"I do not know," Tomasi said. "There are many tinned goods. Also we hunt. Since the appearance of the patrols the Sukuma have hunted with bows and arrows."

"Some of the men are Sukuma? What other tribes, Tomasi?"

"Some Hehe. Some Makonde. Some are Kenyans and some Ugandans."

"He's got an international brigade up there," Crown said.

"Where do these men come from?" Nguvu asked Tomasi. "I have said."

Nguvu shook his head irritably. "I mean how does Rukuma recruit them? How does he find them?"

"My brother came for me," Tomasi said. He looked at Nguvu and giggled. "Rukuma is a great leader. He calls and men follow him."

Nguvu controlled himself. "No doubt," he said dryly. He stretched his shoulders, rotating his head. "All right, Tomasi," he said, straightening, "tell us about this Rukuma who is a great leader. What does he look like?"

"He is very tall, very strong. A powerful man. His voice is deep. He commands. I do not know his age. He is between young and old." Tomasi looked at the last bottle on the tray.

"Take the beer," Nguvu said. "What tribe is Rukuma?"

"I do not know." Tomasi reached for the beer and set the other bottle beside him on the floor and adjusted his crotch. "He speaks many languages. Swahili. English. Others that I do not recognize. But he is Tanzanian."

"He is Tanzanian?" Nguvu said, surprised. "How do you know that?"

"He has said so. He has said that Tanzania is his homeland."

Nguvu looked at Crown. "That is unlikely," he said in English. "We would have known. His passport was Algerian."

"He could be lying to them," Crown said. "This kid wouldn't know the difference."

"True." Nguvu turned back to Tomasi. "What is Rukuma's purpose, Tomasi? Why has he gathered these weapons and these men? What did he tell you you were fighting for?"

"For many things," Tomasi said. "Rukuma said we would drive out all the *wahindi*, the Asians, and all the *wazungu*, the Europeans." He glanced guiltily at Crown. Crown smiled and nodded and Tomasi went on, his voice going dreamy. "He said we would make Tanzania a true country of the people. He said as we grew stronger we would unite Kenyans and Ugandans and Tanzanians into one people. He said we would make all of Africa one great and powerful nation and we would be its leaders and be respected by all the countries of the world."

"And you believed him," Nguvu said coldly.

Tomasi looked down at the bottle dangled between his legs. "My brother believed him," he said defensively. "I followed my brother."

"And your brother is dead."

Tomasi nodded.

Nguvu looked at his watch. It was nearly midnight. "All right, Tomasi. We have learned enough for one night. You have spoken well. The duty sergeant will take you to a tent where you may sleep. There will be guards at the tent, but they will be there only to protect you. Tomorrow we will talk again. I wish you to search your mind for any more information you can give us that will help us in dealing with Rukuma—weapons, forces, transport, plans, whatever you have seen or heard. You understand?"

"I understand," Tomasi said. He stood, wincing as he came up.

He's had a day, Crown thought. He's tired. Also gullible. And if he was looking at the photograph I think he was, then his brother's the one who tore off the tourniquet. The one I shot.

Colonel Mongali closed his notebook and the duty sergeant led Tomasi away.

Nguvu leaned back in his chair. "Well," he said, "there is much to do."

"I'm about through, aren't I, General?" Crown stretched his legs. It was still raining hard outside and the tent was cold.

"I should like you to stay at least through tomorrow, Seth. I want Tomasi to go over the map with us and I would like you to be here when he does."

"Right. Be glad to." He studied Nguvu. "What do you think?"

"Rukuma has a surprise for us? We shall have a surprise for him. We will not wait until the end of the long rains. We will go in with a full force as soon as we can arrange staging. Within twenty-four hours, I think. Now that we have one of his men, Rukuma will either be moving out or preparing for a fight. It will be difficult either way. I am considering an air strike."

"Yes?"

"Our pilots are not likely to hit the camp," Nguvu said with a slight smile, "but the sound of bombs can be wonderfully disillusioning. You will recall the effect of Turkish cannon on the Arabs in Lawrence's *Seven Pillars of Wisdom*."

"I missed that one, General." The general looked very good in the lantern light, very competent.

"They were charged with patriotic fervor, but the cannon unnerved them and they ran away."

"You think Rukuma's bunch will bolt?"

Nguvu shook his head. He noticed that his aide was still dutifully taking notes. "Thank you, Colonel," he said, standing. "You may go now. Thank you for your help."

"It was nothing, sir," Mongali said. He packed his briefcase.

"Some of them will bolt," Nguvu said to Crown. "More usefully, it will keep them busy while we negotiate the bamboo. But it will be a nice question of timing."

"You've got a madman on your hands, you know. Does he really expect to take over the country with fifty men?"

Colonel Mongali nodded to the duty sergeant and ducked under the tent flap out into the rain.

"In 1964 the mutiny in Dar of forty soldiers paralyzed Tanzania," Nguvu said.

Crown got up. "Things have changed a lot since then."

"Yes." Nguvu lifted the lantern from the table and lowered it to his side. "What has not changed is the African taste for revolution." He offered Crown the lead. "Come, my friend," he said, swinging the lantern like a watchman. "Let us get some sleep."

Robert Fuhrey finished his lunch of cold stew on the grass outside the thatched shelter on the rim of Oloito Gorge. He cleaned his spoon and bowl with ashes from the night campfire, the .45 awkward on his hip, and nodded to John Kegedi and went in preoccupied to his worktable. John was entertaining Mohammed and Kulaka with an oration, a politician's shrill plea for belt tightening. He was pretending to address their tapeworms. Lazing in the intermittent sun, they scraped the stew pot and belched their satisfaction and guffawed.

Until yesterday, when Cassie had come over with Abdi to deliver Seth's message, Fuhrey had left the heavy automatic in his tent. She had insisted impatiently that he wear it. He saw that she was worried and agreed. Now he pulled it from its stiff holster and laid it on the table beside the harvest of skull fragments he and John had dug so far from SCK. Its vulgarity beside the skull fragments annoyed him. Darkened with hardener, weathered, numbering more than two hundred now, they were valuable beyond price. The .45 reduced them to a joke: Death with a pistol at his head. Fuhrey reholstered the .45, unbuckled and lowered the pistol belt to the ground. He was ready to begin the skull's assembly.

Collectively he had designated the fragments OG-SCK

1001, the first find in Seth Crown's *Korongo* in Oloito Gorge. He would give the assembled skull that designation in his monograph. But the skull that would be also had a nickname: Tom. The day after he had learned of the attack on the camp, back at Oloito excavating, Fuhrey had remembered one of the verses of an anonymous eighteenth-century English lyric he'd memorized in high school, "Tom o' Bedlam's Song." Bedlam was an insane asylum in London, the Hospital of Saint Mary in Bethlehem; Tom was one of the lunatics the overworked keepers of Bedlam discharged to beg in the streets; the song was his begging song. The verse Fuhrey had remembered came late in the lyric. His mind brought it up as it brought up snatches of song. *The gypsy Snap and Pedro,* it went,

> *Are none of Tom's comradoes.*
> *The punk I scorn, and the cutpurse sworn,*
> *And the roaring boys' bravadoes.*
> *The meek, the white, the gentle,*
> *Me handle, touch, and spare not;*
> *But those that cross Tom Rhinoceros*
> *Do what the panther dare not. . . .*

and the association had seemed right; the rhino that rolled in the gorge's mud pools that had returned to the neighborhood with the long rains, the gentle visionary singer who was mad; and Fuhrey had nicknamed the skull Tom Rhinoceros, then simply Tom, Tom o' Bedlam. Tom lay scattered on the table, flattened by time.

The skull was a puzzle to be worked in three dimensions with no picture to guide. Fuhrey had already fitted·a few of the pieces together, teeth into sockets, two fragments of brow with good joins that started the arch above the left eye. It was odd work and tedious, work not for the verbal but for the patterning side of the brain. You didn't do it consciously. You stared and drifted and thought of other things until the connections came clear. So he could think of other things.

Immediately he saw two small pieces that shared a common curve of cranial suture. He moved one piece next to the other and they aligned. The sutures he had found so far had welded, the plates of the skull. Which confirmed the teeth: it wasn't the skull of a child.

The atrocity at the camp. Two days afterward he had seen the burned platforms, the shattered windows, the splintered door, but he had not seen the bodies, the wounded and the dead, and he could comprehend emotionally what had happened only by its effect on Cassie and Seth. Two days afterward Cassie had been numb and Seth hidden behind a wall of reassurance that seeped a cold, patient rage. Fuhrey had talked to them, stayed overnight at the camp, and come back to work. He didn't know what else to do. No more than Seth would he be run out by terrorists.

That goes there, under the eye.

At the conference last year in Nairobi they debated what was human. One hundred-fifty of them, most of them paleontologists, too many to crowd into the old museum, rattling around the monumental Kenyatta Conference Centre that took its shape from a conical African hut. Richard Leakey, Louis's brilliant, testy son, and Louis's widow, Mary, working in her own right at Laetolil and Olduvai, and opinionated Phillip Tobias somehow slipped in from Johannesburg despite Kenya's ban on everything South African, and a compact wedge of British and a mob of Americans. Everyone who worked in Africa and could get away. What makes *Homo* human? When is a fossil *Homo* and not *Australopithecus* or worse? Richard favored brain size, some minimum critical mass that exploded into thought. Donald Johanson, one of the Americans, favored upright walking, bipedalism. Others favored toolmaking, others brain shape even if the brain was small. The human brain, someone said, was selected for success in manual skills. The shape of the modern brain gave evidence: a disproportionate share of its bulging cortical surface was devoted to operating the fingers and the clever muscular thumbs. No other genus of animals had a brain like that. The human brain was selected for manual skills, and yet human beings had learned to talk. The human brain evolved for tolerant co-operation, and yet human beings had learned to kill, or always known.

John Kegedi came quietly to Fuhrey's side. *"Ikoje?"* he asked. "How's it going?"

"Hapana mbaya," Fuhrey said, looking up. "Not bad."

"We return to the site," Kegedi said in English. "We have opened the level to the mouth of the *korongo*. Should we continue the excavation southward or deepen it back into the slope?"

Fuhrey stood and stuck his hands into his pockets. "The south end's just about run out, isn't it? Are you still finding anything that way?"

"Very little. I think one fragment in two days."

"We won't find much more."

"No. Of this skull at least."

"I know. There might be others."

"It is always possible."

"I figured we'd eventually open up the whole slope." Fuhrey crossed one foot over the other and scuffed the ground, swaying. "The entire level's got to be explored as far back as we can take it. If we could find even one femur in there we'd be home free." He straightened. "Let's do it. Set up a grid and start cutting back. Take a nice big bite out of it, six meters or so. I'd really like to find some artifacts in association with this level. Watch out for flakes. No, watch out for cobbles. Tom here probably wasn't up to making flakes yet." Fuhrey grinned. "Maybe, just maybe, he bashed a few cobbles around."

Kegedi nodded and started to leave.

"John?" Fuhrey stopped him. "I think Seth's right. We ought to be spending our nights at the camp. And I might as well move Tom over there and stay there during the day and work on him. Otherwise I'd have the mess every day of packing him up. Does that give you any problems? Can you handle it over here?"

"Unless you require the Land Rover."

"I can use one of Seth's. It's too bad the damned walkie-talkies won't range that far."

"We have the guns," Kegedi said soberly.

"Okay. Let's plan to leave about six. That'll get us there before dark." Fuhrey looked beyond Kegedi to the two workmen waiting outside the shelter. "It's a hassle, but there's a payoff. We'll eat a lot better over there."

Kegedi smiled and jerked his thumb over his shoulder. "Tell these *walafi* that. These gluttons. They are all mouth."

Abdi had worked through the morning with the young woman of the Effendi and by the hour of the midday meal they had finished the carpentry of the first platform. Now in the afternoon they began the second while his wives thatched the first. His wives worked well together, his senior wife Mama Tele leading them. They sang as they worked. He was blessed in his wives. Slim Jaja's belly was great in front as a melon. He missed her hard brown thighs and the need she brought to the bed, the water that signed her passion. It would be good to sleep with her again when the child was weaned. Mama Tele was comfort for that as she had always been. Equally there was passion in age.

His daughters Moyo and Debba carried the thatch and passed it up to his wives and deftly they wove it into a waterproof covering. When the business of the guerrillas was finished he would go with the Effendi to Arusha for tents. And Moyo was so small she could hardly reach. She would grow quickly and leave respectfully in marriage as his other

daughters had done. The seasons crowded together and the
years shortened. Like a damaged bellows they flared but
also chastened the fire. Through the bad time it had been
better for the Effendi that the years shortened. Now they
might lengthen again. A prayer that the years might
lengthen again for the Effendi and for all.

They repaired the obscenity of the burning. That men
could do this, could murder, men of his color, now that freedom was won. Their hatred shamed the dream of freedom.
Hatred was older than the dream of freedom and more per-
sistent. It was a knifing at a water hole. It was a vain man
jealous of his wife, incensed that she took lovers. It was a
tribe coveting another tribe's ripe fields and in every man it
worked his left hand while he blessed with his right. Sometimes it slept, but it did not die, no more than locusts died.
Men of decency watched for it and dug out its nests. It
spawned again. Nothing was more certain than that it
would spawn again. It was the sadness of the world.

He had not known how to address this young woman of
the Effendi. She worked there on the side of the platform
with skill. He had avoided direct address until the work.
Others had come before her and it was better to wait and
see. With the work he had essayed *bibi* Wendover, Miss
Wendover, and she had laughed, although kindly. Her name
was Cassie, she had said. She called him Abdi, she had said,
and he should call her Cassie. It was not easy to do. He
knew Seth Crown by the old honorific of the officers of the
colonial army. With the coming of Uhuru many scorned the
word, but his friendship with the Effendi was the strength of
his life. It had made him a wealthy man in the things of the
world, four wives, many children, shillings that filled to
overflowing his account at the bank. He possessed more
than he had ever imagined he would possess. Yet he knew
that the possessions were little of it. Loyalty was more, the
great respect the Effendi showed him and had shown him

from the beginning, when he was a gun bearer in cast-off clothing and the Effendi a young man limping back from war. It was a gift beyond price in a time when the powerful regarded Africans as naughty children or as slaves and it had cost the Effendi his wife and his son. The Effendi's grief was a shame that he had borne through many years, until he understood that the Effendi had never blamed him. It was only then, when he gave up the shame, that he saw the true strength that bound them. To the Effendi and to him it was given to stand together against the hatred. They stood as men were meant to stand, proudly, and if they had not so stood and others like them then the world would long ago have withered away.

Abdi laid down his hammer to watch. The burned platform, the charred, blackened boards going to earth and the light new boards replacing them. She was a woman of beauty, strong, with a face finely shaped, her hair caught up in a *kitambi*, a kerchief, with long young legs. With soft hands she worked as hard as his wives. His sons crowded around her, holding boards for her and bringing her nails, Kassim, Rashid, Hashim, the latest of his sons and his joy.

She saw him watching her and stopped hammering. "Your kids are wonderful," she said.

His sons stepped back in shyness from his gaze. "I am glad that they please you. If they stand in your way you must scold them."

"Really, they're helping me." She pointed with her hammer. "Aren't we doing well? We'll be back in business in no time."

He must ask her. It mattered that he know. "May I speak with you?"

"Sure." His tone puzzled her. "Am I doing something wrong?"

"No. The work is excellent. Kassim, go to your mother. Take your brothers." His sons scampered away.

She came around the platform. "What is it, Abdi?"

"I do not mean to be abrupt." He faced her. "Do you wish to marry the Effendi?"

She answered without hesitation. "I want to spend my life with him. I love him. Married or not."

Abdi nodded. "You must excuse me if my questions are improper. For many years I have been his friend."

"I understand."

"I believe that your wish is his also. Will you bear him children?"

"Yes. If he wants children. I do. I think he does. I think losing his son hurt him terribly."

"Yes. It did."

"Is there any chance that Joseph will ever come back?"

"I think that he must not be alive," Abdi said, looking down. "No son would abandon his father so long if he were alive. Even if he hated his father, he would return to claim his inheritance." He shook his head. "No, I believe that Joseph is dead."

"There's so much I want to make up for," she said, pain in her voice. "He's given me my life, Abdi. He means everything to me."

It was as he thought and hoped. Then settled. The Effendi was his brother in all but blood. In fear men called their officers *sir*. He called Seth Crown *sir* in love. The woman who loved the Effendi as he did wanted no honorific. Then her honorific would be her name.

He looked at her steadily. "I am very glad that you have come to this place, Cassie." Her name made her smile.

On toward dusk, the air chilling in the failing light, Nguvu's soldiers waited before their tents for inspection. Crown walked beside the general down the lines. The men's fitness impressed him. At Nguvu's approach they braced in battle gear, steel-helmeted, Kalashnikovs dressed smartly on their shoulders, boots polished, packs trim on their backs. Mortar teams had set up their light Chinese 63's in front of their platoons with carrying handles folded down onto barrels; point men presented walkie-talkies at port arms; sergeants' belts hung with the black pots of grenades. They were soldiers rare in their eagerness. They had worked and walked all their lives. Their country was new, its leaders uncorrupted, its ideals worth fighting for. If many of them were illiterate, they had been born to the warrior traditions of their tribes and they transferred their loyalty passionately to their vigorous little general. After Nguvu had inspected them, Crown noticed, more than one of them broke out in unsuppressible grins.

"Well, Seth," Nguvu said as they rounded the line and crossed over to inspect the other side, "do you think Rukuma will crush us?"

"I think if Rukuma were here he'd be wetting his pants." Crown nodded to Sergeant Mugwa at the head of the line and Mugwa's small eyes crinkled a reply. Mugwa's platoon was easily the sharpest of the lot. Nguvu clapped the sergeant on the shoulder in compliment before he moved on.

At the end of the line, satisfied, Nguvu crisply saluted the parade officer. The officer barked dismissal and the men cheered and rushed their tents to unload for mess. The young officers followed Crown and Nguvu to the officers' mess, talking guardedly behind. Crown sensed their tension. Tanzania was a peaceful country. They didn't get much chance to ply their trade. They watched guerrillas train in Dar for Zimbabwe and South Africa and ran exercises on dusty parade grounds. Rukuma was only cleanup, but Olmoti itself would test them. They knew it and they were ready at the mark.

"The air strike is set," Nguvu said to Crown at table. "Tomasi was very helpful with the trails, don't you think? We will stage half the company from the base of the mountain to avoid the rivers. They ought to catch up by late morning. Two jets will bomb and strafe the bamboo at fourteen hundred hours."

"You should be in place by then," Crown said. The officers were listening. "I hope the weather doesn't blow it for you. The fog'll be thick up there tonight."

"It is predicted to clear," one of the officers said.

"We are cautioned not to trust prophecy," Nguvu said, smiling and setting down his fork.

"The ministry receives the satellite pictures now," said the officer.

"Good, Captain. I am glad. If only they are able to read them."

Laughter. The officers dug in heartily, chicken and groundnut stew and fried plantains, their last hot meal but one.

Hands fought the tangle of the tent flaps. The duty sergeant pushed into the tent waving his arms. "General Nguvu! General Nguvu! You are called to the radio. *Mwalimu* himself calls! It is urgent!"

Nguvu was already up. "Nyerere?" he said. "Calm down, Sergeant. It is not the end of the world." He stepped over the bench and walked out, the sergeant following him.

Crown looked around. Momentarily the officers were silent. The weather officer caught Crown's eye and shrugged. Then the talk began.

The duty sergeant came back. "Bwana Crown," he said, containing himself now. "The general wishes you to come."

Crown jogged across the parade ground. He heard the high, eager voice crackling from the radio tent as he crossed, *Mwalimu*, the Teacher, the President of Tanzania. Inside the tent Nguvu gestured him to a chair.

"*. . . we don't know the extent of the forces,*" Julius Nyerere was saying. "*He has bombed Bukoba. He's an absolute lunatic, John . . .*"

Nguvu was rigid. "Amin has invaded the West Lake District," he said aside sharply to Crown.

". . . *and raping. Looting. He means to annex the district down to the Kagera River. He's claiming it for Uganda. There's already been a broadcast. We'll see about that. I think it's another one of his stunts, John,*" Nyerere went on, his voice becoming more measured, "*but this time he's gone too far. We will meet him head-on.* Field Marshall *Idi Amin Dada. I want that* snake *out of my house.*" He paused. "*We will counterattack in force. I am mobilizing the army here. The People's Defense Forces are already fighting at Bukoba. You are placed farthest west. How quickly can you leave?*"

Nguvu picked up the microphone stand, its base olive-drab before the webbing-covered bulk of the radio. "Immediately, *Mwalimu.* We were preparing to attack the guerrillas tomorrow. It is fortuitous. The troops are ready. We can leave here tonight."

Rukuma's surprise, Crown thought. How the bloody hell did he know?

"*Wonderful. How is your transport? We're short here.*"

"We are also short."

"*Commandeer what you need. Ngorongoro has lorries. Take them. Use my authority. We'll straighten it all out later. If I were a swearing man, John . . . Why is East Africa saddled with such a lunatic? Why has the OAS allowed him to survive? It's absolutely absurd.*"

"*Mwalimu?* What about the guerrillas?"

"*We must attempt to contain them. But they are secondary. We're talking about a force of several thousand men, John. This is no border skirmish. It's a major invasion. Can you leave a small detachment?*"

Nguvu looked at Crown.

"Leave me some men," Crown said. "I'll beef them up with Masai."

"I will handle it here, *Mwalimu*," Nguvu said into the microphone.

"*I'll count on you*," Nyerere crackled back. "*Let us talk no more. We speak for other ears. Go. Stay in touch with me. Other forces will follow.*" Then there was static.

Nguvu set down the microphone. His shoulders slumped and for a moment he stared at the radio. Then he straightened and turned to Crown, oddly smiling. "Can you see my colleagues crossing from Dar all the way to Victoria in taxicabs and garbage lorries?" He shook his head. "Our friend on Olmoti knows more than we thought. He has been in touch with Amin."

"Tomasi said he had Ugandans."

"It is more serious than Julius has seen. Rukuma cannot be merely contained. If he is co-ordinating with Amin he may also be preparing an assault. But I cannot stay to counter him."

"How many men can you spare me?" Crown asked grimly.

Nguvu studied him. "It is not necessarily your fight."

"It's my fight. It's the Masai's fight. No one's going to be safe around here."

Nguvu looked relieved. "How many men do you need?"

"It's not so much men as armament. I can pull out any number of *moran*. But while they're sneaking around with spears I need some firepower. Kalashnikovs, grenades, maybe a mortar. What about the air strike?"

"We had ordered up a tenth of the air force. Nyerere countermanded. It is already gone to Bukoba."

"Bloody Christ," Crown said. "All right. Ten men. Can you leave me the guards on the camp?"

"Besides the ten men?"

"Yes."

"That is fifteen men."

"I won't do it otherwise, General. I won't leave that camp unguarded."

"I understand. Very well."

"Give me Sergeant Mugwa. He can hold the fort and keep an eye on Tomasi while I arrange for the Masai. Leave me all my vehicles. I'll bring the *moran* up in the lorry and we'll go in from here."

"How soon?"

"Maybe twenty-four hours."

"You will be finished before we even begin. Bukoba is on the other side of Victoria. It is better than seven hundred kilometers and the district is serviced by only two roads. Dirt roads. Swamp roads in the rainy season."

"I don't envy you."

Nguvu brushed it aside. "Nor I you, my friend."

"We're still ahead of the game."

"Yes? How so?"

"The son-of-a-bitch can't be expecting us," Crown said. "Especially now with Amin out there howling. Rukuma thinks he's in the clear. He's going to get one fearsome bloody surprise."

Eleven

PAST NGORONGORO, the hard rain slanting through the tunneling headlights, the gearbox whining, Crown ground down the mud-slick mountain road. The Land Rover's eccentric wipers stuck and hissed, working out of rhythm to clear the flat windshield beaten by rain. A field car of drivers and an officer had followed him as far as the turnoff to the lodge to pick up extra transport. They'd be lucky to make the rim. Shouting, muddied men struck their tents at the mountain camp, lorries lined up for light. Rukuma's scouts from wherever they watched in the lower forest would see Nguvu moving out and climb to the bamboo to report. Mugwa's detachment would look like a cleanup crew dawdling behind. They'd keep Tomasi hidden. Tomasi hated being handed back to Mugwa. The poor bastard thought he was a hero. Maybe he was. If he led them to Rukuma, Crown would personally decorate him. He'd lead them all right. Mugwa would herd him up the mountain with a prod.

So Amin was in it. Idi Amin Dada, the mad butcher. Boating on Victoria he sported with the crocs while the bloated bodies of his victims, black skins bleached white in grotesque patches, washed up on the shores. African leaders despised him and sabotaged him where they could. Kenyatta allowed the Israelis to refuel in Kenya after Entebbe and constricted Amin's access to the sea; Nyerere made room for his exiled predecessor to bide his time in Dar. But Arab fanatics supported Amin and Palestinians manned his personal guard. The West made him its bogeyman, proof that post-colonial Africa went bestial. And Rukuma trucked with him. Rukuma had better watch his dreamy speeches to the recruits: Amin had dreams of his own.

With Amin at the west lake, Tanzania might be at war. Better to move on the guerrillas now. The force Crown could muster might not finish them off, but it could scatter them and slow them down.

This time he'd take Abdi with him. Robert could stand a shift at guard, John Kegedi. There wouldn't be much more rain. Nguvu would have to fight the swamp west of the lake, but the forest on Olmoti would dry out fast enough. With the ending of the long rains the Serengeti would dry and yellow, the lions lay up along the watercourses, the game retreat again to shade. It seemed like months since he'd met Cassie coming into camp, since they'd driven this road in darkness up to Ngorongoro. Years. If it had all happened before she came, would he have cared? Not in the same way, but he would have done what he was doing. What else was there to do?

He protected something now. A piece of a country that had been good to him. A camp where he worked, where he lived, a place he wouldn't let them run him out of. A woman whose life he could no longer distinguish from his own. But he also protected something before. He couldn't even name it. Kinship came close. Husbandry. It was older than those, too old to have any single name. Human community was rooted in it and whenever that community was damaged it grew up to restore. It was older than human community and tougher, and its diseased absence made men monsters.

Crown was wary of the guards. When he left the main track for the track to the camp he turned on the Land Rover's interior light, and closer to camp he began intermittently blowing the horn. The rain cut down on visibility. The guards would be out in the rain unless Abdi had fixed up shelters. Crown blew the horn steadily up the last stretch of road and at the entrance to the camp he braked the Land Rover to a halt and jumped out and stood in the headlights to be recognized. Then one of the guards stepped into the light, grinning and lowering his Kalashnikov, and he was home.

Cassie ran to embrace him. The others met him at the porch, and surprised by his grimness stood back: Abdi, Fuhrey, John Kegedi, Mohammed and Kulaka and the guards. He told them quickly about the invasion and led them into the dining room. Behind him the sergeant translated for his men. Their cots were made up smartly, their kits packed and ordered at the foot of the cots in a line. Crown noticed the fragments of the skull laid out on one of the big tables and smiled at Fuhrey and led them to another table and sat down. They wouldn't like what he had to say, Cassie least of all.

He told them: Tomasi, the strength of Rukuma's force, Amin, Nyerere, Nguvu, Mugwa's detachment waiting, the *moran*.

"I must also go, Effendi," Abdi said.

"I hoped you would. We'll need you."

Fuhrey shook his head. "I wouldn't be any use to you."

"I know. Nguvu wouldn't want you up there anyway. I had to talk him out of evacuating you. Don't worry about it." Crown indicated the worktable. "I see you're making progress."

"We've got it. All we have to do now is put it together."

"Do it. Can you take a shift on guard, you and John?"

"Absolutely."

"So can I," Cassie said. She was sitting next to him and he saw she was wearing the .38 he'd given her.

"Good. We'll get the canvas on the lorry tonight. I'll leave at dawn with Abdi for ole Kipoin's. Nguvu left us rations. We ought to be able to haul the *moran* in one trip."

"How many?" Cassie asked. She was gripping the edge of the table. Crown heard the generator idling. He hadn't noticed before.

"Maybe thirty," he said. Abdi nodded.

"Against machine guns?"

"You'd be surprised. We won't send them in straight-on."

"Bwana Crown," the sergeant standing beyond the table said. "It is true we are ordered to remain here?"

"*Ndiyo.* To guard the camp." The sergeant told the men sitting on their cots. They looked relieved enough. "Right," Crown said. "That's it then. Let's get the lorry set up and turn in. Abdi, how about a beer?"

Abdi stood. "I will open one for you, Effendi," he said.

In the bedroom later, in the darkness, Cassie said: "Do you want to talk about it?"

"It's pretty obvious." His hand found the small of her back and she moved to him.

"You can't take me?"

"It's not your show." Her face was close, her hair loose on the pillow.

"Because I'm a woman?"

"Because it's a stalk and a fire fight and you're not trained for it."

"How will I know?"

"When we come back."

"How long?"

"Two days. Tomorrow and the next day." Her skin was warm but she was shivering.

"And if you're not back then?"

"Let it go, Cassie," he said gently. "It has to be done."

She held him. She was silent and she was still shivering and then she said: "I love you. I have gone with you, you know? I was with you this morning and last night and yesterday. Tonight when you drove in. I'm with you wherever you are. I will be. Remember that I will be."

"I know."

They went down into flesh, slowly, and when they were there and completely there her shivering stopped.

"Cassie?"

"Yes. Now."

"This."

"Seth. Seth."

"Yes. This now."

"Yes."

"Cassie."

"Oh yes. My god. My god."

It left him afterward too quickly, the other coming back, and wanting to delay its going and wanting to take something of it with him he whispered: "For you?"

"For me?" She stroked his temple, smoothing back his hair. "Always, Seth. More than once for me. Did you know? More than once for me."

Through the window, like distant thunder carrying, they heard Nguvu's lorries rumbling west across the plain.

Runners went out from the *manyatta* of ole Kipoin in the morning.

"The *moran* will wait for thee on the main track eastward," ole Kipoin told Crown, standing with him beside the Mercedes lorry outside the *boma*. Abdi sat in the cab on the driver's side and the children of the *manyatta* climbed laughing over the canvas-topped stake racks mounted on the bed.

"*O*," Crown said. "How many have been summoned?" An hour after dawn the sky was clear and blue, the sun up over the highlands. The day would be hot.

"So many as there are at the encampments," ole Kipoin said, counting with hand gestures. "Perhaps *osom*. Perhaps the thirty that thou asked. More might be sent for but it would delay thee."

"It is enough."

Ole Kipoin stared beyond Crown, watching the cattle graze. A fly drank unminded at the corner of his eye. "I would go with thee against this barbarian," he said, "but it is not my place."

"It is my duty, my *olaitoriani*. I will perform it."

"Too many of the Masai have left the old ways these years." Ole Kipoin looked back to Crown. "Thou knowest?" He showed no pain in his face but his mouth tightened with disapproval.

"*O*."

"It is not so with this age group. They are senior *moran* of promise. They follow the old ways. They will perform this duty bravely. Lead them well, my brother."

"I will do so faithfully."

Ole Kipoin stepped back. "Send word." He raised his hand.

Crown returned the gesture. Then he reached above him and opened the door of the lorry and stepped up to the running board and slid in. "Let's go," he said to Abdi in English. Abdi started the engine with a roar and the children squealed and jumped off the back. When the children were clear Crown slammed the door as Abdi engaged the clutch and turning from the *manyatta* they pulled away.

That afternoon Fuhrey worked at the table in the dining room of the lodge. If he concentrated too long on the puzzle of the fragments he found himself staring. A few were large as quarters and they were easier to place. Most were small as a little fingernail. Spread on the table they made an illusory archipelago, brown-white islands on a wooden sea, the maxilla beside them with its teeth and the matrix-thickened eye sockets like island cliffs. The brain could read anything into them it wanted, and did, fancifully, but there was only one real arrangement their shapes would fit. He was certain the brain saw the real arrangement almost immediately even though it had to be coaxed tediously to divulge what it saw. In the meantime the real arrangement interfered with the fanciful somewhere deep in the brain to set up a disturbing moiré, and the moiré was tiring as all illusions and sooner or later he stared.

Cassie came in to watch. She sat down opposite him and he glanced up to smile at her. She was wearing a khaki shirt loose outside her shorts. It was patched and faded, one of Crown's. Her hair was tied in a square of paisley. Her tan was reddened and her nose was sunburned and he saw that she was distracted. She was worried about Crown.

"Want to help?" Fuhrey asked.

"Sure. What do I do?"

"Did you ever work jigsaw puzzles?"

"Lots."

"It's the same operation. A little tougher. There's no picture. Some of the pieces are missing and we'll end up with an ovoid instead of a plane."

Cassie touched one of the fragments hesitantly. "Do they break?"

"They're treated with hardener. Just don't flip them. I think I've got them all face-down. Convex. At this stage it's a little easier to build with an outside curve than an inside."

"Okay." She sat forward.

"Tom thanks ye," Fuhrey said, changing his voice.

"Tom's a good boy."

She came to it with a fresh eye and she quickly saw two fits and moved the fragments together. She found another fragment and fitted it to one of the pairings she'd made and then for a time they searched. They might have been playing Martian chess, Fuhrey thought. In a way they were.

"What was it like?" she asked, studying the board.

"What was what like?"

"For Tom."

"Not bad. Assuming he wasn't too different from his immediate descendants, he only had to work half-days to feed himself."

"Hunting?"

"A little. Scavenging. Gathering. Hard to tell."

"What did he do the rest of the time?"

"Socialized. Groomed his buddies. Sniffed around."

"Not wars? Not slaughtering the innocents at the next campsite?"

"That's the Ardrey theory. Probably not. Co-operation's more adaptive than aggression." Fuhrey moved two fragments together, but the fit was loose. He replaced them where they were. "I've gotten to the point where I'm doing this in my sleep."

She looked up at him then and smiled. "It's hard work. Are you glad you chose it?"

"Christ yes." He grinned, boyishly. "You could take everything that's been found between ten and six million years b.p. and put it in a shoe box. Tom just about doubles it."

"That's marvelous."

"Six million years is crucial. If we've got it right, *Ramapithecus* speciated into *Homo* and *Australopithecus* around that time. If Tom's *Homo,* or *Homo*-like, then he's going to be the link. If he's in between *Rama* and *Homo* then we've connected the line all the way back."

"Is he?"

"I don't know. First we have to put him together."

They worked. She was staring as he had stared before. He wondered what she saw. She stared as if the fragments had been cast there for sortilege. For divination by bones. It was still practiced in Africa and he'd seen it done. This fragment stood for man, this for the essence of manhood, this for woman, this for the essence of womanhood, and that one for danger and that one for success, that one for enemies, that one for friends, that one for the arrow of time. Their shapes and their scars defined networks of relationships. How did they fall? Which overlapped another, which turned away, what of the orientation of their markings? The network hypothesized a sequence of cause and effect to order the future. But this wasn't a kit for sortilege. This was a braincase to assemble.

One of the guards came into the dining room and sat on his cot. He was a thin, coffee-colored man with a broad nose. His fatigues were dark with sweat.

"*Ikoje?*" he called over to Fuhrey. "How's it going?" He began field-stripping his Kalashnikov.

"*Polepole,*" Fuhrey said, turning around. "Slowly."

"*Yule ni mnyama gani?* What kind of animal is that?"

"*Yule ni mwanaadamu,*" Fuhrey said. "It's a human being."

The guard grunted and busied himself with his rifle. Fuhrey faced back to the table.

"I caught some of that," Cassie said.

"He didn't realize Tom was human. He's thinking about it. He doesn't look too happy with the idea."

"Maybe you'd better get the guards together and tell them what you're doing. They might decide to dump Tom out the door."

"Lord. Maybe I'd better."

"Oh, here," Cassie said, "I see." She moved one assembly

of three fragments over to another assembly of five. They touched each other only at one short edge but the fit was sure and there clearly was the curve of the cranium.

"Bravo," Fuhrey said. "That's fantastic. I ought to let you take this project over. You'd have it done in no time."

"Thanks, no." Cassie drew back her hand. "It's all in that curve, isn't it. All the millions of years. Everything that came with it." She shook her head. "It's grim. I keep seeing a skull."

"I did at first. After a while it's something more. What's an analogy? There's a scanner they're experimenting with for the blind. A videocon built into a hat that's attached to a box you wear on your back. The box has a grid of sixty-four rubber projections. They press a rough patten of the camera image into your back. At first you feel them in your back, but after a few days' practice you see the image in your head."

"That sounds like a Kafka story," Cassie said.

"Which?"

"A man condemned to death. I don't remember the title. They don't tell him his crime. He's strapped to a table under a machine set with needles. It swings across him. Tortures him. It's slowly shredding him. Finally he realizes it's cutting the name of his crime into his body. After sixteen hours, just before he dies, he reads it in his flesh." She covered her mouth with her hand.

The idea intrigued him. "There's a connection," he said. "It's all wired in. Loyalty, aggression, altruism, sex, religion, everything."

"You think we're robots?" she said, lowering her head and straightening.

"No. It's like language. There's a deep structure of grammar built into the brain. We can invent hundreds of different languages, but the possibilities aren't infinite. They're limited by the deep structure they specify." He shrugged. "There's a deep structure of behavior too."

"We don't choose?" She was deadly serious.

"Within limits."

"Seth didn't choose?"

"He chose. So did you. What did you want him to choose?"

"What he chose," she said quickly.

"So he did."

"We could have gone away."

"Could you?"

She hesitated. "No."

"So it's a choice within limits. That's what I mean."

"Lovely."

"We don't get off the hook just because we evolved larger brains, Cassie."

"Is that why you want to make the connection all the way back?"

"Sure."

"To show that we're determined by our biology?"

"That's one reason. Don't you think we are?"

"I know why you see it that way."

He was surprised. "Why?"

"Because you feel religious about science."

"What other way is there to see it? Not the religious canard, which by the way I don't agree with, but why one does science?"

"*One* does science," Cassie said sharply, "because at each step along the way it's possible to do. You don't find out something to prove something, or because you want to. You find it out because historically it's there to find and you have the tools to find it. How you take it is another matter entirely. There's a lot more going on in the world than science, Robert. For one thing, there's a lot more slippage, a lot more freedom."

"Oh, freedom." He started to say more but she stopped him, standing abruptly to go.

"You really surprise me," she said. "I've never seen you mean-minded before. A choice can be a choice and also not a choice. You forget I've done physics. It depends on the point of view you take. It depends on the operations you specify to isolate whatever part you're studying. That's not wishful thinking. That's wired in too. Not just into the brain." She gestured, dismissing it. "Into the universe."

"Don't go away mad," Fuhrey said.

"I'm not mad," she finished, rounding the table, looking aside at him. "I'm just exasperated you think it's so simple." She passed the guard. He had turned away from the unclean thing on the table. He was expertly reassembling his weapon, and she saw the delight on his face.

The *moran* were waiting on the Serengeti track as ole Kipoin had promised, two groups of ten and one of eleven assembled from three encampments, one man more than Crown had counted on. They saw the lorry approaching where they milled beside the track, eastward toward Olduvai, and waved their spears or twirled them to flash in the sun. Their shouts scattered the tommies that grazed a space around them on the plain. When Abdi stopped to load them they crowded the cab, clamorous to hear more than the runners had known. They called Crown *aputani*, father. They were nervous with eagerness, jumpy, some of them shivering despite the afternoon heat. They were warriors whose elders had forgone war and they wanted a fight.

Once, moving south from the hard plains beyond Mount Kenya to take up new land for grazing, the Masai had terrorized East Africa, but they had laid down their battle shields long ago, respecting the orders of their *il'laibon*, their hereditary priest-kings, to make peace with the white men. Crown knew the story from his own days as a *moran*. Before the turn of the century the old *laibon* Mbatian had prophesied the coming of white things attending a formidable,

headless snake. The white things would not come in his lifetime, Mbatian had boasted, flailing the air with his
herdstick, beating them back to the sea, but he could not
prevent them from coming in the time of his sons. Mbatian's
two sons had divided the Masai—one of them had worked a
Jacob and Esau swindle on the other, stealing disguised into
Mbatian's house for his dying blessing—and the British had
built their headless lunatic railroad through Masailand, the
Masai had signed the treaties of 1904 and 1911 and voluntarily removed themselves south of the tracks, surrendering
their northern lands, and the fighting between the Masai
and the other tribes around them had come to an end. War-
riorhood was a long haul, junior and senior *moran*hood ex-
tending from the fourteenth to the twenty-fifth year. Forbidden to make war, the *moran* were reduced to guarding
cattle, to collecting *hongo* from travelers who presumed to
cross Masailand and to working security for the Council of
Elders when it policed tribal disputes. Since they couldn't
hunt men, they went together naked into the bush and
hunted cattle-marauding lions, for sport. They'd do. At sur-
prising guerrillas who counted on sentries and bully ordnance they'd do damned well.

This bunch was ole Kipoin's pride, senior *moran* eighteen
to twenty-five years old, tall, lean, smooth-muscled Nilotics
handsome as Pharaohs and vain. Their bodies were painted
the color of rust with red ocher mixed with shining fat.
Their hair was thickened with ocher and braided in the
back into long single pigtails. They wore ocher-colored blankets fastened like togas at the shoulder, their high, muscled
buttocks protruding arrogantly behind; and wooden plugs
or buckhorns of snuff in the stretched lobes of their ears;
collars beaded white and black, green and black, red and
black at their necks; beaded belts; ankle bracelets; tough
bullhide sandals. They carried rations of *loshoro*—cooked
cornmeal mixed with milk—in narrow swallow's-nest gourds.

Shortswords hung from their belts, a spare pair of sandals,
knobbed clubs. The spears they hefted were light and keen,
designed for throwing, three balanced parts fitted together:
a spike at one end like a poker; a dark hardwood shaft; a
flat, leaf-shaped blade of polished iron eighteen inches long,
no wider at its widest than three fingers of a man's hand and
sharp enough for shaving. The Masai knew better than to
waste an edge on shaving. They plucked their beards with
iron tweezers and whetted their spears for flesh.

The *moran* listened to Crown respectfully, flies walking
on their faces and in and out of their mouths. When he was
finished they racked their spears, shouting and laughing,
and leapt to the bed of the lorry. Two of their three leaders,
Simel and Sitonik, young men Crown knew from the Council, rode standing on the running boards baring their strong
teeth to the wind, all the way up the mountain. The cab was
awash with their smells of rancid fat and cattle dung. Abdi
twitched his nose. Crown breathed in the nostalgic stink of
his adolescence and settled back to daydream.

They arrived at the camp late in the afternoon, coming in
easily on the drying road, Simel and Sitonik hidden under
cover now with the others in the back. Mugwa was the
highest-ranking army man at hand. Rank might have been a
problem, but the sergeant deferred to Crown immediately
and Crown took charge. Mugwa's men had built a camouflaged shelter for the *moran* in the forest behind the
camp. Abdi unloaded the Masai out of sight at the edge of
the clearing and they jogged back silently to inspect the
shelter and spiked their spears in the ground at the entrance
and stayed in. The army had moved on. Rukuma's scouts
probably weren't watching. If they were they'd report a
lorry come in to pick up the cleanup crew. So the *moran*
were set, and Mugwa and his commandos ready at their one
remaining tent. Mugwa would lead his own men. Crown
would lead the *moran* with Abdi. They'd go up together at

dawn, Tomasi showing them the way. Tomasi had a guard, courtesy of Mugwa. He was so glad to see Crown he couldn't stop pumping his hand.

Crown didn't want to chance a campfire. It was warmer anyway without the rain. The *moran* at least were hot with anticipation. Mugwa's men were seasoned, but they looked eager enough. They carried rations back to the shelter for the *moran*. Save their *loshoro* for the climb.

In early evening, at the quick African dusk, Crown left Abdi with Mugwa and walked to the shelter and ate with the *moran*. They were old as soldiers in any country's army, tougher and smarter and better disciplined than most. Crown knew many of their parents, knew their genealogies and bantered with them in Masai. They were boyish then, politely respectful. They had seen him in Council and knew his position with the tribe. Ole Kipoin was right: they followed the old ways. Then an old way for them, if he could remember it right.

"Do you know the story of the caterpillar called Kunju?" he asked them.

"*O*, my *aputani*, my father," Simel answered for them all. "It is a good story. We would be honored if you would tell it again."

"If *moran* have ears to hear when their bellies are full then I will tell it."

"We have ears, my *aputani*," Sitonik said.

They settled back to listen. The unfamiliar rations made them belch. They fed on milk, milk mixed with blood in the hot seasons when the cows went dry, and alone among the age grades of the Masai went into the forest to kill ceremonial bulls and roast meat. But milk was their staple. Milk made them strong and they blessed it and painted their bodies for the rituals of their youth with milk-thinned chalk that glared in the sun. If not Mbatian's prophecy, milk may have saved the hides of the invading milk-white British. It was the color of Crown's skin that had drawn the elders to his parents' house when he was born in Masailand. They spat on him in blessing.

"*Lomon lolkurto oji Kunju oo ndokitin osero,*" Crown began. "'The News of the Caterpillar Which Is Called Kunju and the Things of the Forest.'" He found the story intact in his memory. He hadn't heard it in thirty-five years.

"There was formerly a caterpillar who goes into the hut of a hare. And the hare comes walking back and he sees the footsteps of the caterpillar and he says, 'Who is in my hut?'

"The caterpillar makes his voice big. 'I am the warrior son of the Long One,' he says, 'whose anklets became unfastened when we fought in Kurtaile. I crush the rhinoceros to the earth. I make cow's dung of the Of-the-arm, the elephant. None dare venture against me!'"

They laughed at the caterpillar's audacity. Crown could hardly see them in the darkness under the shelter. Outside it was lighter, the moon early and nearly full filtering white through the cedars. Lunar rovers abandoned there, plastic bags of trash, gold-foil engines of burned-out rockets, and here under a shelter lean neolithic men listened to a story older than Aesop.

"The hare arises to go. '*He!*' he says. 'You say you are the one who makes the elephant into cow's dung? Then I could be next!' And he goes to see the jackal, and says to him, 'I pray you, my father, come and speak to the big man who is in my hut.'

"And they go, and when the jackal nears the hut he cries, '*Waa Waa,*' the jackal's cry, and he says, 'Who is in the hut of my friend the hare?'

"'I am the warrior son of the Long One,' the caterpillar says, 'whose anklets became unfastened when we fought in Kurtaile. I crush the rhinoceros to the earth. I make cow's dung of the elephant. None dare venture against me!'

"And the jackal says to the hare, 'I will not venture against such a man.'"

They wanted the story exact, retold word for word as they had heard it since childhood. It advised them in virtue: close observation, the tactical advantage of the bluff, the uses of cowardice and gullibility. Its speeches repeated hypnotically for memory's sake, the repetition one tool from the kit of an ingenious and portable culture. The story itself was bare bones, but in the darkness they saw the jackal like a yellowish, short-haired fox, the hare with its yellow fur and its bright round eye, the caterpillar hiding plump in the smoky mud-walled hut, and saw the men the animal costumes disguised.

"And the hare goes to see the spotted one, the leopard, and says to him, 'Let us go so that you can talk to the big man who is in my hut.'

"And the leopard says, 'Let us go.' And they go, and when they arrive the leopard says, 'Who is in the hut of my friend the hare?'

The caterpillar responded as he had responded before, Crown said. Some of the *moran* chanted it with him, quietly, to themselves.

"'*Pasa!*' says the leopard. 'If he can crush the elephant and the rhinoceros, he can crush me.'

"And the hare goes and calls the rhinoceros, and he says, 'Come, I pray you, drive away the big man who is in my hut.'

"The rhinoceros comes, and he says, 'Who is in the hut of my friend the hare?'

"'I am the warrior son of the Long One,' the caterpillar says, repeating the refrain.

"Now when the rhinoceros hears these words, he says, '*He! Ai!* He can crush me to the earth! I had better go away.'"

They laughed at the *He!* and the *Ai!*, the rhino like a

timid farmer curling its toes and backing off. The story
scaled up in size, inflating like a bladder, to be punctured
with the caterpillar's pretension at the end.

"And the hare goes and calls the elephant, and he comes,
and he says, 'Who is in the hut of my friend the hare?'

"And the caterpillar responds as before, and '*Aiigaa!*' the
elephant says. 'He can make me into cow's dung. I won't
venture against him.'"

Crown had lain in the darkness in the encampment of his
young manhood, his age group at ease around, and the
young girls had slipped in among them, girls that in any
Western culture would be children, girls uncircumcised,
with small buddings of breasts but beaded and knowing,
and never lifting the girls' maiden aprons they had moved
together in innocent orgy and made love passionately with
hands and mouths. Like all *moran,* the *moran* of his encampment might never be alone, not even to relieve themselves. They had painted each other's bodies, dressed each
other's hair, exchanged with each other the milk they were
forbidden to drink from their own family cows. Until they
were one, intimate and equal. Like these, Crown thought.
And but for Cassie I would give all that I know and have to
be one of them again.

The *moran* had quieted, anticipating the end.

"And the hare goes to the frog, and says to him, 'Come,
please, and see if you can drive out the big man who is in
my hut whom the others have not been able to move.'

"And the frog says, 'Let us go.' And they go, and the frog
says, 'Who is in the hut of my friend the hare?'

"'I am the warrior son of the Long One,' the caterpillar
says, 'whose anklet became unfastened when we fought in
Kurtaile. I crush the rhinoceros to the earth. I make cow's
dung of the elephant. None dare venture against me.'

"But the frog moves closer to the house, and he says, 'I
have come! I am strong, and I am a leaper, with buttocks

like a post, and Engai the great God has put vileness in me!'

"The frog moves closer, and the caterpillar trembles, and trembling he says to the frog, 'I am only a caterpillar! I am only a caterpillar!'"

They howled with laughter. To be one of them again. Tonight he was, and would be tomorrow.

"Well," Crown finished, "the animals seize him and drag him out of the hut, and they all laugh at the trouble he has given them to put him out."

Simel hissed to silence the *moran*. "We have seen this frog, my *aputani*," he said, chuckling. "He is the man called Mugwa. Engai has surely put vileness in him."

"He is a reliable man," Crown said. "Not all have the fortune to be born Masai."

"I know why you have told us this story the night before the raid," said Sitonik.

Crown smiled in the darkness. "Good."

"I will not tell its meaning, but will leave my brothers to discover it for themselves."

"Let them think on it," Crown said. He stood. "I will leave you now, my sons. I will come again for you before dawn and we will do this thing of duty. Sleep well."

"We are honored to be chosen, my *aputani*," Simel said for them all.

"*O*," Crown said. "I see Masai."

He found Mugwa and Abdi sitting on the ground outside the tent, talking quietly and watching the forest mists drift past the moon. Mugwa was smoking a pipe.

"The sergeant tells me of the old days of elephant hunting, Effendi," Abdi said when Crown sat down beside them.

"When was this?" Crown asked Mugwa.

"Back long time ago, Grandfathers' days. Back when no guns."

"Your people?"

"My people. Other people. Kill damn elephant with

spears." Mugwa drew on his pipe and the bowl glowed red.
"Take maybe hundred men with spears, maybe ten runners.
Spearmen hide in forest. Hide behind trees, rocks, hide in
bushes. Runners know where they hide. So runners find
some damn elephant, get him mad, make him chase them.
They take turns so they can run fast enough he don't catch
them. Run him into the forest past the spearmen. They stick
him good. Stick him everywhere. Hundred spears, hundred
sticks. Finally damn elephant weak. Spearmen make a sur-
round. Crowd him in somewhere he can't get out. Blood everywhere, crap, piss. Damn elephant slip. Fall down. Come
down like damn mountain falling. Elephant get down, can't
get up. Spearmen come in and finish him off. Then they all
fagged out. Sleep. Next day they go after damn elephant's
insides. Every man cut his own hole into the hide. Damn
thick. Crawl in like the vulture. Man cuts up parts he likes,
liver, breads, big heart, guts, belly fat. Guts everywhere.
Hard to see. Every man in a big, big hurry. Wants to get it
all for himself, feed his family. You know what happen?
Long time ago? One man in there slicing away, another
damn man grab his balls. Thinks they're breads, best breads
he ever found. Cuts them right off." Mugwa slapped his
knee and laughed his thick laugh. "Cuts them right off. So
after that, man don't go into no damn elephant alone. Gets
his wife. Wife follows him into elephant holding his balls.
True. Wife holds back his damn balls."

They laughed with him, looking at each other amused.

Mugwa knocked out his pipe. "I got packs for you. You
want to check them?"

"Might as well," Crown said.

They stood. "How many grenades you want?" Mugwa
asked.

"I think we'll skip the grenades and load on more clips,"
Crown said, looking down at the sergeant. "We've got to
keep up with the *moran*."

"Fine damn boys," Mugwa said. "Take out those bandits easy." He turned and led them into the tent.

Later they slept, Mugwa's men taking shifts to guard. On toward morning a hyrax screamed.

Twelve

SUNLIGHT BRIGHTENED the forest floor as the line of men climbed, Crown in the lead with Abdi and Tomasi, the *moran* following, Mugwa and his commandos bringing up the rear. The light beamed down in bands through the high, leafy canopy, dividing and redividing across trailers of liana, raising mists where it struck the spongy compost and flashing their eyes, making the forest seem to move. In rain the forest had been gloomy and still; now it came alive. Duikers whistled. Bushbuck blurred chestnut across the trail. Birds darted and swooped in the canopy, green warblers, clacking hornbills, red and blue trogons, bright touracos gliding to a perch. Wild orange sweetened the air; cedar freshened it; wild coffee and pepper made it pungent above the musty gasses the compost released. Mountain taberna bloomed with white flowers and orchids spiked pale green on the dark branches of African mahoganies; lizards skittered around the trunks. Crown saw, and saw the cheap scarred milling on the loaded rifle clip that curved up like an iron

tiller at his hand, the stain of fear that darkened Tomasi's
back.

The trail led them eastward around Olmoti on a gradual
ascent. It was one of the trails the guerrillas used. Least
used, Tomasi had said. It was less direct and longer than the
trail the Chaggas had cut before, but better for surprise. It
would cross the bamboo and approach the camp from
higher up. They meant to sweep the camp before the guerrillas could retreat into the denser bamboo downhill. That
was a hole in the plan. Assuming the guerrillas retreated.
That was a gaping hole.

Crown stepped off the trail and signaled Abdi to take his
place behind Tomasi in the lead. The *moran* began passing.
They nodded to him respectfully. They used their spears as
walking sticks. They were lithe at climbing, not even breathing hard. A climb was nothing. In a day and an evening
they could walk a hundred kilometers. But the humidity
heated them and some climbed naked, their blankets rolled
and tied across their chests. Their gourds, hung on thongs
over their shoulders, clicked against their belts. They'd cool
out up above. Their nakedness was natural. The Masai
weren't a prudish tribe, not compared to the others. Nakedness had become a political issue. Nyerere had pushed
through a law requiring the Masai to wear pants. They
obeyed it, most of them, in town, but hardly ever went to
town. Elders went to town to drink in low-roofed *dukas*.
Harvey's Bristol Cream Sherry was the latest fad. *Moran*
weren't allowed to drink. Nyerere should have left the
Masai alone. Tanzania was lucky they'd accepted Uhuru
peacefully. They'd make formidable guerrillas. Trained in
weapons and riled, they'd soon be pasturing their cattle in
Dar. They already had a country within a country, but submitted to the larger authority, and ran it well except for
overgrazing. The *moran* hadn't turned out as a favor to

Nyerere. They were here because Rukuma had violated the laws of their land.

Mugwa came up. Crown waved him past and stepped back onto the trail behind him. He was heavily armed, a Kalashnikov on his shoulder, a pack lined with clips, black grenades hanging from his webbing belt ringing his waist. He went bareheaded. Against regulations he'd ordered his men to leave their helmets behind, packed in the lorry with the camp gear. He wanted them light and fast and counted as much as Crown did on surprise.

"I have thought again of the planning," Crown said in Swahili. "The opening downhill is bad."

Mugwa shrugged. "If we go quick enough we get them," he said without looking back. His hair was clipped military style. Rolls of flesh padded his short neck.

"We could position two of your men below the bamboo."

"Damn thin already. Bandits get away, what they do? Go shoot bushbuck?" He glanced around at Crown. "I talk blunt," he said, facing ahead again. "We got our damn hands full. They up there loafing, we all right. They up there cleaning weapons, we all right. They up there lock-and-loaded, we got plenty damn trouble. Better stick to plan. Hit damn bandits right away hard. I make sure we blow weapons *banda*. Stores *banda*. Then they stuck like old elephant hunter. Lost their balls. *Vema?* Okay?"

It was the best they could do. "*Vema*," Crown said, not liking it.

They climbed. Tomasi halted them in late morning at a spring. Cedars dominated now and it was darker in the forest and cooler. The going was easier without the tangles of vines the guerrillas had left at intervals to obscure the trail. The floor was thick with cedar needles drying aromatic and loose. The spring was hardly more than a seep and they took turns kneeling to drink and the water was fresh and cold. From that point on, Tomasi said, they must go silently.

Crown passed the word and they tightened their gear. The *moran* slung their gourds across their backs. Crown took up the lead again behind Tomasi and they climbed.

They came to the bamboo. They heard it before they emerged from the thinning forest onto its margins. They heard what sounded like gunfire. It startled Crown until he remembered what it was. Moisture trapped between the joints in the hollow bamboo expanded in the sun and the brittle tubes exploded. It was a fine sound like a carnival firing range and it would cover their approach.

Tomasi had trouble locating the opening into the bamboo. Crown and Abdi helped him look. At lower altitudes bamboo was good for as much as a foot of growth an hour and even this high, with the rains, it had overgrown the trail. Abdi signaled first. The trail through the bamboo was assembled from rhino trails and Abdi pointed to trefoil prints no more than two days old. With the noise of the bamboo they'd be lucky to hear a rhino before it charged them. Tomasi looked worried. Crown gripped his shoulder hard and turned him to his work.

They walked bent over, the bamboo catching and jerking the projecting barrels of the automatics and the spears of the *moran*, young stalks cutting them like blades of dry grass, clouds of flies swarming at their faces, biting, diving for their eyes. They knocked aside the thick webs of orb weavers and dodged the panicked spiders when they jumped. Cane rats scurried past their feet and they kicked at them. They crawled on their hands and knees over matted breaks flattened by storm that gave way under them and balanced across broken poles like sewer pipes that bridged deep, washed-out *korongos*. The bamboo blocked the stinging sun, but the sun heated the tunnel of the trail and they sweated despite the altitude, their skin and their lungs and their throats burning, chafed by the sharp crystalline silica dust of decayed bamboo. The bamboo fired. They were two hours crossing. When they assembled on the high, alpine meadow above the bamboo belt it was early afternoon.

The *moran* wrapped themselves in their blankets against the cold and followed Crown, Mugwa and his commandos separating, working northward through the golden grass. They were south of the camp and above it and Tomasi had said no sentry watched that unlikely approach. The grass was tall and golden and everywhere there were wild flowers fed on montane mists and grown enormous, blue gladiolas and orange, fireball lilies, yellow everlastings, beds of bushy russet heather, branching candelabra of scarlet aloes. They worked past stands of giant groundsel with craggy trunks and clusters of thick leaves at their crowns like bunched plantains. They started coveys of partridge hidden in the grass that exploded into the air and whirred off to better cover. Beyond Mugwa's line Crown saw a family of greater kudu bolt like deer from the nest where cows and calves had laid up for the day.

When Nguvu was in it, Crown thought, when it was a question of superior force, the terms were different. They were only going to round up criminals then. Now they advanced through a landscape of antelope and wild flowers to kill men. Men and women. It was bloody business. It wasn't what he'd signed on for.

Rukuma set the terms, didn't he?

Someone always sets the terms. That's the drill.

When was Africa anything but bloody business? The settlers' jape: miles and miles of bloody Africa. It was crude and physical and you took it personally or you didn't survive. When Sidanu was living, at the ranch in Kenya, they'd heard Joseph scream one night from his crib and raced to the nursery to find his thrashing infant body covered with *siafu,* biting red ants, the crib and the floor seething with them. They got him out, but the *siafu* had locked their mandibles into his skin and had to be removed painfully one by

one. Crown cleared the nursery with kerosene and boiling
water and pyrethrum. First the *siafu* swarmed over the help-
less body; then, on signal, they bit, all at once. And with one
mind killed chickens, lambs, calves, the wild young of cats
and jackals in their dens, and drove larger animals to frenzy.
Engai stayed aloof on his sacred mountain. Down below the
earth oozed with casual brutality, and sooner or later you
cleared it with brutality of your own.

He itched.

Mugwa signaled. Crown stopped and Abdi and the line of
moran stopped and closed up behind them and Mugwa and
his men pulled away, Tomasi leading them down toward the
bamboo. They would enter it again just south of the camp
and take out the sentries and wait. First the *moran*. Beyond
the near rise was the sunning place. Below the sunning
place was the camp. Crown marked the time.

Fifteen minutes. The sunning place was an outcropped
lava platform. Tomasi had said the guerrillas took the sun in
the morning to warm up after the cold night. No one was
there. Crouching, his Kalashnikov armed and in hand,
Crown led the *moran* running down to the platform and
looked for the trail. It began just north and below the outcropping. He jumped to it. It was narrow. They went single
file. Crown and Abdi and then the *moran*. It tunneled
through the bamboo. Their eyes adjusted to the gloom. The
bamboo fired around them. Crown saw light ahead and
heard voices. Swahili. Tomasi's map. The circle of men's
banda directly beyond the tunnel. Rukuma's larger *banda*
three hundred yards north, to the right. The women's *banda*
between. The ordnance and the stores north toward
Rukuma's, downhill. The mouth of the tunnel. Abdi, the
moran crowding in behind.

Crown broke running from the tunnel and veered right.
The weight of the Kalashnikov held out from his waist unbalanced him and made the running awkward. He hit his

position and swung the Kalashnikov around and braced. The circle of houses began twenty feet in front of him. It surrounded a large clearing. Rukuma's guerrillas were out in the clearing, any number of them. The ground sloped away so that the far houses were lower than the near houses and showed more roof. Farther downhill, beyond the far houses, the bamboo glared yellow. Everything was as brilliant and fixed as if the sun had stopped.

They were huts, really, bamboo huts. Yellow-ivory spotted brown. Thatched. They'd sleep four at best. Grass in the clearing. Up here long enough for grass to grow. Settled in. How many guerrillas? Most of them. Maybe all of them. That one with his head shaved. He's laughing. He's just told a joke. A near bunch and a bunch across the clearing and they're all in fatigues. Olive drab. They'd cooked. You could smell it. What? Meat. Stewed. Groundnuts. You could smell the slit trenches too. They're loading packs. M-16s leaned against the packs. The one lacing up his boot. Pots and gear. Blankets spread out in the sun. Olive drab also. Good equipment. Right, they're getting ready to move out. We got here just in time. Those two over there field-stripping a mortar. Long greasy braids and that one with a beard. Two coming out of the far hut. But they've all got their rifles. They've all got their bloody goddamned rifles.

The sun moved. Abdi was clear and veering left to the other flank. The *moran* spilled from the tunnel. They divided around the near hut, fanning out. The guerrilla with the shaved head saw them and his mouth snapped shut. The *moran* drew back their spears screaming a battle chant, *Aiii! Aiiii!/ Aiii! Aiiii!*, and the guerrillas shouted, scattered, dove for the cover of their packs. Coming around a hut Crown saw a spear punch into a guerrilla's chest and splash out through his shoulders. The *moran* closed with the guerrillas, clubbing. A guerrilla was up on the far side with an M-16. He couldn't decide to shoot into the mix-up of guerrillas and *moran*. Crown fired a rattling burst from the Kalashnikov and cut him down.

The firing sprang Mugwa from hiding. Crown saw the commandos rushing the circle of huts from the south, automatic rifles crackling, picking off guerrillas escaping between the huts. The guerrillas away from the melee of the *moran* were down behind their packs and the commandos used the huts as cover and pinned them there. Abdi reached Crown blowing from the run and they withdrew north. Leave the fire fight to Mugwa. They're ripped. Get Rukuma. You didn't come up here for a slaughter. It's Rukuma you want.

There was standing bamboo north of the circle. The grass around the tunnel mouth was beaten down. A woman came out of the tunnel with an M-16. She was thin, chocolate-brown, in men's fatigues with the sleeves and the pants rolled up. She saw them and swung the barrel of the M-16 with its conical barrel cover toward Crown. Abdi shot her and she screamed and dropped the M-16 and fell.

Crown jumped to the tunnel entrance firing but the tunnel was empty. He ran it. It was cut straight through the bamboo and it opened on another, smaller clearing on a steeper slope. He looked out quickly and ducked back. Angled to the left was the women's *banda*, downhill. They'd seen only the one woman so far and the others must be there or up at Rukuma's. Then a woman cut across the clearing making for the tunnel on the other side and Crown fired and missed and she was into the tunnel and screened. Rounds tore the bamboo over his head. He pulled back into the tunnel backing Abdi behind him and crouched and another burst ripped the bamboo.

"It's coming from the *banda*," Crown said.

"The firing is high," Abdi said. "I think that the angle is wrong."

"I'm going out." Crown crawled on his elbows to the end

of the tunnel. He had to turn the Kalashnikov to keep the
long banana clip from dragging. From the ground he could
see only the thatched roof of the house. The clearing was
grass with outcroppings of black volcanic rock. He could
have used a grenade about now. Rukuma could be going for
the machine guns. "Abdi," he said over his shoulder. "Cover
me."

"I am here, Effendi," Abdi said.

Crown crawled out into the clearing keeping low, watching the house. So long as he could see only the thatch he
was out of the line of fire. When Crown was well away from
the tunnel Abdi began pumping short bursts at the women's
banda to draw their fire. They fired back high and Crown
made it to one of the outcroppings and around the side and
then looking down he could see all the house, the barrels of
M-16s at the door and the near window. Up on his knee he
swept the house with a long, sustained burst, emptying the
clip, the bamboo splintering, shatterings flashing in the sun,
and heard a woman scream. He ducked down behind the
outcropping and locked in another clip but there was no
more return fire and the screaming had stopped. Abdi ran
crouched across the clearing. Crown met him at the mouth
of the tunnel where the woman had run and Rukuma's
banda and the ordnance and stores *banda* were up the tunnel and where the hell was Mugwa? But there was still
firing behind them at the circle of men's huts.

"Hit it," Crown said.

The tunnel through the bamboo to Rukuma's part of the
camp was longer and it turned in the middle so that they
couldn't see to the end. They ran to the turn and dropped
prone. Crown rolled out firing but the second half of the
tunnel was clear. It didn't make sense unless Rukuma was
making his stand at the buildings. He'd had time to go for
the Brens by now. Waiting wouldn't cut it either. Make up
your mind. Wait for Mugwa or get going. Get going then.

Crown worked forward to the end of the tunnel, Abdi watching at the turn. Rukuma's *banda* was twice as big as the women's. It had a porch and the door was open and the shutter flaps on the windows cranked up and Crown couldn't see anyone inside. He fired a burst at the house. There was no response and he fired again, sweeping across the wall just below window level. One of the poles supporting the porch roof splintered and the roof collapsed on that side. Crown heard shooting then in the bamboo and backed up into the tunnel and then he realized it was only the bamboo exploding.

So the house was empty too. Wasn't that amazing. Rukuma would have heard the fire fight. All or most of his men were back there. What would you do? If forty men couldn't stop whoever was attacking the camp then there wouldn't be much chance that you could stop them so what would you do? Even if you had mortars and grenades and light machine guns? Hell, I'd do what I could. I'd sure as hell give it a try. But if you were the messiah who was going to weld all of Africa into one great superpower what would you do? I'd fly over them and zap them with angels and archangels. Besides that. If you weren't brevetted for the Second Coming yet. You'd get the hell out, wouldn't you? I wouldn't. If you were Rukuma you would. Sure you would. Take off for the bamboo. Crown suddenly understood where Rukuma had rounded up all the equipment. The M-16s, the mortars, the grenades, the quality blankets and fatigues and boots. Indochina: Vietnam or Cambodia. The business of his mysterious flight to Bangkok. What did they call Cambodia now? Democratic Kampuchea? There was plenty more where that stuff came from. Vietnam was something like the third or fourth best-armed country in the world just from the ordnance the Americans dumped when they abandoned ship, and Cambodia wasn't far behind. The Americans, he thought. You're an American too. I didn't get into that mess,

though. That wasn't my mess. I was just over here mindin'
my taters, as my daddy used to say. That wasn't your mess,
but this is your mess, isn't it. Right. Hell of a mess. Just a
hell of a mess.

Crown loaded another clip and called Abdi and then he
was running to the near window of the *banda* with his
Kalashnikov up and Abdi at the tunnel covering him but the
house was empty. Abdi came across and they rounded the
house and saw the trail that led downhill through thin,
widely spaced bamboo to the stores *banda*. Rukuma would
be crazy to hole up in the ordnance *banda*. If he's set a defense anywhere it must be the stores. Unless they really did
just take off. Take off down the mountain and leave the
others to fight it out. Rukuma wasn't enough of a bastard to
do that, was he? Who said he wasn't? That's what he did at
the camp that night. There'd been no women at the men's
huts and one at the tunnel and two at the women's house so
he'd have the one woman with him and how many men?

There was an outcropping down the trail directly above
the stores *banda* and they crawled to it for cover. Low and
flat-roofed, the stores *banda* was built of rock piled between
bamboo uprights and caulked with mud. The roof was rusty
iron corrugate with thatch laid over the corrugate. The
banda was windowless and the wooden, corrugate-faced
door was shut. Crown fired downhill into the door, the
rounds punching the sheet iron and racketing. When he
eased off someone kicked the door open and he saw the
bipod and the flared barrel of the Bren and pulled back
behind the outcropping and the stuttering .303s tore the
rock. They'd have to wait for Mugwa now to come up with
the grenades but at least whoever was inside the stores was
pinned. It wouldn't be Rukuma inside the stores, you could
count on that. It would be more of his disciples. Rukuma
was damned prodigal with his disciples.

Crown fired intermittent bursts to keep the guerrillas

pinned at the machine gun. Abdi worked his way back to
the house and beyond it to the tunnel mouth to cover the
rear. The rock of the outcropping beside Crown's face was
charcoal gray and porous, bubbled like pumice, and the
heavy rounds from the Bren screeched and gouged it as they
ricocheted. Crown listened for firing in Mugwa's direction
beyond the bamboo. Quiet over there. They ought to be
mopping up by now. The *moran* took out enough of the
guerrillas in that first charge to even up the odds and
Mugwa had them down in the open. The surprise worked
but it was bastard luck that they'd had their rifles out. It
was bastard luck too about the women. Why was it any
different with the women? They weren't exactly grinding
mahindi when you came on them. That one Abdi took out at
the tunnel wasn't. The two at the *banda*. To hell with the
women. To hell with them all.

Then Abdi was beside him with Mugwa and one of the
commandos. The commando looked like Mugwa, short and
broad. Mugwa must have hand-picked him. Buttocks like a
post.

"What you got here?" Mugwa asked. His face was
scratched and one sleeve of his fatigue blouse was torn.

"*Kuna* machine gun," Crown said. "There's a machine
gun."

"*Wapi?* Where?"

The Bren fired and Mugwa knew.

"It's in the stores *banda*," Crown said. "Can you put a
grenade down there?"

Mugwa grunted and handed the commando his Kalashnikov and unclipped an M32 from his belt. He pulled the cot-
ter-pin ring and held down the safety lever and bobbed up
to find his range and dropped back as the rounds flared off
the rock. He waited a beat and then he bobbed up again
and tossed the grenade and they flattened behind the outcropping and seconds later the grenade went off and the ex-

plosion blew a litter of bamboo past them overhead. Mugwa
bobbed up once more to check the damage and stayed up
and took back his automatic. "Burn their butts, by damn,"
he said. He was around the outcropping and running down
the trail and Crown came out running to cover him and then
Abdi and the commando. The grenade had blown the door
off the stores *banda* and peeled back the roof. Food tins
were scattered across the slope and the two guerrillas who
had manned the Bren were thrown torn against the exposed
rear wall.

They sheltered in front of the stores. "Where that damn
weapons *banda?*" Mugwa asked.

"There." Crown pointed. The ordnance *banda* southwest
and farther downhill through sparse bamboo was built like
the stores but twice as massive. Southward the bamboo
thickened again to a screen glaring in the sun.

"What you think?" Mugwa asked Crown. "Think more
damn bandits over there?"

"That's the only place left."

Abdi and the commando watched around the side,
crouched in the rubble of the ruined front wall.

"Better reconnoiter," Mugwa said. The technical term in
Swahili surprised Crown. "I go out. You cover me. *Vema?*"

"*Vema,*" Crown said.

Mugwa worked cautiously down the trail. Halfway to the
point where the trail turned toward the ordnance *banda* he
dropped to his belly and swept the bamboo with fire. There
was no return fire and he got up and ran, Crown firing over
him now, but he hesitated at the turn, looking toward the
bamboo farther south as if he'd seen something Crown
couldn't see from above, and an M-16 pocked from within
the bamboo in the direction Mugwa was looking and he
jumped and seemed to dance and then a round hit one of his
grenades and he disappeared in a yellow roaring flash and
Crown flung himself behind the protection of the stores as

the other grenades went off thumping and shrapnel sung past the stores.

Crown was up then and out on the trail and Abdi and the commando furiously raking the bamboo where the M-16 had been. They ran down the hill through the gray drifting smoke and flattened at the turn and fired clip after clip into the bamboo until they had shattered it as far to the south as they could sector without hitting the ordnance *banda* and they didn't look at the twisted broken body bloody on the ground.

Whoever had fired from the bamboo wasn't firing now. They pushed up and ran along the trail to the ordnance *banda*. It looked even bigger up close. A rusted padlock hung from the latch and the door was open. The commando kicked the door. His face was contorted. The door swung squeaking on its hinges and when it swung back he kicked it again.

"Is the camp secure behind us?" Crown asked the commando in Swahili.

"*Ndiyo*," he said. He clicked the empty clip from his Kalashnikov and flung it angrily up the slope.

"Let's blow this son-of-a-bitch," Crown said in English to Abdi. He pushed the door back against the wall. There were steel canisters of rifle rounds stacked on the dirt floor inside and wooden crates of grenades and mortar shells and the polished blue-black tubes of mortars. Crown used a mortar tube as a brace to prop open the door and dragged one of the grenade crates onto the sill.

They ran, the commando covering their rear, back up the trail to the shelter of the stores. When the commando came up Crown steadied the Kalashnikov against the wall and fired at the grenade crate. The rounds went in high, spraying the wall above the door. Crown fired again and hit the crate and light flashed and he ducked back and then the booming, rolling explosion shook the ground, grenades thumping and the rounds popping like strings of fire-crackers, mortar shells whining, shrapnel and blown rock spraying overhead. The concussion smacked the stores *banda* and wrapped around them and their ears rang. They looked out to swirling smoke, hot rounds still popping, and as the smoke cleared they saw the bamboo flattened in a great circle around the hole where the ordnance *banda* had been and the smoke drifted over to them the acrid stink of cordite.

The commando spat. *"Vizuri,"* he said. *"Vizuri sana.* Very good."

Moran knelt over the bodies of their wounded brothers at the clearing within the circle of men's huts. On the other side of the clearing, well away from the *moran,* the commandos had herded together the guerrillas they had captured. The guerrillas sat on the ground looking sullen, their hands behind their heads. Crown counted eight of them. It wasn't likely, he thought, but maybe Rukuma hadn't gotten away. Maybe they'd caught or killed him. He wouldn't necessarily be wearing his halo. He might be in there pretending to be a mere disciple or he might be one of these holy martyrs sprawled all over the clearing. Tomasi would know.

"What happened to Tomasi?" Crown asked the commando. They had run back from Rukuma's part of the camp.

"He stayed within the bamboo when we attacked," the commando said.

"Perhaps he is hiding, Effendi," said Abdi.

"Tomasi! Get your butt out here!" He wouldn't know the English, Crown thought, but he'd appreciate the tone of voice.

Tomasi appeared in the doorway of one of the huts. Crown waved him out. The captured guerrillas watched him cross and Crown heard them cursing. Tomasi avoided looking at them.

He was eager. "It is as I said, Bwana Crown," he started.

"*Tulia!*" Crown ordered. "Be silent! We want to know if Rukuma is among the dead or the captured. Have you searched for him?"

"*La,* Bwana."

"Go and search."

"I am afraid."

"You will be protected," Crown said. "Go and search." To Abdi in English he said: "Take this pitiful bastard and check all the bodies, *mzee.* Check the ones they've captured and check those two back at the stores. See if Rukuma's anywhere around and get a complete count, will you?"

Abdi nodded and took Tomasi's arm and led him off.

Crown turned to the commando. "Tell your men to prepare for the return to the lower camp."

"*Ndiyo,*" the commando said.

Simel noticed Crown then and trotted over. He had retrieved his spear and cleaned it.

"How many have been killed of the *moran?*" Crown asked him in Masai.

"Ten and one, my *aputani.*" Simel counted by hand gestures as he spoke, a circle of thumb and forefinger and then a forefinger pointed alone. He extended two fingers, holding down the others with his thumb. "Six are wounded."

"We must leave the bodies here. Some of those whom we attacked have run away, but I do not believe that they will return. They will not desecrate the bodies."

"The vultures will clean the bodies."

Crown hadn't noticed: the vultures on the ground beyond the huts. Since the Masai didn't dig in the earth they didn't bury their dead, except the *il'laibon.* "Are those who are wounded able to walk?"

"Some are able."

"Cut bamboo to make carriers. Use the blankets."

"*O.*" Simel gestured. "We killed many more than they killed of us."

"I see that the *moran* fought well. Go and prepare. We must leave quickly to arrive below before the night."

Simel rejoined the *moran* and two of them left to cut poles for stretchers. Crown counted the commandos. Six, two of them bandaged but on their feet. So three dead and Mugwa. Poor bastard. Poor tough marvelous bastard. He was almost done and he'd done it well against ugly odds and he ought to have been promoted and decorated for it. He ought to have caught up with Nguvu at the west lake and had a shot at Amin's boys. They'd be feeding the crocs by now. And then gone home, back to his pocket valley and his wives. All these people dead. One man's megalomania and all these people dead. Crown joined the *moran* to check the wounded.

Abdi came back with Tomasi. "Rukuma has escaped, Effendi," he said, shaking his head.

"Bloody hell."

"It seems five of the guerrillas and one woman escaped with him if the count Tomasi has made is correct."

Crown looked at Tomasi. Tomasi nodded sheepishly. "Bloody hell," Crown swore again. He pushed Tomasi aside and crossed with Abdi to the guerrillas sitting on the ground. "Where is your leader Rukuma?" He asked them angrily. They stared ahead. "You," Crown said, picking out the guerrilla he'd noticed earlier whose head was shaved. "Where is Rukuma?" The guerrilla didn't answer. "Shoot him," Crown said to Abdi.

Abdi unshouldered his Kalashnikov and clicked off the safety.

"Rukuma is gone," the guerrilla said.

"You murderous bastard," Crown said under his breath. In Swahili: "We have seen that Rukuma is gone. Where would he go? Where would a brave leader go who leaves his followers to be killed and captured?"

"He has gone to safety," another guerrilla with a deep

voice said, "so that he may fight again." He glared at Crown. "There will be many, many battles and one day there will be victory. Victory for the people and death to the *wahindi* and the *wazungu* who oppress our land! Death to the *wabenzi!*"

He must be Rukuma's shouter, Crown thought. "To hell with it," he said to Abdi. "Let's get moving."

Tomasi guided them down a different trail, the trail Rukuma's scouts had used to watch Nguvu's movements. It was shorter than the trail they had followed coming up and it led close to the army camp. Once they negotiated the bamboo it was obvious and Crown wondered why the army patrols hadn't found it.

The commandos had tied the guerrillas' hands behind their backs. After the bamboo Crown put the guerrillas second in line to Tomasi and himself, for insurance. Rukuma could be set up in ambush anywhere along the way.

They came out of the cedar zone into the lower forest. The birds were nesting. Behind Crown a wounded guerrilla moaned. Sunlight filtered through the canopy low and red.

Heading home, Crown thought. Idly he thought: if you were Rukuma now, just you and Mary Magdalene and five disciples on foot in the bush, what would you do? And saw suddenly, as he smugly, stupidly hadn't seen before: saw the scouts on the porch of the *banda*, saw the big man silhouetted in the doorway listen and laugh: why the trail was obvious: why whoever had used it last hadn't bothered to lace its vines and branches back: what Rukuma would do: where Rukuma would go.

"Abdi!" he shouted down the line. "Come on!"

They ran out the trail. At dusk, stumbling, they came to the camp. There was broken window glass and a dump of Mugwa's gear. The helmets were gone and the rations, and the freshly cut branches that had camouflaged the lorry were strewn on the ground.

Thirteen

"Turn off the lights, Chaudi," Rukuma said. "Unless you are night-blind. On the plain the moon is light enough." Rukuma rode where Crown had ridden before, in the left front seat of the lorry, the woman guerrilla Kare beside him, the guerrilla Chaudi driving, the four others who had escaped the attack on the camp on the stake bed behind, under the canvas, and the warm night air blew into the cab through the empty frame of the broken window where Rukuma braced his massive arm.

Chaudi switched off the headlights. Their eyes adjusted and the stars came out. The track west across the Serengeti opened a dark wound through the tarnished silver grass.

"There is blood in the air," Rukuma said. He thought: under the moon the zebra become invisible.

The woman Kare covered his hand with her own. Her hand was cool, the bones long and thin, the palm rough with the dignity of calluses. There was consolation in her hand. He shook it off. It retreated to her lap, down by her belly.

The wire snares of the poachers. The zebra caught and choked. The carcasses of the flayed zebra, fat-yellow and meat-maroon. The scraped and salted hides.

He remembered hunting. He examined the memory for knowledge useful to him now and found none and pushed it away uneaten.

The hides like fingerprints.

He was thirty years old.

"What will we do?" Chaudi asked. Kare glanced at him sharply.

Rukuma thought: they imagined that they had won. Seth Crown imagined. The general's soldiers, the pretty buck *moran*. When they saw that the lorry was gone they would know that they had lost. He outran them everywhere. It was not even a setback.

"Rukuma? What will we do?"

"Do not question, Chaudi," Rukuma said. "Drive." Millions and millions were nameless, Rukuma thought. Their only weapons were their lives. Africa was a river of weapons. Asia was a flood.

The nameless saw the satellites streak across the night blackness. They saw the high cloud-trails of passing jets. The nameless scratched out a bare subsistence on the thin surface of the earth. Each one of those who exploited them weighed down a thousand of the nameless. More. Ten thousand. For want of names the nameless ballooned with *kwashiorkor*.

Rukuma had watched the fighting from the bamboo. Crown was a hunter. Rukuma had thought that Crown might come out hunting when the general and his soldiers went off to play with Amin, but not so soon. He had forgotten about the *moran*. It didn't matter. He had killed the ugly little sergeant. His men had killed soldiers and *moran*, the tourists at the camp before, the decadent scholar of *kifaru*, the Kenyans at the post. With forty of the nameless

he had eliminated as many as twenty of those who exploited
them. The nameless were then two hundreds of thousands
ahead, less the forty or so that were lost. In the mathematics
of namelessness forty was a naught.

To lay waste. It was simple. He was surprised no one had
conceived of it before. It required no ideology, no education, no base of capital, no technology other than what
might be found and gathered. It required no history. The
nameless had no history. They copulated and squatted and
brought forth nameless as invisible as the zebra under the
moon. It required only to violate the exploiters equally and
everywhere as they violated the nameless. To lay waste. Not
even the bombs, not even the missiles could prevail against
so simple a principle. It would spread as Christianity and
Mohammedanism had spread. It would bathe the earth in
blood, not as Christianity and Mohammedanism had bathed
the earth in blood, to the obscene thickening of privilege,
but as a *shamba* is bathed with water by the long rains. And
then the earth would flower for the nameless.

He had intended to sweep down on Ngorongoro and restore his transport. He had intended to ravage Seronera and
complete the ravaging of Crown's camp and return to the
mountain to rest. He saw now that he had planned on too
small a scale and there could be no rest. Guerrilla warfare
was an inadequate means. He must go among the nameless
himself. He must shrug and shed his skin and swim up
among the nameless and mass them for larger revolution.
But first he would finish what was begun.

"Stop the lorry," Rukuma said. "Leave the engine running. Come around to the back with the others, Kare, curious Chaudi, and I will tell you what we will do."

Crown had felt exhausted before, at the army camp, waiting
stricken, waiting infuriated for the line of men to come in off
the trail. He felt only anger now, a cold boiling of the blood.

Walking out. To achieve the lodge at Ngorongoro and borrow a car. If Nguvu hadn't already commandeered every vehicle they had. To descend to the Serengeti. To cross to the
camp. To make it safe. It wasn't safe with Rukuma loose. He
might run. He might not. You've consistently underes-
timated the bastard, Crown thought. It's cost you. It could
cost you a hell of a lot more.

He'd thought of leaving a note and going on, but he
didn't know if any of the commandos could read. He was
obligated to the commandos and even more to the *moran*.
When the commandos arrived they saw the signs as quickly
as he and Abdi had but they felt no urgency. They would
rest and then walk out to the lodge, contact the district
police at Arusha, turn the guerrillas over to them, go back to
Arusha or go on to the west lake. They were soldiers and
Tanzania was skirmishing at war. The wounded *moran*,
even those their brothers had carried down the mountain,
attached no importance to their wounds. The *moran* would
rest at the camp and carry their wounded home. He had
gone ahead then with Abdi, Abdi as implacably angry as he.

They kept their packs, lightened of everything but clips,
and kept their Kalashnikovs. The moon brightened the
track. The track cut through the dark forest, crossing the
saddle between Olmoti and Ngorongoro. Tree partridge had
flown in late and cackled to their nests. Hyrax had screamed
after sundown. Otherwise the forest was still.

You always ended up on foot in bloody Africa, Crown
thought, yet there were sectors of the forest around them
where no man had ever walked, not European, not Nilotic,
not Bantu, not even Dorobo. Nowhere else on earth was the
night darker even under the moon. It didn't bother him.
He'd hunted too many years to feel uneasy in the bush. But
the convulsion of fear at the camp when he saw the broken
glass bothered him. Its shape was Rukuma's laugh that he'd
never heard. He'd wondered if he could stay on his feet. It

had felt like dying and he'd thought that it was death, a convulsion of mortality around his failure to foresee what Rukuma would do, but it wasn't death. After fifty you got to know death. You slept less and you talked to it. You explained what you were about. It didn't seem to mind. It yawned and crawled in with you, inside the bag of skin you wore. It was just another scavenger. Death was a scavenger in Africa. In Africa death came and went in the space of a single afternoon, cleaning up the flesh and even the bones. Robert was lucky to find so much as a rare gnawed skull.

If you had a purpose in life then death was probably harder. He'd never had much purpose. His purpose had been simply to live and do no serious harm. He'd never understood the Rukumas of the world with their fanatical grasping at purpose. The world didn't have a purpose. No animal he'd ever seen had any purpose. They were so many bright, unstrung beads thrown up into the air. Human beings too. You went on. These dominated or those. This happened or that, this was learned, that was forgotten. Pain taken away here was given over there. Maybe this time around the Europeans were doing the giving. Next time the others would. It had been the Masai before, the Arabs, the Portuguese, hell, the Egyptians, the Babylonians, all the way back. The whole great cage made no sense except for the curiosity of its construction. What was the sense?

Abdi stopped him.

"*Ndovu*," Abdi whispered. "Elephant."

Crown listened. The track turned ahead, following the ridge of the saddle. He heard the rumble of elephant stomachs around the bend.

They went up. The cows stood in the track in the moonlight.

"We may avoid them through the forest, Effendi," Abdi whispered.

"There isn't time." Crown unshouldered the Kalashnikov

and clicked off the safety. The cows heard the click and
their heads lifted and they started to turn. Crown fired into
the air and the forest fired, the cows trumpeting and crashing off the track, birds squawking from the canopy, colobus
monkeys belching a relay of alarms. When the track was
clear Crown led on and the forest reassembled the machin-
ery of its silence.

They crossed the saddle and began the march uphill, up
Ngorongoro.

That clutch of fear, Crown thought. It wasn't death. It
was the dropping weight of his obligation to Cassie. He'd
said two days. She expected him back tonight, in the lorry,
and Rukuma had the lorry.

But there were guards at the camp.

But the guards were looking for the lorry to come in.

"And when that work is finished?" Kare asked, climbing into
the cab of the lorry.

"Then we will see," Rukuma said easily. He swung in beside her. "I have heard that the *Mzee* Jomo Kenyatta is
dying. Perhaps we will go up into Kenya and see what we
can make of that."

Close to Crown's camp, on the track through the open forest
south of the plain, the lorry slowed and Rukuma and then
Kare jumped from the cab. Chaudi switched on the headlights and accelerated, smoothly shifting gears. The guerrillas rode standing in the back of the lorry. They were
wearing the helmets the soldiers had left behind. They held
onto the stake racks and they swayed with the lorry's lurching on the rough track. Rukuma shouldered his M-16 and
watched them go. When the lorry was well away, he led the
woman across the track and cut northwest toward the lake.

They ran among fever trees blotched with shadow, using
the moonlight. The lodge wasn't far and they could hear the

grunt-laughs of hyena prowling at the lake shore. A resting
giraffe loomed in silhouette and they swerved to avoid it
and went on. If the camp was guarded, the guards would be
expecting the lorry. If it wasn't guarded then the assault
would be child's play. Rukuma smiled. In this way also, he
thought, the privileged were like children. They took their
privilege for granted and with it their safety. Someone grew
food for them and placed it on the table. The sun arose for
them in the morning and set for them at dusk. Not one day
in ten thousand required of them their utmost exertion. This
day would.

Rukuma heard a radio blaring from the lodge. He worked
silently toward the bright windows through the cover of
trees. The lorry was louder, turned back north now on the
track into the camp, and its bouncing headlights greened
the sparse forest canopy. The lorry would decoy any guards.
They would already have moved behind the lodge to challenge it. Rukuma noticed an elephant skull mounted against
a tree opposite the lodge porch and led the woman there
and they crouched and readied their rifles.

The lorry geared down. Light spilled across the roof of
the lodge and then the engine idled and someone shouted in
Swahili and there was a burst of automatic-weapons fire and
Rukuma dashed for the porch door, the woman behind him,
and at the second burst he threw open the door and stepped
up into the light.

"*Simameni!*" he shouted into the room. "Up! All of you!"
Soldiers bolting, knocking over tables, beer bottles clattering
to the floor. Surprised. Unarmed. A bar. Two Africans in
workmen's clothes. Others in the dining room beyond.
"Cover them!" Rukuma told the woman urgently.

He rounded the near couch and slammed a soldier aside.
The dining room. A white woman. An African and a
mzungu at a table and something there and a sergeant fumbling for his pistol. Rukuma fired from the waist. The ser-

geant jerked with the banging clatter of the burst and
crashed against a cot and fell and the cot flipped and
clapped over the body upside down and the sergeant's protruding booted feet drummed on the floor. Rukuma swung
toward the table where the people had ducked.

"Get up!" he ordered. "Hands first! *Move!*"

They came up, their hands in the air. The woman was
armed. "Unbuckle the belt!" Rukuma barked. "Drop the
belt!"

She was staring at him. Was she stupid? Then she lowered one hand slowly, lowered the other hand, worked the
buckle and slipped the pistol belt to the floor.

Rukuma swung to the white man. "How many guards?"

"Two." The white man's voice came out choked and he
cleared his throat.

"We have seen to those." Kare had turned off the radio
and behind him Rukuma heard his men pushing into the bar
and he relaxed. They would have circled the lodge and rec-
onnoitered. "Kare!" he called over his shoulder. "Go into
the compound! You will find women and children!"

The white woman was glaring at him. "They're nothing to
you," she said. "Can't you leave them alone?"

She was angry. How interesting. How very interesting
women were. "I shall give the orders," he told her. "Kare!
Do not bring them into the lodge! You should also find a
cook! Confine them to the compound!" He heard the porch
door bang as Kare went out. "Come around the table," he
said to the white woman. "Turn the chairs on this side of
the table and all of you sit."

They did as they were told. The white man arranged the
woman's chair. Rukuma watched them as he backed to the
doorway. He glanced into the bar. There were only two soldiers. It had seemed more. His men had forced them against
the inside wall so that they faced it and their hands were on

their heads. "Chaudi," Rukuma said. "Bring the two workmen and come in here. Let the others guard the soldiers."

The workmen shied from the overturned cot and Chaudi
shoved them forward to the last cot in the row and pushed
them down. He took up position behind Rukuma. Rukuma
laid aside his M-16 then and spun a chair from a nearby
table and sat, stretching out his legs.

God, Cassie thought, he's enormous. That booming voice
and he looks like a defensive guard or a heavyweight boxer.
Seth. We need you and I can't find you. My god what is
happening.

"Now, woman," Rukuma said, "you will tell me your
name."

"Cassie Wendover."

"What is your nationality?"

"American."

"Why are you here?"

"I'm a tourist."

"The tourists were evacuated from this district." Rukuma
clasped his hands behind his head. "Why were you allowed
to stay?"

To hell with you, Cassie thought. She shrugged.

"Come, you waste my time. If you are concerned for the
women and the children . . ."

"I'm a guest of the owner of the camp."

"A guest. Yes. I see. You are Seth Crown's mistress."

Cassie started. "Yes," she said then. "And you're Rukuma."

He smiled and crossed his legs. "No doubt you have
heard of me. You will be concerned for the safety of your
mpenzi. Your lover. He is alive and unhurt. He is returning
from the mountain. It will be a long walk for him. He was
kind enough to make us a loan of his lorry."

"How the hell did you get away?" the white man asked.

The white man changed color like a chameleon when he was angry.

"It disappoints you? But where are your manners?"

The porch door banged. Kare came into the dining room. She was breathing hard. "They have run away into the forest," she told Rukuma.

He chuckled. "Like chickens scattering before a herd. Never mind. They are harmless."

"Thank god," Cassie said. He's gone bust, she thought, unless he's got more men outside. They lost but somehow they escaped. Found the truck at the camp. This woman: rangy, long-armed, a long, narrow face. Much darker than Rukuma. She hates. She's almost as frightening as he is.

"Replace Chaudi here," Rukuma said to Kare. "Chaudi, locate the radiotelephone and destroy it. Then go back and guard the lorry."

Kare moved in behind Rukuma to take Chaudi's place.

Rukuma looked to the white man. "Your name?"

"Robert Fuhrey. I'm a scientist. I have a dig at Oloito Gorge." Fuhrey pointed. "This is my assistant John Kegedi. Those are our workmen, Mohammed and Kulaka."

"What do you dig for?"

"The earliest men. The Old Ones."

Rukuma laughed, throwing back his head. He was still smiling when he straightened. "How very patronizing you are, Robert Fuhrey. Your field of specialization is paleontology, correct? Like the famous Leakeys you are searching for *Homo habilis*. No? Earlier? *Australopithecus?*"

"Yes."

"Which is it, Dr. Fuhrey?"

"I don't know yet."

Rukuma took in the bowl of the partly assembled skull on the table, the litter of bone. He stood and walked to the end of the table and picked up the skull. "And here is what you have found."

Fuhrey stiffened. "Yes."

"And you are frightened that my nigger hands will be clumsy with it and ruin your careful work." Rukuma turned the skull on the tips of his fingers, admiring it. "No, Dr. Fuhrey. Have no fear. I am familiar with skulls. Have you dated it yet?"

"Only roughly."

"Yes? And?"

"Between six and seven million years."

"Marvelous. Is it not then quite the oldest find so far?"

"Yes."

"And it is human?"

"It may be. It's certainly hominid."

Rukuma ran a finger around the inside of the bowl, feeling the irregularities of the braincase. "Then this is my ancestor," he said. He held the skull out toward Kare. "Do you see, Kare? This is our ancestor."

Kare's tongue worked behind her lower lip. "It is a dead thing," she said.

"But once it was alive, woman, even as you and I. It is the ancient father of our fathers. You should respect it. It has seen all the years of Africa."

"The *mzungu* digs up our graves."

"He proves our case. We entered the world long, long before the *wazungu*. Did you know, Kare? When they crept north from Africa into the cold regions they were chilled to the heart and they put on clothing. The sun ceased to caress them and they bleached out like corpses." Rukuma studied the skull in silence. When it no longer spoke to him he set it carefully on the table and returned to his chair. "You," he said. "John Kegedi. You are Tanzanian?"

"*Ndiyo.*"

"Don't you speak English?"

"I speak English."

"Why do you work for the American?"

Kegedi smiled slightly. "It is my work."

"You are also a paleontologist?"

"No."

"But you went up to university. Where?"

"Nairobi."

"Why do you not use your education to help your people?"

"All Tanzanians work for the people. I dig for research. During term I teach."

"What do you teach?"

"Soil chemistry. Agriculture. Also paleontology."

"Do you teach that Africa is the birthplace of man?"

"Yes."

"Good. Then you have my permission to continue, *mwalimu*." Rukuma winked. "Tonight my permission is necessary. The great *Mwalimu* Julius Nyerere's permission may be necessary at other times, John Kegedi, but mine is necessary tonight."

Kegedi had stopped smiling. He nodded.

Rukuma turned to the workmen. "And you. Why do you work for the American?"

"*Hatuelewi*," Mohammed said nervously. "We do not understand." He pulled at his cheek.

"Why do you work for the *Mwamerika*?" Rukuma asked in Swahili.

"He pays us, Bwana."

"Does he pay you well?"

"*Ndiyo*, Bwana."

"Continue to work for him, but give a tenth part of your wages to the poor. Tell them that Rukuma taught you to do so in the name of the people. *Unafahamu?*"

"*Ndiyo*, Bwana. We understand."

"We surely understand, Bwana," Kulaka said.

"*Vizuri*. Good. Be certain that you do. I will know. I have powers and I will know."

Rukuma stood and walked back into the bar and spoke

quietly to one of the guerrillas. Kare watched in the dining room. A lion roared from the plain and the workmen shifted uneasily on their cot. When Rukuma returned to the dining room he was no longer smiling. He sat on the end of the table, one foot on the floor. "The conversation has been charming," he said coldly, "but the hour is late. Your friends have given us a full day. We are weary and we still have some distance to go."

Cassie saw the two soldiers pass the dining-room doorway with their hands on their heads. They shook. "No!" she blurted. She started to get up. The woman guerrilla's rifle swung around to her. Fuhrey jerked her down into her chair.

"Good, Dr. Fuhrey," Rukuma said. "You are not as impractical as I thought."

"You bastard," Fuhrey said. "You don't have to kill them."

"We are not prepared to take prisoners."

An M-16 stuttered from the yard, a burst, a second burst.

"Quickly now," Rukuma told them. "What vehicles are in camp?"

"Three Land Rovers," Cassie said.

"Good. We will take two of them and leave you the third and the lorry. The kitchen is stocked?"

"Yes."

"Excellent." The guerrillas came smiling into the dining room and Rukuma turned to them. "Strip the camp of weapons," he ordered in Swahili. "There will be gun cases."

"I saw them in the bar," one of the men said.

Rukuma nodded. "Also the rifles of the soldiers. There is a pistol on the floor behind the table where the *wazungu* wait. Take the Africans into the bar and tie their hands and feet. Behind the dining room is a kitchen. Two of you stay with me. The other two go into the kitchen and load the tins of food that you will find there into one of the Land Rovers in the garage. The garage will be behind the building where the lorry came in. Instruct Chaudi to wait for us at the Land Rovers. Be certain also that they are fueled." He looked around at Cassie. In English: "Where are the keys?"

"I have them," Cassie said.

"*Upesi!*" Rukuma ordered the guerrillas. "Be quick!" He watched as they swept the dining room of weapons and led the Africans away.

"Robert Fuhrey," he said then. "Listen carefully. You will deliver a message to Seth Crown when he returns to his camp. Tell him that he has proven himself to be an enemy of the people and must now come to judgment for his crimes. Tell him that I have taken his woman for a hostage. But tell him that Rukuma is a compassionate man and is willing to make an exchange."

The guerrillas filed past the doorway. They were hung with sporting guns.

"He must come to me alone and unarmed," Rukuma continued. "He must surrender himself voluntarily and privately. If he notifies either the police or the army, then his woman will die. If he comes privately then I will exchange her life for his." Rukuma turned up his hands. "What could be fairer than that?"

"Where will he find you?" Fuhrey asked sharply.

"There is a cabin in Ngorongoro. We will wait for him there."

"Why the hell should he trust you?"

"Don't, Robert," Cassie stopped him. "It's all right. Rukuma is a man of his word."

"But how generous of you," Rukuma said.

The cabin, Cassie thought. The cabin above the river where we loved. "Tell Seth it's my show," she said quickly to Fuhrey.

"And she is also brave," said Rukuma.

He waited for the guerrillas. When they returned they

had buckled on Crown's pistols. Two stopped beside
Rukuma and the other two went into the kitchen through
the dining-room door. There was swearing from the kitchen
and one of the guerrillas backed out and held the door open
while the other found the light.

"Take the woman," Rukuma said to Kare. "Wait for us in
the garage."

Kare motioned with her rifle and Cassie walked past her
into the bar.

Rukuma stood. "Are you right-handed or left-handed, Dr.
Fuhrey?"

The screen door banged.

"I'm right-handed."

"Hold him," Rukuma ordered. Fuhrey stood. The guerrillas took his arms. "Bring him to me and force him to
kneel. No. Turn him the other way. Yes. *Vizuri*."

Fuhrey looked up.

"I want to fix this night in your memory, Dr. Fuhrey,"
Rukuma said. "So that you will not forget the message I
have given you. So that you will not forget Rukuma."

Rukuma bent and took hold of Robert Fuhrey's left forearm holding at the wrist and just below the elbow and lifted
it abruptly and broke it hard across his knee.

Walking out from the army camp on the track through the
forest, climbing Ngorongoro, Seth Crown heard two cars
gunning up the western approach, going fast. They came on
as he climbed and slowed above him and turned off the
main road. He was glad for the co-ordinate of the sound. It
meant he was approaching the rim. The only tracks off the
main road at that height led to the lodges and down into the
crater.

PART III

The Last Safari

Fourteen

Now LATE AT NIGHT the moon was far in the west toward setting, the air was cool and still and Seth Crown and Abdi on foot in the open forest stalked the lodge of the tent camp. On the drive down from Ngorongoro in the borrowed Range Rover Crown's walked-out legs had numbed. His shoulder was raw where the strap of the Kalashnikov had cut and his mouth was dry. It would have been a good night, he told himself. It would have been a good night to sit late and sore on the porch drinking beer. It would have been a good night to listen to the lions roaring from the plain, to hear one big scarred male start with moaning and thunder into full roaring and grade off into hoarse coughing and hear the others in the pride roar one and another in answer and single them out and try to follow their wanderings by their roars. It would have been a good night to stop on the porch and watch the zebra pound onto the lake slope after sundown like fat ponies, stallions skittishly alert, and listen to their cropping as resonant in the darkness as ripping canvas. Or to do no more, talking on the porch, than watch the moon, to notice it and later to notice it again and see the slow silver casting of its face shifted westward. But even without the climb on Olmoti, without the botched bloody raid, even without the long, hopeless march from the army camp to the lodge on Ngorongoro for the car, what I hear up ahead finishes that, Crown thought. What I can already figure up ahead finishes that.

There was a time, so long ago now it seemed almost a mythical time, when he entertained tourists. He entertained tourists and sometimes he pointed a moral. In that mythical time he would shoot a golden tommy for the pot and save back a haunch and at night, after he had seen the tourists to their tents and buttoned them into their tents as a father buttons his small children into their pajamas, at night he would enact for them a story of Africa. He would hang the haunch high in the big acacia behind the tents for the hyenas. When the camp was quiet the hyenas would follow in the scent, giggling between the tents to the tree, collecting, whining, growling, yelling, leaping high for the meat and thumping to the ground and groaning and wedging up grunting through the pack to leap again. Protected behind thin canvas walls, the tourists would gather a tale to take home. That was in another time, when even the walls of a tent were an assurance of security. Now in this time the generator was still running, there was no sign of the guards and the hyenas that snarled up ahead tore something more substantial than a tommy haunch.

Abdi saw the guards first, the remains of them that the hyenas had dragged apart. He moved cautiously into the open with his automatic ready but Mama Tele called from the porch and Crown knew then that Rukuma had come and gone.

He was running, shouting. "Cassie!" Mama Tele was shaking her head and he pushed onto the porch and into the bar and saw the white sling on Fuhrey's splinted, bandaged arm. "Where is she?" he asked urgently.

"Rukuma," Fuhrey said, looking quickly down at his arm, lifting it, reddening. "He took her hostage."

"What hostage? What the hell are you talking about?" It just goes on, Crown thought. Whoever wound it wound it tight and it just goes on and on.

"For you, Seth. God I'm sorry. He surprised us. He had your lorry. There was nothing we could do."

"For me what?"

"He wants you. He said he'd exchange her for you. He's taken her to the cabin in Ngorongoro."

Crown slowly turned around. Abdi was behind him and he looked at Abdi and Abdi stepped aside and Crown walked out into the yard. Three hyenas still worked at the remains of the soldiers. When the hyenas saw him walking toward them they whined and tucked tail and scuttled and only as he started to squeeze the trigger of the Kalashnikov did he check himself and fire over their heads.

After a while Abdi came out. "Effendi?" he said. "There is much that must be planned."

Crown went in. John Kegedi was there, Mohammed, Kulaka, Mama Tele. Fuhrey told him what had happened and the rest of Rukuma's message and how later Abdi's wives had returned from the forest and freed the Africans and Kegedi had splinted his arm. Crown thought of the cars he had heard turning off the road on Ngorongoro. The crater was a good choice with the tourists gone. The park boys wouldn't spend much time there with no tourists to guide and in any case they didn't go armed. Rukuma's instincts for self-preservation were remarkable. He traveled light and he knew exactly what he wanted and he made it all very simple. He made it as simple as a primer. He took you through the alphabet one letter at a time and at each letter you learned a useful verse. You're at X now, Crown told himself.

As a personal favor to his most inept pupil Rukuma is personally going to teach you Y and Z. And if it frees Cassie from this terrible hell I've put her through I will accept it with whatever is left of my dignity and feel nothing but gratitude.

"Hear me out," Crown said, leaning forward in his chair. "We've got the Range Rover from the lodge and the lorry and Robert's Land Rover. John and Robert will go with me in the Range Rover. They'll drop me at the Seneto Hill track and go on to Arusha and fix up Robert's arm." He turned to Abdi, Abdi slumped staring on the couch beside the chair. "Abdi will take the lorry and pick up the *moran* and return them to ole Kipoin."

"Effendi—" Abdi interrupted.

"Wait," Crown said. In Swahili he said: "Mohammed, Kulaka, you will remain here." He looked to Mama Tele. "You and the other women must dispose of the bodies of the soldiers, Mama." She nodded. "The *fisi* have torn them very much but there is also the sergeant. You must take them into the forest and bury them. Use the Land Rover. One of the men can drive. No one must know of what has happened here until the woman Cassie Wendover is returned. You understand? No one must know."

"*Ninafahamu,*" Mama Tele said. "I understand."

"You cannot trust this man, Effendi," Abdi said in English.

"Don't start," Crown told him. "It's set. It was set when we lost the lorry. There's nothing left to do but run it out." He stood. "Let's go."

Abdi was on his feet. "Effendi. It is very late and all are weary. Not even Rukuma will expect you to cross the crater unarmed and in darkness. Let us all rest until dawn and then go up. Nothing will change in the hours left to the night."

"Bloody hell," Crown said. He looked around. "John? What about you?"

"He's right."

"Robert?"

Fuhrey's arm pressed hot against the bandaging and it throbbed. "Christ, whatever you think best, Seth. You could use some sleep. It won't help Cassie if you don't get there."

Crown glared at them. "Right," he said then. "Dawn it is." He swept up his Kalashnikov and strode from the bar into the dining room and they heard him letting himself into his apartment. He slammed the door.

Abdi held up his hand. "This cannot be allowed," he said quietly to Fuhrey and Kegedi. "The Effendi will be murdered and Cassie will also be murdered. You must go with him as he says but in Arusha you must notify the police and convince them to send a force. When you return, join with the soldiers at the lodge. I will bring in the *moran* but I will appeal to the Masai chieftain ole Kipoin for a sufficient number of those who have rested to surprise the guerrillas in the crater."

"Be careful," Kegedi said. "This man Rukuma is brutal."

"I have seen that," said Abdi. "Let us pray that he is also one of those who takes much time to gloat."

Crown lay on his bed in the darkness. It was almost three. He had pulled off his boots and wound the clock and set the alarm for six. He hadn't undressed and he hadn't bothered to turn back the bedcover. He wouldn't be sleeping there again. The room was so dark that open-eyed he could see the yellow drifting forms the brain hallucinates to pretend there is light in darkness, the spirals and S-curves and yellow misshapen corners. He could see them and he watched them drift from left to right across his field of vision and start up again left and drift.

The bastards were right about waiting until dawn, he

thought, but it didn't make things any better. It would have
been better to go, to keep moving. If he kept moving he
wouldn't have to think about it. To hell with them, though.
Just to hell with them. To hell with Abdi and John Kegedi
and to hell with Robert with his bloody broken arm. Right.
It's their fault. Wonderful. And where were you, pal? What
were you supposed to do?

Cassie, Crown thought, trying to see her but seeing only
the yellow drift of his brain, I can't tell you how sorry I am.

What was he? Rukuma. What was he? You keep forget-
ting that you've wounded him, Crown told himself. He was
all set to go when you went up. He had these amazing connections. He'd come out of Algeria and he had backing
there and he'd been supplied from Vietnam or Cambodia
and he had some kind of connection with Amin. He was
loaded for elephant and he was going to march down the
mountain and absolutely devastate the countryside. With
that much firepower and with most of the army off at the
west lake he probably could have occupied Arusha if he
could have gotten there. He was wounded in his transport
first and then Mugwa and the *moran* took out most of his
men. He's on the run now. He's got four men and a woman
and two cars and he's holed up in the crater and he's lost
most of what he's spent months, maybe years, building.
Which is a very nice, a very balanced and objective tactical
assessment and the most awful bullroar. What Rukuma is is
the implacable bastard who has Cassie's life in his sadistic
murderous hands. And there's not even the ghost of a guarantee that he's going to make an exchange. She could already be dead.

She'd better not be. I tell you and I tell you here in blood
she'd better not be.

What the hell could you do about it if she were?

The yellow was tinged with green. The colors were flat,
dead, the kind of colors you'd expect the brain to make. You

got a good idea of what the body was really like when it decomposed. What it was really like was a mass of seething, idiot cells strung together on a rack and flapped and squeaked by a blind gray parasite swollen inside a skull.

He wouldn't dare. She's his leverage until I arrive.

You should have got out of it when they found the head. It was none of your goddamned business. You're not a policeman, are you? You're not a district officer, are you, or a soldier? The Tanzanian Government has never been graced by your employment in any capacity whatsoever. You're a former professional hunter so-called who decided in his declining years, after he managed to be away from home on veterinary business while his wife was raped and murdered, after he botched raising his son so badly that his son ran away from home and has never since been heard from, to take up innkeeping, and who then proceeded to drink and bull his way through the most important two decades in the modern history of East Africa. You've had just a hell of a productive life, haven't you. You spent the first half of it helping your clients prove their manhood by knocking off the game and you spent the second half helping the tourists renew their tender sensibilities by polluting the national parks. You've lived most of your adult life, up to fifty-three years, at the same level of moral and emotional maturity that a thirteen-year-old boy reaches the day he discovers his first pubic hair. Well hey, *mon,* look how it averages out. You get to make up for it now all at once with only a few hours of the easiest kind of work.

And if not when they found the head, then you should have got out of it when the general came. It should have been obvious when they sent along a full-fledged American-trained general of the army that it was too big for an innkeeper. If it meant a general and a company of soldiers it was too big. But Nguvu needed a tracker and Cassie was watching so you sucked in your belly and you were Nguvu's blushing boy. You'd go into that godforsaken forest and show him the way. You'd fight a small war and at the same time you'd keep your bloody camp running and con the bloody tourists, play the white hunter in puttees and pith helmet for the bloody tourists. Hunted with Hemingway, chaps. Rather a better fisherman than a hunter, don't you know? Bit of a sot, but hell on the rhino. Slip us a bit more of the *bangi*, chaps, and we'll tell you another one. Did you know why polacks don't hunt elephant, chaps? Polacks don't hunt elephant because the bloody decoys are too heavy.

And when you lost them, when you failed them and they were cut down in their innocent trust of your superhuman white-hunter powers, you should have got out then. You shouldn't have gone up with Mugwa, poor tough Mugwa hot after his damn bandits. Mugwa and his honey tree. Mugwa and his witches. Mugwa the leaper. Rukuma shot him. Rukuma or one of his gang. That's another debt Rukuma owes you that you won't get to collect.

Even as late as the night Nyerere radioed the camp from Dar about Amin you should have got out of it. It would have been harder to do. The whole thing kept winding up tighter as it went along. Rukuma had a known force then even if he didn't have any transport. But they could have mobilized the villagers. Called up the militia. You could have taken Cassie and gone off to Dar or up to Nairobi. You could be lying beside her on the beach at Mombasa right now, talking away the night.

You didn't get out of it, though. What you did was butt in where you had no business. Really, what you did was the same as what Rukuma was doing except that in your case you had a sort of quasi-official sanction. What you did was take the law into your own hands.

It's too late for that now. It's too late for accusations. You got into it by arrogance and by choice and now you're into it all the way.

Wasn't it wonderful how it worked, though? he thought
bitterly, letting the worst come now. Wasn't it wonderful
how they stuck it to you? Not to you directly. You could handle that. That was easy. That was no more than anything
else you'd been through and it was the same for everyone. It
never mattered very much and it didn't matter very much
now. It was always something you did alone and in a way it
was chosen and because it was chosen and because you did
it alone it was the very core of your freedom. They knew
about that, so they didn't go after you directly. They waited
until you loved someone and then they went after her.

They took Sidanu, he told himself then at the ugly bottom
of it, and now they've taken Cassie and if only I hadn't
loved them I'd never have known the difference. If I'd never
met Cassie and never loved her I'd never have known the
difference.

That's enough of that, you sodding bloody coward, he
thought then with sudden rage. That's enough of denying
the woman you love. You can take that and stick it and take
the self-pity and stick that too. No one's asking you to like it.
All you have to do is do it and do it without whining and
without dumping your bloody garbage on people who love
you. Without dumping your bloody garbage on Cassie because she didn't ask for any of it. All she asked for was you.
So why don't you shut up? You're worn out and most of the
garbage is because of that. So why don't you shut up and
get some sleep while you still can?

But god damn them all. God damn and damn them all to
hell. God damn Dominick and his bloody rhino and god
damn Nguvu, god damn Julius Nyerere, god damn and burn
in deepest hell Idi Amin, god damn Mugwa and the
Chaggas and Tomasi and the guerrillas and the army and
Olmoti and its stinking forests and its crawling bamboo, god
damn Tanzania and East Africa and Africa itself huge and
brutal and risen out of the oceans like a monstrous thicken-

ing tumor on the earth, god damn all this teeming life that
goes on to no end except its own repetition, its own obscene
drooling endless consumption of itself, and god damn forever and in hellish torment Rukuma. Damn him and forever
damn him. God damn him forever into hell. Cassie, Cassie,
Cassie, how I love you and how sorry, how very very sorry I
am to put you through this. Because we lose either way.

Crown woke at four minutes to six and shut off the alarm
and stared at the dark ceiling above the bed. Then he got up
and lit the lamp and laid out a change of khakis that Mama
Tele had washed and pressed the week before and that still
smelled fresh from drying on the grass in the sun. Then he
stripped and went into the bathroom to wash and shave.

Crown found Abdi waiting for him in the dining room.
Fuhrey and Kegedi had slept there. Abdi had already waked
them and they were dressing, Fuhrey awkwardly because of
the arm. Abdi's wives had removed the sergeant's body during the night and scrubbed the floor clean of blood. Crown
noticed the skull on the table. It wasn't finished and he
wouldn't see it finished but it was found and it was worth
having known about. That it went that far back and in
Africa was worth having known.

"How's the arm, Robert?" Crown asked.

"It'll keep," Fuhrey said. It was sharply and hotly painful
but the splint immobilized it and he saw no reason to worry
Crown.

"Let's get moving," Crown told the two men. "We'll wait
for you outside."

He walked out through the bar and Abdi followed him.
Behind him he heard Fuhrey ask Kegedi to tie his boots.
The sky was deep blue, the last morning stars fading, and
pink dawn glowed beyond the lake and the air was warm.
The high, scattered clouds, feathery cirrus, were pinkish
white and moving eastward with the winds, flaring up and

separating as they came. Zebra grazed at the lake shore and
eastward in the forest a lone giraffe browsed the high
branches of a fever tree. Crown watched the giraffe and
then turned and looked toward the tent platforms with their
new wood and their new bleaching thatch.

"Finish rebuilding," he said.

"I will do so, Effendi," Abdi said somberly. His eyes were
red from lack of sleep but like Crown he had changed into
clean khakis. "We have finished all but three."

"Buy good tents. Don't let the Indian cheat you. The best
are British." Crown unbuttoned the left breast pocket of his
bush jacket and took out an envelope. "Keep this," he said,
handing Abdi the envelope, Abdi taking it and studying it,
turning it over. "You're already authorized to sign on the
business accounts. This covers the rest. I've deeded you a
half interest. The other half's for Cassie. *Mzee?*" Abdi
looked up. "Take care of her, will you?"

"Effendi—" Abdi started.

"It's all right," Crown said. "I haven't worked it all out
yet but I got through a lot of it last night and it's all right."

"You must at least carry a knife, Effendi."

Crown shook his head. "Nothing. I'm not going by my
rules now. I'm going by Rukuma's rules." He looked impatiently toward the lodge and back at Abdi. "Bring in the
moran. After that's done you might take the Land Rover up
to the rim and wait for Cassie."

"I will do so, Effendi," Abdi said, straightening and folding the envelope and putting it away. "I will watch for her
and I will take care of her faithfully. She will be as a daughter to me."

The porch door banged. Fuhrey and Kegedi came around
the end of the porch and waited there apart from Crown
and Abdi and then through the breezeway from the compound came Abdi's wives and children and the cook.

"They wished to see you off, Effendi," Abdi said. "I pray it does not trouble you."

"It's fine, *mzee*," Crown said. He went to them and spoke to them, the children somber and standing back until he knelt and called them close, crowding around him then and when he hugged them looking shyly across his shoulder to their father. Then Crown stood and the cook gave him a thermos and pumped his hand and Crown turned to Abdi's wives and they surrounded him as the children had done and embraced him, Mama Tele holding him hard and Jaja awkward with the bigness of her belly under her bright flowing dress. Then he left them and returned to Abdi.

"*Kwaheri, mzee*," he said, looking at Abdi steadily. "Good-bye. You're the finest man I've ever known."

"Effendi," Abdi said, choking. "Effendi."

"Don't worry, *mzee*. It's all right. Take care of things. Take care of all those wives of yours."

Abdi nodded, trying to smile. "*Nenda salama,* my Effendi," he said thickly. "Go in peace. *Tutaonana tukijaa-liwa*. If God wills I will see you."

"*Kwaheri*, my great friend." Then Crown was walking away with Fuhrey and Kegedi past the lodge and through the open forest toward the Range Rover where they had left it the night before eastward on the track.

Watching him go, his height and his confident walking and the youthful straightness of his back, Abdi thought: it is not yet *kwaheri*, my Effendi. Not if I can help it is it yet *kwaheri*. If there is any pity from Allah and any new, bright knife of justice among men it is not yet *kwaheri*.

The sky seen through the forest spaces was lighter, filling to the light blue of day.

Kegedi stopped the Range Rover at the turnoff on the rim of Ngorongoro Crater and Crown got out. They had already said good-bye. Crown closed the door and Kegedi pulled away, watching in the mirror. Fuhrey turned in the seat and looked back through the rear door until the trees filled in around the curve of the road and blocked his view. He thought of Crown and he thought of Tom who had died alone and unburied in SCK at the beginning of the world and he promised Crown silently that he would find a more fitting name.

Crown didn't watch them go but stepped off the road and crossed the grass to the sheer rim, the wind from the crater blowing his hair. The green crater opened away vast to the blue, distant wall. The river that ran from the wall to the silver-pink lake was darker green and from the high rim Crown couldn't see the cabin. You've got a long safari ahead, he thought, and it's your last. Better get going. He left the rim for the steep red-dirt track and started down.

Fifteen

WHEN THE WOMAN guerrilla shook her awake Cassie was startled to see sunlight in the cabin. She was certain she had lain awake all night. Apparently she hadn't. She'd have to do better than that.

The night before, crowded into the front seat of the Land Rover between Rukuma and the driver, she had stupidly allowed herself the self-indulgence of rage. Rukuma describing in detail how he broke Robert's arm, spitting an anti-American diatribe, Rukuma swaying heavily against her on the turns, the driver working the gearshift, clumsily slamming it into her leg and his elbow jamming her side, kept the rage hot going up the mountain. She didn't notice that they were descending into the crater until the steepness of the track forced her to brace herself against the dash and looking out she saw the dark void swallowing up the headlight beams. The windshield pressed her in front, Rukuma and the driver on the sides. Then the woman in the seat behind her unaccountably, gratuitously, viciously pulled

her hair and rage turned to panic and she jerked away and
the woman slapped the back of her head sharp and hard
and it was all she could do not to fight her way from the car.

There was more. At the cabin Rukuma lit the lantern on
the table beside the fireplace and ordered her onto one of
the camp beds. She sat at the head of the bed with her
knees drawn up and her back against the wall, watching
them and hating them, trying to control her fear. The driver
settled at the table with a revolver to guard her. The woman
spread blankets on the floor beyond the beds. The other
guerrillas began carrying in the chop boxes they had loaded
in the kitchen at the lodge. Rukuma saw the first box in and
spoke to them in Swahili and then he lay down on the next
bed and turned on his side away from her and immediately
fell asleep.

After the last box the guerrillas barred the door and
talked among themselves in the kitchen. They swaggered to
the end of the bed and their eyes were yellow in the light.
They looked at Rukuma and looked at each other. One of
them, the one who was smallpox-scarred, pointed to her and
said something, a phrase, and they grinned. The woman
called across the cabin and they laughed, throwing back
their heads so that their brown faces shone in the light and
Cassie could see the pink roofs of their mouths and their
white wet teeth and the wet pink tips of their tongues. The
scarred guerrilla started to shake the bed. The woman came
over to watch and caught the rhythm of the shaking and
swayed her hips in time. Cassie held onto the frame with
both hands and the scarred guerrilla shook the bed harder
and her back banged against the wall.

Then Rukuma had spun to his feet between the beds. The
scarred guerrilla let go the bed and the woman stopped her
hips. Rukuma shoved the guerrilla stumbling away and
berated them all in Swahili. They slunk to the blankets the

woman had spread and lay down. Rukuma lay down on his bed.

Cassie waited for them to sleep. When the cabin was quiet she stretched out on the bed on her back. She watched the yellow lantern light flickering on the rough wooden ceiling. The bed shook then to her heartbeat. She listened to Rukuma's heavy breathing. The cabin smelled of kerosene and rank, metallic sweat. The guard shifted restlessly in his chair. Sometimes he yawned and when the lions roared from the crater he talked to himself. Once he blew his nose. He played with the lantern, turning the wick up and down, changing the light. He spun the cylinder of his revolver. The lantern flame flickered slowly and Cassie's heartbeat slowed and slowly the bed stopped shaking. It was the bed where she and Seth had made love.

Now in the daylight the fear was better, retreated behind an intense, guarding vigilance. She could hear every sound and sense every movement in the cabin. The woman guerrilla stood over her. Quickly she sat up.

"Slut," the woman said in English. "Rukuma orders me to feed you."

"Bring her to the table," Rukuma called.

The woman followed her. Rukuma ate with a fork from a plate, European style. Two of the guerrillas sat opposite him on upended chop boxes. In the center of the table was a smoke-blackened iron skillet of eggs scrambled with coarse corned beef, the orange tallow from the beef thick on the eggs, and the two guerrillas ate from the skillet with their fingers.

"Sit," Rukuma said, patting the empty chair beside him. "Bring her a plate, Kare."

"I'm not hungry," Cassie said. "Is there coffee?"

"Our food is too mean for you?" Rukuma asked. He shrugged. "There is *chai*."

"I'd like that."

"Kare, bring the memsahib *chai.*"

The woman left them and came back with a mug of tea cloudy with milk and set it in front of Cassie, deliberately slopping it. Cassie tasted the *chai*. It was hot and sweet. Rukuma refilled his plate and ate silently, working across the steaming mound. The guerrillas were watching her. She kept her eyes down.

Rukuma finished and pushed back his chair. "*Vizuri,*" he said. Cassie thought: *vizuri* meant *good*, but he said it as he said almost everything, with mockery. He raged or he ordered or he mocked, and there was a lightless hole in him where decency or compassion or simple fellow-feeling ought to be. God knew what crawled in that hole.

"We must get to know one another," Rukuma said, mocking. He folded his arms and leaned back in his chair. Cassie couldn't sort his features. He was light brown. Without the distortion of the mockery, without the eyes constricted and cold, he would have been handsome. High cheekbones and a thin, expressive mouth. "When did you come to East Africa?" he asked her.

"What do you want with Seth?" she countered. "What's he done to you?"

"I will ask the questions, woman. After I am finished it may be that I will answer yours."

"In time for your attack on the camp," Cassie said. "I arrived in time for that."

Rukuma grinned. "Splendid." He spoke to the guerrillas in Swahili. They listened, their hands stopped on the way to their mouths, and smiled and went on eating.

"It wasn't *splendid*. It was cold-blooded, brutal murder."

"But how indignant you are at the death of a few tourists. Where is your indignation when Africans and Asians starve?"

"I didn't personally cause their starvation," Cassie said.

"Nor do you work to alleviate it. It comes to the same thing."

"I care about them. A lot of Americans care about them."

"Oh yes. They send little packages."

"You've got African governments now to help. Why not work with them?"

"They were corrupted with Western evil even as they were forming. Their so-called leaders want industry. They want to drive fine cars. They want cities where they can amuse themselves in nightclubs and bed their mistresses in fine apartments. They want to go to the moon."

"You sound like a country boy."

Rukuma laughed. A great joke. "Yes, I am a country boy." He straightened and looked at her. "But allow me to enlighten you. A few stories. Incidents. Little things. In Nairobi there was a man of middle age. Within his tribe he would have been a respected elder, but he was no longer within his tribe. He supplied music in a whorehouse. This was not a Western whorehouse but an African. You must not imagine brocaded curtains the color of French wine. A tin roof. A dirt floor. A row of shacks out the back door behind the bar. The man supplied music on a wind-up gramophone. For many years he had worked on the coffee estate of a white bwana. The white bwana was a drunkard. Two bottles of whiskey a day. As his drunkenness progressed through the day he would call in this man, who was a young man then. The bwana designated the young man his gramophone *toto*. You know the word *toto*? It means *boy*. The gramophone *toto* would crank up the gramophone. The same records, played over and over to cheer the bwana in his drunkenness. Remarkable records. I had never heard their like before. 'What Are the Wild Waves Saying?' was one of them. 'St. Louis Blues.' 'Making Whoopee.' 'Gas Shell Bombardment at Loos, 1915.' 'Funiculi Funicula.' Eventually the bwana committed suicide. His gramophone *toto* was presented with the gramophone and the remarkable collection of records. He moved to Nairobi and set himself up as a disco jockey. We were happy to have the machine and the records, of course."

"In the whorehouse," Cassie said.

"Yes, in the whorehouse."

"And you kill people for that."

"Don't be stupid," Rukuma said coldly. "It is merely a symptom of a disease."

The two guerrillas at the table stood and wiped their hands on their fatigues. One of them spoke to Rukuma and he nodded and they crossed to the sleeping area and picked up their automatic rifles and went out through the kitchen. The night guard was sleeping, Cassie noticed, rolled in his blanket on the floor.

Rukuma smiled. "Your lover should be started on his way by now," he said to Cassie. "Supposing, of course, that he will come."

"He'll come," Cassie said.

"You are confident of that?"

"Yes."

"Good. So am I. I know something of this Seth Crown. He is truly a heroic bwana, is he not? Brave and courageous. Willing to give up his life for many ideals. Now this time for the lady he loves. You should be flattered."

The woman guerrilla came to the table with a mug of *chai* and sat down to listen.

"Why do you want him?" Cassie asked Rukuma. "Because he led the attack on your camp?"

Rukuma slammed his hand on the table. Cassie jumped, but the woman only raised her eyebrows and lifted her *chai* away. "You are so tender about violence," said Rukuma angrily. "You are all so very Christian about violence so long as you are the ones behind the rifles. You may murder freely in Vietnam, you may invade Cambodia without warning, bomb it, your Nixon and your Henry Kissinger may, but let those of us who are looking at the barrels of your rifles counter your violence with violence of our own and you are bewildered. You ask, 'Why, Rukuma? Why are you doing this terrible thing to us? Have you no decency?'" Rukuma shook his fist. "Where was the decency in Vietnam? Where was the decency in Algeria when tens of thousands of Algerians were murdered and in seven years not one Frenchman was brought to justice? Where was the decency when the brave men of Mau Mau were hounded from the forests and confined to concentration camps while the toadies of the British took over Kenya? Where is the decency when Africans live in poverty while the wealth of oil and uranium and diamonds flows out to America and Europe and Japan?" Rukuma turned off the anger as quickly as he had turned it on. He smiled. "It is impossible that you could understand."

"I understand," Cassie said quietly.

"No. It is impossible." He raised his voice to lecture. "There is meaning in violence, woman. It cleans. It brings fearlessness and self-respect. The *totos* discover in violence that they are men. Violence unifies them. No longer are there masters and servants, tribes, this town against that town, this region against that region, this people against that people. Suddenly there is only the people, one people. They know what they want. They know who they are. They lead themselves and they no longer listen to the false prophets in Western suits who talk hypocritically of socialism and land reform and the nationalization of wealth while they grow fat in exploitation."

Chilled, Cassie asked: "When does the violence end?"

"When there are no more whites in Africa. When there are no more twins to whites living hidden inside the black skins of traitorous Africans. When Africa is all black and all one nation and all its resources flow to its own benefit."

"Why do you speak to her?" Kare asked Rukuma in Swahili. "She is an *mjinga*, a fool. We should kill her and be done with it."

"In time, Kare," Rukuma said. "In time."

Cassie didn't understand the Swahili. "You can't kill everyone," she said.

"Why not?" Rukuma asked lightly.

My god, Cassie thought. No one's learned anything. She shook her head.

"You are thinking of Hitler," Rukuma said.

"Among others."

"Yes. At this point in the discussion Europeans always think of Hitler. Unless they are German. If they are German they think of Dresden or Hiroshima." Rukuma stood and walked to the sleeping guard. "Chaudi," he said, teasing him awake with his toe. "You have slept enough." Chaudi mumbled in Swahili and sat up, rubbing his eyes. He stood and scratched. "Kare," Rukuma said. "Chaudi's belly rumbles. He is hungry." The woman took her mug of *chai* and left the table for the kitchen and Chaudi followed. Rukuma sat down again facing Cassie. "I have not told you other stories. You would find them instructive. The common sport in Australia for many years, which was hunting down aborigines. I suppose there was a shortage of foxes. The torturers in Algeria who pushed bottles into the bodies of their captives and went home complaining of the difficulty of their work. The disappearance in Kenya of former Mau Mau who questioned the *Mzee*'s fulfillment of the dreams they fought for and their comrades died for. The *Mwalimu*'s—"

"Is there a toilet?" Cassie interrupted impatiently. "If there is I'd like to use it."

Rukuma smiled. "You do not like my stories. Of course. It is only a poor outhouse, but I will be glad to escort you to it. Perhaps we will see your lover approaching as we go."

I hope so, Cassie told herself. And I hope to god he's got

an army behind him. Because this man's insane. This man's had his heart cut out.

Seth Crown hesitated at the edge of the forest, studying the crater floor ahead. The grass under the fever trees beside the track was waist-high and lush. Beyond in the open it browned, rolling up to a near hill, the track curving smoothly to the low, rounded crest. He would follow the track to the lake and curve around the shoreline and follow the curving line of the river to the cabin. The cabin was halfway across the crater, a little more than eight kilometers away.

Wildebeest grazed ahead of him grunting and lowing, the bulls wandering with the cows less territorial than they had been when he and Cassie had come up to the crater before. Zebra mingled grazing with the wildebeest, the small fat crater zebra; and black-feathered ostrich cocks and drab ostrich hens; tommies flicking their restless flags, a bulky lone eland; and quick and white among the grazers and the periscoping ostrich the small cattle egrets darted after insects. It was pushing eleven o'clock. The lions and the hyenas would be laid up resting after their dawn patrols. Crown left the forest and started toward the hill.

The sun warmed his back and the wildebeest nearest the track bellowed as he approached them and scattered. They weren't used to a man on foot in the crater. Coming up to the crater with Cassie the first time had been the real beginning, Crown thought, the elephant in the forest, the wildebeest, the flamingos wheeling from the lake, lying in at the cabin and the rain and the night stars afterward. Cassie was right about the connections and how quickly they could lock in. He still had time to figure it out. In the daylight with the garbage gone he still had time. You never knew everything you needed to know until it was too late. Maybe now he'd know.

There's really no point in pulling a long face about it, Crown told himself then. Let the wildebeest pull the long face, that's their drill. You're off on a fine long walk. It never was more than a fine long walk, so why pull the long face?

It all depended on how you looked at it. If you flayed the thing out you could find a machine. The machine was self-propelled and it was fitted with a variety of sensors. The sensors monitored the machine and the immediate environment around the machine. When the information that the sensors were tuned to came in above a certain threshold level, the sensors kicked a switch that started the servomechanisms and the machine responded. Eventually the machine wore out or another machine smashed it or it smashed itself on the environment because the sensors were coarse. That was one way you could look at it. That it wasn't the machine's fault or the other machines' or the environment's. That the fault was in the tolerances. Hell, if you looked at it that way there wasn't any fault, and it was a legitimate way to look at it and maybe it was the right way. It sure as hell answered a lot of questions.

Or you could flay the thing out and find meat. That was another way to look at it. More complicated and not as pleasant as the machine business even if you had been a hunter and were used to the work. Machines were easy. But knock down a hyrax and open it up and there in miniature were the same bones and muscles and organs as yours. The same with a monkey, the same with a lion, the same with an elephant and almost the same with an egret or an ostrich or a mamba. People like Robert traced it back and back, all the casual transformations, until it disappeared into the rocks. Until the meat that made the meat got too small to see. It started out as ocean water. The ocean water writhed and eventually it started to sway and then to crawl and a long time after that it started to walk. It was almost like watching waves breaking into spray against a shore but slowed down, slowed down until it hardly seemed to move at all. Remember the time you took the old Dorobo into Mombasa to see the ocean? Crown asked himself, walking in the crater. He'd never seen the ocean before. It was in the monsoon season. He'd been a fine guide but the safari had folded from the bloody mud. You and he drank your way from bar to bar, the bars very wondrous to him, down to the beach and the water was oily gray, broken with whitecaps, crashing white and thundering on the beach. But instead of being delighted as you thought he'd be the Dorobo was terrified. *What is it?* he'd shouted over the roar. *What is it for? Why is it boiling like that?* If you looked at the thing as so much meat then you weren't much better off than the Dorobo. The Dorobo didn't want to look at it. He wanted to head straight back to the forest.

It *was* meat. It twitched like meat, it hurt like meat, it rotted like meat. It was enormously clever, but not so clever that it ever escaped itself or the ocean it came from. Sooner or later it always went back to the ocean. All of it. Every particle of it. It washed into streams and the streams washed into rivers, it washed from divides and down the combining slopes of mountains, and the rivers ran into the ocean and no small pure thing escaped.

It began as meat and it ended as meat, but between beginning and end it was something more. There was so much more than anyone dared to allow. They'd legislated so much away. Put pants on the Masai. The Masai with their cattle like household pets and their unshakable confidence in their natural rank among the game of the savanna and their unburied dead. If the milk gives out, drink blood. If the blood gives out, sit in dignity and wait to be taken. Engai lives high on his mountain and has business of his own herding the fine white cattle of the clouds. They put pants on the Masai and slept in soft beds and only at the climax of rare, feverish couplings did they sense dimly how much they had

legislated away. It was meat, but you couldn't see it if you
flayed it. If you flayed it, it came apart in your hands.

When Crown reached the lake, though he was urgent to
go on to the cabin, he impulsively left the track that was
now only two parallel lines of shatter in the thick crater
grasses and walked toward the shore. The flamingos
watched him, swaying up their heads, and close to the water
he stopped and abruptly raised his arms and the flamingos
lifted to his command in a great sheet and beaten by num-
berless wings color flooded the air.

Nice day, Crown thought. Going on, the flamingos settling again behind him on the lake, he thought: whatever it
was, it was absolutely undivided unless you divided it, and
there was no better place to see it than the crater. Imagine
Robert's little man coming up here on a day like this! They
always painted them as hunters with clubs and spears facing
off a mastodon or a saber-toothed tiger, or the women with a
folded leaf or a basket gathering seeds, digging for grubs
and roots. Working, sweating it out, looking grim because
they didn't have a flush toilet back at the cave with a *London Illustrated News* beside it to read. They never showed
them laughing except the bloody kids. Christ, you'd wake
up in the crater and spend the first few minutes just watching the clouds roll back. You'd swing your club over your
shoulder and go out prowling and you'd spend most of your
time just taking it all in. Nice day, man. Rhino print. Fresh.
Woman rhino. Hell of a hunt the day before yesterday,
wasn't it. Got enough meat to keep us maybe two, three
days. Slept with my woman last night, damn fine. Hey,
hyenas moved out of that old den over there and look at
that, this morning it's full of bat-eared foxes! Four moons
ago it was full of wild dogs and who dug the son-of-a-bitch
anyway? Maybe today I name me some more animals. That
one funny-looking with the beard and the long face. Grunts.
Call him, let's see, call him *t'gnu*. Hey, *t'gnu!* Yes, you an-

swer me, *t'gnu*, don't you. That stink one laughs, drags his
belly, man one and woman one got same parts, call him . . .
fisi. Stinkword, *fisi*. Sound like stink. Ah man, hell of a day,
though! Never seen such a day!

You don't have to get giddy now, Crown told himself. You
can drop the giddiness. You've made it most of the way
now. Just along the river now and up to the cabin and
you're in.

And what then? You want to think about that now or did
you mean just to wing it?

Not wing it. I'm beginning to see how it works and I'm
pretty sure I know what to do. Assuming just the minimum.
Assuming just a little luck.

Then there were wild dogs in the track ahead where it
crossed a dry, shallow wash, a pack of them patched brown,
black, yellow and white, thin-legged, with alert, scooped
ears, grin-panting, dug in, and Crown stopped in the track
and one of the bitches saw him and was up and studying
him, not yet signaling any alarm, uncertain of what he was
on foot in the crater where of men only the Masai walked
combining their silhouettes with the silhouettes of their cattle. He could backtrack and go off to the right into the river
and maybe he could pass them that way. He couldn't go
through them. He'd seen them running tireless on the Serengeti, wheeling around a line of wildebeest, hamstringing a
cow and pulling it down. They weren't the sort of dogs you
could pet and they were bloody curious.

He backed, watching them covertly, remembering not to
stare, and stepped off into the grass dislodging hoppers that
snapped whirring from his way and the pack was up and he
calculated making a run for the river and then the dogs took
off up the wash away from the river, fanning out, and he
stopped in the grass. When the dogs were well up the wash
he pushed to the edge and looked along where they had run
and there were two lions, big males with full, black-rufous

manes, crossing the wash slack-mouthed and panting in the heat of the day. Deployed in an open line the dogs watched the lions pass and while they were distracted Crown cut running across the wash and put some distance behind him before he slowed winded to a walk.

It's less than a kilometer, he thought, catching his breath and cooling out from the run, walking on. You had a little fun there and you're almost in. And farther up the track he thought suddenly: it's simple. It's so damned simple I'm surprised no one thought of it before. You could do the machine or you could do the meat, you could work any number on it you wanted, but it all came back around to a place like this. It was just a place like this. A fine wide crater with hazy blue walls. Nothing more because it didn't need any more. It was absolutely complete as it was. Game in the crater, a fringe of forest, a river running clear and cold down to a lake. Robert's little man here too, standing naked in his dignity like the rest of the game.

Crown caught a movement in the bush along the river.

The guerrilla stepped out and leveled his automatic. "*Simama!*" he called. "Halt!"

Crown stopped in the track.

"What is your business here?" the guerrilla called.

"I'm Seth Crown!" Crown shouted in Swahili. "Rukuma orders me here!"

The guerrilla ran awkwardly through the grass to the track, carrying the M-16 high. Facing Crown on the track he brought the M-16 to waist level. "Put your hands behind your head! *Upesi!* Be quick!" He worked past Crown, behind. "Walk!" he ordered. "*Upesi!* Do not lower your hands!"

"I'm not armed," Crown said.

"Silence!" the guerrilla barked. Wasn't he nervous, though. "Move!" He prodded Crown's back and Crown set off briskly. Now we'll see if it holds up, he thought. With luck it will. God knows I'm due a turn of that.

On the track in to the cabin another guerrilla emerged from the bush and stopped them. The first guerrilla frisked Crown then and then they walked into the yard past the two Land Rovers and the first guerrilla hailed the cabin.

Cassie came out, the woman guerrilla behind her guarding her with an automatic. Crown saw that she was safe and he smiled. Then the big man appeared dark in the doorway and looking up, stunned, Crown dropped his hands.

"Joseph," he said. "*Joseph.*"

"My name is Rukuma," Seth Crown's son said.

Sixteen

"WHY?" SETH CROWN ASKED. The woman guerrilla had searched him. She had searched him roughly, letting him know her hatred, and then Joseph, Rukuma, had led him with Cassie to one of the fever trees at the edge of the yard and the three of them had sat in the soft grass. The woman and the two guerrillas who had brought him in guarded them.

"But I wished to see you, *baba*," Rukuma said, smiling. *Baba* meant *father*. Rukuma plucked a stem of grass and chewed it.

He's not mocking now, Cassie thought. The smile isn't. It was better when it was.

"You could have come home anytime," Crown said. "I'd have welcomed you."

"Home. Yes." Rukuma turned his head and spat out the stem. He looked at Crown. "Have you become stupid?"

"Apparently."

"I am Rukuma," Crown's son told him, his voice flat with boredom. "Joseph is dead."

"I feared that thou were," Crown said in Masai. Cassie glanced at him and then at Rukuma.

"Sentiment," said Rukuma. "You wish to play with languages? I have several more now. Would you like to try French?"

The resemblance was there. Cassie wondered why she hadn't noticed it before.

"You went to Algeria," Crown said.

"Yes."

"Vietnam?"

"The weapons? No. Kampuchea."

"I'm surprised they can afford a foreign policy."

The woman guerrilla walked away.

"The weapons cost them nothing. They were a gift from the American people." Rukuma smiled then at Cassie. "After the little packages," he said to her. He leaned back on his elbows in the grass. The sun through the foliage dappled his face. Cassie felt chilled. His serenity chilled her.

"And Amin?" Crown asked.

"Amin makes messes. People who make messes are useful."

"I expect he thought he was using you."

"You think this, *baba*? How very astute you are."

"Why?" Crown asked, reverting to his earlier question. "Because of your mother?"

Rukuma shook his head. "The Western mind. Monkey mind. It looks for reasons." He sat up. "Tell me a reason. Tell me why your clients came so far and at such great expense to hunt."

"I understand," Crown said.

"You gave me enough reasons this morning," Cassie said.

Rukuma gestured, quickly grinning. "But there is no end to reasons." He dropped the grin, looking to Crown. "There

is a white bwana inside each of us, *baba*. He must be driven
out. Is that a good reason?"

"I understand," Crown said calmly.

Rukuma studied him. "Your old age has made you simple." There was anger in his voice.

"When can Cassie go?"

"What trap have you set for me, *mzungu?*" Rukuma
asked, using the word for white man.

"None. I followed your orders."

"Then perhaps she may leave tomorrow morning. Perhaps. Afterward."

"She doesn't need to see."

"Yes. Most certainly she does." Rukuma pushed up lightly
and stood. He was tall as his father and thicker, more heavily muscled. He looked down at them. "You will have much
time to say *kwaheri*. For now you may sit in the Land
Rover. We will speak again later."

"You may not believe me," Crown said, looking up, "but
I'm glad to see you."

Rukuma turned abruptly away. He barked orders in Swahili to the two guerrillas and strode across the yard to the
cabin.

"Easy," Crown said to Cassie. "He told them to shoot our
legs out if we try anything. Get up slowly and we'll walk to
the Land Rover."

"There must be something we can do," Cassie whispered.

Crown took her hand. "Not at the moment."

Arusha was hot, a dry wind blowing through the streets
dirty with litter. Fuhrey felt feverish. He'd never really slept
and now after the long drive his eyes stung and a hot sharp
pain burned from his arm. Kegedi was stuck behind a bus in
the market district, a diesel Mercedes, red and rusted,
crowded with Africans. The Africans in the back of the bus
were jammed in among cardboard boxes and crates of

scrawny chickens and they stared out the back windows
happy at the entertainment of the Range Rover. The bus
was forced to stop in every narrow block to wait for vendors
to pull their carts from the street. The carts held fruit, vegetables, groundnuts, flowers. Everything was rotting in the
afternoon sun except the groundnuts. When the bus started
up again after a stop it swirled smears of black diesel fumes
over the car and the Africans pointed to the fumes and
laughed with great good will.

Kegedi found a side street wide enough for the car and
turned off. He threaded side streets and worked in beyond
the bus and the main street was ahead. When they neared
the intersection they saw that it was barricaded.

"Jesus Christ," Fuhrey said.

Kegedi pulled up to the barricade. He worked the door
and jumped out and slipped past the barricade and around
the corner. He came back shaking his head. "There is a parade," he told Fuhrey. "The member for Arusha is in town."

"Can we walk?"

Kegedi checked behind. The bus blocked their retreat, the
passengers spilling from the doors. "Better to wait," he said,
straightening. "It is only a small parade."

The passengers crowded around the Range Rover. Some
of them climbed onto the fenders and looked back through
the windshield and smiled. They were careful to leave the
hood clear so that Fuhrey and Kegedi could see. Fuhrey
heard brasses blatting and the beat of drums. The first line
of marchers entered the intersection, women in pink sandals
and bright print dresses and kerchiefs carrying a banner.
The banner spelled out TANU, the initials of the Tanzanian
African Nationalist Union, the national political party. The
big man at the center of the line wore a blue silk business
suit that shimmered in the sun. He greeted the crowd left
and right, turning his head and expansively raising his arms.
More lines followed of men and women and then the band

and as the band passed the intersection it struck up a tune and the marchers started singing and then groups of singing schoolchildren went by ordered by forms, the oldest children first, so that they tailed off as they passed. That was the end of the parade. Kegedi leaned out the window and called in Swahili and the bus passengers jumped from the fenders and two of the men swung the barricade aside. Kegedi drove into the main street and followed the parade until it turned off. He drove on to the police station and parked.

"You do the talking, John," Fuhrey said as he came around the car.

"If you wish," Kegedi said.

The police station was a long, low, thick-walled building of reddish-gray concrete. Inside it was cool. A *polisi* in khaki with sergeant's stripes on his sleeves sat at a battered desk opposite the door laboriously filling out a form. He looked up as they came in. When he noticed Fuhrey's arm he frowned and laid down his pen.

"*Hujambo*, Bwana," Kegedi said formally.

"*Jambo*," the *polisi* said. He straightened and folded his hands on the desk. His brown face was thick and lined and his close-cropped hair was gray.

"We have come for help," Kegedi said in Swahili. "An American woman, a tourist, has been kidnaped and taken to Ngorongoro Crater. A small band of guerrillas is hiding out in the crater. Five men and a woman. They are heavily armed. A man has gone to the crater to negotiate with them for the woman. We believe the man and the woman will both be killed. We wish to lead a detachment of *polisi* there to rescue them. There are soldiers at the lodge above the crater. Some are wounded but some could join the detachment."

The *polisi* blinked. "*Jina lako nani?*" he asked. "What is your name?"

"John Kegedi."

"Show me your identity card."

Kegedi pulled out his wallet and found his card and laid it on the desk. "There is little time," he said impatiently.

The *polisi* studied the card. When he was satisfied with it he squared it carefully in front of him on the desk and turned to Fuhrey. "Who is this man?" he asked Kegedi.

"*Jina langu daktari* Robert Fuhrey," Fuhrey said. "I am an American scientist working at Oloito Gorge."

"What is wrong with your arm?"

"It was broken by the leader of the guerrillas."

The *polisi* frowned. "Show me your *pasi*. Your passport."

Fuhrey reddened and looked at Kegedi. "Hell, John," he said in English, "it's back at camp."

"We came quickly to report these crimes," Kegedi told the *polisi*. "We did not stop for passports."

"You do not have a *pasi?*" the *polisi* asked Fuhrey.

"*Ndiyo*. I have a *pasi*." Fuhrey held up his arm. "My arm is broken. We drove six hours to find help. People will be murdered unless the *polisi* come."

The *polisi* nodded. "Where is your *pasi?*"

"My *pasi* is at my camp at Oloito Gorge," Fuhrey said carefully.

"*Wageni* visiting Tanzania, foreigners, are required to carry *pasi* at all times." The *polisi* looked stern now. "You will have to wait for the captain of *polisi*."

"Yes," Kegedi said, relieved. "Let us speak to the captain of *polisi*."

"The captain of *polisi* is not in. You will have to wait for him."

"When will he return?" Kegedi asked.

"Perhaps in an hour."

"This man requires treatment of his arm. We must go to the *hospitali*. We would return to see the captain in an hour."

The *polisi* picked up Kegedi's identity card and studied it.

"You are a *mwalimu?*" he asked. "A teacher?" Kegedi said
he was. The *polisi* handed back his card. "You may go to the
hospitali," he said. "I will assign a man to go with you. Wait
here." He stood and started down a side hall. He stopped at
a door and turned back to them. "Do not attempt to leave,"
he called. "If you attempt to leave you will be charged."

"We will wait," Kegedi said. The *polisi* opened the door
and went in.

"God *damn* it," Fuhrey swore. "God *damn* it."

"We will lose very little time, Robert," Kegedi said. "You
would have had to go to the hospital in any case."

"You could have gone on."

"The captain will help us."

"I hope to hell."

The *polisi* came back with a younger *polisi*. The younger
polisi, in khaki shorts and knee socks, was strapping on a
pistol belt. "How did you arrive here?" the sergeant asked
Kegedi in Swahili.

"We have a car."

"This man will go with you to the *hospitali*. Return here
when you are finished."

"Of course," Kegedi said.

They went out, the young *polisi* dawdling. When he saw
the Range Rover he hurried and climbed quickly in behind.
Kegedi started the engine and worked the clutch hard,
squealing the tires. The young *polisi* chuckled.

Abdi in the lorry had found the *moran* at midmorning hik-
ing down the mountain road from Ngorongoro. They carried
their wounded on the makeshift stretchers and they were
singing. Abdi supposed they were singing victory songs. He
had spoken to Simel, mixing Swahili with his smattering of
Masai. Simel had understood and quickly the *moran* had
boarded the lorry. Abdi had worked it around on the road
then and driven down the mountain and across the Seren-

geti to the turnoff and southeast toward the *manyatta* of ole
Kipoin. There had been no question of leaving the wounded
and going on to the crater. The wounded needed attention
and in the absence of the Effendi any further assault required the permission of the chief.

When he came to the watercourse on the track to the
manyatta Abdi saw that the rains had washed out the ford.
He turned northeastward then, taking the lorry fast over the
rolling savanna, following the watercourse and scattering
the game, and looked for a better ford. Some kilometers
above the washout he found one. He halted the lorry and
got out to inspect. The near bank dropped off abruptly to
the water but the opposite bank had been cut away by
flood. Abdi spoke to Simel and Simel directed the unloading
of the wounded. Other *moran* jumped down and hacked at
the dense bush with their swords, opening up a track. Then
cautiously Abdi inched the big lorry to the bank edge, going
in at an angle, and dropped one front wheel and then the
other, ground forward, dropped the doubled rear wheels,
the stake bed hanging on the bank but pulling clear, and
gunned across the shallow and up the slick opposite slope.
The *moran* crossed behind the lorry. When Simel knocked
on the rear window of the cab Abdi steered southeast again.

At the entrance to the *manyatta* the women and children
swarmed over the lorry, shouting and questioning and helping down the wounded *moran*. Abdi left them and entered
through the thorn *boma* to the circle of houses and looked
for ole Kipoin. Simel had run ahead as soon as the lorry had
stopped. Abdi saw him with ole Kipoin crossing the common. He waited for them inside the entrance.

"It is bad," ole Kipoin said to Abdi in awkward Swahili
when he came up, taking Abdi's arm and going on. "This
one, Simel, explains. I go with you. We take *moran*. Is it
enough?"

"There are six in the crater, my father," Abdi said. "They have weapons. It is enough if we surprise them."

"Other Masai in crater," ole Kipoin said. "They help." Outside the entrance he called sharply to the *moran* in Masai and they separated from the crowd and reboarded the lorry. Ole Kipoin nodded to Simel and he joined the others. "Now quick," the chief told Abdi. "We go."

In the cab with ole Kipoin beside him Abdi started the engine and swung the lorry around in the direction he had come.

"Not this way," the Masai said, raising his voice over the noise of the engine and gesturing with his club. "Other way. Not so far."

"The lorry cannot cross the watercourses if the banks are steep," Abdi said, braking and turning.

"Places to cross. My people's land. Masai cross with cattle. Not-Masai not know. I know." Ole Kipoin pointed northeast. "That way."

Abdi settled back to drive. He was smiling. It would cut at least an hour off their time. They would reach the rim before sundown. Pray, Abdi thought. Pray that the Effendi and Cassie were still alive.

"We hunt down," ole Kipoin said sternly, as if he'd heard. His lips moved as he searched for words in the unfamiliar language. "No walk this land no more. My brother dead, take all this one's life, we hunt down." He spat out the window to seal the pledge.

Midafternoon, Rukuma crossed to the Land Rover and angrily flung open the door. "Come out, *mzungu*," he said to Crown. "There are questions you must answer." He told the guerrillas to watch the woman. "Come," he ordered Crown. "We will walk."

On the track that followed the river to the lake Rukuma said: "Where are the soldiers who attacked my camp?"

"I left them at the army camp," Crown said. "Where you found the lorry."

"They would not have remained there. Where would they have gone?"

"To the lodge. Some of them were wounded."

"Which lodge?"

"The crater lodge. They intended to radio for orders. They had prisoners."

"Yes?" Rukuma was interested. "How many?"

"I didn't count. Maybe ten."

"Where will they take them?"

"Arusha. They'll turn them over to the police."

"Are they still at the lodge?"

"Probably. They were pretty bushed."

"And they do not know that I came to the crater? They do not know you are here?"

"No."

"No," Rukuma said. He looked at Crown. "What about Abdi? He was with you at my camp. I saw him."

"He knows. I told him to stay away. He was to pick up the *moran* and take them back to their encampments. After that he's supposed to drive to the rim and wait for Cassie."

"And the others I left at your camp?"

"I sent Kegedi and Fuhrey in to Arusha to take care of that arm."

Rukuma faced his father. "There is something more, *mzungu*," he said harshly. "You are too calm." He folded his arms, his biceps straining the sleeves of his fatigues.

"There's nothing more," Crown said. "I did what you asked me to do."

"Are you tired of living? Do you go so easily to your death?"

"No."

"Then what is it?"

"You said an exchange. I came to make that exchange."

Rukuma laughed. "You trust me?" he said, mocking.

"I trusted Rukuma," Crown told him, looking into his eyes. "I trust Joseph even more."

Rukuma looked away and turned and began walking again. Crown kept pace beside him. After a while Rukuma said, "You value this woman so much?"

"Equally with your mother."

"Yes. You loved my mother. I learned very much about love from that."

"It mattered."

"Not to the Boers."

"Especially to the Boers."

"Exactly. It made you vulnerable."

Beyond now on the savanna were wildebeest. "Everyone's vulnerable, Joseph."

"*Rukuma,*" Crown's son said savagely, swinging around. "*Rukuma.* Say my name, *mzungu! Rukuma!*"

Crown nodded. "Rukuma."

Rukuma stared at him and then the anger was gone and they walked.

"I am not vulnerable," Rukuma said after a silence.

Crown said nothing.

"I was called," Rukuma went on. "It came slowly, after I left you. No," he said, shaking his head, "I heard no voices. I only saw and slowly understood what I was seeing. I saw my mother. I saw Uhuru. I saw the *Mzee* with his drunken brooding face. I saw black men dressing as white men and learning to exploit. In Algeria I saw a people united by the violence of their struggle."

"How long were you there?" Crown asked, watching the wildebeest.

"Several years."

"Did you study there?" The herd shifted subtlely, adjusting to their presence on the track.

"Yes. Marxism, tactics. They trained me."

"Why?"

"For their own reasons. For Zimbabwe. For alliance with the P.L.O. Nothing important. I had my own reasons. I came back to Dar and worked with the groups there. When I was ready I went to Kampuchea."

"Why?" Crown asked again.

"There were Chinese in Dar. They directed me there. I went for weapons, but I found a purity. I saw that what I was called to do could be done."

"They've murdered a fifth of their population."

"To kill a poisonous tree you must dig out its farthest roots," Rukuma said. He stopped. A hyena lounged ahead of them in the track. It saw them and came to its feet, its tail going between its legs.

"What's the tree?" Crown asked. Watching the hyena, he remembered the lone hyena at the lake that oddly hunted flamingo. They don't kill to eat, he'd told Cassie. They kill by eating.

"The West," Rukuma said.

"All of it?" Bedlam in the crater sometimes. At night. You had to have eyes for it. Otherwise you missed it.

"All of it, *baba*," Rukuma said. "Root and branch."

Crown studied him. "Back how far? Back to the Stone Age?"

"You cannot even conceive it, can you." Rukuma extended his hand toward the hyena. The gesture triggered it and it swung off the track and trotted away, looking back at them over its shoulder. "Here, *baba*. I give you your freedom. You are free to go." He was grinning.

"No."

"You have no guarantee that I will spare the woman. If you go then at least one of you will live. Come, go on. I allow it. Take this chance Rukuma gives you."

"No," Crown said.

Rukuma shrugged then. "As you wish. You are hungry for suicide."

"We're two men, Rukuma," Crown said. "That's all we are. I came to make an exchange. Whatever follows from that exchange is your business."

"Yes," said Rukuma, looking down. He scuffed the grass with his boot. "Well," he said finally, "you have had your chance." He glared at Crown. The glare shaded to mockery, a smile playing at the corners of his mouth. "Come, *baba*," he said. "Let us return to the cabin."

The doctor at the hospital was Indian, a small brown man in a lab coat that had once been white. When he came out to collect Fuhrey from the confusion of the crowded waiting room he was beaming.

"Dr. Fuhrey, Dr. Fuhrey," he said, leading Fuhrey down the hall, the *polisi* staying behind with John Kegedi, "how very excellent to make your acquaintance. I myself have been frequently to Olduvai. Yes! Yes! I recognized your name immediately! I am a devoted student of your excellent profession. I follow the conferences and the papers. Most difficult to find the papers here in Arusha. You must tell me all the latest news." He turned in to an examining room. "Sit here, my good friend," he told Fuhrey, patting a wooden examining table covered with a worn leather pad. "Let us have a look at that arm. However did you break it?"

Fuhrey explained as the doctor slipped the arm from its sling and began unwrapping the bandages.

"But that is remarkable." The doctor's voice rose to a squeak. "I have never heard of such a thing! This must have been a man of truly remarkable strength, yes?"

"Yes."

"Yes! And over his knee! Extraordinary! Here now, very carefully, very carefully I will remove these splints. This is fine work, Dr. Fuhrey."

Fuhrey looked down at his arm cradled in the doctor's thin brown hands. It was swollen at the break, purplish-red, and the imprints of Rukuma's fingers were bruises above and below. The doctor palpated the break. Fuhrey winced.

"Excuse me," the doctor said. "I do not mean to hurt you. I am accustomed to the Africans, Dr. Fuhrey. Truly I believe that they feel no pain." He glanced up from the arm. "And the man who did this was a terrorist, you say? How very strange! What object would send a terrorist so far into the bush?"

Fuhrey felt himself sweating. "I don't mean to be impolite, Doctor, but please work quickly. It's not over out there. I've got to get back to the police."

The doctor bobbed his head. "Of course, of course, how thoughtless of me. Here," he said, holding open the sling, "Let us use this to give the arm support. We must go now to the X-ray room for X rays."

"Is it absolutely necessary?"

"Oh yes. Necessary. Necessary. We must see if the fracture requires reduction. You cannot dig for *Australopithecus boisei* with a bent arm! Come, please!"

He led Fuhrey out of the examining room and around a corner. The X-ray room was dark. The doctor switched on a bare overhead bulb. "Wait here, please," he said. He left the room and came back with film plates and fitted one into the X-ray table. The plate was bent and it stuck. He struck it sharply with the heel of his hand, one corner and then the other, and it wedged into position. "There, Dr. Fuhrey," he said. "You see the quality of our equipment. It is impossible to acquire new machines. Impossible! I myself submitted an order for X-ray equipment more than three years ago. This machine is a legacy from colonial days." He maneuvered Fuhrey to the table and arranged his arm on the plate. "Yes. I know that it is painful. You must remain very still." He guided the cone of the tube over the arm. "Still, Dr. Fuhrey.

I shall make the exposure and return immediately. Very quickly! We will work very quickly!"

But it seemed the plates wouldn't be ready for at least half an hour. Fuhrey went out to the waiting room and told Kegedi to go back to the police station alone. The young *polisi* didn't like the arrangement. Kegedi pointed out that his identity card was in order, that only Fuhrey's passport was in question. Finally Fuhrey brought the doctor and the doctor convinced the *polisi* that he should wait for Fuhrey in the waiting room and let Kegedi go.

"Well, Dr. Fuhrey," the doctor said, "that is what we must contend with." They sat in his consulting room at the rear of the hospital, Fuhrey on a brown leather couch, the doctor at his littered desk, Indian rugs scattered on the stained wooden floor. "Quite confidentially I do not know why I remain here, except that my dear wife's family is here. The Africans are mistrustful of Asians. Supplies! We are short always of supplies. You should see the surgery! The flies! I have explained and explained to them, but they pretend not to understand. They have lived with flies, a fly is nothing, they do not even brush them from their faces. Flies walk in and out of their mouths! What is one to do with such a people? Those who live in the cities are riddled with venereal disease, those who live in the rural areas are riddled with parasites. I have seen parasites never reported in the medical texts, my good friend. Yes! Jiggers, tapeworms, roundworms, liver flukes, nameless things. Horrible. How is it that they survive? Can you tell me that? You have worked in Africa. How do they survive?"

"They're tough," Fuhrey said, distracted.

"Tough, yes! That is surely exactly the correct word for them. Tough! But also lost in superstition. A country woman comes to me with a surpassing pain in her abdomen and tells me an uncle bewitched her! Imagine! We approach the twenty-first century, Dr. Fuhrey! An uncle bewitched her!

No," the little doctor said, smoothing back his thin black hair, "it is hopeless. Truly hopeless. Nothing will ever come of Africa. A most terribly backward land." Mercurially the doctor was beaming again. "Forgive me for speaking of my troubles, Dr. Fuhrey. You deal with far more exalted things. Your digs! If you will do me the enormous honor, if it is not too much trouble with your painful fractured arm that you have broken certainly in the line of duty, beyond the call of duty I should say, would you be so kind as to tell me about your latest work?"

Fuhrey realized he hadn't thought of his work since the night of Rukuma's attack. Last night, he corrected himself. Only last night. He told the doctor. It was something to do.

Eventually a technician brought the plates. The fractures were partial, the bones cracked but not completely broken. Plying Fuhrey with questions, masterfully the Indian doctor cast his arm.

The cast was still warm when Kegedi returned. "I spoke with the captain," he told Fuhrey grimly. "I am not sure he believed me. He agreed finally to order an investigation."

"When?"

"Tomorrow."

"For Christ's sake, John, tomorrow's too late."

"I know. I tried very hard to convince him."

"We'll have to get back up there ourselves."

"Not possible," Kegedi said.

"Why not?"

"He will not allow you to leave until he has confirmed your passport. He has wired Dar, but the American Embassy is closed until tomorrow morning."

Then it's hopeless, Fuhrey thought. I'm useless anyway with this arm and John can't go it alone. The doctor was right, about the land at least. The land itself defeated you.

Abdi drove eastward on the main Serengeti track. He estimated he was no more than ten kilometers from the upgrading of the track at Olduvai. Ole Kipoin's word was good. He had directed Abdi to easy fordings and quickly they had left the district of the Masai for the reserve area east of the park. The Serengeti was golden again after its brief greening at the time of the long rains, the wildebeest retreated again to the woodlands. Tommies watched the lorry go. Treeless the golden plain stretched ahead and black in the distance were the highlands.

When they reached the rim at sundown they would stop at the lodge. The soldiers would join them with their automatics, leaving a few behind to guard. They would have to go on foot. Night would cover their advance. It would be a stalk at night down the Seneto Hill road and into the crater. The cabin by the river was screened within a grove of trees. They could use the river itself as cover and spread out then around the grove, the Masai going in first, silently, to overpower the guards. How many guards? The guerrillas were six. It might be that Rukuma would set no more than two to guard since he expected no attack. Another would be guarding Cassie and the Effendi, perhaps inside the cabin. Abdi and one of the soldiers might storm the cabin. It was a possible plan.

It was a possible plan if the Effendi was alive. If the Effendi was not alive it would at least bring swift retribution, though how bitter the taste of that retribution. Cassie might still be alive if Rukuma kept his word. Abdi had no faith in the guerrilla leader's word. A man who killed so easily knew nothing of honor. Let him die without honor then. The others the soldiers could deliver to the police. Abdi wanted Rukuma for himself. He would leave the body unburied for the scavengers of the crater.

You tell yourself great tales, old man, Abdi thought wearily. There will be time for tales when you have earned the right.

Strange that the gorge, Olduvai, was hidden from the track. They would pass it before they saw it. Strange that

the Europeans dug there for the bones aged to rock and
read their secrets. The skulls told Abdi little but there was
mystery in the bones of the ancient animals. From hunting
he knew the bones of animals well. The animals that lived
before were giants. The horns of the sheep of old were
wider than his outstretched arms. The elephant was larger,
the rhino, even the cats. He had heard that as the world
aged the animals got smaller as if the strength of the world
were weakening. What strength was taken from the world
with time? Did the grasses become less nutritious and the
green browse of the trees? And at the same time men grew
taller. It seemed that evil came into the world and slowly
filled it. The time was evil now. When men murdered men
for empty dreams the time was evil. Perhaps the world
would end soon. Perhaps fire would burn it clean as Africans burned the dead grasses to make room for new green
shoots. Something must be accomplished against evil before
it overwhelmed the earth. A handful of men was not
enough. In the greener time it might have been, but in this
sere declining time no longer was it enough.

Suddenly the engine stalled, lurching the lorry, and
caught and ran and stalled. Startled, Abdi pumped the ac-
celerator and the engine ran briefly and died and the lorry
rolled unpowered in the track. Abdi braked and shifted to
neutral and worked the ignition and the engine caught and
as quickly died. Petrol, Abdi thought, reading the gauge, his
throat tightening, *petrol.*

Ole Kipoin watched curiously. "Is it sick?" he asked.

Abdi didn't answer. The needle of the fuel gauge registered below empty. Had he refueled the lorry that morning?
He couldn't remember. It seemed to him that he had. He
jumped from the cab and plucked a stem of bush from the
roadside and stripped it. He unlocked the fuel cap and unscrewed it and fed in the stem until it scraped the bottom of
the tank. When he withdrew it it was dry.

He threw down the stem and went to the cab. "The lorry has no more fuel," he told ole Kipoin in a strangled voice. "We must go from here on foot."

Ole Kipoin got out and walked with dignity to the back of the lorry. "The machine has died," he told the *moran* in Masai. "We will walk to the crater. Come."

They started out, Abdi and ole Kipoin in the lead. Stricken, deeply shamed, Abdi hung his head. They would not reach the crater before morning. In his criminal stupidity he had forfeited the Effendi's life.

Seventeen

THEN AGAIN IT WAS NIGHT, the sky above the crater clear and struck with stars and the waning moon silvering the yard outside the dark cabin, and to an impulse of compassion or of mockery Rukuma had given them blankets and allowed them to bed down together in the back of the Land Rover, a guerrilla posted to guard them behind the car where he could watch the doors. Lying beside Seth in the light darkness of the car, the windows misting from their breath and the scent close and nested of the game the car had carried, Cassie let the last of her vigilance go. It had no place there. She didn't need it. She hadn't needed it since he walked into the yard.

He was touching her. His fingertips traced the shape of her ear, her temple, her forehead, her nose, the bones of her cheek. Neither of them had stopped touching, through the afternoon except when Rukuma took him away to talk, through the evening after they had eaten at the table in the cabin with the guard. They touched now and she gave her hand lightly on his.

When Seth walked into the yard alone and unarmed and looked at her and smiled, before she had known what he was doing she had understood that it was rare. It was something she had never seen before. It surprised her and at first it even frightened her. From somewhere he had recovered it as he might have recovered a lost language or a temple complex overrun with jungle and it changed the terms. What had been unbalanced was balanced, force with force.

She was finding now that she could approximate it. She couldn't do exactly as he was doing. She hadn't lived that long or lived that way, if how you lived was part of it, and she already saw that it was. But she could approximate it and learn.

Rukuma's attacks were to kill his father. To wound and then to kill. She couldn't think of him yet as Joseph. They were for other purposes too, ugly and devastating purposes that she would have to confront, but they were first to kill his father. Seth had come to the porch of the cabin entirely resolved and then he had also had that to resolve. And he had done it easily and without any distance, and before the rarity of it even Rukuma had faltered. She would learn to think of him as Joseph, as Seth did.

"Listen," he said then beside her in the car. "We don't have to push our luck. The man back there can't do us both. We'll wait until the moon is down. I'll work the door and jump him. You'll take off for the river. They'll have to deal with me before they can come after you."

"No."

"Cassie?"

"No, Seth."

"There's no certainty about the other way. You can't count on it."

"Please."

"I suppose I could force the issue," he said.

"Don't shame me, Seth."

"Not shame. There's no shame. It's a decision you have to make."

"I have. No."

Her lips and her throat. Her hand on his and her lips and her throat.

"They'll want to hunt him down," he said. "You've got to convince them not to. Tell them I said so. Tell them to bring in the authorities and let them handle it."

"All right."

"It really has to stop somewhere. It can't just go on. Someone has to stop it. That's why I'm doing it this way. Because someone has to stop it."

She was crying.

"No," he said gently.

"I can't help it."

"We don't have to be here," he said, holding her. "We can be anywhere we like. Where would you like to be?"

"With you."

"That's easy. But where would you like to be with me? California?"

"No."

"At the camp?"

"Yes."

"Fine. We're at the camp. What are we doing?"

"Making love."

"We're good at that, aren't we? We may be the best anyone's ever been at that."

"Yes."

"Good. Now, we've done that."

"When did we?"

"Say for the moment that we have. What would you like to do now?"

"Take a picnic."

"Marvelous. I've a wicker basket with silver and china set in the lid. I ordered it from Harrod's. Very fancy. All these pockets and compartments. What goes into it?"

She tried. "Artichokes," she said, not seeing or tasting them. "Cheese. Bread. Pâté. Champagne. Apples. Chocolate."

"Hell of a picnic."

"Seth?"

"No. You're doing very well. So we pack the fine basket and walk down to the lake. We've got flamingos on the lake. We chase away the usual collection of local fauna—"

"Let them stay."

"Right. They stay. We spread out the checkered tablecloth and invite the boys over."

"And the girls."

"And the girls. Mama Fisi hunkers down and eats—"

"Chocolate."

"She'd like that. Bwana Simba tries his paw at an artichoke and swears off gazelle. What about the giraffe? We've got two of them looking over our shoulder from either side."

"Champagne. Because it tickles their throats. And apples for the elephant."

"Perfect. And since it's sundown, a great streaming sundown—"

"I can't, Seth. I can't."

He shifted so that her head was against his shoulder. "We don't have to," he said. "We don't need fantasies. We never did. Being here is as good as being anywhere."

She pressed against him, his lean, long body that he had kept hard.

He's accepted it, she thought. He's accepted it and turned it to your advantage and you aren't making it easier on him. He doesn't owe you that much. No one owes anyone that much. He's worked through the anger and the denial. You can too.

No, she thought, I can't. I wish I could but I can't. I'm not ready to and there isn't time. Later there'll be time. I'll have to carry that through tomorrow. God knows it's light enough with what he's carrying. He needs me now and here, completely here. He's arranged an afterward for me. Afterward I can work on the rest. Afterward I can answer for all I have to answer for. Now and tomorrow are his.

"There's a certain amount of housekeeping," he said. "Can you think about it now?"

"Yes," Cassie said, touching. "Tell me."

"When you leave here, stay on the track. That way if anyone comes down they'll find you. Walk calmly and watch ahead. Give the game a wide berth. If you see any of the local Masai, get over to them. Otherwise Abdi should be waiting for you at the rim." He was stroking her hair. "I've deeded you half the camp. You can keep it if you want or you can arrange for Abdi to buy you out."

"I'll keep it," she said. "What needs to be done?"

"Finish rebuilding the tents. Abdi can teach you the business side. I'd go ahead with that water hole as soon as possible. The game needs it and it's a great attraction for the tourists. With Abdi as a partner you shouldn't have any problem about the licensing. The government collects enough on the operation." He stopped. "Let's see, what else? Right. Joseph. When they bring him in he's going to need a good barrister. There's an Indian in Dar. Abdi knows him. Pay him well, will you?"

"Yes."

"It won't be the easiest thing you've ever done."

"He's your son."

"Something. I don't know what he is."

"Yes you do."

"Yes," he said. "I do."

"What about tomorrow?" she asked carefully.

"It should be all right. After I say what I have to say to Joseph. The woman worries me more than he does. Watch out for her. What's most important is that you stay calm. You know that he'll keep his word and you expect him to. But don't let the woman get you alone."

"I won't."

He was silent, thinking, and then he said: "I'm sorry. I wish I could tell you how sorry I am."

"No. Never that. I love you."

They went on to the work of the night. It was the work the night was given them for, Cassie thought, even if it had been given to them in mockery, and they had much time for it and they could do it well. I write my love into your body now, she told him silently. Not with a torture of sentencing needles but with my hands and my mouth and my flesh surrounding you and it is not a sentence and you have committed no crime. I write my love into your body as a gift I give you freely, what I have to give and so little against what is coming but all there is and all. You cannot take it with you where you go. I will not pretend that you are not going and I will not pretend that you can take with you what I give. I will not even pretend that now is now and there is no other now because now is also the knowledge of tomorrow and the knowledge of the tomorrows that might have been. Only that you will know this before you go and know it well, know it in this sweat and lust of body, of the body's holy work, that defies all mockery, and that it might somehow ease the going that you choose freely on my behalf when nothing is owed. And that I believe I would have chosen on your behalf, although I cannot say with certainty because it was not given to me to choose, beloved. I will not use those words either. I will not use those words cheapened and worn away but I will say with absolute certainty that I love you and I will never forget you. So I give this that is also not

owed and is freely given, now for now but equally for tomorrow and equally for me and in the words of your name,
Seth Crown, and in the uncheapened unworn words that
will also always be your names to me, Oloito, Ngorongoro,
Serengeti, Masai. Seth. Seth Crown. Seth Crown.

In the cabin Rukuma looked up from the game of dice the
men were playing on the floor and saw Kare across the table
in the lantern light watching him. "Why do you stare at me,
woman?" he asked in Swahili, swinging around heavily to
face her. The men heard his tone and stopped the game.

"This *mzungu* is your father," Kare said.

"What of it?"

"You did not tell us so before."

"Are you my mother that I come to you with tales?"

"This is a matter of importance," Kare said. The men
were listening.

"Yes? And what is the importance?"

"You have told us that the *wazungu* are evil. That they
brought their corruption to Africa and that all of them must
be killed. And yet your father is a *mzungu,* and you carry
his blood."

"And that is as far as you have understood it," Rukuma
said coldly. He looked down at the men. "Do you hear her?
Does this question also trouble you?"

"I have thought of it," Chaudi said.

"Ah. You have thought of it. There is much thinking
going on in this *banda.* I am surprised that the walls do not
shake with it." He looked back to Kare. "Why do you think
I kill this man?"

"It is a thing of much omen," Chaudi said behind him.

"*Asante,* Chaudi. Thank you. I see you have not learned
what I have taught you." Rukuma was still looking at Kare.
Stubbornly she stared back at him. "This is no omen,"
Rukuma went on. "There are no omens. That is village

superstition. I kill my father to rid the world of another *mzungu*. I kill my father to show you and all who will learn of it after that my purpose is stern and absolute. That one *mzungu* is like another. That *wazungu* are not powerful as so many believe but weak, easy to capture as hyrax, and that they bleed and die. Do you know how you capture hyrax, Kare?"

"A woman does not hunt," Kare said.

"You find him in his hollow tree. You find the small opening by which he enters and leaves. You push a sharpened stick into the opening until it touches him and you twist. He screams. You twist and he is tightened on the stick, his pelt is tightened, and when the stick has found sufficient purchase you withdraw the hyrax from the tree and snap his neck."

"It is true," one of the other guerrillas said. "I have done this many times."

"So you kill your father," said Kare. "It seems to me that much that we have done has been directed to this. Many lives have been lost for this. My sisters were lost for this." She leaned forward, her long dark arms on the table and her face in the lantern light a dark mask. "Do we work for Africa, Rukuma," she asked, challenging, "or do we fight your private wars?"

Jerking up, Rukuma slapped her hard, snapping her head aside and bringing dark blood to her mouth and she pulled back cowering and covered her mouth with her hand. Rukuma's hands were fists and he towered above the men on the floor. "Any of you?" he raged. "Any of you? Do you think what this whore thinks? Do you? Do you dare?"

The men scurried back from him, not looking, looking down. "No, Rukuma," they mumbled. "We follow you," Chaudi nervously said.

"And you, whore?" Rukuma spat at Kare. "Who do you follow?"

"As I have done," she answered him. "I follow you." As if to herself she said: "But I am not a whore."

Rukuma sat down again. He inhaled deeply to slow his breathing and then he smiled. "No, Kare, you are not a whore. You are only a poor woman who thinks too much. But here," he said, his head swinging toward the men, his voice softening, "part of the fault is mine. I have not spoken to you of what we are to do. When the business of tomorrow is done we shall have accomplished our work here for now. We shall leave and go up into Kenya, avoiding the customs at Namanga, and stop for a time in Nairobi. I have followers there. We shall band with them. We shall put aside our uniforms and become as men of the city. The *Mzee* Jomo Kenyatta is dying. With his going will come a time of confusion in Kenya. He has governed that country for many years and it is swollen with corruption. There will be many who covet the high offices. We shall align with some against others. We shall offer an arrangement of assassination."

"How will this help us, my leader?" the scarred guerrilla asked.

"The men we aid will thus become our accomplices," Rukuma said. "When they have taken up office they will be in a position to make changes. We have worked from outside. Now we will begin to move inside to work from within. The changes will be of our proposing." Rukuma waved his hand, dismissing them. "There is more, but that is as much as you need to know at this time."

Kare touched her swollen lip and looked at him. "What of the woman?" she asked, almost whispering.

Rukuma frowned. "That is not yet decided."

"I do not tell you your business," Kare said then, "but she has seen you and would recognize you. She has seen us all. Also she is a *mzungu*. She must be killed."

"Kare," Rukuma said too quietly. "You have thought

enough for one night. You would show great wisdom to leave the thinking to me."

Holding Cassie, her body under the rough blanket indistinct in the moonless predawn darkness but warm against him all along its length, Seth Crown told himself so now it's almost finished. You've been lucky. You couldn't have asked for a better way through the night. You gave yourself away to her and she did the same for you. How many people can count on a night like that? See how much luck you've had?

I would like never to leave this woman's arms, he thought. It's going to be dawn soon. The lions have picked up their roaring.

What's left?

Cassie will be all right, won't she? She will if she gets out of here. Afterward she'll be all right. She's got Abdi and he'll take care of her and she's got the camp and she's young. She'll pull out of it. I hope it doesn't take her as long as it took me. I wish she'd come along about twenty years ago. That's what I was doing. Waiting for her.

And when they catch Joseph, which they will, they'll hang him. The people who follow him will be there in the crowd. They'll look at each other and nod. Then they'll find another Rukuma to follow.

And you think you're going to stop it.

No. I never said that. Just Cassie. That's the best I can do. It isn't enough but it's the best I can do and it's enough for me.

Fine. Leave it at that. Do you want to think about the rest of it now?

Not much.

Your mother wanted you to be a parson. It was the only big argument you ever had with her. Probably everyone's mother did. You were burned out on religion before you were fourteen. What you wanted to be was Masai, and

thanks to your dad and thanks to your mother's tolerance
you managed that. You weren't having any religion then.
Are you having any now? Isn't it about now that the chap-
lain comes around to make sure there aren't any atheists in
foxholes?

Are there any atheists in foxholes?

No, what there aren't any in foxholes is back doors.

Seriously, what do you think about it now? he asked himself.

Nothing. I don't think anything about it. Dust to dust.
Meat to meat. In between it's not only meat but before and
after it is. That's the news from this particular foxhole. I
guess I never really understood why it bothered people the
way it does. Why they cared where they went afterward or
whether they got the deluxe accommodations. It always
seemed to me it said a lot about what they thought of what
they had while they were still here. That was the pity of it
and that seemed to me the lie of it. That they didn't see
what they had while they were still here. I don't know of
any religions among the game animals. Maybe now that
they're teaching them sign language the chimps will come
up with one.

Don't start tearing down. Who the hell are you to say?
You've had about as good a life as anyone could have. Let
other people believe what they want to believe as long as
they don't start shooting. Maybe they need it.

That's enough thinking, he told himself then. That's
enough brooding and going on. That was someone else's
book. That was in another country and the poor bastard's
dead. You don't have to do that. All you have to do is hold
onto the center and see it through. You don't have to justify
it. It's clean and straight and it justifies itself or it doesn't,
and it stops it or it doesn't. It's no different from going in
after something you've wounded or a client has wounded.
Someone has to do it and you happened to be in the neigh-

borhood. And you're lucky you know how to do it and you're lucky it turned out to be Joseph and you're lucky you had all this time with Cassie before. It's work. Do your work.

"Cassie?" he said. "Are you awake?"

"Yes."

"I love you. Don't ever forget that I love you."

She held him, warm in his arms, and there was roaring in the crater and in the imperceptible paling of the sky the first small stars went out.

Then it was dawn. The woman guerrilla came for them, throwing open the back door. They got out of the Land Rover. The air smelled of wet grass and the waking birds clacked and throated in the trees of the open grove that surrounded the yard. They could hear the river splashing over rock. The morning within the crater was damp and cold, deeply shadowed, but above the sky was pink and blue and streaming with mountain fog that the sun had not yet burned away. The fog streamed gray at the level of the rim. Higher it was golden where it caught the sun.

The woman motioned with her automatic. Crown led off, holding Cassie's hand. They walked out into the center of the yard. The grass wet their boots and Crown felt the wet soaking cold of the dew. Three of the guerrillas watched from the cabin porch. They were armed, the one called Chaudi, the one who was smallpox-scarred and of the other two the one who had not stood guard the night before. In the center of the yard the woman motioned Cassie back. Cassie pressed to Crown and held him. The woman swore at her and Crown took her shoulders and gently moved her away and looked at her and nodded. She faced the woman then and the woman backed in front of her holding the automatic and the three guerrillas left the porch and deployed themselves on three sides of the yard. Rukuma was still in the cabin. They waited for him. The sun broke the rim and the shadow narrowed to the long, edged shadow of the cabin. The dew sparkled beyond the edge of shadow the cabin cast. The yellow-green fever trees caught the sun, light and dark, and the birds quieted to day.

They heard the door. Rukuma came out. He was carrying an M-16. He left the door open behind him and looked out from the porch. He looked at the woman, at Cassie, at each of the three guerrillas positioned around the yard. Then he looked at Crown, steadily, staring. After a time he drew himself up and dangling the M-16 in one hand descended the steps, his boots sounding on the wood, and crossed to the Land Rover on the north side of the yard in the sunlight and leaned against the grill.

"Your friends have not come," he said. He closed his eyes and took the sun on his face, turning his head.

Crown stood with his legs braced apart and his hands on his hips. "They did as I asked."

"Better for them," Rukuma answered, distracted. "I am surprised Abdi did not come."

Crown shrugged.

Rukuma opened his eyes. "No?"

"He might have," Crown said. "I'm glad he didn't."

"How is he?"

"He's fine."

"Yes," Rukuma said. "We are all fine."

"I have something to say," Crown told him, dropping his hands.

Rukuma shook his head. "I have no wish to hear it." He straightened and seemed to shudder. He looked to Kare. "Hold the woman," he called.

"This woman is the age of thy mother, Joseph," Crown began quickly in Masai.

Rukuma turned back surprised. "Speak English."

"She is the age of thy mother when thy mother was murdered by men of another color than her own."

"No," Rukuma said.

"If thou kill her thou will be killing thy mother, Joseph. Let her go. After—"

"Silence!" Rukuma shouted, finding the rifle.

"After thou hast done this thing thou must do, let her go."

"Seth!" Cassie screamed.

"This must end, Joseph," Crown said steadily, watching the rifle come up. "This must end now."

"Silence, man! Silence!"

"What language is this?" Kare called past Cassie. "Kill him, Rukuma! Kill him!"

"Dost thou understand? The bargain is made. Spare this woman thy mother, Joseph. End this now."

"*Seth!*" Cassie screamed again.

"Free her!" Crown shouted in Masai, thinking then suddenly *Damn! What's the rush?*

"*Silence! Silence!*" Rukuma bellowed or Joseph, and there might have been silence, but looking down startled he saw the automatic rifle alive and loud jumping murderously in his hands.

But there's plenty of time, Seth Crown thought all at once, impacted, falling, falling like floating, seeing the others there in the yard frozen, shouts and Cassie's scream and the cracking burst from the rifle frozen in the shadowed frozen air, there's plenty of time, see how far away is the earth I fall to, a lifetime away, I might have been dropped without the billowing silks of a parachute from a plane. More luck. My day for lovely luck. I know enough now, where it led from, how it came. I know enough. Finally you got to know enough.

You knew hunting with red-faced McClanahan in the Mount Kenya forest north of Embu when you were young

and learning your trade, hunting elephant when men like
McClanahan could still pay off the overdrafts on their farms
by going out for ivory no more than a month a year. That
last day they broke camp early in cold fog. The *totos*, the
men everyone called boys, shivered in their ocher blankets
striking the patched khaki tents. McClanahan was already
drinking. McClanahan loved three things: gin, hunting and
the cannon-barreled Hollis he packed for elephant. They
had enough ivory, rows of yellow tusks nested on the rust
ground martial as racked scimitars, ready to be loaded into
the lorry. They had bull *vilaiti*, the thickest and heaviest, all
of it over sixty pounds. They had the smaller, finer *calasia*
from the cows. They even had a little of the finest straight
calasia that would be quartered lengthwise and carved into
ornate walking sticks, four only to the tusk, to support the
bent weight of Asian patriarchs who dealt in pearls and
ginseng and the maidenheads of virgins bought at market in
Calcutta and Macao. It was a foul day for hunting.

But McClanahan roared to go, roared for his Hollis, and
they went, hot for the hundred-pounder they'd missed the
day before. They pushed through the forest with the *totos*
behind them and when the bull charged them out of the fog
they burst from the trail like a covey. McClanahan went after the bull. It turned on him. You ran to back him up but
you didn't have a clear shot and the Hollis boomed late
through the forest. McClanahan rode to his farm with his
totos in the back of the lorry and you lashed the ivory under
him for a bed. His boys loved him. They sat stricken until he
swore them to song and then they sang him home on chants
they'd made up over the years to his drunken rampages and
his kills. Lingering broken on his deathbed he took gin
against the pain and his urine went black. His last request
was to be buried with the Hollis. You did that for him while
his widow packed for home, cleaned the big Hollis and oiled

it and wrapped it in skins and nailed it with him into his coffin.

The boys did more. The boys drove a length of water pipe into the grave the night after the burial, down into the coffin, and for a month of evenings after, just at sunset, they brought a bottle and a funnel to the grave and decanted generous shots of gin through the pipe to thirsty McClanahan. That was how they were, the men everyone called boys.

The men everyone called boys taught you most of what you knew. Out in the bush they taught you to travel light. Look for a honey-guide bird and follow it. It would lead you to wild honey and if you dawdled it would come back to scold you. The juice of the roots of a certain bush leafy and compact as the topiaries of formal gardens would clarify a muddy water hole. Certain trees and shrubs bore edible berries and you could make tea from the bark of one of the acacias. You could eat the flowers of the blue water lily, the fruits of the doum palm and the baobab. Where there were no water holes, in desolations of thorn scrub, you sucked water from the hearts of edible wild sisals, peeling back the spikes; or cut sections from the pulpy trailers of a coarse, ragged vine; and the plump tubers of one desiccated shrub held water quenching and cool as the upwelling of a spring. But where there were water holes there were almost always catfish and you could spear them with a sharpened stick. If the water holes were dry you could still dig catfish from the crusted mud where they buried themselves to wait for rain. Grilled over wild olive wood their flesh was fine as the flesh of lake fish. So you learned to travel light and later, in desolations worse than thorn scrub, you were grateful that you knew.

There was still time.

Sidanu met you coming back from war as if she'd waited. She was supple, the color of mahogany, her skin cool and smooth. Walking out one evening to an *ngoma* she told you about the thunderbolt her uncle had found. It appeared on the plain after a rainstorm. The grass was scorched where it fell. It was heavy and cold, but it shone in the night like the embers of an evening fire. Her uncle brought men and they carried it into the *manyatta* and put it in a box and it shown through the iron of the box. "When was this?" you asked her. "Before the war," she said. "Before I went to Nairobi to train." She had trained as a surgical nurse. "Did you see it?" "Yes." "Where is it now?" "My uncle sold it to an *mhindi.*" She could debride wounds and suture them, give inoculations, examine at clinic and diagnose. Her uncle found a thunderbolt and kept it in a box.

The *moran* and the young girls danced jumping at the *ngoma*, jumping shining in the firelight, and one here and one there fell down frenzied, spittle bubbling from slackened mouths. You walked out to the *ngoma* with Sidanu and contented in late darkness, Sidanu gliding in grace beside you, afterward you walked home. Joseph helped herd the cattle you raised together on the ranch. The name of the wheat you grew was Equator.

You knew the faces of lions lifted blood-red from a kill. Each day at dusk the sacred ibis returned to their swamp in a rush of wings.

Bush Africa was the life of men before they softened into cities. Bow hunting with your brother *moran* you were surprised by a rhino and one of your brothers was disemboweled. You helped load his guts back into his belly while he watched. A brother sewed him with sinew from his bow and you made a litter to carry him home. Only a little way from the water hole he complained of the roughness of the ride and only a little way farther he got down and walked, walked half an afternoon back to the encampment. In a month he was healed enough to hunt again.

Remember the old Dorobo who came around to trade

skins with the Masai for snuff and magic and Kunoni iron?
He was a little man. He wasn't much bigger than you were
then and one of his eyes was clouded. He hunted with
poisoned arrows, hunted even elephant alone with his bow.
You couldn't pull his bow. Your dad tested it with the spring
scale from the dairy and it pulled a hundred pounds. The
Dorobo taught you tracking. He taught you how to make
snares from the inner bark of a dozen different trees, chew-
ing the bark to fiber and rolling the fibers into cord between
the palm of your hand and the flat of your thigh. You were
bloody about hunting then. You wanted to take every animal that crossed your sights, to trap out the stream banks
and fish out the pools. The Dorobo taught you craft.

When you'd proved yourself he invited you to his poison
camp. You brought along a blanket roll and a caged cock.
Three days you walked beside him into the deep scrub.
From a cairn hidden in a thorn copse he uncovered a blackened cooking pot and six blackened seashells the size of
soup bowls. First you gathered thorn scrub for the fire and
then you cut the green branches of an aloe. He dug the acid-
smelling black roots of the bushy, fragrant-flowered tree the
Masai called *ol morijoi,* the acokanthera. He masked himself
with a greasy cloth while he pounded the roots on a rock
and he made you stay upwind. He said even the dust of the
roots could sicken. You carried the pot to a far water hole
and carried it back and set it on the fire. When the water
was boiling the Dorobo loaded in the pounded roots and the
branches of aloe and for half a day you fed the fire while the
water boiled brown and the smoke from the burning thorn
stung your eyes. Then the Dorobo dipped the seashells full
of the brown water and set them directly on the embers to
boil and the water reduced to paste. That was the poison.
You brought the cock. The Dorobo opened its struggling
beak and dropped a dot of poison on its tongue and set it
down. It blinked once. It stretched to crow. Before it made

a sound it quivered and died. The Dorobo nodded and
called you closer. He held up his arm. He nicked his arm
with his knife so that a trickle of blood ran down and he
touched his knife to the poison and touched the poison to
the trickling drop of blood and the poison ran coagulating
up the blood like a spark up a fuse and just before it reached
the wound the Dorobo smiled and casually flicked his
thumb and wiped its death away.

The next time the Dorobo visited the mission his cache of
skins was poor and you asked him why. Gravely he informed you that it was forbidden to make poison if a man
became unclean. You told your dad. You wondered how a
man became unclean for poison-making. Your dad didn't
know and he questioned the Dorobo. That night after sup-
per your dad led you out onto the porch, away from your
mother. You sat in the rocker beside him and he explained
that the Dorobo had a venereal disease. What was that? He
told you. It took a long time to tell.

So much of what you knew you couldn't say, even now
when you finally knew enough. If you said *grief*, if you said
sunset, if you said *woman*, if you said *campfire* you returned
through the wilderness of a lifetime that revealed itself to
you now moment by moment as you sought, and at each
revelation the sense of each single word altered and enlarged. *Plain* was such a word and when you spoke it you
saw giraffe in heart-shimmer undulating on the horizon,
impala sprung bounding to flight, grass and grass and
golden grass and gray granite kopjes mounded in the gold,
elephant mounded in the gold. You saw lines of grunting
wildebeest and scatterings of quick tommies and you
watched again the ordered morning takeoff of vultures by
size, smaller to larger, as the warming morning thermals
gave them lift. You saw thorn scrub, the wind whistling
through the holes that insects drilled in the jagged branches
and you saw the black bossed buffalo laid up to rest always

in triangles, cows and calves protected within, the biggest
bulls keeping sentinel at the points. You saw black line
storms advancing on spars of lightning and clouds of lacy
alates blowing from termite mounds after the first greening
rains and you felt yourself reaching up as the game reached
up to drink the freshening wind. You saw all the safaris you
had made out across the plain to hunt or to search for silence. You smelled coffee brewing and roasting meat, you
tasted again the smoke of the whiskey you had drunk and
heard the good talk of years of evenings. And always when
you smelled coffee you remembered when you were a boy in
the years of world depression when they couldn't sell coffee
from Kenya and they burned it for fuel in the engines of lo-
comotives and the coffee air drifted down green Kenya for
miles and miles.

It went back to that. What you knew was gathered now
into Cassie for safekeeping, Cassie was close and fresh in
what you saw, but now it went back. You were a boy of fourteen running a logging crew in cedar forest. The crew knew
its skill. You were charged to choose the trees. You let the
Africans choose and worked beside them. It was dark in the
forest. The floor under your feet where you worked was
springy with bedded needles. You pulled one end of a cross-
cut saw. An African pulled the other. The saw was blued
steel, flat, six feet long, its cutting edge deeply serrated, with
oak handles bolted to the ends, and each tooth was precisely
set. At first you thought to push as well as pull and the saw
bowed and sung and stuck. You learned its delicacy. You
pulled. Exactly at the extremity of your body's swing the African pulled in common time and you let the saw glide. You
cut a virgin cedar, the tall trunk straight and the first blue-
green needled branches high, and when it fell crashing it let
down high sunlight onto the brown floor. You cut logs from
the trunk. You brought up wedges, hammers. You set the
wedges and swung the hammers, gandy-dancing. The ham-

mers flashed in the sunlight in the space the tree had made. Smooth-grained in its long growth the log gave to the driving of the wedges and cracked like close thunder and split open to its heart. Cedar oil flowed golden in the light to fill the channel of its heart. You cupped your hands to the oil and lifted it to your face. Heart of cedar, oil of cedar golden in the light, it warmed your hands and streamed down your arms and dripped through the sunlight to the forest floor. You looked across to the African. His cupped hands were lifted to his face and cedar oil streamed down his arms.

Cassie!

Her hair was golden as the golden oil. Her hair was golden as the plain. Her hair was golden as the sun above the crater and finally you knew, a man, game in the crater, a river running to a lake, a man in the crater fallen

Eighteen

CASSIE SCREAMED Seth Crown's name once more. He had turned to her as he fell and his shirt had bloomed bright flowers of blood where the slugs went in. His shoulder hit the ground first and he slumped over onto his back and now in rage Cassie jammed her elbow backward into the woman guerrilla's belly. The woman bent, blowing, and Cassie jerked free and ran. She saw Rukuma's rifle still aimed and it didn't matter and then she reached the body and dropped to her knees. She saw the eyes fixed and staring and spreading from under the body was blood. She moaned. She rocked forward moaning, taking him into her arms.

Rukuma thought: let her. Catching motion he swung to Kare. She had slung her rifle to restrain the white woman and now it flew to her hands. She would kill. Whore. She would kill the woman. *Damn* she would not. "Kare!" Rukuma shouted. Her head flicked his way, the rifle. Now he knew he fired. The burst drove her backward. She staggered and flung her arms. Her legs buckled and she collapsed and menacing he swung beyond to Chaudi.

"Rukuma!" Chaudi screamed. "No!" He let go his rifle and shot his hands into the air.

Rukuma swung to the next guerrilla and the next. They shook their heads frantically and pointed their M-16s away. "You *see?*" Rukuma shouted, his voice pitched high. "Did you *see?*" His body jerked and he stamped his feet. He almost danced. "She would have murdered me!" He ran to Kare. Sprawled, she bled from the mouth, staring at him. He saw his mother. He spun around. The white woman rocked his dead father. The white woman cradled his father's head. Bullets of flies buzzed in. Go, Joseph. Go now. It is dead here. *Go.* "Chaudi!" he shouted. "Start the Land Rover! *Upesi!* Hurry! We must leave!"

"Rukuma?" Chaudi called, running in. "What of the woman?"

What of the woman? Thy father's woman. She cradles him. They bury the dead. "Leave her! Start the car!" How can they bear? "*Upesi!*" he called to the others. "Hurry! Load!"

Cassie watched the Land Rover pull away. She still held Seth, kneeling in the center of the yard. His blood was drying on her hands. She had closed his eyes. She stared now at the car as it bounced up the track and turned at the river and disappeared from view beyond the trees. She could hear it going fast eastward beyond the trees and the smell of its oily exhaust drifted back to her. She felt no rage now nor yet any grief. She felt dulled. They had run. Whatever Seth had said to Rukuma had shaken him. To Joseph. They had left the other Land Rover but she had no key. The yard stank of exhaust. Before it had stunk of guns. The sun was higher and hot and there were flies. She should cover him. It was no longer any use to hold him. He couldn't know that she was there.

She lowered his head to the grass and stood. Standing dizzied her and she knelt again and kneeling she thought to arrange his hands. Why had she never been taught to prepare the dead? Why was it left to strangers? Why was death invisible in her country when here death was everywhere and commonplace? Death was the ground of the crater whatever moved or soared, and there were specialized animals and birds here that thrived on death. You interlace the fingers on the chest, she thought, like this. Oh, the flies. Damn the flies. She swept them away with her hand and they clouded back and she swept them away. They're horrible. They can't wait. She stood and now she wasn't dizzy and she ran for the cabin. The dead woman's face crawled with flies. She would have to cover her too.

The cabin was a shambles. The guerrillas had knocked over chairs and left blankets strewn on the floor. Cornmeal was spilled in the kitchen. It ground under her boots. She pulled the blankets off the beds and then she noticed a belt and holster hanging from one of the bedsteads, the wooden handle of a revolver. She wadded the blankets and carried them out. She fanned the flies from Seth's face and protected it with one of the blankets while she straightened his legs. Then she covered him, tucking the blanket tight. Somehow she would have to shelter him from the sun. She went to the woman, Kare, and arranged her and covered her as she had covered Seth. Kare was a stranger, Cassie thought, yet she wanted to kill you. First Seth and then Joseph Crown had saved your life. It welled from Seth into Joseph and it was so powerful it carried beyond his death. You have your physics now, she told herself, wondering. It no more looks like common sense than your father's physics did. Four pounds of plutonium incinerated a hundred thousand people at Nagasaki and two people, one who hated you and one who loved you, died in Ngorongoro Crater to spare your life.

The scavengers would come. Somehow they knew. She walked to the cabin again and belted on the revolver.

Abdi, ole Kipoin and the *moran* had reached the lodge on the rim of the crater a little after dawn. Abdi had left the Masai outside and gone in to find the manager. The commandos were still sleeping and Abdi followed the manager from room to room on the lower level of the lodge rousing them. Beyond them in their rooms, through the glass outside walls, he could see the crater opening to day. He was weary of carrying the ugly rifle. He ached from the climb up the mountain, from lack of sleep. There was more to do. Whatever was left to do he would do. He dreaded what they would find at the cabin. The manager said he had seen no vehicles leave the crater, but he also had not heard them going in.

Abdi waited for the commandos outside on the tarmac with the Masai. The *moran* lounged on the stone steps of the entrance under the jutting wooden roof that covered the drive. The lodge manager had no more vehicles to loan. His face had told Abdi that he wanted the soldiers and their prisoners to leave his lodge. He was a young African from the city and soldiers with brutal automatic rifles, wounded soldiers, soldiers guarding sullen guerrillas frightened him. He had seen the *moran* on his steps with their spears and he would go no farther with Abdi than the front doors. The *moran* frightened him too.

The commandos came out and the *moran* greeted them warmly. Ole Kipoin looked at Abdi and Abdi nodded. Ole Kipoin spoke to the *moran*. The commandos took the lead with Abdi, the Masai behind them, walking up the tarmac to the road. They would walk into the crater.

There were vultures on the ground now beyond the dead

woman. One had flapped in and soon after more had followed. When Cassie waved her arms and shouted at them they fluttered and hopped away but didn't fly. She'd never studied them before. They were bigger than she'd realized. Their feathers were mottled dusty brown and their gray necks were like swans' necks but shorter. Some had buff-colored beaks and some black. The tall bird with a white ruff and a red head set neckless on its shoulders and a long, pointed beak like the beak of a cartoon crow was a maribou stork.

"Go away," she told them. They watched her. One shook itself, fluffing its feathers. Another fanned a wing and poked its head underneath.

The slight breeze changed direction and she smelled them and gagged.

"God damn you," she said, walking toward them. "Go away." They backed off. She counted six. Then beyond them she saw two faces peering from the grove, pug noses and alert, scooped ears and grinning mouths. So they knew too. They saw the vultures and followed them in. Was it scent with the vultures or did anything motionless on the ground where nothing had been before attract them? Dully she pulled the revolver and ratchetted the cylinder. Five bullets and there were more in the belt.

She didn't want to shoot them. She wanted no more death in that hot clearing buzzing with flies. She didn't want to hear another gun, but she'd have to scare them off. Standing beside Kare's blanket-covered body she raised the revolver over her head and fired. Crashing into each other, feathers flying, the birds squawked and flapped away and when Cassie looked to the trees the hyenas were gone. She was shaking. She tried to holster the revolver but she couldn't fit the barrel. She guided it with her left hand.

Seth was too heavy for her to move. Probably she could move the woman. If she could start the Land Rover she could position it beside Seth so that it protected him. She could drag the woman and lift her into the back. There were wires you could find that led to the ignition that you could cross. She wanted to sleep. After her father died she'd slept around the clock for days. She couldn't sleep and she couldn't leave without Seth. Abdi was supposed to come for her but he was supposed to wait on the rim. She would have to start the Land Rover. She could try to do that and then she could wait.

She looked up. The vultures watched from the trees.

Halfway down the Seneto Hill road Abdi heard the car. It was coming up the hill, its engine straining in low gear. It could be no other. There were no other cars in the crater. The Effendi might be in it and Cassie or it might be only the guerrillas. It would pass them climbing at no more than ten kilometers an hour.

Abdi stopped in the road. "They come," he said to the leader of the commandos in Swahili. "We must hide."

"If the hostages are there," the commando said, "we must storm the car quickly." He looked back at the Masai. "Instruct the *moran* to conceal themselves above the road," he told Abdi. "Let them attack after we have shot out the tires and drawn their fire."

Abdi hurried to ole Kipoin and spoke to him. Ole Kipoin relayed the instructions in Masai and silently the *moran* climbed the steep, forested slope above the road and took up positions behind the trees. Abdi crossed the road to the commandos stationed now on the lower slope, the barrels of their Kalashnikovs resting on the dirt berm. He unshouldered his own Kalashnikov and slipped down beside them. Let them come, he thought. Let them come and let all be well with the Effendi and with Cassie.

The car labored around the switchback. Chaudi was driving and Rukuma rode in the left front seat. Rukuma was

wary. It had been too long since his father had descended
into the crater. Someone should have come by now. All the
way from the cabin he had watched ahead.

Then he saw, sunlight glinting off the barrel of a rifle.
"Chaudi," he said quickly. "Stop. They wait ahead." Chaudi
hit the brakes and the Land Rover jerked to a halt. "Out!"
Rukuma yelled over his shoulder. "Behind the car! Fire on
them!"

He threw open his door for a shield and jumped from the
car on the side away from the berm. The three guerrillas in
the back seat spilled from the car behind him. There was a
rattle of firing from the road ahead. Slugs tore the near side
of the car and the tires hissed and the Land Rover settled
slanting. Protected now behind the car the guerrillas returned the fire. Chaudi bellied across the front seat and
slipped to the road beside Rukuma. His M-16 was out of
reach in the back of the car.

"Take the rifle," Rukuma said, passing Chaudi his own.
"Fire across the bonnet." Chaudi looked at him confused
and Rukuma shoved him against the open door, stepping
behind him. "*Hit them,*" Rukuma barked. Chaudi stuck the
rifle through the window frame and fired, shell casings eject-
ing into the car. Rukuma looked to the back. His men
weren't watching him. He jumped off the road and scrambled up the slope.

Abdi saw him. "One of them runs!" he shouted over the
firing. He popped up and sprayed the slope but the man was
higher and screened by the trees. Abdi ducked behind the
berm again. Who ran away? It had to be Rukuma, running
as he had run before on the mountain. He must not escape.
Where was the Effendi? Abdi set aside his rifle and cupped
his hands to his mouth. "Ole Kipoin!" he called up the road.
"One climbs the hill to escape! Send *moran* to stop him!" A
spear stuck from behind a tree and twirled in the sun to sig-

nal and Abdi saw *moran* starting to work across the slope
and climbing.

The leader of the commandos was beside him. "None at
the car are European," he said.

"It may be that they are inside," Abdi answered.

"None are inside. They would use them as shields. I will
silence them with a grenade."

He is right, Abdi thought. If Rukuma had hostages he
would not have run away. There is danger to these men.
"Do it," he told the commando.

The commando unhooked a grenade from his belt and
pulled the safety. He didn't lob it but signaled his men for
covering fire and when the Kalashnikovs rattled and the
firing stopped from the car he darted up and rolled the grenade down the road. "Grenade!" he shouted, ducking behind the berm.

The grenade blew, muffled under the Land Rover, and almost instantly the petrol tank exploded, a flash of yellow
flame and a gust of heat and a roar, and glass and metal
sang past the berm and there were screams from the wreckage. The commandos went over the berm firing and ran
down the road, dividing around the burning car. The guerrilla at the side door had been blown against the slope. He
had lost his rifle. His fatigues were burning, his hair, and he
was screaming. Two of the commandos pulled him off the
slope and rolled him in the dirt, beating out the fire, but before they had finished he convulsed and lay still. They found
the other three guerrillas dead behind the wreckage.

The *moran* who had not gone after the runaway slipped
down the slope and ran to Abdi at the car, eager to see. Ole
Kipoin walked down behind them. "My brother here?" he
asked Abdi. "Where my brother?"

"At the cabin in the crater," Abdi said grimly. "We must
go on." Abdi turned to the commando leader. "Stay with the
car," he said. "When it no longer burns push it off the road.

They had a second Land Rover. It must still be at the cabin.
We will bring it back. Watch for the one who escaped."

"He will not return here," the commando said.

"The *moran* may catch him," said Abdi.

Ole Kipoin and his *moran* had started down the hill. Abdi
slung his rifle and worked past the car to join them. The
moran walked jauntily now, he noticed, twirling their flashing spears. For them a battle was better than the sleep of a
long night. It had been a long night for all.

Panting, sweating in the heat, Rukuma pulled himself up
the slope. He had heard the explosion of the car and he
knew it meant the fight was finished and they were free to
follow him. He wasn't even armed. Stupidly he had left his
revolver behind at the cabin.

Who had they been? The firing had sounded like the
firing at the mountain camp. They must have been the commandos from the lodge finally alerted and coming down to
the cabin. But coming so late they could not have known
before that morning. His father had kept his word. Well, he,
Rukuma, had kept his word also. Out of what? He had not
meant to leave the white woman alive to identify him.

Above was the next higher switchback but the slope was
treacherous with loose rock pushed over from the road cut.
Rukuma pulled himself upward on saplings and branches of
bush, thorns tearing his hands. He lost footing and rock
tumbled down the slope behind him and momentarily he
hung, his stomach knotting, and then his feet found purchase and he climbed. He crawled scrabbling up to the
berm and got a leg up and the other leg and then he was
standing on the road. He looked down the slope. He could
not see the lower road for the trees but smoke billowed up
from the burning car. He started to turn and then his eye
caught the glint of a spear. *Moran.* Then Abdi had come

and alerted the commandos. But why had he waited until morning?

Rukuma ran up the road and around the switchback. He could not keep to the road. The *moran* would climb straight up the slope and so must he or he would lose his lead. At least they would have no guns. Their spears would slow them. The forest was thin on the slope but above the rim it was dense. He knew tracking in the forest as well as they. He had learned as they had learned, from an elder of the Masai.

He crossed the road and leapt over the inside berm and climbed. He climbed at an angle now to improve his footing and to move aside from the *moran* climbing behind him. His lungs ached in the thin mountain air and sweat soaked his fatigues and his hands were slippery with blood. It was Kare's fault, he told himself, wiping his hands painfully, one and then the other, on his fatigues. She had confused him. It became a matter of opposing her challenge with his own and he should not have let it go so far. But his father had stood in the yard of the cabin and he had not seemed afraid. His father should have begged for his life and he had not begged. He had spoken out of the past in the language of the past and Rukuma had seen in Kare fallen there in the yard his mother, Joseph's mother, fallen in the house. He had seen it!

It didn't matter. He needed none of them, Kare or Chaudi or the others. He had done what he had to do. They would have been an impediment. He had no past now and another *mzungu* was dead. Joseph had been purged. Now there would be only Rukuma. Rukuma's vision. Rukuma leading. Rukuma who survived. Someone must survive for the nameless. Someone must harden his heart for the nameless as all others had hardened their hearts against them. How long had the nameless suffered? How many had died? Who wept for them, ever? None, ever. Jomo had said it for all time, in the days before he was corrupted by authority, though he denied the saying later at his trial at Kapenguria. Jesus Christ was an English gentleman, Jomo Kenyatta had said.

The slope shallowed and leveled and Rukuma entered the mixed cedar forest of the rim plateau. There was no sign yet of the *moran.* For a time now he must run. He must keep running. Savagely in passing he tore a low, leafy branch from a tree. The *moran* would find the stump but that was all they would find. With the branch he would thread into place the growth he disturbed behind him. The forest floor would preserve no mark if he ran on the sides of his boots. They would say that Rukuma turned invisible, he told himself, light-headed with the narrowness of his escape. They would say Rukuma released broad wings and flew away. They could track as long as they liked. They would never catch up with him now.

But why, he asked himself then, and again a little farther on, and again after he had worked well into the forest and the plateau began to slope to mountainside, *why had he feared to kill the white woman?*

It was nearly noon. Cassie had managed to start the Land Rover. She had pulled it to the center of the yard, beside Seth's body, and rigged a blanket from the door to the uprights of two chairs she had carried from the cabin. She had dragged the woman's body then to the back of the car and lifted it inside and covered it. The blanket shaded Seth's body from the high, hot sun and Cassie sat in the shaded grass beside the body protecting it from scavengers. Now and again a vulture dropped down to pick at the blood dried on the grass where the woman's body had lain. She let it. The grass would be cleaned and there would be no sign that murder had stained the crater. The rangers would come eventually to clean the cabin. The crater would go on as it had gone on before, when she first came up with Seth to see it. The crater would go on as it had always gone on.

She had thought through the morning of what she might have done. It was easy enough now to see that she might have left at the very beginning. After that she might have left after the raid on Seth's camp when it was clear he was in danger. If you looked backward, events had causes and causes had effects. But looking forward there was increasing uncertainty, paths of choice that divided and divided until they became too complex to follow, and sometimes choice itself was taken away. Joseph had taken her choice away. Seth understood even that. Last night he had offered her a choice, to run or to risk Joseph. She had chosen then and she had chosen right. Any other choice would have undercut his own. It had freed her. Seth had freed her. He'd left them all free, for the briefest moment even Joseph. For the briefest moment Seth had pried open the door through the wall and held it and they had slipped through.

That was as far as she had thought. She had heard the firing, heard the explosions echoed across the crater, and dulled again and numbed.

Then Abdi was running to her from the track, across the yard, calling her name, the *moran* behind him and ole Kipoin. At the sight of the blanket-wrapped body he stopped, struck. A terrible cry tore from him and he stood rooted, tears welling from his eyes, and Cassie went to him and they clung to each other.

Ole Kipoin came on. He slipped under the shelter and uncovered his brother's face. Cassie heard him hiss. He said nothing but he spat his blessing and covered his brother again and stood and rejoined the silent *moran*.

Still weeping, Abdi held Cassie away from him. "I tried to come," he said hoarsely. He released her and hung his head. "The lorry. I did not check the petrol. It ran out of petrol and we were forced to walk. I would have come yesterday." And, whispering: "It is because of me that the Effendi is dead."

Cassie raised Abdi's head between her hands. "No," she

said, her face wet with tears. "He didn't want you to come. You were right not to come."

Abdi looked at her as if he hadn't heard. "Once before I failed the Effendi," he said. "Now again I have failed him."

Cassie held him. His thin, hard body was shaking. "No," she whispered. "Abdi? No. Stop. There's no blame. Stop."

He straightened then and stood apart. "Who did this?" he asked. His face was hard now and his voice cold.

"Rukuma."

"There is blame. There is blame for me but centrally there is blame for the man who killed him. There is blame for Rukuma! He escaped us at the road. I saw him." Abdi's hands were fists. "I swear by Allah I will kill him!"

Cassie stared at him. He didn't know. "Did you recognize Rukuma?"

"Why should I recognize him?"

"Abdi," Cassie said. "Rukuma is Joseph. Seth's son."

She might have hit him. He winced and pain tightened his mouth and pinched closed his eyes. When he opened them again he could find no place to rest them. He glanced at Cassie, at his hands, at the ground. "*Mti ukifa shinale,*" he said to himself, crooning, "*na tanzuze hukauka.*"

"I don't understand," Cassie told him.

He stared past her at the body. "It is a saying of bitterness. 'When a tree dies at its roots, its boughs dry up also.' Joseph did this?"

"Yes."

"It is obscene."

"He killed the woman guerrilla afterward. She's in the car. She was going to shoot me. Joseph protected me. Abdi?" He looked at her. "Seth asked me to tell you and the Masai. He doesn't want you to hunt for Joseph. He wants you to contact the authorities and leave it to them. When they find him he wants us to arrange for his defense."

Abdi said nothing. It was obscene that a son would murder his father. It was obscene that the lorry would fail of

petrol from carelessness and that none had come from Arusha. The death should be revenged. But the father and
mother were dead and the father wished that revenge not
be taken on his son. The Effendi wishes me to give up revenge, Abdi thought. "What the Effendi asks of me I will
do," he told Cassie.

He left her to explain to ole Kipoin. She took down the
blanket and moved aside the chairs. Abdi came back.

"Ole Kipoin will inform the Council of Elders," he said.
"It is their authority to decide."

At ole Kipoin's direction the *moran* impaled their spears
in the ground behind the Land Rover, as they would do as a
sign of peace at the entrance to a house. Cassie opened the
back door and solemnly the *moran* lifted the body in its
wrapping and carried it to the doorway and arranged it on
the floor bed beside the body of the woman. They waited as
Cassie closed the door. Then they retrieved their spears and
nodded to her, their young faces somber, and turned and
walked away across the yard.

"They go to crater *manyatta*," ole Kipoin told her as he
got into the car. "Rest. Later they come to encampment."

Abdi drove, past lions sleeping in the shade of the trees
along the river, past the wildebeest keeping their territories,
past zebra and antelope laid up resting in the afternoon,
past the wreckage of the Land Rover pushed off on the
slope below the road. The commandos were walking out
and Abdi stopped and spoke to them and drove on. From
the height of the rim Cassie looked down into the crater and
she could not see the cabin, only the curving river and the
shining lake pink with feeding flamingo and the green savanna. Then they were driving through the forest. Screened
behind them through the forest the crater made a space of
immensity where the sun shown down. Cassie listened as
Seth had taught her to do. She could hear the crater's silence. It seemed to her it breathed.

Nineteen

IT CAME ON SUMMER and the dry season when the plain bleached to the color of wheat straw and the air shimmered with the heat of the sun. In every direction on the horizon there were mirages that looked like distant, pale-blue lakes. Because of the altitude it was never truly hot on the Serengeti even in the dryness of summer but tourist agents who knew the plain only from guidebooks discouraged their clients from traveling there in summer and it was true that the game retreated to the woodlands then and the viewing was less interesting than in the green time between the short and long rains when the game was out feeding on the new grass. Yet there were tommies on the plain and impala, scattered families of wildebeest and grazing zebra, in the open forest around the tent camp there were giraffe and sometimes elephant, and there were always birds at the lake. Summer was the dry season and the ordinary life of the plain went on and only the operators of the tour companies and the big commercial lodges missed the tourists.

One morning early in summer, in the dining room of the
lodge at the tent camp, Robert Fuhrey sat studying the
small, brownish-white skull he had finished reconstructing
the evening before. He still wore the cast on his left arm. He
planned to drive to Arusha at the end of the week to have it
removed. Now that the skull was finished he meant to spend
the rest of the season digging further at Oloito Gorge before
going back to Harvard to teach in the fall. He was tired of
wearing the heavy cast and he was glad he'd be rid of it.

He stared at the skull and seeing it staring back at him
complete he grinned. He guessed that the volume of the
brain would come in at somewhere around six hundred cc's.
The lab report of the potassium-argon ratio of the tuffs
where the skull had been bedded had established its age securely at between 6.5 and 6.9 million years b.p., probably
about 6.7. It was more than two million years older than
Lucy, the australopithecine that Donald Johanson had
found at Afar, the oldest previous hominoid find after *Ramapithecus*, and now that it was completely reconstructed
there was no doubt that it was *Homo*.

The brain volume argued that genus designation and so
did the doming of the cranial vault. The ear openings were
positioned farther forward than those of the australopithe-
cines. There was no indication of a bony crest at the top of
the cranium like the crest that the smaller-brained australo-
pithecines evolved as an attachment site for the powerful
muscles of their much more robust lower jaws. The palate
was shallow but wider than the palate of the australopithe-
cines and the molars and especially the canines were reduced. On the theory that *Homo* and *Australopithecus*
branched off from *Ramapithecus* some time after about nine
million years b.p., SCK-OG 1001 was almost certainly the
first of the hominids and the earliest direct ancestor to modern man. And it was distinct enough by even the most conservative standards to rate designation as a separate species.

As the leader of the team that found it, Fuhrey had the right to choose its species designation and for weeks in his spare time he had been drifting through a dictionary and thinking about possible names. He wanted the species designation to be a tribute to Seth Crown. He wanted Seth's name attached to something more substantial than the name of a *korongo*. He'd discussed a long list of possible species designations with Cassie but not until this morning had he found one that met all his requirements.

Cassie had changed. There were days when she worked on the camp and seemed almost lighthearted and there were days when she sat on the porch looking out across the plain. She was different from when he had known her before at Stanford, different even from the first weeks of her time with Seth. Fuhrey had tried to formulate the difference. His formulas were pedestrian. That grief had burned her away to simplicity. Or she knew her own mind now. She escaped formulation. She was alive.

He had returned too late from Arusha to be of any use to her. Abdi and John Kegedi had dug the grave facing the plain on the slope north of the lodge, between the lodge and the lake. Cassie had retired then, after the burial, to the apartment that had been Seth's, and when she emerged again a week later she was changed. Fuhrey had felt awkward with her, as if she were much older than he, as if he were a schoolboy. When they talked about his work he saw it differently. She changed that too. What had happened changed it. It was less important and more.

He saw that it wasn't going to answer all his questions. He saw that he was naïve ever to have believed that it would. There was more mystery in the world than he had thought and more novelty. He had always understood that at ground the world was opaque, but he had imagined that his work and the work of others like him might someday shatter that opacity and allow them to see through. He

knew now that the capacity of the world was proof against
any shattering. He should have been terrified. Instead he
was relieved. His work could go on. It was not a progressive
devastation. It wasn't certainly predictive nor could it ever
be. It was historical. The skull on the table had been a living
man.

Fuhrey crossed through the bar to the screened porch.
Cassie sat at the far end. He went to her and turned out a
chair and straddled it. "I'm going to draft the report today,"
he said. "I think I've found the right species designation."

She was very far away, out on the plain. She was remembering the two Masai herdboys, how they stood back shyly
from Seth and then came forward bowing their heads for
the blessing of his hand. She returned slowly to the porch
and looked at Fuhrey. "Wonderful," she said.

"Do you know the word 'regulus'?"

She shook her head.

"You know I was leaning toward 'coronator.' 'Homo
coronator.' It's just too junky. The other species designations
are all descriptive. 'Homo habilis' is 'adroit man,' 'Homo
erectus' is 'upright man.' 'Coronator' would be 'man who
crowns.' But that suggests some sort of crest structure on the
cranium, and that kind of structure doesn't show up on the
hominids. 'Regulus' isn't exactly descriptive either, but it's
not misleading and it picks up two or three different mean-
ings that fit. Okay. A regulus is the refined part of a charge
of mineral ores that's been smelted in a crucible. It sinks to
the bottom of the crucible. When the charge has cooled you
turn over the crucible and tap it out and the regulus appears
on the top. With antimony the pattern looks like an irregular
star. Like the frost patterns you get on a cold window.
'Regulus' is a word from alchemy. It means a minor king or
a little king."

"Yes."

"And kings wear crowns. Regulus is also a bright double star in the constellation Leo."

Cassie smiled.

"The alchemists called the star regulus of antimony the 'little king' because antimony combines readily with gold. Gold was the king of metals. So 'Homo regulus.' 'Refined man.' Man the minor king of creation. 'Man crowned.' And the type specimen is SCK-OG 1001." He turned up his hands. "What do you think?"

"I like it," Cassie said.

He studied her. "How are you?"

"I'm fine."

"I worry about you."

"Whatever for?"

"You seem so far away."

"I'm here," she said simply.

"Okay. I'm here too if you need me."

"I know. I like 'regulus.'"

He nodded. "Good enough," he said, getting up. "I'll put it in the report."

At the dining-room table, next to the skull, he unzipped the brown cloth case of his portable typewriter and rolled in a sheet of paper, snapped down the paper bale and returned the carriage. He thought, remembering the format, and then he typed:

Evidence for an Advanced Pliocene Hominid
from Oloito Gorge, Tanzania
R. Fuhrey
Harvard University, Cambridge MA USA

Then quickly he composed the brief abstract that would precede the detailed report in the journal:

A cranium with mandible, SCK—OG 1001,
collected this year from Oloito Gorge,
is attributed to a new species of the
genus Homo, designated Homo regulus.
It is probably 6.7 million years old.

That's a start, Robert Fuhrey thought. Now I've got to
spell it out. It really is only a start. It still is after all those
millions of years and who can say where it will lead?

That afternoon Abdi returned from Arusha in the lorry with
the load of new tents. He backed the lorry into the space between the tent platforms and the shower buildings and Cassie joined him and they unloaded the tents onto the platforms. The tents smelled of preservative and waterproofing
compound and new canvas. Their brass grommets were
bright. In the afternoon heat Abdi and Cassie began setting
up the new tents. It was heavy work and before long they
were both sweating. At another time Abdi might have
stopped work until early evening when it was cooler but he
wanted the work finished and so did Cassie. They wanted
the camp restored the way it was.

When they had unfolded a tent on its platform and
threaded its ridgepole they raised it together, pulling on its
guy ropes, and then Abdi held it in position while Cassie
pegged the ropes.

"Did you remember to pick up the lotion for the baby?"
she asked Abdi as they worked.

"*Ndiyo*," he said. "I have given it to Jaja."

"I don't think it's anything serious. It's diaper rash or
prickly heat. If it doesn't get any better we can take him
into Arusha when Robert goes to get his cast removed."

"I stopped at the police station," Abdi told her. She
looked up from the rope she was fastening. "The investigation is ended," he said. "They have found no sign of
Joseph."

She hammered, carefully driving in the peg, and then she brushed back her hair. "Are you surprised?"

"No. He is clever at escape."

"They'll find him. Someone will."

"I wish only that it had been here," Abdi said. "Then we could have done for him as the Effendi asked of us." He passed her the next rope.

"I know. Is there anything else we can do?"

"It is for the police to do. He is a criminal."

"I know. Fine."

"He is not Joseph to me," Abdi said with vehemence. "Joseph was a child. Somewhere his life was taken. This other one is nothing of Joseph except the ugliness that was left when his life was taken. My sadness is only for the Effendi, that he had no other sons or daughters to survive him."

The tent was fast, the second in the row. Cassie gave her hand to Abdi and he helped her up. She studied the tent secure on its new platform under the clean new thatch that had dried watertight in the sun. "Seth would like your tents," she told him. She was smiling.

"I bought the best that were sold, my daughter," Abdi said gravely. "It is what the Effendi would have done."

The bar in Nairobi where Rukuma stood leaning on the zinc counter, nursing a beer, was filling up with men. It was one of the better bars along the river road in Nairobi. It was tin-roofed and dingy but it had a wooden floor. The bartender was playing his transistor radio and as more men came in talking he turned it up until it blared. The announcer on the radio was a woman. She was reading rapidly in a singsong voice. She had been reading for hours as Rukuma listened and she no longer read the words for their sense. She was reading an official account of the life of Jomo Kenyatta. The *Bwana Mzee* Jomo Kenyatta was dead.

Rukuma had come into the bar in the morning to escape
the streets. When the news of the *Mzee*'s death had been
radioed from the coast the government had declared a
three-day period of mourning. Offices and factories, markets
and garages and shops had emptied their workers into the
streets. Everyone was talking. Strangers talked to strangers.
They were not festive but neither were they somber. They
were excited, curious, expectant. The *Mzee* had lived forever. He was born before the British came in any numbers
to East Africa, the woman sang from the radio. He had been
a water-meter reader in Nairobi in 1922. He had studied
abroad in England and lived in exile there until after the
Second World War. He had come back to a hero's welcome after the war, and then in 1952 he had been arrested
on trumped-up charges of managing Mau Mau and tried at
Kapenguria and sentenced to seven years' hard labor in the
northern desert. He was already an old man then. For seven
years he cooked beans and mealie-mush for the other political leaders and the Mau Mau generals who were imprisoned
with him at Lokitaung. He was released to desert exile but
finally he was brought back to Nairobi and from prison and
exile, after Uhuru, he became the first President of inde-
pendent Kenya. He was President for life and the country
had known no other. Now he was dead. The Vice President
had temporarily assumed his office. The government promised new elections in ninety days.

The news of the *Mzee*'s death enraged Rukuma. There
had not been time to reconnect with his friends. There had
not been time to contact the men he had come to Nairobi to
see. He had only just settled into a flat of rooms and tapped
his Nairobi bank account and bought clothing when the
news came. He knew the *Mzee*'s life story. The *Mzee* had
waited into old age to come to power. He wondered that the
Mzee had been so patient. He wondered how long he himself would have to wait. If the *Mzee* had led Mau Mau from

the very beginning instead of denying it as he had done, if he had gone underground and escaped prison, the entire nation would have risen up behind him. The *Mzee* had been rotten with patience because he had admired the British and had chosen British ways. The woman on the radio had been careful not to mention it, but the *Mzee* had taken a British wife in England and sired children there. And after Uhuru, when he might have sought revenge, he had sold Kenya to the West. He had maintained Kenya as a capitalist country and sold out Mau Mau and sold out Africa.

Rukuma looked at the men around him. Most of them were Kikuyu, the *Mzee's* tribe. They were smaller and blacker men than he. They made a little money and they took it home. It bought them dirty rooms and drunken weekends and bright swatches of *amerikani* for their wives. If they saw a Mercedes in the streets they looked at it not with loathing but with envy. They imagined that someday they might ride in such a machine or even own one. An uncle did, a brother-in-law. They were poor material for revolution. Country people were better material, but they had no skills. They could attack and defend, pull triggers, give up their lives, but they could not run governments. The time was late for revolution. Too late. It might already be too late.

No! Rukuma told himself angrily. It is not too late! He drained his beer and slammed the bottle on the counter. The bartender looked up and frowned. "Another," Rukuma ordered.

The bartender brought him another, shoving it across under his face. "Five *shilingi*," the bartender said.

"It was not five *shilingi* before," Rukuma told him.

"Five *shilingi*," the bartender said. "If you can't pay, get out."

Rukuma paid, the coins ringing on the counter, and the bartender took the coins and the empty and moved away.

"He overcharges you," the man beside Rukuma said. "It is only three *shilingi*."

"I know the price of beer," Rukuma said.

"You should not allow him to overcharge you," the man said helpfully.

Rukuma straightened to his full height. "Mind your business."

The man looked up at him. "I meant no offense, brother." He raised his bottle. "Will you drink with me to the *Mzee?*"

"Drink yourself," Rukuma snapped. "To hell with the *Mzee*."

Others around him heard and there was muttering. He listened to it. It sickened him. Since he left Ngorongoro he had been sickened. He had walked out over the highlands. He had stolen clothing from a village *duka* and hitchhiked to Arusha and crossed the border and ridden dirty buses to Nairobi. The villages were squalid, and the cities. The countryside was squalid with its emptiness of wild animals and its pitiful *shambas* of crops. Its very vastness was a squalor.

He was tired of the muttering. He left his beer and pushed through the crowd of men and kicked open the door and walked outside.

Outside was bright day. He strode down the middle of the sidewalk and the crowd divided before him. There were professional beggars working the street on stumps bound up in rags. An old man was catching locusts in the gutter, tearing off their wings and stuffing them into a plastic bag. In a tin hovel wedged among identical tin hovels at the edge of the city the old man would fry the locusts in groundnut oil and feast. There was nothing Rukuma could do for these people. Why had he ever thought he could? They wanted only to fill their bellies and ride in *motokaa*. They knew nothing of dreams. He felt alone. He had orphaned himself. He had cut himself off from what he had been and he had not yet become what he meant to be and he was weary, weary of the effort.

He leaned against a wall. Stop this, he told himself. You are being a fool. The *Mzee* endured seven years in the prison compound at Lokitaung. Do you think he did not despair? Have not all men who would lead great movements sometimes fallen aside in bitter despair? Is that not a test of the core of their determination? Believe that you will do what you have set yourself to do. Believe that you will come in wrath to stand at the head of all the millions of nameless. It is not yet time for that. It is not yet your time, but it is nearly time and it will be time soon. The nameless have waited long. When all is ready you will lead them. You have swept away your past and with it your weakness. Believe that you have. Are you not glad?

Are you not glad? Rukuma asked himself, starting off again down the crowded sidewalk, mocking. *Are you not glad? Are you not glad?*

At the end of the day, after Cassie had showered and changed, she walked out as she always did just at sunset to the grave above the lake. It was still bare, marked with a temporary stone John Kegedi had brought from Oloito that was cleaved on one face to the fossil impression of a branch of whistling thorn, but rhizomes of the tough Serengeti grasses were already reaching out to weave a cover over the dry earth of its mound. Cassie sat in the grass beside it and watched the sun set, the sky streaming pink and then red and going purple toward Lake Victoria to the west.

She had only begun to know the plain. When she wasn't working she watched it. She had not yet been able to return to the crater eastward in the highlands, but when she felt ready she would. She wanted to know it too. She wanted to know the life of this place. She meant to live here. She had written to the Livermore attorney who was the executor of her father's estate to transfer her funds to her bank in Arusha. There was nothing left for her to do in the United States. There was a life of work for her in East Africa. The frontiers had filled and closed in America long before she was born. East Africa was still a frontier, hungry and raw.

"Robert's started on his monograph," Cassie said aloud to the grave. "We got four tents up today. Abdi's very proud of them. I wish you could see Jaja's baby. He's gained five more pounds and he's already beginning to crawl. Seth? I miss you."

The umbrella thorns blurred, losing focus against the evening sky. Cassie thought: I wonder how long it will be until I can sit beside his grave without this welling of tears from my eyes? It isn't grief. I'm almost past grieving. It's love, and every day the depth of it overwhelms me.

"I know the time will come when I'll forget how you looked," she told him. "We didn't even take any pictures. It's absurd. I was a tourist and I didn't even take any pictures. I'm working on it. You'd want me to. I'm learning the plain. The plain will be your face and the crater. The life on the plain and in the crater will be your life. And I'll live here. I don't know yet what I can do. I'll do something and it won't be murderous and it won't be hate."

She brushed the tangled grass beside the grave, smoothing it. "Right now," she told Seth Crown, "what I can do is keep this camp and care for this child I carry that we made. I haven't let Abdi know yet. It will help him to know. He's still grieving for you, Seth. It will help him to know that we made a child and I'll tell him tonight at dinner but I wanted to tell you first. I'm sure now. We'll go on. We'll have a son or a daughter and we'll go on."

She stood then and walked back to the lodge. She would sit down to dinner at the big table in the dining room with Robert and Abdi and Abdi's wives and children. She was getting to know Abdi's wives and the children. She hadn't even taken time before to learn their names. There was everything to do, but for now, in summer, it seemed to Cassie that carrying Seth's child and restoring the camp and knowing the human beings she lived with was beginning enough.

Kenya/Tanzania, April 1973—
Kansas City, Missouri, March 1979

In appreciation: Dr. Tumaini Mcharo.

Glossary

NOTE: (M) following a word means the word is Masai. Most other words defined here are Swahili.

amerikani brightly printed cloth.
aputani (M) father—a term of respect.
asante thank you.
baba father.
banda shed, cabin, garage.
bangi marijuana.
bibi Miss, Mrs.
boma fence made of thorn brush.
bwana Mister.
calasia cow-elephant ivory.
chai tea.
daktari doctor.
Dorobo a hunting people, the Wa N'Dorobo, now scattered, believed to be the aboriginal inhabitants of East Africa.
duka shop.
Effendi colonial military usage: Sir.
fisi hyena.
haya okay (as permission).
hongo a bribe; monetary tribute travelers paid to cross Masai-land.
hospitali hospital.
Hujambo hello (formal).
il'doinyo orōk (M) the black mountains. The Crater Highlands of North Central Tanzania.
il'engat (M) wildebeest (plural).
il'laibon (M) Masai hereditary priest-kings (plural).
il'oipi (M) photographs.
il'oitigoshi (M) zebra (plural).
jambo hello, hi (informal).
karibu welcome.

kifaru   the rhinoceros.

Kihehe   Hehe—the language of the Hehe tribe of Tanzania.

Küngereza   English—the language.

kilemba   kerchief.

Kiswahili   Swahili—the language.

korongo   ravine.

kwaheri   good-bye.

kwashiorkor   severe malnutrition.

la   no.

laibon (M)   Masai hereditary priest-king.

leleshwa (M)   a termite-resistant African shrub.

loshoro (M)   traveling food: cornmeal porridge mixed with
   milk.

mahindi   corn, maize.

manyatta (M)   Masai village.

mhindi   an Asian; an Indian.

mjinga   fool.

moran (M)   young warrior Masai.

motokaa   motorcars; automobiles.

mpenzi   lover.

mwalimu   teacher.

The Mwalimu   affectionate title Tanzanians accord the President of their country, the honorable Julius Nyerere.

Mwamerika   an American.

mzee   old man—a term of respect.

The Mzee   affectionate title Kenyans accorded the President of
   their country, the late honorable Jomo Kenyatta.

mzungu   European, white man or woman.

ndiyo   yes.

ndovu   elephant.

ngoma   a dance.

nyingi   many, much.

nyumba   house.

nyumbu   wildebeest; gnu.

O (M)   an acknowledging interjection: yes; I understand; I
   hear you.

olaitoriani (M)   chieftain.

ole (M)   Mister.

ol morijoi (M)   the poisonous acokanthera tree.

osom (M)   thirty.

pasi   passport.

polisi   policeman, police.

pombe   home-brewed beer.

rukuma (M)   the black club that Masai chieftains carry as a badge of authority.

sana   very.

shamba   garden plot; farm.

shauri   as used here, a private feud.

shilingi   shilling, shillings.

siafu   biting red ants: safari ants.

simba   lion.

toto   colonial slang: boy (for *mtoto*).

twende   let's go.

uhai   magic powders and potions. In the nature of things, frequently poisonous.

Uhuru   Freedom; the East African word for independence.

Uhuru ni Kazi   the Tanzanian national motto: "Freedom Is Work."

Upesi!   hurry! be quick!

usivute sigara   no smoking.

vema   okay.

vilaiti   bull-elephant ivory weighing more than sixty pounds per tusk.

vizuri   good.

wabenzi   slang: the people of the Mercedes-Benz, *i.e.*, the new class of Africans, often with government connections, come to wealth since Uhuru.

wageni   foreigners.

wahindi   Asians; Indians (plural).

walafi   gluttons.

waragi   banana gin.

wazungu   Europeans; white people (plural).